HIGH STAKES

The first bomb had all but destroyed the magnificent glass dome of Deng Xiaoping International Superport, and dozens of people were injured. No one knew where or when the next explosion would take place.

Yet there they were in the next terminal—representatives of the four most powerful aviation manufacturers in the world—seated at the same banquet table, trying to make small talk instead of corporate war.

Cutthroat competitors, they only had one thing in common: the exclusive contract to supply the Chinese with supersonic transport aircrafts for the new superport. It could mean billions for their companies and powerful international status for their governments.

And one of them would sacrifice anything to get it.

Anything—including their lives.

CHINA DOME

OTHER BOOKS BY
WILLIAM H. LOVEJOY

WILLIAM H. LOVEJOY

CHINA DOME

PINNACLE BOOKS
WINDSOR PUBLISHING CORP.

The first granddaughter should have her own book,
and so this one is dedicated with love to
Alena
and to her rightfully proud parents
Jodi and Jeff Statler.

PINNACLE BOOKS are published by

Windsor Publishing Corp.
850 Third Avenue
New York, NY 10022

The P logo Reg U.S. Pat & TM off. Pinnacle is a trademark of Windsor Publishing Corp.

First Printing: March, 1995

Printed in the United States of America

THE PEOPLE OF CHINA DOME

PACIFIC AEROSPACE INCORPORATED

Dan Kerry, Vice President for Far Eastern Development
Peter James (P.J.) Jackson, Executive Vice President and
 Chief Operations Officer
Kenneth Stephenson, Chairman of the Board and President
Charley Whitlock, Director of International Security
Terry Carroll, Chief Astroliner test pilot
Don Matthews, Astroliner copilot
Jeff Dormund, Astroliner flight engineer
Cliff Coker, Astroliner test pilot
Dennis Aikens, Manager of Production and Chief Engineer
Mickey Duff, Assistant Director for Aeronautical Engineering

AEROSPATIALE-BAC

Jacqueline Broussard, Marketing Director
Henri Dubonnet, Chairman of the Board, Managing Director
Stephen Dowd, Security Director

BBK ENTERPRISES (Boehm-Bussmeier-Kraft)

Gerhard Ebbing, Director of Production
Matthew Kraft, Managing Director of BBK
Ernst Bergen, Director of Security
Hakim al-Qatar, Director, Investment Group

TUPOLEV DESIGN BUREAU

Pyotr Illivich Zemenek, Chief Engineer
Josef Vladimirovich Treml, Assistant to the Engineer
Yuri Yelchenko, Director of Security

CHINA

Sun Chen, Chairman of the Committee for Airport
  Construction
Yichang Enlai, Director of Security, Deng Xiaoping
  International Superport
Zhao Li, Superport Manager
Chou Sen, General, Commander, Southern China
  Defense Sector
Hua Peng, Major, Squadron Leader

OPENING SHOTS

ONE

From twenty miles away, the place looked like a green felt pool table, with streaks of muddy tan spoiling the cloth. There was a random scattering of dark gray balls strewn over its surface by some colossal cue.

The table must have been in the recreation room of a giant's castle because there was a child's toy city far to the south of the pool table, tiny high-rises built of white blocks haphazardly stacked around a spill of blue water.

Dan Kerry's vantage point was located in the left seat of a Cessna Citation II business jet, and he was impressed with his first view of what the newspapers and the brochures were billing as a Superport. As he got closer and lower at six thousand feet above ground level (AGL), the definition improved, and he was able to pick out a few of the features of the airport.

Kerry was impressed, a condition which didn't often affect him.

He depressed his transmit button and asked the air controller for permission to circle the airport so he could see what twenty-one billion dollars American could buy. The air controller, who spoke in British-tinged English, proudly granted his wish, but reminded him that he was observing Visual Flight Rules (VFR). The air control radars had not yet been certified, and the Instrument Landing System (ILS) was not yet functioning.

"Cessna Five-Seven, you are cleared for one circuit. Please go to five thousand feet and maintain a four-mile distance from the airport. You have a DC-9 on approach at your bearing one-eight-zero."

"Roger, Deng Xiaoping Air. I copy five thousand and four mile separation. DC-9 behind me. Five-Seven out."

Kerry continued to bleed off speed and altitude as he rolled into a shallow right turn and took himself out of the approach pattern.

"At least VFR isn't a problem this morning," Jim Dearborn, his copilot, said. "You can just about see infinity."

"On a clear day, you can see the People's Republic?" Kerry paraphrased the title of John DeLorean's book.

"Right, boss." Dearborn gave him a look that told him he was stretching a bit far.

Dearborn was correct, though. In the west were a few high-flown, wispy cirrus clouds. Otherwise, it was a magnificent day, with the sun shining on an endless series of rolling, emerald-colored hills, some of which achieved an elevation of 3,000 feet. To the south, across the border and down in the New Territories, random areas of cultivation near concrete villages could be seen.

"Time to go to work," Kerry said. "The airplane is all yours."

"I have the airplane, roger."

Kerry waited until he felt Dearborn signal his command of the jet by gently rolling the control yoke, then released the wheel, lifted his feet off the rudder pedals, unbuckled his harness, and stood up in a half-crouch. He slid out of the cramped space past the throttle pedestal. Stretching his back and shoulders muscles first, Kerry slipped through the open cockpit doorway into the passenger cabin. The ceiling was low for his height, and he had to walk with a bent neck.

He had six passengers with him, all of them assigned to his Tokyo office, and all of them sitting or kneeling between the seats on the port side of the Citation, peering through the porthole windows at this new Disneyland. The airplane leveled out, then put her left wing down a few degrees as Dearborn started into his huge circle.

Kerry grabbed a pair of binoculars from a cardboard box labeled for Budweiser resting on the floor and slipped into the first seat on the left side. Behind him, Charley Whitlock looked up from his own binoculars.

"This son of a bitch ought to be declared a city, Dan."

Whitlock was Director of International Security, a graying man in his late fifties. Though he had the subtle beginnings of a paunch, he was still hard-muscled and fit. His hair was curly and full-bodied, a forelock dripping over a forehead furrowed with the experiences he had gained as an LAPD cop, then as an agent of the FBI specializing in antiterrorist programs. He had a law degree but had never taken a bar examination.

"My hundred bucks to your ten that we're going to find better controls than a city has, Charley."

"Maybe. I'm going to have to be convinced."

Whitlock was a born skeptic, and Kerry appreciated the fact.

Sitting sideways in the seat, Kerry raised his binoculars to his eyes and rested his elbows on the armrest.

He rotated the binoculars and studied the perimeter first, defined by a pair of chain-link fences running parallel to each other, twenty feet apart. They enclosed an area that was rectangular, and he knew from his briefing notes that the grounds of the airfield were fifteen miles long by nine miles wide. One hundred thirty-five square miles. Deng Xiaoping International Superport was the largest airport in the world, surpassing the massive complex built with Middle Eastern oil money outside of Riyadh, Saudi Arabia. The new Denver International Airport in Colorado, which carried a tab of nearly three billion dollars, paled by comparison. Considering that the labor costs in China were considerably less than those in the United States, twenty-one billion bought a great deal more.

There were fifteen runways. One quadruple set of runways ran east-and-west on the southern side of the seven passenger terminals, next to the commercial and industrial sector, and another triplet of north-south runways were placed perpendicular to them, at their western end. On the northern side of the terminals, crossing in front of the massive tarmac, an east-west group of five airstrips intersected a north-south set of three runways on the eastern end. Each of the parallel runways was about a quarter-mile apart. In the wide and open spaces between runways and taxiways, the grass and weeds which gave off the color of green were chewed up by the tracks of construction vehicles, revealing a hot, dry, and dusty color of tan.

The steel-and-fiberglass reinforced concrete that had been poured into those landing strips so far could be counted in the millions of cubic yards, and they weren't finished yet. The north-south runways on both sides of the terminals were still under construction. Kerry counted more than fifty mobile cement trucks—painted in a rainbow of yellows, reds, blues, and greens—in queues, waiting their turns to pump sludge into two-foot deep forms. At the construction sites, yellow hard-hatted ants scurried about in seemingly inane responses to the commands of some queen of the hill. Working ahead of the concrete pour, massive land-leveling equipment was in operation—landscrapers and bulldozers supported by a bevy of water and gas tankers, pulverizers, steamrollers, and dump trucks.

All of the runways were three and a half miles long, about a half-mile longer than the sixteen-thousand-foot standard for international aircraft. Kerry wondered if the Chinese weren't expecting space shuttles to utilize the facilities, and maybe they were. Everything he had read indicated some very long-range planning.

But they weren't ready for the shuttles just yet. Great white *Xs* were painted on the finished and unfinished ends of fourteen of the runways, denying access. Only one, Runway 9R-27L, was open to specially cleared aircraft like his Citation or the DC-9 which had just put down. The DC-9 VIP transport looked miniscule against the great plains of concrete and asphalt surrounding it.

They weren't showing up yet, but the prospectus called for acres of gardens to be spotted throughout the complex. Rivaling the botanical gardens of major cities in the world, these were intended to offset the harsh reality of so much concrete and blacktop surface.

A maze of taxiways interconnected the runways, the tarmac surrounding the terminals, and the subordinate facilities, and Kerry could imagine, when full operations got underway, that the ground controllers were going to have their hands full. They would have a lot of high-tech automation working for them, like traffic control lights at intersections, masterminded by computers monitoring the landing and takeoff frequencies. However, the planning documents he had seen projected over two thousand flights a day. That was double, and even triple, the traffic of most major airports, and it was a hell of a lot of aircraft to move from one point on the ground to another without denting a few fenders.

Dearborn increased the rate of his turn as they reached the west end of the complex, turning to the south, and Kerry shifted his attention to the structures, scanning each with his binoculars. The bulk of them were located to the south of the runways, and the results, so far, were amazing. There were a lot of very happy, very wealthy architects somewhere in the world. Even though the complex was over a year from completion, design awards were flowing into the Orient like the Mississippi River at flood stage.

The official name of the airport, as proclaimed by the Chinese, was Deng Xiaoping International Superport, but he could see why the insiders in the aviation industry were calling it China Dome.

The guiding design precept was a parabolic dome. Every structure was fashioned similarly, as a half-hemisphere a bit over two times wider than it was high, faced in smoked gray glass. The only exceptions to that rule could be found in the control towers, which were domes raised on top of tall, inward curving stalks. They looked something like overgrown mushrooms, Kerry thought.

There were ten control towers spaced around the airport. The major tower, for air control, was twenty stories high, located to the southwest of the main terminal. The other towers were shorter, five stories tall, and controlled ground traffic. There were so many of them because the spacing of the terminals interfered with the controllers' vision. When moving aircraft into parking positions adjacent to the seven terminals or near the maintenance and commercial compounds, it was helpful if the controller could see the airplanes. On top of which, the smaller towers would control the local movement of helicopters, and a hell of a lot of helicopter traffic was envisioned.

Kerry had read the specifications. The major terminal structure was over twelve stories—150 feet—high and four hundred feet wide. It was much larger than a standard city block, and it would house over a thousand businesses and offices, as well as a hotel. It sat in the center of a shallow arc of domes, the ends of the arc farther from the runway than the center. Three of its slightly smaller kin were emplaced to either side of it, separated from each other by a quarter-mile. In his view, the black domes appeared to be sitting all by themselves in a sea of grayish-colored concrete. The far dome, on the eastern end, had several aircraft parked near it, and a few trucks sitting around, but the shortage of vehicles and activity at the other domes made them seem desolate.

The construction activity was focused on the interiors now, and the smoked glass prevented him from seeing how far that might have progressed. What seemed strange to him was the lack of automobile parking lots that usually peppered the outskirts of major airports. In the far southeastern corner of the property, however, was another set of domes, and they were dedicated to ground transport. To reach the terminals, one used the underground rapid transit system or helicopters. The planners intended to discourage the use of automobiles and urge travellers to make use of the rail-based people mover which would eventually extend beyond the airport and on into the city.

Dearborn made the next turn, headed back east, and as they passed the grouping of two dozen domes in the southwest corner of the field, Kerry looked them over. These were aircraft maintenance facilities, enough to support maybe fifty separate air carriers. The architectural principles were the same except that the domes had four flat sides where hangar doors were located. Extremely large aircraft could be sheltered inside by way of each of the four doors.

Beyond the maintenance structures, and spaced down the southern border of the airport, more domes were under construction. Perhaps twenty of them looked to be complete, or near completion, and another twenty were rising out of the soil. Thousands of workers and hundreds of trucks, cranes, and other equipment were toiling away. The pace appeared frenetic to Kerry, and he supposed that every subcontractor on the project had been led to believe his one-year deadline could be advanced to next week.

According to the planning documents, these buildings, and as many more as were needed, would be leased to the companies that required physical space on the grounds of the airport. They were to be serviced by the seven runways on the southern side of the airport, and the traffic would be cargo-oriented.

Dearborn leaned back in his seat and called through the cockpit doorway, "You coming back up here, Dan?"

"No. Go ahead and take us in, Jim."

Kerry found the release handle under his seat, spun it around so that it faced backward, and locked it in place. He snapped the seat belt buckles together and snugged the belt up.

The rest of his team began returning to their seats as Dearborn brought them around on final approach.

Kerry thought he had the best of the best working on his team. Alyce Williams handled the computer systems, and Barry Metcalf was a genius when it came to radar, infrared detection, and electronic countermeasures. Ricardo Alvarez understood the finer points of physical layout and design related to population control. Mickey Duff, also an ex-fighter pilot like Kerry, and also with a degree in aeronautical engineering, knew the inside of aircraft as well as he knew the outside. Each of them carried an assistant director title with the company, but were on loan to Kerry's operation. Clay Tompkins, a narrow-faced and intelligent man with a Ph.D. from Harvard, wasn't an administrator, and Kerry had borrowed him from the Economics Division of Pacific Aerospace Incorporated.

There were another twelve people assigned to Kerry's front-line office, which was based in Tokyo, and they were all specialists in one field or another. This trip, however, was focused on facilities, operations, and security, and so he had brought the appropriate people with him.

Whitlock gave up his ground search as the landing gear clunked down, settled into his seat, and locked the seat belt in place.

"I'll give 'em one thing, Dan. That's the cleanest airfield I've ever seen. Most of them start out that way, and over the years, they tack on new buildings and functions and get to be a real maze."

"It's probably still a maze, underground," Kerry said.

"No doubt. But the view from here is nice."

"What do you think of the perimeter?"

"I'll let you know after I've walked it, but I think the perimeter is the least of our worries."

Whitlock leaned against the window and stared ahead at the approaching field. He said, "I can't believe they built that mother without one contract in place. That's gutsy as hell."

"It's a different kind of airport," Kerry said, but he agreed with Whitlock. In the past couple of decades in the United States, government entities didn't start building expensive airports without guarantees that someone was going to use them. Denver International had relied on its contracts with United and Continental as its go-ahead signal, and when Continental's financial problems had resulted in the airline's downsizing its commitment, DIA had had to scale back its terminal designs and the number of gates available. They were still a couple of runways short of what the founders had foreseen. In some quarters, it was still known as Pena's Folly, named for Federico Pena, the mayor of Denver at the time the project was initiated and who subsequently became Secretary of Transportation.

The Chinese Ministry of Transportation, on the other hand, had simply created a special commission called the Committee for Airport Construction. The Ministry had simply ordered the committee to build Deng Xiaoping International Superport to 21st Century specifications and expectations. The committee was not to worry unduly about costs.

Ninety percent of the architects and eighty-five percent of the engineering firms involved with the project were from Western nations. *Aviation Week* had reported that the Chinese were stunned when they realized they did not have the expertise available within their own country to construct their dream. Currently, a shake-up was taking place in Chinese universities, and a large number of faculty had been recruited from prestigious institutions around the world.

"From what I've heard, Charley, the People's Committee for Airport Construction is knee-deep in applications for contracts and leases. They've got three or four bidders for every slot and space available."

"Un-damned-believable."

"Look at us," Kerry reminded him.

"Yeah, there's us."

Whitlock knew as well as Kerry—the honchos back in California kept drumming it into them—that this contract was a make-or-break proposition for Pacific Aerospace Incorporated.

The Citation skipped lightly on the runway, then settled down. Dearborn didn't bother jamming on brakes or reversing engine thrust. He had all of the concrete in the world ahead of him.

Halfway down the runway, he turned onto a taxiway at some temporary ground controller's direction, then headed back toward the terminal on the eastern end. Six minutes later, he followed the arm-signalling instructions of a man on the ground and parked the Cessna next to the DC-9.

None of the skyways projecting from the dome were in operation yet, and they would not have accommodated the Citation, anyway.

As the engines spooled down, Kerry and his team unleashed themselves and began to gather their briefcases and overnighters.

Kerry unlocked the door, shoved it down into its airstair position, and was first off the plane. He stood next to the airstair and looked around. Several aircraft were parked in the line, most of them corporate jets. The DC-9 appeared to be a converted VIP transport for Air France. There was a Boeing 737 and a couple of Aerospatiale airplanes.

It was hot on the ground on August 2, and a mild breeze swirled heat at him. From ground level, the airport seemed even more monstrous. The dark-glassed dome nearby seemed far removed from its sisters. The rest of them were all in the next two counties. Or provinces, perhaps.

Three hundred yards away to the west was one of the smaller ground control towers.

Close-up, he could see that the dome's outer shell was constructed of triangular units, each smoked-glass pane framed in a similarly colored aluminum, and each unit appeared to stand about twelve feet tall. He knew, though, that each component would be of a slightly different size in order to achieve the curvature required for the dome.

"It's really impressive engineering," Alyce Williams said as she stepped to the ground.

She was a petite woman, in her midthirties, and very brainy. Her dark hair was full and shoulder-length, and it framed an oval face that was clear and blue-eyed. Unlike most computer slaves he had worked with, Kerry found her to be people-oriented.

"About ten of those triangles would build me all the house I'd ever need," Kerry told her.

"That's because your girlfriends never spend more than one night at your place."

Williams was always getting on him about his lady friends. She was happily married to a computer expert teaching in the computer science program at UCLA, and she thought everyone in her immediate vicinity should also be married, and happily at that. Kerry had been married once, but he and Marian had apparently missed out on Alyce's formula.

"They quickly learn how inadequate I am," Kerry said.

"B.S."

Whitlock stepped off the airstair and said, "Pretty damned stark. I think this is what Mars will look like, when we build our first port there."

"You're too impatient, Charley. You have to wait until they plant some trees," Williams said.

"I'd rather go find some now. I'm bushed after that flight."

Kerry grinned at him. They had departed Tokyo three and a half hours earlier, and it was only eleven in the morning, local time.

By the time the rest of his people had climbed down from the Citation, Kerry saw several figures emerge from a ground-level door in the dome.

"Here comes the welcoming committee," he said.

There was another welcome waiting for them.

A dull, flat boom pounded the warm air, and the successive concussion wave buffeted the aircraft, knocked Alyce off her feet, and rocked Kerry back against the side of the Cessna.

He looked to his right in time to see the fifty-foot concave stalk supporting the nearby control tower throb convulsively, spew flame, disgorge pieces of itself, then buckle.

The finely fashioned smooth dome at the top tilted, struggled, then came crashing to the concrete.

Glass exploded into the air.

TWO

Mickey Duff pushed himself up from the tarmac where he had thrown himself on top of Alyce Williams in an attempt to protect her from flying debris.

"Jesus Christ!" Whitlock said. "That's the first time I've seen a cost overrun in action."

Kerry reached down, gripped both of Williams's wrists, and helped her to her feet.

The people who had been coming to meet them were also regaining their feet. The area around the dome, once swept meticulously clean, was now littered with tiny glass fragments and a few pieces of metal.

"Anybody hurt?" Kerry asked.

Barry Metcalf displayed a small cut on his forearm, but that was the extent of the injuries.

Kerry looked to where the tower had once stood. A thirty-foot-high section of the base remained upright with flames beginning to gush forth from the open top, but the top section had tumbled sideways, towards them, and the dome rested on its edge on the ground, crushed and mangled. As he looked, he saw the flicker of flames erupt within the wreckage.

And he thought he heard a yell.

He had already dropped his briefcase and carry-all, and he simply started running.

It was only three hundred yards.

He heard feet pounding on the cement behind him and glanced back to see Mickey Duff.

Sirens were beginning to warble from around the field.

The closer he got to the wreckage, the more debris he encountered. He dodged large chunks of aluminum framing and huge sections of skin from the tower base. Sidestepped a chair. Leapt over a file cabinet.

He heard a man screaming. He thought he heard moaning.

He did hear flames crackling, and through the bronzed glass that was still intact, the darkened interior seemed to get brighter.

About half of the dome was still in one piece, resting on its side, though much of the glass remaining in frames was cracked or starred. He was aware that safety glass had been used, holding itself together by some film bonded between layers, but there were still thousands of tiny fragments littering the pavement. Along the edge resting on the ground, there were openings to the interior, but they were jammed with twisted metal and furniture and bulkheads that had broken loose and spilled down from the inside.

The dome seemed both gigantic and precarious, rising above him. Kerry picked the most likely gap in the wreckage, veered toward it, and slid to a stop on the slippery glass fragments. He grabbed a stairway railing protruding from the opening and tried to lever it out of the way. It was snagged on something.

Duff banged to a stop next to him, wrapped his big hands around the lower bar of the railing, and the two of them twisted it to one side.

Kerry stepped through the triangular opening and found a desk blocking his way. He and Duff raised it and shoved it aside.

Looking up, he saw that the top floor of the control tower had apparently been one large open space, ringed on the outer edge with built-in consoles. The desks had probably been grouped in the middle of the floor. What looked like an electrical fire was spreading rapidly from a cabinet thirty feet above him. He tasted ozone in the air.

He could hear someone groaning.

"Hey! Where are you?" Duff yelled.

Someone called back in Chinese from below the jumble of equipment stacked in front of them.

He and Duff began tossing cushions, papers, chairs, and cabinets aside, trying to work their way into the pile.

The sirens got louder as they worked. The flames above spread quickly, licking at the material coating the walls. The air lost vibrancy.

More men arrived and piled in next to them—Metcalf, Whitlock, Alvarez, and two Chinese he didn't know. They set up a kind of bucket brigade, shifting debris from the interior to try and clear a path.

They found the first man, the screamer, beneath a heavy computer terminal. Both of his arms were broken, the bones protruding through the flesh, and it appeared as if his hip had been smashed. He was in so much pain he wasn't coherent, and Kerry couldn't get any information out of him about how many people were in the tower.

Metcalf found a wooden door, pulled the hinge pins to free it from its broken frame, and they eased the man onto it, trying to be careful with him, but having to fight his thrashing about. The two Chinese carried him outside.

Kerry called out to the moaner, "Hold on, we're coming. Can you understand me?"

"I . . . hear you."

"How many are in here?"

"Six."

He figured that most of them must have been on a floor under the top floor. They had some digging to do to get through the floor.

Whitlock had found a fire axe.

"Let me up front, Dan," he said.

August 2, 11:12 A.M.

Jacqueline Broussard pushed through the glass door and stepped out onto the apron. She had been with her group on the upper floor of Terminal Seven when the control tower erupted. Inside the dome, with its dual-paned insulated glass, the explosion had gone almost unnoticed.

When someone finally yelled out in some panic, the preparations for lunch ceased abruptly. People who had been milling about in conversational groups ran for the elevators which were at the core of the building, on the other side of bridges that spanned an open atrium.

Broussard had found an unmoving escalator near the edge of the dome and took the seven flights downward at full speed, beating the first elevator to the ground floor by seconds and pushing her way through the pair of steel doors to the tarmac outside.

She saw two men emerge from the wreckage carrying another man on an improvised stretcher. Dozens of fire trucks, ambulances, and cars, all painted a bright, sickly yellow, had begun to arrive, circling the remains of the tower. The sirens died away, but the blue and red strobe lights continued to rotate. Firemen clad in yellow slickers and carrying red fire extinguishers converged on the collapsed structure.

She was about to launch into a run toward the tower to help when a firm hand took hold of her upper arm. She looked back to see Mr. Yichang, who was the director of security for the airport.

"Please, Miss Broussard."

"But they need help."

"It will be taken care of," he said. "Additionally, there may be more explosives in the area. We will wait."

Yichang's men quickly set up a cordon, keeping the visitors away from the scene of the explosion. She saw others of his men going back inside the dome. No doubt they would begin an intensive search for explosive devices within the terminal itself.

Broussard hated the role of spectator. She much preferred to be where the action was taking place.

This was, however, Yichang's jurisdiction, so she forced herself to stand still and consider just what message was being sent, and more important, just who was supposed to receive the message.

August 2, 11:21 A.M.

Ric Alvarez and Kerry found the moaning man and freed him from a steel beam pinning him to a smashed wall. Kerry was afraid he had a broken back. The two of them also discovered the next victim, but he wasn't a survivor. A twelve-inch length of steel rod protruded from his right eye.

"Vaya con Dios," Alvarez said.

By then, a couple dozen Chinese men, most of them in

yellow slickers, were swarming around them. Kerry felt the evil eye from a couple of them.

"I think they want us out of here," he told Alvarez.

"Their turf, after all."

They backed out of the way, found Whitlock, and worked their way out of the second floor into the top floor space, climbing over the jumble of equipment and furnishings, then back to the makeshift opening in the dome. They had to slip around yellow-coated men trying to get inside. The fire in the consoles was extinguished, the place reeked of electrical burns, and fire extinguisher foam coated the flooring and dripped from above.

Outside, the air was sweeter, but chaos seemed to be the order of the day. Firemen rushed around, supervisors yelled at them, emergency vehicle lights pulsed, handheld radios chattered in Chinese. A gray pallor of thin smoke had dimmed the sun.

Kerry brushed debris from his suit coat and slacks. The back of his hand was bleeding, but not badly, and he ignored it.

"I want to see the other end of it, Dan," Whitlock said.

"I'll go with you."

The two of them walked around the wreckage of the dome to where some thirty feet of the supporting column still stood, leaning backward, supporting the severed base of the dome. It appeared to be twisted, torqued counter-clockwise, and a number of sheets of aluminum skin which were the same color as the window glass had sprung free along their bonded edges.

There was a ground-level door, with a neat sign on it. Lettered in Chinese, French, and English were the words, "Authorized Personnel Only." Kerry assumed the warning was the same in the other languages. To the right of the door was a small, black-faced panel with a slot for magnetic security cards. Access to the tower was denied to those without the cards.

The door was sprung, hanging open by a couple inches, and Kerry pulled on it. It grated, but opened a few more inches, and he and Whitlock stepped inside.

They found a hallway with two more doors, one of them secured by a magnetic card lock. That one, to the left, was a steel door with a steel-mesh imbedded window. It appeared to be the access to the subterranean passages. Directly ahead, the second door closed off a storage or equipment room. On the right, a circular stairway led upward. It was lit by the sun pouring in from above.

And flames, perhaps. Kerry could hear them crackling.

"I don't think," Whitlock said, "I want to see anything up there until the fire's out."

"That would be wise, gentlemen," a voice spoke from behind them.

Kerry turned to see a Chinese man motioning them outside. He was slight of stature, but immaculately turned out in an off-white suit, white shirt, and blood-red tie. Kerry hadn't seen shoes polished to that blinding a luster in a long time. He figured the man for a military or law enforcement history. His jet-black hair was longer than military, though, combed backward along the top and sides. The dark eyes were penetrating and direct, set in a face full of hard, flat planes and angular bones.

He wore an ID card with his picture on it clipped to the breast pocket of his suit jacket. It would be the same card magnetically programmed to open locked doors.

"I am Yichang Enlai. I am Director of Security."

Kerry stepped outside and offered his hand. "Dan Kerry. I work for Pacific Aerospace Incorporated."

Yichang's grip reflected his face, hard and firm, though he did not choose to test muscles.

"I know," he said. "You are the Vice President for Far Eastern Development. And this gentleman is Charles Whitlock, your security assistant. I have read your dossiers."

Kerry thought Yichang was trying to impress him with his thoroughness, but his knowledge might have been expected. PAI—as well as other potential contractors, he assumed—had been required to submit background information and photographs on each of the key people who would be working on the China Dome project.

Whitlock stepped outside and shook hands with Yichang.

"If you gentlemen will follow me?"

Yichang turned on his heel and headed for the terminal.

"Maybe there's something we could help you with," Whitlock said.

Yichang looked back and smiled. He smiled something like Dracula might have smiled, Kerry thought.

"We will take care of it."

Kerry and Whitlock fell in behind him.

Kerry looked at Whitlock, who shrugged his shoulders.

Beijing, China
August 2, 11:47 A.M.

Sun Chen was the Chairman of the Committee for Airport Construction, and he worked out of a large but spartanly furnished office on the fifth floor of a high-rise office building. A large woven carpet of pastel greens, reds, and yellows depicting rural scenes supported the spindle-legged table he used for a desk, two long couches perpendicular to, and in front of, the desk, and a long, low table between the couches. A set of three panels on one wall captured in artistic watercolors the essence of his birthplace in the Eastern Highlands.

Sun had been born to a mining family on the Shandong Peninsula, which juts into the Yellow Sea like an accusing finger pointing at South Korea. His early life had not been an easy one—his four-room household had necessarily contained his parents, his grandparents, his two brothers, his sister, and his uncle's four-member family. His grandfather, father, uncle, and oldest brother had labored for ten-hour-long days in the mines.

Sun's quick intellect had attacked the entrance examinations for the university with fervor and determination, and his success had directed him away from the mines and into government service. He was considered by his superiors, he knew, as a fine accountant and a superb manager. And he was proud to be managing one of the most important projects the Republic had ever undertaken. It might not rank alongside the Great Wall or Mao's revolution in architectural or political history, but Sun thought that it would help the People's Republic to achieve significant strides in economic progress.

Sun Chen counted himself among the blessed. In a nation of 1.1 billion people, with only one thousand universities and technical colleges enrolling 1.7 million students, he had found the way into, and through, the system. And purely by chance, he had found himself a university student at the right time in China's evolution. There is a major conflict between economic progress and Communist philosophy. The ideology commands that all of the people be educated equally, but those principles prevent persons with special skills or talents—who might further the nation's economic standing—from advancing beyond the norm by denying them the educational opportunities and facilities necessary for superior development. The educational leaders over time have wavered between their desires to conform to Communist principles and their wishes to achieve rapid modernization. Chen happened to enter his university program at a time when the Communist educational philosophy was under suppression and the ministers of education were attempting to propel the nation into the current century.

The philosophical wavering back and forth helped no one, he thought. The deficiencies in the system had been strikingly evident when he had sought out the architects, engineers, and construction contractors necessary for his project, and found them to be nearly nonexistent. Those who were available were lacking in their knowledge of the materials and techniques required for a project with the scope of Deng Xiaoping International. Even the best construction managers, necessary to supervise the thousands of workers, were not up to the task. He had been humiliated by the requirement to extend contract bids internationally, and the education ministries had been ordered to implement changes in higher education opportunities and programs immediately.

His humiliation had been short-lived, however. Bringing in foreign expertise from Europe, the Americas, Asia, and Australia had proven entirely beneficial, even if expensive. Chinese subcontractors learned from the foreigners, the contractors spent their yuan in the local economy, and best of all, the worldwide public relations explaining this openness had vastly improved China's image. Sun had modestly accepted the praise heaped upon him by the leadership for his farsighted strategy of contracting with outsiders. He did not admit, nor did others, that it was the accident of limited educational opportunities.

That learning development, in conjunction with the philosophy rampant during his education, remained with Sun. It was the guide he followed as he reached for the completion of Deng Xiaoping International Superport.

He was well aware that the Superport was only a tool. It was to be used to support a greater concept in which he also believed. He was aware, also, that he and his project were the keystone in the arch. Without the airport, the tremendous leap into economic power for China could not be achieved.

Sun took his responsibilities very, very seriously, and he allowed very little to interfere with his timetable.

On the wall opposite the Shandong Peninsula watercolors was a series of aerial photographs, beginning on the far end of his office with the view of the farmlands and rice paddies that had been selected as the site of the airport. The photographs advancing toward his desk along the wall displayed the stages of construction over the past three years. It seemed to have taken a long time before visible progress was made. Nearly a year had gone into site preparation— leveling, backfilling, and excavating for the subterranean passages.

The latest photographs showing the field of smooth gray domes were exhilarating. The vision was almost in place.

Sun Chen sat back in his stiff desk chair, sipped his tea, studied his photographs proudly, and waited to hear from Deng Xiaoping International. The first gathering at the site of aviation industry people, who might or might not be future participants in the enterprise, was taking place today, starting with a luncheon at noon.

The administrator of the airport, Zhao Li, was to call him precisely at twelve o'clock. Sun expected a happy progress report.

As he waited, Chen pressed the intercom button and ordered more tea from his secretary.

He would dearly have liked to have a frosting-covered biscuit, but he was on a strict diet. At 235 pounds, he was very much overweight for his short frame, and the obesity was revealed in the firm roundness of his cheeks. His lips appeared too full, and his eyes had all but disappeared into folds of flesh. Sun was heartened, however, by the fact that he had lost seven pounds in the last month. He was well on the way to his goal, just as he was with the Superport north of Hong Kong.

Just as the secretary placed a fresh cup of tea in front of him, the telephone set rang.

He picked up the receiver, and the receptionist told him, "Director Yichang, Chairman."

A call from the security man was not what he had expected, or wanted. It foretold problems.

Pressing the button for the blinking line, he asked, "What is it, Director Yichang?"

"Chairman, I must inform you that Control Tower Six was destroyed by a bomb."

Sun's heart sank. He knew precisely where the tower was located on the schematic of the airport. His eyes went to the picture on the wall and found the tower. His mind tried to erase it.

"In front of the visitors?"

"I am afraid so, sir."

"How, and by whom?"

"Our first estimates, not yet confirmed, suggest that nearly ten pounds of plastic explosives would have been required to sever the interior support columns. The perpetrators are unknown at this time."

Sun felt the anger boiling up within him.

"This is a disgrace, Yichang. To you, to me, and to the nation."

"I am devastated, Chairman."

"I want the perpetrator captured immediately. There will be an extremely public and extremely short trial before he is executed."

"Of course, Chairman, but—"

Sun slammed the telephone into its cradle.

Then remembered that he had forgotten to ask about fatalities.

THREE

Deng Xiaoping International Superport
August 2, 1:22 P.M.

The sixty-five guests of the Chinese government made a tremendous amount of noise as they ate, Broussard thought. Silverware clinked against china, crystal rang as water goblets collided with stemmed wineglasses. And above it all was the incessant buzz of animated conversation, some of it taking place in about six different languages, though English was predominant. Her observation was that most of the people here, despite their lofty titles, were salespeople at heart, and salespeople loved to talk.

Most of them were men, she had also observed. There were only eight women in the group, but they too were animated conversationalists.

Although it had started almost an hour late, the meal was excellent. A variety of platters—dim sum, *har gow,* hot pepper chicken—were spaced around each of the seven circular tables. Set up on the observation level of Terminal Seven—which she would have named Concourse Seven, but she was not in charge—the location of the tables provided them with a magnificent vista of the airport grounds. That was unfortunate since they were marred by the platoons of construction workers already cleaning up the debris from the destroyed control tower. Their host, Mr. Zhao Li, had offered no concrete information about the tragedy, though he had apologized profusely for the incident.

By the occasional glances most pairs of eyes took toward the remains of the tower, she was certain that it was in the back of everyone's mind. Who knew where another bomb might be located? She herself was a trifle uneasy, and the only ones who seemed oblivious to the high potential of danger were Zhao Li and the American Daniel Kerry.

Jacqueline Broussard thought the seating arrangements interesting. Most of the people in the room represented airlines from around the world which had an interest in obtaining gate access at Deng Xiaoping International. They were here for the orientation lectures and the tours.

The diners at her table were different from the rest of the people attending the session, and she had been surprised, when she found her seating card, that Zhao had decided to put them all together. Of the seven others at her table, she had met Pyotr Zemenek twice before, at aviation conferences in Europe, but other than her deputy, Francois Miter, across the table from her, she knew the others only by the files she had compiled on them.

Zemenek was Chief Engineer for the Tupolev Design Bureau in Russia, and he was accompanied by his assistant, Josef Treml.

Wilhelm Stuttmann, Deputy Director for Sales for the German consortium of BBK Enterprises, sat on her left, and the BBK Director of Production, Gerhard Ebbing, was seated next to Miter.

On her right was Clay Tompkins, an economist for Pacific Aerospace, and two seats away to her left was Daniel Kerry, PAI's Vice President for Far Eastern Development.

The only thing the eight of them had in common was the

fact that they all coveted the single—very single—contract the Chinese would offer for supersonic transport aircraft. The eight of them represented the only four companies in the world capable of manufacturing SSTs in the numbers sought by the Chinese. They were competitors for the one customer that could keep their companies afloat. By all rights, they should be at each other's throats.

Zhao Li should have known better than to put them together.

Or perhaps he did. He frequently looked over at them from his table. Was civility in a hostile environment part of the Committee for Airport Construction's screening process?

The initial chit-chat around the table had been mostly inconsequential. She, Stuttmann, and Tompkins had exhausted the weather, the explosion, and the fine meal as topics. Tompkins wanted to talk economics without revealing any trade secrets, and economics bored her to death.

Tompkins ladled more of the shrimp dumplings onto his plate.

"I hope our security people are eating as well as we are," he said.

"I am sure that they are," she told him.

Each of the SST contract competitors had brought their security teams and a few other experts along with them. A side conference was taking place concurrently, with the emphasis on the operations and security measures for people, aircraft, and facilities in place at the airport.

Broussard did not really care what security people or computer people talked about, and she certainly had no interest in making polite conversation with people who would cut her throat as soon as possible. She was more interested in spending time with Zhao Li or Sun Chen.

She had been studying Kerry, though. He did not seem

particularly intimidated by his luncheon companions, and he and Josef Treml were engaged in a debate about friction coefficiency at various altitudes and speeds above Mach 1. Pyotr Zemenek was listening to the conversation with careful intensity, either trying to pick up breakthrough information from Kerry or monitoring the secrets his assistant might be giving away.

Kerry was an interesting study. He was tall and ruggedly handsome. His hair was a light blond, or graying with silver, or sun-bleached, or all three. His face was deeply tanned, and his gray eyes appeared to survey his surroundings from sockets that were set in a permanent squint. He had an easy smile that revealed teeth so straight and white that she was sure they were not his own. His face was accented by the small lines of wrinkles at the corners of his eyes and mouth. The light gray suit he was wearing went well with his eyes, and it was tailored smoothly to his wide shoulders.

The suit coat was also blemished with soot, wiped-off grease, dirt, and several long tears, but he seemed unaware of its condition. His right hand, gesturing with his fork as he made some point about fuselage skin temperatures, displayed a long cut on the back of it, now beginning to scab over.

His actions right after the explosion in the tower fulfilled some of the expectations she might have had about him from the cold facts listed in his dossier. He was supposedly a war hero, with a number of decorations to his credit. Broussard remembered reading about a Silver Star and an Air Medal or two among the listings. He had flown fighter aircraft in the Vietnam conflict. Though he was a graduate of the Air Force Academy in aeronautical engineering, he had not made the Air Force a career.

There was an attraction in his physical presence which normally would have intrigued her, but his whole easygoing manner suggested a high degree of arrogance and self-importance. She told herself that she was not impressed.

Red-jacketed waiters began moving among the tables, delivering dishes of ice cream. Broussard declined, and as she did, Kerry stood up, circled the table, and spoke to Tompkins, "Clay, switch chairs with me, will you?"

"Sure thing, Dan."

Kerry sat down in the vacated chair and turned it toward her, extending his hand.

Surprised, she took his hand in her own for a brief moment. His hand was hard and firm and warm, not the hand of a man who sat behind a desk for long periods.

"I wanted especially," Kerry said, "to meet the representative of Aerospatiale-BAC."

"Did you?"

"Certainly. Your people have the most experience in the industry, and my bosses want me to learn as much from you as I can."

Well, that is direct enough.

"I am not a technical person, Mr. Kerry."

"It's Dan, and I know. You've studied at the Sorbonne and at Oxford, emphasizing public relations and international relations. You've built yourself a nice reputation with the French directorate of information before moving to Aerospatiale, and you have a lot of admirers."

"Know your enemy?" she asked.

"You've got the same file on me," he grinned.

"Of course."

"And I'd bet you know the history of your company like it was your own."

She did. The consortium of Aerospatiale, the British Aircraft Corporation, Rolls-Royce Bristol Engine Division, and the *Societe Nationale d'Etude et de Construction de Moteurs* was assembled in November of 1962, and by February of 1965, the first two supersonic transport prototypes were under construction. Concorde 001 made its first flight in March of 1969. Since certification in 1974, the Concorde had had two decades of safe and successful flying experience.

"And my superiors told me to be wary of you, Mr. Kerry."

"Dan. I'm sure they did."

She was aware that Kerry kept his eyes trained on her face, on her eyes, and seemed completely at ease in doing so. Most men let their attention wander to other parts of her being.

And yet, behind the nonchalance and open friendliness, she felt he could be absolutely ruthless. With the past hour's assessment, Broussard decided that she agreed with Henri Dubonnet, her chairman of the board, who had told her that Daniel Kerry was not to be trusted.

And yet, she too was a spy of sorts. There were important secrets to be learned from Kerry.

Zhao Li got up from his table and moved toward the podium.

"Well," Kerry said, "it's about tour time. If we can stand to walk on our blisters by the end of the day, I'll buy you a drink at the hotel."

I'm not drinking with you, Daniel Kerry.

"That would be nice, Dan. I'll look forward to it."

August 2, 2:36 P.M.

Yichang Enlai had missed the luncheon, over which he was supposed to preside, with the security personnel from Aerospatiale-BAC, BBK Enterprises, Pacific Aerospace Incorporated, and the Tupolev Design Bureau.

Instead, he had supervised the gathering and recording of evidence at the scene of the bomb blast in conjunction with the investigators from the national police, then allowed the impatient and tidy people from the maintenance division to begin cleaning up the mess surrounding the tower. They could not touch anything on the inside until the investigators had had their look.

He had joined the group at his table—Charles Whitlock of PAI, Ernst Bergen of BBK, Yuri Yelchenko of Tupolev, and Stephen Dowd of Aerospatiale-BAC—as dessert was being served, and he had had only a few minutes in which to familiarize himself with them before they began their tour.

The specialists with each team—the computer and facilities people—went off with Yichang's own assistants, and he led the foreign security chiefs across the wide expanse of the observation deck—which was subdivided into functional spaces by several interior bulkheads—toward the elevators. He explained features as they walked.

"Each of the six subordinate terminals has facilities which could become available to as many as ten air carriers. Besides the observation deck, with its restaurants and coffee shops, there are six more floors above ground level. The first two floors are devoted to airline operations such as ticketing and baggage handling, and the other four floors are planned for offices and shops.

"The main terminal"—he pointed toward the largest dome a thousand meters away—"has twelve floors in addition to the observation floor, eleven restaurants, seven lounges, one hundred shops and stores, a three-hundred-room hotel, and facilities for up to fifteen air carriers. The carriers housed in Terminal One, as you know, will be restricted to those utilizing supersonic transports."

The five of them crossed one of the many bridges over the

open center of the dome's floors and boarded one of the elevators at the core of the dome. At three points on the perimeter of the dome, transportation between floors was by escalator. The elevator doors were made of glass so that passengers could look out on the atrium of each floor as they descended. The open central section on each floor allowed natural light filtering through the dome to penetrate the inner layers. In this terminal, gardeners and florists were already beginning to plant many of the tropical plants that would adorn each level. The planters were finished in red-and-black tiles, the accenting color scheme of Terminal Seven.

Yichang pressed the button for Sublevel Three.

Whitlock asked him, "Have you learned anything significant about the explosion, Mr. Yichang?"

"These things take time, Mr. Whitlock."

"Still, there must be something."

"Three people are dead, and three are seriously injured. The explosive material was plastic, probably C-4. It was attached to four support columns, and at this time, we think that it was detonated remotely."

Yichang hated detailing those facts, but he was also burdened with the knowledge that these four men were supposed to be experts in his own field. They were concerned with the precautions taken at Deng Xiaoping International Superport and with the safety of the very valuable prototype aircraft their respective companies would be bringing to the airport. Chairman Sun Chen had ordered Yichang to be very open with them, and the order was antithetic to anything in his previous experience as a military policeman, then a national police investigator.

Yelchenko asked, "What of the perpetrators? I think that you must have suspects in mind."

Yichang Enlai steeled himself to giving up what he considered trade, as well as state, secrets. "There are, quite naturally, a large number of people who oppose this enterprise, Mr. Yelchenko. They range from disenchanted . . . nationals of my country to outright terrorists to persons of other nationalities. We have quite a large database of potential suspects, and we are currently searching it."

"This does smack of terrorism, does it not?" Dowd asked.

"That is our first thought, yes," Yichang admitted.

They lost the atrium concept at the first floor, and their view through the glass doors of the elevator was of a tiled wall, laid with an intricate black-and-red design. Dragons and flowers predominated.

He explained the baggage management system on the first sublevel and the engineering spaces on the second sublevel as they passed them.

The elevator came to a soft halt on the third sublevel, and the glass doors slid back smoothly and quietly.

Yichang stepped out of the car onto the wide platform. This was the main transit level. One more level down, not accessible by the standard elevators, was the maze of 130 kilometers of maintenance tunnels which carried power, water, sewage, and communications conduits.

The transit level consisted of twenty-seven kilometers of tunnel which, reminiscent of the domes above, was constructed with an arched roof. It was finished in crisp white, with yellow and blue accents, to give it a bright and vibrant feeling. As yet, there were no signs in place to direct incoming and outgoing passenger traffic to their proper destinations, but the sign frames were attached to the walls and over portals. Additionally, a few television monitors mounted in the walls would assist travellers with information about flights and gate locations, though their screens were now blank.

In the center of the tunnel, in a depressed pit so that the floor level was at the same height as the passenger cars, were the rails for the trains.

On a standard near the barrier isolating the rail pit was a large square button impressed with the legend in Chinese, French, and English, "Train Stop."

He pressed the button.

"When we become fully operational," Yichang said, "a two-car people mover will arrive every one and a half minutes and stop automatically. Each car can carry forty people. At the moment, we have trains scheduled every ten minutes. It is completely computerized."

"What is the route?" Ernst Bergen asked.

"The people mover makes a circuit of the seven terminals, the maintenance area, the commerce area, and the transportation transfer area, where people can change to ground transport by automobile, bus, limousine, or train. At the terminals and the transfer area, the trains will stop automatically when the airport becomes operational. Someone wishing to get off at one of the maintenance hangars, for instance, must push a button to order the stop. The computer then adjusts the speed of all trains to account for the unscheduled stop."

"What about your security personnel?" Whitlock asked. "Are they tied to the trains?"

"No. We have available electric carts on Sublevel Four if we need to move quickly underground."

Yichang heard the train coming, and the entire group swivelled to watch it zooming around a curve in the well-lighted tunnel toward them. It was extremely quiet. The wheels had a hardened rubber surface, and the rails—continuously welded, with very few joints—were coated with some Teflon-impregnated substance that had once been explained to Yichang. The chassis of each car rode on an air-cushioned suspension.

The two cars were aerodynamically designed, almost free-form in their flowing lines, and the upper halves were entirely transparent, made of a clear, acrylic plastic. As they approached the station under the power of the electric motors mounted to all four of the wheel trucks, they slowed smoothly from 75 kilometers per hour to stop cleanly, and exactly, in front of his group.

The white ceramic tile of the flooring was delineated with dark blue ceramic pieces that formed entrance and exit lines precisely in front of the train's doors. As the train came to a stop, sections in the two-railed, blue-painted divider that kept the crowds from falling into the rail pit slid back to allow them access to the doors. The car doors also slid aside automatically.

Yichang led his party aboard, and a few seconds later, the sensors in the floor of the train and the floor of the tunnel detected no additional passengers and notified the computer. The computer closed the doors, and the train accelerated smoothly. Along the front panel below the windscreen was a series of square buttons, and he pressed the one marked, "Terminal One."

"Between the terminals," Yichang said, "the people mover only achieves a top speed of forty kilometers per hour."

Whitlock settled into one of the cushioned seats lining the side of the car. "I wish I had one of these in California, Mr. Yichang. I could give up my old Pontiac."

Yichang knew that PAI had occupied the facilities in Southern California that had been formerly owned by Lockheed Aircraft. He also knew that Whitlock spent a great deal of his time lately working out of the PAI offices in

Tokyo. He was not certain how he should take Whitlock's remark.

"Disconcerting, however, to not see a driver up in front," Stephen Dowd said. "I certainly like to see the operators."

"One becomes accustomed to it rapidly," Yichang said.

The train whisked past Terminals Five and Three—Two, Four, and Six were on the other side of the main terminal—and slid to a stop at the far end of the platform under Terminal One. Up to six of the two-car trains could park simultaneously at the platform.

As they stepped off the car, Yichang said, "In the morning, we will examine the surface facilities and the perimeter by ground transport. This afternoon, I want to show you the central command and communications arrangements."

"We'll also get to see the maintenance tunnels, won't we?" Charles Whitlock asked.

Yichang gritted his teeth.

Everything they ask for, the Chairman said.

"If you insist, Mr. Whitlock. They are dismal, I warn you."

"But that's how your terrorists got in, wouldn't you say?"

"Perhaps. We have a large number of construction crews with access on the surface, also."

He led the way to the elevators, and they rode to the tenth floor. Exiting the car there, Yichang piloted them down a long and wide corridor to a door marked for access to authorized personnel. He bent over to slide the edge of his ID card through the magnetic strip reader slot in the door access panel.

Behind that door was only a small anteroom, blindingly white, with a steel door and a mirror in one wall and a second steel door in the adjacent wall. The door to the right led to the security center, and the one directly ahead provided entry to the communications center. He would show them the communications capability, first. Yichang pressed his thumb to a reader panel, and the computer identified him by his thumbprint.

A speaker in the ceiling issued a smooth voice in English. "You have guests, Director Yichang?"

"Yes. Please stand before the window, gentlemen."

One by one, each man stood in front of the window until the technicians on the other side of the one-way glass compared his features with the pictures they had, then pressed his thumb against the reader so that the computer could compare it with the prints previously submitted. As each identification was confirmed, a small tray opened in the wall, and a laminated photo ID appeared.

Whitlock picked his out of the tray and clipped it to his breast pocket. He had been wearing the identification badge issued by Pacific Aerospace, and he dropped it in his jacket pocket.

"I suspect that this will not open doors for me, Mr. Yichang."

Yichang smiled. "I am afraid not, except lavatories for authorized personnel."

When they entered it, they found the communications center in frenzied activity. A dozen technicians were still installing consoles and electronic components. Some systems were functional already, and some were undergoing various stages of testing.

The outer wall was curved since it was also the outer wall of the dome. The glass here was darker, dimming the natural light, and the room's lighting was controlled by computer so that it maintained the same degree of luminosity day and night. Almost the entire perimeter of the room was occupied by electronic consoles, and the center floor contained master consoles where supervisors would direct the operation.

"This is the nerve center for the entire superport," Yichang said. "From here, for example, we can monitor every vehicle that enters the transfer point. Trains, buses, taxis, and limousines have bar-code identifiers on their windshields which are read by sensors mounted over the incoming and departing traffic lanes, and cars entering the parking garages have their license plate numbers entered into the system. We know, from one moment to the next, how many vehicles are on the grounds, and we can identify them precisely.

"The people movers record and report the number of people utilizing them. Within thirty seconds, I can tell you how many people are in the airport or, for example, how many are in Hangar One."

"Bloody damned amazing," Stephen Dowd said. "Do you keep a record?"

"I know where you are going with that question, Mr. Dowd, but yes, we will keep a record for ninety days. And yes, my people are examining the records currently on computer file. We will compare the numbers for each day against the number and the names of workers reported by the subcontractors."

"That's bound to be slightly inaccurate, though," Whitlock said.

"I suspect so," Yichang said. "Most of the subcontractors enter the field on the surface, where we do not have electronic tracking. We do have a portable electronic scanner that records the entry and exit of each worker, but there are bound to be a few exceptions. I do not think we will identify the bombers that way, but we will go through the exercise, anyway."

"This center," he continued, "is also the hub for all telephone service, data transmission, security checkpoints, baggage control, lighting systems, air conditioning, almost everything. Air traffic control is maintained at another center, in the base of the main control tower. Both centers are supported by a fiber-optic system that rings the airport. There are two systems, actually, one being a backup. Fiber optics in a bundle this size"—he held up his hand, his thumb and middle finger joined—"transmits millions of bits of information at nanosecond speeds. In comparison, the use of copper wire is similar to using wheelbarrows alongside the Mach 2 airplanes your companies have built."

Most of them appreciated the analogy, Yichang thought.

Whitlock raised a finger.

"Mr. Whitlock?"

"Perhaps this is a sensitive question, Mr. Yichang. If you're controlling telephone and data transmissions here, I suspect that some of the airlines and the companies using the systems will have a concern about the integrity of their proprietary information."

"Ah, secrets. Yes, we have considered the necessity of trade and industrial confidentiality. This center monitors only usage and maintenance, for billing purposes. Each company issued a lease will also be issued scrambling devices for their voice and data networks, the encoding selected by the user. We do not intend to eavesdrop."

"We will want to examine the encryption and network schematics," Whitlock said.

"My assistant is providing that information to your computer persons," Yichang told him.

"Great."

"Eight thousand kilometers of fiber-optic cabling is utilized in the system, gentlemen. The control tower, in one instance, obtains information from sensors imbedded in the runways and aprons. They will know, even in the densest fog, exactly where every aircraft is located. Here, this is a monitor of the control tower system."

Yichang stepped over to one console and spoke to the operator in Chinese. Though Yichang had been born in Hengyang and raised by parents who spoke the Yue dialect—called Cantonese by outsiders—the language of the Superport was the official language of the nation, known as Mandarin by nonChinese. Chinese preferred to call it *putonghua,* common language.

The screen in front of the operator came to life with a symbolic depiction of Terminal Seven. Small and large symbols of aircraft ringed it in their parked positions, and next to each symbol was a set of descriptive information, shown in Chinese characters. Yichang said to the operator, "Convert to English."

With one press of a key, the Chinese characters transformed themselves into English letters. Next to one of the airplane icons was the legend:

MYSTERE-FALCON 92176
AEROSPATIALE-BAC
ARR: 2 AUG/0942
DPT: 3 AUG/2000 EST. (PENDING)

The others were identified similarly.

"Each identification is backed up by a complete record in the database," Yichang said. "Such things as fuel loaded or maintenance performed is recorded, along with the monthly billings."

"Our Citation is now a permanent record of Deng Xiaoping International Superport?" Whitlock asked.

"Absolutely. And before your pilot takes off, he will complete a form which will be read by the computer scanners. Our records will contain information about when the airplane was constructed and when it last had airframe, engine, or avionics overhauls. We think that information contributes to safety, and poorly maintained aircraft will not be allowed to land here."

"What did this entire system cost you?" Bergen asked.

"I believe the number is well over two billion dollars, American. It seems high, but we have the advantage of foreplanning. At older airports, new technology in communications, or perhaps in security, is added piecemeal. Here, we have tried to envision, and provide for, what may become available in the future. The fiber-optic network contains millions of unused circuits. The antenna complex, which is located in the northwest corner of the airfield, now contains radar and microwave transmission antennas, in addition to weather sensors, but there is a large amount of room for expansion. Individual air carriers may move their own computer systems into their facilities, but the networks they will use are already installed and will be part of the leasing arrangements."

Yichang allowed the security chiefs to wander about the room examining consoles for fifteen minutes, then led them through a connecting doorway into the security center.

"On the far side of the communications center is the computer center. Two levels down is a backup computer system, and both are supported by batteries and emergency generators, in the event of a power failure. Here, we have the hub for all security at the airport."

It was a large space, again adjacent to the outer wall of the dome, and again with controlled lighting so that the television monitors could be viewed without glare. One wall contained five rows of television monitors. The opposite wall abutted a series of small, glass-faced cubicle/offices for Yichang's various assistant directors along with his own office against the curved outside wall. Two rows of desks in the center of the room, each with three monitors molded into its desktop, faced the monitor wall.

"In each of the airport terminals, as well as at the maintenance section, and in three current locations in the commercial area," he told them, "there are security substations. Terminal One has two hundred and sixty television cameras monitoring the hallways and public areas, and there are a proportionate number of cameras located in the other terminals and structures. The cameras are all hidden from view, and each camera has a two-hour loop videotape to provide backup to the live action seen on the monitors. Additionally, in the event of a fire, the cameras closest to the fire will automatically swivel and focus on the problem area. There are exterior cameras monitoring the fences and the transfer area. In this center, we can tap into any camera on the airport, or we can link a camera to computer files to identify suspect persons."

Yichang swept his arm toward the cubicles and desks. "My assistants are in charge of every activity that takes place in security—from walking patrols to internal criminal investigations to providing guards for the transfer of cash. We maintain a close liaison with the fire control division. We monitor for interference, or tapping, into the telephone and data transfer networks. We maintain our own criminal and suspect database, and we are in contact with the national crime database. Currently, we are seeking an agreement with Interpol in which we will share information."

Yichang could not help smiling. He was very proud of what he had accomplished. It helped, of course, to have almost unlimited funds available when building such a security system. And the Chairman had recognized the importance of having a world-class operation when the Superport entered into competition with the world.

"This is very impressive," Charles Whitlock said. "But we still have the problem of a terrorist or two running about, don't we?"

Yichang thought it condescending of Whitlock to include himself in the "we."

"Yes, Mr. Whitlock. We still have that problem."

Newport Beach, California
August 1, 11:49 P.M.

Peter James Jackson's home on Upper Newport Bay reflected his $400,000 per year salary. P.J., as he preferred to be called, had laid out 2.2 million dollars for the smallish, six-bedroom Tudor-style house and let his wife, Valerie, charge another $100,000 on the Gold Card for the furnishings.

He was comfortable when he was home, which wasn't often. Jackson thought he earned his salary by putting in seventy- and eighty-hour weeks as Executive Vice President and Chief Operating Officer of Pacific Aerospace Incorporated.

Jackson had come home early today at five in the afternoon after a hellish board meeting where he and Ken Stephenson, PAI's president, had been lambasted by the outside directors. He had said hello to Valerie, walked straight through the house shedding his coat and tie, and right out the big sliding glass door to the patio. Grabbing a one-liter bottle of Black Label from the patio bar, he had carried it down the long sloping lawn to the dock where his forty-foot Hatteras was secured. Though he had once commanded naval ships, the Hatteras had never been to sea under Jackson's command. He had never had the free time.

Valerie left him alone while he sat on the afterdeck all evening, sipping scotch and staring at the sparse water traffic on the bay. She knew what these moods were like.

The lights from houses across the bay reflected like a second set of stars on the water's surface.

He had ignored the telephone extension on the boat all evening, letting Valerie pick up in the house, but when it rang this late, he grabbed it from the table beside his deck chair.

"Yeah?"

"P.J., it's Dan."

The connection was surprisingly good. Kerry sounded like he was next door.

"Middle of your afternoon, there. You taking the day off?" His words were a little slurred, but not bad.

"Have you been drinking?" Kerry asked.

"Damned right."

"Bad board meeting, then?"

"This line secure?"

"I think so. I'm calling from the communications center at the airport. I remember places like this from my first trip to Tomorrowland. I think I was about ten years old at the time."

"The outside directors," Jackson said. The outside directors represented about fifteen billion dollars in Pacific Aerospace investment, and they carried a hell of a lot of weight.

"Let me guess," Kerry said. "They're getting antsy about October first."

"Paranoid's a better word. Their eyes are dark and sunken. They see all the cash that's been flowing out. They wonder why no revenue has shown up yet. I don't think they've really figured out the game plan."

"Any ultimatums?"

"You might say that. The president and myself are out on our respective asses on October fifteenth, if we don't have a contract."

"There will be some trickle-down?" Kerry asked.

"Damned right. I fire you before I clean out my desk."

"I better go back to work, then."

"Good idea. Say, what the hell are you doing? What's the place like?"

"We're on a break from our tour. And you've never seen an airstrip like this, P.J. I'll send you the brochures. They're handing out brochures like they own a printing plant. They probably do, but the tour hasn't reached it yet."

"Are you getting any take from the opposition?"

"Nothing worth commenting about," Kerry said. "I'm taking the Aerospatiale rep out for a drink later."

"She as good-looking as her picture?"

"Won't do us any good. She doesn't like me."

"Then why in hell am I spending good money on a single guy like you? Tell me that."

"You're paying for my mind, not my bod. Besides, I don't think a Concorde upgrade is going to hurt us, anyway."

"Shit. You'd better be selling the airplane, buddy. I like my house."

"You're never there."

"I lose it, and Valerie'll cut me off in more ways than one. You start convincing people."

"I'm convinced."

"You don't count."

August 2, 6:31 P.M.

Dan Kerry wasn't the type to pay for guided tours when he was travelling. He preferred wandering about on his own. He often missed the highlights—Big Ben, the Eiffel Tower, the Golden Buddha, the Dolphin—of London, Paris, Bangkok, or Copenhagen when he toured that way, but he frequently stumbled into more interesting situations.

He had been in southern China before, and had gotten to know Hong Kong in a similar accidental manner in four previous visits. The first time, on an R&R tour out of Vietnam in 1972, he had been chiefly interested in discovering the locations of every nightclub on the island and in Kowloon. He came close to succeeding in that quest.

At China Dome, he was content to take the tour and listen to the tour guide, Superport Administrator Zhao Li. The man was intensely proud of his airport, and the pride crept through in enthusiastic bursts of hyperbole as he enumerated the virtues. So far, he hadn't pointed out one vice. Zhao was a round-faced man with dark hair forming a majestic widow's peak and large, wire-rimmed glasses. When he really got into his message, the glasses vibrated on his nose.

On their journey through Terminal Seven, the larger Terminal One, Hangar Three of the maintenance complex, and several structures in the line of commercial spaces, they travelled both overland by bus and underground by way of the people mover.

This examination of the grounds was a first for outsiders. Though the airport had been under construction for nearly three years, nonChinese visitors had been politely turned away until now. Only photographs released to the Western press had detailed the progress and a few of the features. Kerry knew, also, that this tour was aimed more at the representatives from International Air Transport Association (IATA) air carriers than at Kerry, Broussard, Stuttmann, or Zemenek, though Kerry was certain it was intended to impress all of them. The agents of American, United, El Al, Air France, TWA, Quantas, Lufthansa, and others were here to be enticed. They would go back to their respective headquarters, extolling the promises of China Dome and urging the pertinent executives to get in line for space and gates at the new aerodrome in southern China.

It was going to be an expensive endeavor for them since the Committee for Airport Construction, which with a few changes in its membership would eventually become the Committee for Airport Operation, would require the major airlines serving the Deng Xiaoping International Superport from the Americas, from Europe, and from western Asia to service it primarily with supersonic transports (SSTs).

That was why it was called a Superport.

Seventy percent of the traffic through China Dome would be comprised of SSTs, and the balance—primarily from nearby Asian, Indian subcontinent, and Pacific nations—would be of conventional jet aircraft. This was going to be the fastest airport in the world.

And the air carriers who wanted a piece of the action, and the huge chunks of money that would be flowing, would have to go along with the people who controlled the airport.

The IATA members vying for space at the airport already knew where their supersonic transports were coming from.

From the Chinese.

All SSTs utilizing China Dome would be owned by the Committee for Airport Operation and would be leased to the air carriers desiring to participate.

Which is why Kerry, Broussard, Stuttmann, and Zemenek were present for a first glimpse of Deng Xiaoping International. They represented the four manufacturers vying for the SST contract to be awarded by the Chinese on October 5.

The initial contract could be worth fifteen billion dollars. Kerry didn't see it as dollars, though. He saw it as jobs. He saw the old Lockheed plant in California swarming with the engineers, machinists, mill workers, electronics technicians, and airframe specialists laid off from Boeing, Martin-Marietta, Lockheed, Hughes, and other defense-related industries when the Pentagon went into a downslope configuration.

He saw Hangar Three, and the others, peopled with employees of PAI.

The vendor who captured this contract would not only build and certify the initial order for eighty SST aircraft; they would also provide the pilots who flew them, the technicians who maintained them, and the replacement parts that kept them flying. They would establish maintenance facilities all around the world in order to service the aircraft on the outbound legs of their routes. It was an enormous and very international undertaking. Staying on the positive side, Kerry knew that when PAI secured the contract, they would have to create training programs for flight and maintenance personnel. They would have to recruit talent from twenty or thirty nations to staff both China Dome and the foreign facilities of the airlines that secured leases.

Kerry had some misgivings about the fact that the center of all of this supercharged progress was located in the Orient, but the reality was that the hub of commerce was moving from the Atlantic to the Pacific Rim, and he was excited about the prospects. It made life more vibrant.

They were in a large open dome—ready to be configured into spaces designed by the lessee—in the commercial section when Zhao Li finally looked at the large gold watch on his wrist and realized what time it was.

He turned to the group standing behind him and said, "I am afraid I must apologize to you all, once again. I have exceeded my time limit, and I am certain that you must be hungry and tired. It is difficult for me to remember the mundane things, like time and appetite, when so much of significance is taking place all around me. Come, we will go down to the trains."

Kerry took one more look around the dome as he fell into line behind a visibly weary man whose visitor badge said he was from New Zealand.

The interior was a large and echoing vacancy. All of the support services, like telephone, electricity, and water, were in place, but the outfit that leased the place could subdivide any way they liked. It could be one business or twenty. It could be one floor with a very high ceiling, or it could be five floors. It could house light industry—plastics, electronics, or an international bank, or a stock exchange. There were twenty of these domes to be completed in the first phase of construction, fifteen in the second phase, and more as necessary according to Zhao. The Chinese had done well to leave the options so open.

They walked down inoperative escalators to the transit level on the third sublevel. Zhao had explained that a second subterranean tunnel also served the commercial domes, providing access for cargo handling by way of rail cars shuttled about by electric locomotives.

The final leg of the trip to the transportation transfer facility was a short one, and Kerry barely had time to meet a man from Pakistan and a woman named Misty from Ireland. Misty had great big green eyes and loads of red hair. She also talked a mile-a-minute.

The people mover rails gained altitude as they neared the transfer point, and when the train slid to a stop, they were at ground level, but inside another dome. The group filed out onto the platform, and Kerry checked the signs. Some aimed passengers toward the parking garages, via moving sidewalks that weren't yet moving. Some pointed the way toward the bus and limousine pickup areas.

Directly across the platform, resting on another set of rails, was a seven-car train that appeared to be a near design match for the people mover, though the dimensions for each car were greater in width and length.

"I must make one more short speech before I send you on to your hotel," Zhao Li said. "And I should provide a short history lesson. Many of you know that Hong Kong consists of the Island of Hong Kong, the Kowloon Peninsula, the New Territories north of Kowloon, and over two hundred and thirty islands.

"The British gained control of the Island in 1842 and then the Kowloon Peninsula in 1860 through treaty agreements with China."

Kerry noted that Zhao did not elaborate on the 1842 Treaty of Nanjing, the result of the Opium War. The war broke out because China objected to British merchants smuggling opium into China.

Despite the objection, Britain won.

"In 1898," Zhao continued, "they leased the New Territories for a period of ninety-nine years. Hong Kong has been known as a British Crown Colony, though it was officially redesignated as a dependency in the 1970s. In 1984, China and Great Britain arrived at an agreement for the transfer of Hong Kong to Chinese control upon the expiration of the New Territories lease."

Personally, Kerry thought the British were damned short-sighted. Ninety-nine years looked like a long time back in the midnineteenth century, he supposed.

"Under that agreement, Hong Kong will be a special administrative area of China, similar to Beijing, Shanghai, or Tianjin. The administration of the municipality will be local, subject only to the defense and foreign policies of China. Hong Kong also will maintain its capitalist economy, within the Chinese socialist system.

"Though Hong Kong will shortly come under Chinese administration, we envision the proud history of commerce to continue without alteration, and in fact, we expect it to grow significantly. That is the reason for Deng Xiaoping International Superport."

Zhao gestured toward the south. "Some of you came here by way of Kai Tak Airport in Kowloon, I know. For the others, let me explain the geography. The airport is located eight kilometers north of Lo Wu, which is on the border between the New Territories and the People's Republic of China. By way of the Guanzhou-Kowloon Railway, which some of you know as the Canton-Kowloon Railway, it is thirty-six kilometers, or twenty-one miles from Kowloon.

"The rapid transit train that you see here is currently operational only to the border. However, we have reached an agreement whereby we are beginning to construct the rails for the rapid transit system in the New Territories, following the Guanzhou-Kowloon right-of-way. The construction should be completed within the year, and then Kowloon will be but thirteen minutes from this platform by way of the rapid transit train.

"Unfortunately, at this time, I must send you on your way by bus. However, I hope that your needs will be met satisfactorily, and if they are not, please do tell me so. Your luggage has already been delivered to the President Hotel, and you need but sign for your rooms or meals. Until we meet in the morning, I wish you an enjoyable stay."

While Zhao walked among them shaking hands, Kerry looked for the rest of his party. They weren't on the platform, so he assumed they were going to be either late or early. He wouldn't worry about them since, as he had learned over the years, the Chinese were generally exceptionally solicitous of their visitors. The little things, like securing transportation or manhandling luggage, were always accomplished quietly and efficiently.

He looked for Jacqueline Broussard, but found her in the midst of a half-dozen admirers, or would-be admirers. She spoke animatedly with all of them as they drifted down the platform and through a short tunnel into another dome. In the immense labyrinth of passenger platforms and driving lanes, two buses waited for them, and they climbed aboard.

Kerry found himself seated in the second bus next to an operations executive from Lufthansa, and the two of them passed the time exchanging their positive reactions to China Dome. Even the German called it China Dome.

The Lufthansa rep was as enthused as if he had spent the day in a motivational sales seminar conducted by a propagandizing hypnotist.

Listening to the German, he halfway worried that Broussard, who was in the first bus, would get away from him. He remembered being ditched by promising young ladies when he was thirty years younger and sixteen inches shorter in Clovis, New Mexico.

The bus made its way south, passing through patches of fertile farming land with rice paddies and vegetable gardens, barren lands of rocky hills, and small villages constructed primarily of concrete. As they neared Kowloon, the high-rise apartment buildings appeared, then the neon garishness of the business district. Even in daylight, with the neon turned off, the signs advertising a million businesses dominated the facades of buildings. Many of those buildings, taking up a full block, could house a thousand tailor shops, leather shops, camera merchandisers, and exotic furniture dealers inside. Tai Ping Carpet Salon, Yangtzekiang Garments, Town and Country, Jersey House, International Dress Shop—the signs said it all, Kerry thought. He considered the configuration of those blocks and blocks of small businesses as the world's first urban malls.

The driver swung off Chatham Road onto Austin Road, then took them down the bustling, overpopulated main drag of Nathan Road to give them a feeling for the zestful, sleepless life. Miraculously, the driver found a place to park in front of the hotel.

Kerry descended to the sidewalk to see Broussard near the big front doors, still surrounded by her gaggle of admirers. She was certainly equal to the admiration. Standing about five-ten, she was taller than two of the men next to her. Her bearing was regal, enhanced by the straight line of her back and the shoulder-length dark hair that cascaded to each side of her face, an elongated oval with high cheekbones. Liz Taylor eyes, he thought, almost violet in color, and large enough to give the impression of childish awe. If she used very much makeup, she used it well. There was just a touch of color in her cheeks and on her full lips. The lower lip appeared fuller when she smiled. She wore a light pink travelling suit over a lacy white blouse, and none of it did much to hide her full figure. The calves of her legs were finely turned creations that flowed smoothly into ankles that seemed too fragile for her. She also carried a shoulder bag that matched her tan high-heeled shoes and probably had the same capacity as a fifty-five-gallon fuel drum. And surrounding her was an aura of sensuality that attracted the admirers, but didn't show up at all in her photographs.

Kerry decided that he didn't want P.J. Jackson to meet her. P.J. was happily married to Valerie, but he might reconsider.

Not that Kerry had much going for him. That aura she carried also emitted sparks when she was near him.

She looked over at him, then to a chorus of dismay, excused herself and walked toward him. Kerry halved the distance by meeting her in the middle of the sidewalk. Her eyes were slightly smudged, showing some fatigue which was probably caused by jet lag.

"I used you for an alibi," she said.

"Happy to oblige. Shall we make it for dinner, on top of that drink?"

"I want to freshen up first."

"No hurry. It's customary in Hong Kong for the dinner hour to begin around nine."

"You've been here before, then?"

"A few times."

"Can we find somewhere besides the hotel for dinner? I am a little tired of the mob."

"Sure. We'll take the ferry over to Victoria."

They turned and entered the hotel together, then headed for the registration desk.

As they waited in line, Kerry said, "No."

She swung her head to look up at him, her hair shifting nicely with the movement. He noticed how long her throat appeared to be.

"Were you talking to yourself?"

"I was," he admitted.

"And what were you saying to yourself?"

"I was saying that I didn't think you'd respond well to Jackie."

"You were quite correct!" she told him.

FOUR

Mach 2.6

The numerals of the digital velocity readout were orange because that was what Terrence Carroll wanted them to be. He could select and change colors at will for each of the instrumentation readouts. It was kind of like playing with a new computer program.

His preference was to have the minor readings appear in blue and the critical monitors—indicated air speed, heading, altitude, altitude above ground level (AGL), the RPM indications for the four turbofan engines—provided in the more attention-getting orange.

His copilot, Don Matthews, had his own panels set up in the same color scheme, but with a few more selections in orange. Jeff Dormund, the flight engineer seated at a right angle to them aft of Matthews, had an entirely different color layout in green and yellow.

"That stretches the envelope pretty tight, Terry," Matthews said.

"We won't try for more speed. Anything fall off?"

"If it did, it's ten miles behind us."

"Jeff?"

"I'm in great shape. All temps and pressures right where they're supposed to be."

The top end design speed for the Pacific Aerospace Incorporated Astroliner was Mach 2.4, but that was with the maximum load of 168 passengers, a four-person cabin crew, and the cargo bays crammed to capacity. They were pushing the parameter for this test of the control surfaces. Later, the flight control computer would be programmed to prevent the aircraft from exceeding Mach 2.4. Even in a steep descent, if the computer detected excess speed, it would automatically deploy the speed brakes in order to limit the excess.

In fact, the computer also monitored the altitude in relation to the airspeed. There would eventually be speed limits applicable to various flight levels. That was not only a safety factor in regard to other aircraft at lower altitudes, but also an attempt to control fuel consumption. The thicker the atmosphere and the more friction dragging on the skin of the SST, the rate of fuel depletion climbed substantially.

At 36,000 feet however, they were at an altitude above which the speed of sound remained constant, and with the coast of California forty miles behind them, they were free to do the kinds of things that might get them wet if they reached the surface of the Pacific in one piece.

Terry Carroll knew he wasn't really free. The engineers back at the PAI lab were watching every move he made via the telemetry transmissions made through the black boxes fastened to the deck in the stripped-down passenger cabin. Every instrument reading available to Carroll, Matthews, or Dormund was also repeated on the consoles in the monitoring laboratory at Edwards Air Force Base, and someone would yell loudly if he deviated from the flight profile.

Sometimes, when he got into an argument with one of

the academics or engineers, he wanted to say, "Well, let the goddamned computer fly it, then!"

He didn't, though. He was half-frightened that the response could well be, "We'll do that."

Carroll was afraid the technology was fast approaching the time when bones and a heart wouldn't be necessary to the seat he was sitting in. Already, the machines thought a hell of a lot faster than he could, and as soon as artificial intelligence was able to make the decisions he was paid to make, he might as well head for a warm beach in Florida.

He wasn't ready to retire at forty-eight, and he was certain he wouldn't be ready to retire at seventy. Michelle, his wife of twenty years, would testify that his six-foot frame and 175 pounds were interfaced just where they were supposed to be. He'd been a Scotch-guzzling, beer-siphoning demon in his Navy days, but he'd gladly dumped those habits as the price of being selected for the Astroliner test program. Now, he felt good, and he thought he didn't look his age. His hair was still mostly in place, his cheeks and jowls were firm, and only his nose was out of alignment. That wasn't his fault, though; it was someone else's fist in a nice melee in an Angeles City bar in the Philippines a long time ago.

Carroll shifted the headset with its cantilevered microphone to a new position on his head.

"Don, call in the start of our series. Two minutes."

Matthews radioed the PAI lab at Edwards and made the announcement.

"Ten-four, Zero-One," someone, probably Dr. Dennis Aikens, the chief nerd, said.

"That sucker's still hooked on CB radios," Matthews said, though he prudently did not say it on the air.

"Let's tighten up the harness," Carroll ordered, cinching his own straps another notch.

On the instrument panels in front of the pilot's and co-pilot's seats were three large multifunction displays (MFDs). The eyebrow panel across the top of the instrument panel contained the key, orange-lit readouts, and Carroll had the base engine monitors and skin sensors displayed on the left screen. The center screen provided him with a symbolic representation of the aircraft attitude along with an artificial horizon. The right screen currently displayed the 180-degree sweep of the AN/APN 320 Doppler radar, set to a scan range of sixty miles.

There wasn't another aircraft within thirty miles of them.

Matthews had the instrument readouts on one of his screens, the display from one of the three inertial navigation platforms on another, and as a check against the inertial system, the data-link readings from the NavStar Global Positioning System on the third. The GPS was composed of eighteen satellites in orbit, three of which continually triangulated their flight for them and located them geographically within a few feet of their true position.

"Want the checklist, Terry?"

"On three."

His radar symbology disappeared from the right screen, to be replaced by the test flight checklist.

"Disengage autopilot," Carroll said, resting his hands lightly on the control yoke.

Matthews reached for the center pedestal, below the throttle quadrant, and flicked the switch.

"Autopilot off," he said.

Carroll felt the tremor in the wheel.

It was all his, but it was dangerous.

At this speed, violent maneuvers resulted in violent consequences. It was another sign of the times. The autopilot and its associated computers were better at maintaining stability than humans were. At Mach speeds, if he wanted an alteration in heading, speed, or altitude, he would generally enter the changes into the autopilot and let the computer make the corrections gradually. It was guaranteed to be a smoother transition than that made by an aviator, even though the control systems had a built-in, artificial hydraulic feel to them. It prevented excessive aerodynamic loads resulting from overcontrol by the pilot.

Not that most pilots weren't smooth, he reminded himself. Some of them might hiccup, though, and if it came at the wrong time, anything from a bump to a catastrophe could result.

He could recall times, coming off the *Ranger*'s catapult in his EA-6B Prowler tactical jamming aircraft, when the fog was so thick it seemed to be in the cockpit with him. By activating his data link with the E-2 Hawkeye airborne early warning plane, he could let the air control operator, who could see a hell of a lot better via the Hawkeye's radar, fly him through the fog and cloud cover to regions of visibility and safety. The data link utilized the autopilot for that.

Carroll had learned early-on that there were times to be a macho, hotshit pilot, and that there were other times when it was far more judicious to rely on your buddies.

"Let's go hot mike," he said.

The three crew members switched their microphones to constant transmit on the company frequency, so the scientists on the ground could monitor their conversations during the test. If something went wrong, the guys in the white coats didn't want to have to look for the black boxes—the cockpit recorders—to find out what the last words—likely to be obscene—were.

"Dr. Aikens, Carroll here."

The nerd said, "I hear you."

"We have Mach two-point-six, straight and level at thirty-six thousand."

"Copied. That agrees with our readouts."

"Going to Test Sequence One."

"Five degree up-elevon deflection only," Aikens said.

"Roger. Starting now."

Carroll eased back on the yoke, watching the elevon angle readout on the left screen.

"Two degrees."

A bit more tug on the yoke. It trembled.

"Five degrees."

"Copy," Aikens said.

The long nose of the Astroliner rose slowly.

Carroll translated what he was feeling in the yoke to a verbal report.

"I've got a flutter."

"Flutter? What does that mean? We don't see anything here."

"It means the yoke is fluttering, damn it."

"You can't feel that."

The Astroliner abruptly went into a left bank.

The nose went high, and Carroll shoved it down, trying to counter the bank with light right pressure on the wheel. Matthews put his hands on his own control yoke and assisted him.

Nothing abrupt, he reminded himself.

She continued to roll.

"Throttles, Don!"

"Coming off on the throttles."

"What's going on?" Aikens yelped.

"Shut up," Carroll said. "I'm busy."

Hong Kong Island
August 2, 9:27 P.M.

Figuring they would get more Chinese food the next day, Kerry and Broussard had opted for something with an English flavor, sharing a Beef Wellington at a small restaurant called Toodles on Connaught Road Central along the waterfront in the Victoria District. Victoria was the center of government and finance, and high-rises containing banks, investment firms, hotels, and shops catering to high fashion were the prime focus of the area.

They had a table against a large window overlooking Victoria Harbor, and the lights of Kowloon across the bay rippled on the surface of the dark waters. The silhouette of a junk crossing the harbor blotted out the far lights momentarily. Inside, the illumination was low, augmented by candles on the table, the flickering light reflecting on heavy silverware, fine china, thick white linen, and sparkling crystal. The walls were wainscoted in smooth teak planks and papered in a dark blue fleur-de-lis pattern on a cream background. Red-coated waiters were in too-perfect attendance.

The restaurant couldn't have been more romantic, but Kerry had chosen it for the food.

Beneath the polite, acquaintance-making conversation of the early evening while they made their way through dinner, the magnetic field emanating from Broussard was full of static, and he was quite aware that, despite the setting, her mind was not on romance. She toyed with her snifter, swirling the brandy lazily.

This was the point in a dinner scene when he wished he still smoked. It was time to light up.

He sipped some of his cognac. It had a deep smoky flavor to it, with a deceptive bite. He wouldn't have more than one.

"Tell me about the war," she said.

Just the perfect conversational topic.

"It was there, it was bad, and then it wasn't there."

"You don't like to talk about it?"

"No."

"You are still a pilot?"

"That, I manage to do. My first love."

And only love?

"Do you still fly jets?"

"At every available opportunity, Jacqueline. But now, they're mostly business planes. Once in a while, a friend gets me into an F-15 or F-16, but those times are entirely too rare."

"Have you flown the Astroliner?"

He thought that was where she had been headed.

"Of course," he smiled.

"And did you like it?"

"It is by far the best large airplane I've ever had the pleasure of flying. Have you piloted the Concorde? Or the Concorde II?"

"I am not a pilot."

"But, naturally, your people wanted you to have firsthand experience with the product you're peddling."

She didn't like the way he put that, he thought, but she grinned and said, "I have taken the controls for a few moments. It was exhilarating."

"What feature did you like best?"

She smiled.

He smiled back. Standoff.

"Tell you what, Jacqueline, let's put our companies off-limits for the time. We can bad-mouth the others. What do you think of the Tupolev 2000?"

The Tupolev Design Bureau, back when it was still a

component of the Union of Soviet Socialist Republics, had been first to get a supersonic transport—the Tupolev 144— airborne. The program hadn't progressed much beyond the prototype, probably because of the international popular resistance to the noisy beasts. The Concorde had run into the same problems, which was the primary reason that they flew into only New York's Kennedy International and Washington, D.C.'s, Dulles. Even those two concessions had come hard, with long and bitter legal fights in the courts and in Congress.

With the Chinese announcement of a need for SSTs, however, the Tupolev Design Bureau had been given the seed money by the Russian Republic to revive the program. Russia needed the jobs and economic boost as much as any other country, and probably more so.

"They do not have a chance in the world of obtaining the contract," Broussard said. "We do not seriously consider them as competition. Do you?"

Kerry liked the slight British accent in her speech. No doubt she had picked it up while attending Oxford.

"Personally," he said, "no. But I don't think the policy makers at PAI are taking anything for granted."

He watched her eyes to see if she picked up on the distinction he set up. Kerry set himself apart from the decision makers at PAI, whereas Broussard, with her royal or third person plural "we," had allied herself with the executives at the top of the Aerospatiale-BAC heap. Then again, maybe she was allied with them. She had some kind of special relationship with Henri Dubonnet, but his sources hadn't known what it was. His sources were the investigative agency PAI had hired to run background checks on all of the principals in the competing companies. Like Jackson with his Navy experience, Kerry liked to know the enemy as well as possible. He'd also like to know more about Broussard's connection with the managing director of Aerospatiale-BAC. For professional purposes, he told himself.

She'd be good at poker, he decided. Neither her face nor her eyes provided him with a clue as to how she took his response. She said, "Tell me why you do not think highly of the Tupolev."

"All right. First, while the Bureau had first crack at an SST, they've been out of the business for twenty years. I think, with their first model, they were making use of technology stolen from various parts of the world, and with the collapse of the Soviet Union, I don't think they've had an espionage base that has kept up with technological progress. Simply put, they haven't stolen enough new technology to put anything competitive in the air."

She started to interrupt, but when he looked up, she said, "Go on."

He was setting her up again.

"Second, they've lost a lot of talent and expertise in the last five years, good people bailing out of the Republic through immigration. If they won the contract, I don't think they would have the human resources required to fulfill it—pilots, techs, engineers, scientists. The Chinese have to be weighing that aspect.

"And third, they've tried to build the 2000 model with ideas formulated in the 144 model. And those are out of date. Building the 2000 a few feet longer than the 144 in order to meet the minimum passenger capacity specification of one hundred and sixty and slapping bigger Turmanov turbojets in it won't be enough to do the job."

"Why not?"

Kerry had seen the shadow pass through her eyes. Perhaps it was the uneven light from the candle, but he didn't think so.

"There's evolving technology, Jacqueline, and there's old technology with new paint on it. I think they're trying to get by with the latter."

She grinned at him, but it might have been to cover a sudden tic in the corner of her mouth. "You are certain of this?"

"Hey, our spies have gotten some photos. I'm sure that your spies have done the same."

If, as he and Jackson and others thought, Aerospatiale-BAC was attempting to build the Concorde II by sticking a few new computers and digital instrumentation and 128 inches of fuselage on the Concorde, then he had just given Jacqueline Broussard something new to worry about.

He hoped so. Keeping her worried was part of his job. A preoccupied Broussard wouldn't perform as well in front of the Chinese judges.

"The pictures of the 2000, the AeroSwift from BBK, and the Concorde II have all been published in *Aviation Week,*" she said.

"Long-distance pictures," he reminded her. "Taken at about the time they received their airworthiness certificates."

"We have not seen a decent picture of the Astroliner," she countered.

"That means Charley Whitlock and his buddy Tom Baker"—who was in charge of domestic security—"are doing their jobs. Plus, we haven't been certified yet. The reporters will be all over the airplane as soon as the FAA gets done with it. Hey, maybe we won't pass the testing."

"Do you really think that?"

"Of course not."

"Are you not doing the same as Tupolev, Dan? Pacific

Aerospace did purchase the Boeing prototype plans, did it not?"

The Boeing plans and test data had been a great starting point. Having access to the formulas, metallurgy, wind-tunnel statistics, power-to-weight ratios, wing chord trials, and the like had shaved years off the project. And yet, there weren't too many Boeing concepts utilized in the final version of the Astroliner.

Kerry didn't intend to respond to her question, of course. He said, "The AeroSwift is worrisome, however."

"Is it?"

"You don't think so?"

"We know that there is a great deal of money behind Boehm-Bussmeier-Kraft. The Bank of Dusseldorf has invested eight billion deutsche marks, and several prominent Arabs have joined six German nationals in providing over forty billion more. That would purchase a great deal."

"Yes. They bought the best American, British, French, German, and expatriate Russian minds. They bought technology where they couldn't devise it or didn't want to take the time to develop it. The AeroSwift is an all-new craft."

"Like yours?"

"Shall we make our way back to the mainland?"

Kerry paid the bill, and the two of them left the restaurant and went out onto the busy street. Diners and revelers hopping from supper club to nightclub peopled the street.

"Do you want a taxi?" he asked.

"I would prefer to walk. I need the exercise."

They strolled the avenue eastward, Kerry walking along the curb. The lights from shop windows and the streetlights kept their course well-illuminated. He was careful not to touch her or to offer his arm. He thought that she, too, was avoiding any physical contact.

The night people of Hong Kong swarmed around them and were aware of them. Kerry gave up counting the appraisals she received after one block and fifteen apparently positive evaluations.

Broussard was wearing a short-hemmed white cocktail dress that set off her dusky skin and revealed those fine calves. The bodice was cut not daringly low, but just enough to suggest cleavage and leave the rest to one's imagination.

Kerry had never been short of imagination.

They walked well together. She was three inches shorter than his six-one, and he didn't have to shorten his stride as they strolled through the warm and fragrant night. He figured the temperature at eighty-five and the humidity close behind that. The aura of the tropics and the scent of jasmine coated the air. The island's name, of course, derived from *Heung Kong,* meaning Fragrant Harbor, and tonight lived up to the tradition. The lighted windows of houses dotted the side of the slope leading up to Victoria Peak. There was a tramway operating for the tourists, but he didn't suggest taking the excursion.

At the Star Ferry, they had a ten-minute wait, and they stood in line with a few dozen other people, mainly couples.

"Have you travelled a lot, Dan?"

"I've gotten around some."

"I have been all over the Continent, of course, and to the United States and North Africa a number of times, twice to Beijing now, but this is my first time in Hong Kong."

"How about Japan?"

"Not yet."

"You'll have to visit me in Tokyo."

"Perhaps. I had expected Hong Kong to be a dirty city, full of intrigue. As in my childhood reading. Marseilles is much worse."

"There may be an intrigue or two floating around, Jacqueline, but they seem to keep them out of sight of us tourist-types. No, it's a good city."

When the ferry docked, they boarded on the passenger deck, above the automobiles, and moved to the forward starboard side to watch a few ships moving in Kowloon Bay, which was east of Victoria Bay. Kerry remembered spending a large number of idle hours just watching traffic in the bay. The contrast between modern container ships and ancient and ageless junks was fascinating.

He leaned forward and rested his elbows on the railing.

Broussard did the same, and when the ferry lurched away from her slip, she tilted sideways and pressed her shoulder against his own.

Kerry had a sudden insight. The undercurrent of static he detected in Jacqueline Broussard might be of the clinging variety.

Not that he minded.

Edwards Air Force Base, California
August 2, 10:50 A.M.

Terry Carroll, with Don Matthews and Jeff Dormund in his wake, followed Dennis Aikens out to the tarmac.

Aikens, wearing the two hats of Manager of Production and Chief Engineer, was the skinniest man Carroll had ever seen. At six-seven, he couldn't be carrying much more meat than a medium-sized Saint Bernard. With big, brown Saint Bernard eyes magnified by thick lenses in heavy horn-rimmed glasses and a shaggy mop of similar-colored hair, Aikens seemed more a caricature of himself than himself. Carroll had heard that he had fought his way through undergraduate school on a basketball scholarship, then wormed his way into the Massachusetts Institute of Technology on pure academic ability.

Carroll, after getting the Astroliner out of Mach speeds, had recovered from the inadvertent rolling and successfully landed at Edwards at seven-thirty in the morning. The flight crew and the engineers had spent the last three hours reviewing the tapes from the aircraft recorders as well as the telemetry data recorded by the people manning the flight test lab.

After the air conditioned environment of the lab, the heat rolling off the concrete hit him like a slap in the face. He unzipped the upper six inches of his gray flight suit as he trailed after Aikens. Matthews and Dormund were wearing the same flight suit, with the PAI logo above the right breast pocket. Aikens wore running shoes, blue jeans, and a red-and-white-striped polo shirt that was intended to give him an illusion of breadth. Instead, it made him look like an old-fashioned barber pole, Carroll thought.

Aikens, with a perfect mind that only accepted perfection, was still unable to grasp the fact that the Astroliner misbehaved on her own. For three hours, Carroll and his crew had been interrogated about their history of criminality. "How often have you performed practical jokes in the past, Terry?"

"Fuck you, Dennis."

Not a productive morning.

The field in this section of Edwards appeared deserted but for a row of automobiles parked near the hangar. PAI was leasing the hangar and time on the runway from the Air Force since the Astroliner, like its Concorde cousins, had never been certified for civilian airfields in California. Unlike the Concorde, the Astroliner was relatively quiet, and the PAI bigwigs didn't think they'd have any trouble finding space at commercial airports once they had had a chance to demonstrate the transport. Somebody was supposedly working on getting the legal restrictions lifted, and Carroll hoped that somebody was on the job. The Astroliner wouldn't do anyone any good if it wasn't allowed to utilize LAX or San Francisco International.

One of the positive spin-offs from operating out of Edwards right now was that the PAI aircraft remained out of the media eye. The security types like Tom Baker were happy with the arrangement.

A quarter-mile and a half-pint of sweat later, the four men entered the monstrous hangar which, at great expense to Pacific Aerospace, was air conditioned.

The two airplanes took up almost all of the available space.

The closest plane was the Astroliner. At 247 feet, it was sixteen feet longer than a Boeing 747 and forty-four feet longer than the Concorde. While a 747 had a 195-foot wingspan, and the Concorde an eighty-four-foot span, the Astroliner fell into the middle of that range at ninety-two feet.

She was the sleekest thing Terry Carroll had ever seen. Delta-winged in smooth flowing curves, she had an elongated tail and a swooping vertical tail fin. The trailing edge of the delta wing was not perpendicular to the fuselage, but angled toward the tail, flowing into it in an arcing curve. The thick wings, which carried 200,000 pounds of fuel, were molded into the fuselage in such a way that the wing and fuselage appeared to be one unit.

Slung beneath the fuselage and wing on the aft end was the single nacelle housing the four giant turbofan engines. The nacelle was also molded to the curvature of the bottom wing and was similar to the design of the Tupolev 144. The

Concorde, the Concorde II, and the BBK Enterprises AeroSwift housed their engines in paired nacelles beneath the wings.

Forward, the long and slender nose of the aircraft housed the cockpit with its bronzed side windows and windscreen and was aimed at the hangar doors like a dart. Unlike the Concorde, the Astroliner's nose did not droop for takeoff or landing. A video camera fixed in the nose gave the pilot and copilot a landing view on any of their multifunction screens. Carroll had always thought of the Concorde as an ungainly goose coming in for a landing, with her snout dropped for visibility. No drooping snouts for the Astroliner.

She stood high above them, the bottom surface of the wing a little over twelve feet off the hangar floor. The extreme extension of the tricycle landing gear was necessary to provide clearance for the underslung engine nacelle during takeoff rotation.

The Astroliner's skin was impregnated with a matte silver finish to reflect heat, and it was bonded to the framework with a Super Glue spin-off from a National Aeronautics and Space Administration program. Down the side of the fuselage was a row of rectangular, rounded-corner portholes, again in bronzed glass. There were forty-three portholes, one for each of the four-seat rows, and one for the galley/cabin crew area. A Chinese Red streak of paint shot down the side of the fuselage, encompassing the portholes, and curved up the vertical tail fin. The slanted streak on the tail was broken up into the stylized PAI logo.

The underseat cargo bay, combined with the aft cargo bay, could handle ten tons of baggage.

When the interior was finished, the Astroliner would seat 168 passengers with a 36-inch seat spacing providing adequate foot room. That compared to the Concorde at 144 seats with a 32-inch seat pitch. No one yet knew what the Concorde II was going to do to a passenger's feet, but the highly salaried guessers thought that the British-French consortium was simply adding seats at the same 32-inch spacing. The Astroliner's additional thirteen feet of fuselage length cost big bucks, but the design team had determined that the increase in passenger comfort would be a major selling point.

On the far side of the Astroliner in the hangar was PAI's ace-up-the-sleeve. Parked nose to tail alongside the Astroliner, she hadn't been seen by anyone outside of the company, and she was a dead match for the Astroliner except for the long row of passenger windows. They were missing on the Astrofreighter. The cargo craft had the same red streak and PAI logo.

With no passenger deck floor, her hull could hold 60,000 pounds of freight, accessed by a ramp which lowered toward the front from the fuselage bottom, just aft of the cockpit. Small tractors could zip up the ramp with pallets of freight. Additionally, the ramp could be stacked with boxes, crates, or shipping containers before it was lifted into flight position. PAI thought that if they showed up at the final judging by the Chinese with a cargo version of the airplane, they would garner a few extra plus marks in their column of the evaluation sheet.

Carroll admired his 130-million-dollar airplane from below as he followed Aikens below the wing toward the aft end. A dozen men were hanging from scaffolding, crawling over the wing, probing into opened access panels with high-powered halogen lights, and generally searching for a defect that Aikens swore wasn't present.

They stopped below the trailing edge and looked up. The Astroliner utilized four sets of elevons on each wing. The split panels acted as a singular unit, raising or lowering when operating in their elevator mode, or split—the left side rising and the right side dropping for a left bank—when utilized as ailerons. They were also considered flaperons, utilized as flaps for increased lift during takeoff and landing. The safety factors were redundancy intensified. Two separate systems of electrical control and hydraulic actuation controlled the elevons in each wing. A loss of one system would leave two elevons in one wing and four elevons in the other wing functional. The 4,000-pound hydraulic jacks that actuated each surface were initiated by electrical solenoids.

Aikens called to the crew foreman, "Find anything, Alex?"

"Not a thing, Dr. Aikens."

Someone operating a remote actuator went through the test series.

In sequence, the elevons demonstrated full elevator, then full aileron operation.

Aikens turned to Carroll, "See?"

"I don't give a shit," Carroll said. "I'm the chief test pilot, and this son of a bitch is grounded."

"You can't do that!"

"Call the FAA and ask them," Carroll suggested.

Kowloon
August 3, 6:30 A.M.

Whitlock reached the coffee shop first and asked for a table for two. He ordered breakfast for two—one egg, two strips of bacon, two pancakes, orange juice, and coffee each. Breakfast was the preferred meeting time for Whitlock and

Kerry, and though this one wasn't prearranged, he could be pretty certain his boss would show up.

Whitlock had headed all of PAI's security until Kerry had been named to the newly created Far Eastern Development unit and had asked Whitlock to go with him. He hadn't known at the time why Kerry wanted a security setup for an office in Tokyo, but Marge had just succumbed to leukemia, and he was happy to go to the Far East and get away from the memories. His daughter, who lived in San Francisco, had objected, but she had her own family now, and Whitlock didn't want to be a grandpa hanging around the kids' house.

He was also happy to be working with Kerry. At first, he wasn't sure he could work for the younger man, but Kerry pretty much gave Whitlock his own head. He wasn't a stickler for corporate organization and protocol, and these casual breakfast meetings had evolved out of the way Kerry ran his shop in Tokyo.

Whitlock had finished the rest of his newspaper, and the coffee had just been delivered to the table when Kerry appeared in the doorway to the coffee shop, spotted Whitlock, and came over.

"Good morning, Charley."

"You look too well rested this morning, chief. I guess the French lady dusted you off, huh?"

Kerry sat down and picked up his coffee cup. "We had a perfectly fine dinner. How'd you know?"

"A few of the guys in the lounge last night spent their time sharpening their claws on your name."

"It's nice to be so well loved, Charley. How was your day?"

"Yichang seems to know what he's doing. He's a bit on the defensive side, but I suppose that's understandable. And the systems in place at China Dome are damned nearly impregnable."

"Nearly?"

"I saw a few holes, one of which admitted some guy with a few blocks of plastic explosive. At the right, and diplomatic, time, I'll mention them."

Kerry indicated the newspaper. "Anything in there?"

"A couple paragraphs is all. Explosion at the airport site, several casualties, but no mention that some of them were fatal."

"Somebody has a tight rein on the publicity. How are you reading this, Charley?"

"I'm keeping my mind open right now, Dan. As far as I know, no group has claimed responsibility, but then Yichang may know a hell of a lot more than he's telling us. I get the feeling he does, anyway."

Their breakfasts arrived, and as they dug in, Kerry said, "It has all the marks of a terrorist action."

"It does, but I'm not up to cruising speed about the dissident groups within China."

"I suppose there's bound to be a few that the Western press has never heard about."

"Sure, but motive?" Whitlock asked. As an old cop, he was always interested in the basics.

"The human rights record in China isn't an exemplary one. Even I have some reservations about dealing with them, Charley."

"But the pluses outweigh the negatives?"

"They do. The point I was going to make is that there may be some bunch that doesn't think the boys in Beijing, based on their past history, deserve to enter the twenty-first century."

It was always easy to accept the simplest explanation,

Whitlock knew. But he had long been a fan of chess, if not a master, and he enjoyed playing out the more complicated moves.

"There are others who don't like the looks of China Dome, Dan."

"That's true, Charley." Kerry poured syrup over his pancakes. "Throw a dart at a map of the world, and you'll probably find a culprit. The Japanese will be disenfranchised as the center of Asian commerce. The South Koreans don't like the shift in power, either. And the shift is inevitable, all because of the supersonic aircraft. It's going to be too easy for the West to zip into China Dome to conduct business. The Japanese and the South Koreans are already preparing to move their major industrial and financial headquarters operations to China."

"But they're not alone."

"No. My interpretation is that Europe and the United States always felt that, if a few things went their way, they could wrestle back their leadership roles in international commerce. China Dome, and the resources the Chinese are pouring into the airport and into Hong Kong, has scuttled that. So you're right, Charley. The list of people who don't want to see China Dome open has a lot of nationalities attached to it."

Whitlock drained his orange juice, then asked, "How hard do I push Yichang on this, Dan?"

"On yesterday's event?"

"Yeah."

"We're in a tenuous position."

"I know," Whitlock said. "On one hand, we don't want to antagonize the Chinese because we want our proposal accepted."

"That's why I'm glad you took this job, Charley. You understand those nuances."

"And on the other side of it, my job is to protect PAI, and especially, the Astroliner."

"That's still number one," Kerry said. "If it's any consolation, the others are in the same situation."

"Bergen, Yelchenko, and Dowd are the names, Dan. In the order of BBK, Tupolev, and Aerospatiale. Maybe the four of us should get together and work on a strategy for dealing with Yichang?"

"I'll leave that up to you," Kerry said.

"Today, we'll take a look at the maintenance facilities. I might get a chance to talk to them, then, or maybe get together with Yichang. I'll play it by ear."

"I got a quick glimpse of one of the hangars yesterday. They're meant to impress, and they do."

"The security setup there is going to be important to us, if we get the contract," Whitlock said.

"If you have any recommendations to make, let's you and I discuss them first and figure out how best to go about it."

"Gotcha."

Whitlock knew Kerry had a lot more on his mind than security, but he was always willing to listen to Whitlock's bitches.

PAI had a separate marketing division, and Kerry wasn't really a part of that. His job in the States, as he had once explained to Whitlock, was simply to meet people, establish contacts, open up lines of communication, and be a front man for the Astroliner when it reached production stages. When the Chinese announced China Dome and when the Chinese Request for SST Proposals came up the year before, P.J. Jackson had moved him to Tokyo with a new title and the same job. Kerry had written and submitted PAI's proposal to Beijing, and he was working with Far Eastern government officials in areas such as airport access, noise reduction, access to labor, education and training programs, and the like. Kerry always tried to be upbeat, and he was preparing for the time when PAI, with a secured contract, would need to work with dozens of government bureaucracies in order to develop training programs for workers, monetary exchanges, or local companies to participate with PAI in some phases of the operation. Some nations required that foreign companies establish an in-country entity that included local investors and managers.

In the last thirteen months, Kerry and Whitlock, together or separately, had visited Seoul, Vladivostok, Taipei, Hanoi, Manila, and P'yonyang numerous times. They had been to Beijing a dozen times for extended stays.

There were other PAI representatives doing the same thing in the United States, Canada, South America, Asia, and in Europe. If it came to pass, the contract would encompass the world, and Pacific Aerospace intended to be in a position to move quickly. Kerry was confident, also, that word of PAI developmental contacts and activities around the world would filter back to the Chinese and exert a positive influence on their decision about a contract.

Kerry was paged for a telephone call, and Whitlock ordered more coffee while he left to answer it.

When he came back and plopped in his chair, he had lost some of his morning zest.

"Problem, chief?"

"The damned airplane is grounded."

"Shit. By the FAA?"

"Fortunately, it's internal for the moment. We'll know more tomorrow." He explained the problem.

"Damn," Whitlock said. "I hate to carry baggage like that in my head when I'm trying to concentrate on important things."

"Me, too, Charley. Hell, decision time is less than two months away, and if we're not flying, the decision is that much easier. I want the choice to be easy for them, but not that easy."

Kowloon
August 3, 11:40 P.M.

The back reaches of Kowloon, among the towering and older high-rises, was a labyrinth of passageways, staircases, walkways, and tunnels travelled by both rats and residents who seemed to know where they were going. Large family clusters of children, parents, grandparents, and frequently, great-grandparents were compressed into four-room apartments. Clotheslines strung between buildings carried the day's laundry at fifth-, eighth-, and twelfth-story levels. Paper sacks of trash and pails of wet, stinking garbage were stacked in the hallways and on the stair landings. Chinese faces were everywhere—passing in the halls, peering from behind worn curtains. The doors and windows stayed open during the day in the attempt to capture passing breezes.

Kurt Wehmeier, who was twenty-nine years old and had been on the run from one form of authority or another for over half his life, was accustomed to such places. They were, first of all, more pleasant than the two jails to which he had been confined for two short periods, and secondly, he thought that most of the world's population lived like this. He thought of himself as a representative for the world majority.

As far as he was concerned, the people who frequented
the hotels of Kowloon and Hong Kong were in the minority,
and it was an undeserving minority at that. When he was
younger, living on the streets of Frankfurt, he used to watch
the gentry riding in their Mercedes Benzes and the officers
from Rhein-Main Air Base driving their Chevrolets and
Pontiacs and the enlisted personnel zipping about on Honda
and BMW motorcycles. He would dream, then, about the
things he would do with a million American dollars—the
places he would travel, the people who would be his companions, the houses he would own in America's Hollywood
and on France's Mediterranean coast and on Spain's Costa
del Sol.

The dreams had not come true.

Wehmeier supposed that more than three million dollars
had passed through his hands in the last ten years. He had
travelled the world over. He could name thirty people who
would be his trusted friends into the grave.

But he had never owned a house or an automobile. When
he stayed in luxury hotels, it was for business, never leisure.
He had never taken a vacation.

And here in Kowloon, he was living in the back room
of an apartment that housed five other people. He paid high
rent for his room, and he had seen two rats in it, but he
was comfortable.

And he was content.

Even though he had three million dollars, U.S., in the
bank.

FIVE

Deng Xiaoping International Superport
August 3, 1:20 P.M.

Yichang Enlai led his four charges—Dowd, Yelchenko, Whitlock, and Bergen—into his private office for the first time. They had just completed their lunch, and they all declined tea when he offered it.

His office was not ostentatious, but it was spacious enough to contain his desk, a small conference table in one corner, and two leather sofas angled to each other in another corner. A television set was placed against the window that looked into the security center proper. From his desk, he had a view of the video monitors lining the far wall of the center. Through the large triangular windows of the exterior wall, he had a sun-filtered view of the airport, toward the main runways. Twelve men manned the monitors in the security center now; when the airport became operational, there would be thirty on each of the three shifts.

The five of them took seats on the two couches.

"We are scheduled," Yichang said, "to visit the control towers, but I thought we would take a break here so that I might provide you with the information we have assembled regarding the destruction of the tower."

Chairman Sun Chen, in fact, had pointedly advised him

that it would be in their best interests to involve these four men in the investigation. Yichang had not been in a position to object.

"That is an excellent idea!" Dowd said. "Particularly before *we* visit the other towers."

"I assure you that every structure has been thoroughly searched for bombs," Yichang said.

"Oh, I've no doubt of it, my friend," Dowd said.

Unspoken by Dowd, but clearly present was his skepticism. After all, the public and private areas of Deng Xiaoping International were massive, and there were literally thousands of hiding places—out-of-the-way nooks and crannies in the maintenance tunnels, especially—in which small bombs could be placed. Yichang had commandeered the maintenance forces for his search, however. Over two thousand men had been conducting the search for the past twenty-four hours. Nothing of lethal intent had been located.

He mentioned that fact to them and received affirmative nods in return. Unconvincing nods, nonetheless.

Yichang did not care for this silent disapproval of his efforts. This was his domain; it was not intended for him to be defensive.

"Gentlemen?" he asked, waiting for their comments.

No one apparently wanted to discuss the search.

"What hard facts do you have?" Whitlock asked.

Yichang removed the notepaper from his jacket pocket, unfolded it, and read from it.

"The plastic explosive used was C-4. The engineers say that a minimum of six pounds was necessary—one and a half pounds per support column, and that, quite likely, more than the minimum was utilized. Perhaps three pounds for each column. It was placed at the joints between vertical steel columns, and the four emplacements were detonated simultaneously, or very close to it. That is confirmed by videotape from an external surveillance camera. We have located some pieces which may be from a radio-activated remote control device. At least, it appears to be an electronic circuit of some nature."

"This was," Yelchenko said, "accomplished by a person who knew what he was doing, then?"

"With explosives, yes. As an engineer, he overcompensated. We will assume he is not an architect or an engineer."

"Are we assuming he has fingerprints?" Ernst Bergen asked.

"The area, and the stairway, was dusted for fingerprints, yes, but that will be inconclusive. There are dozens of sets of prints, and there are many that are smudged. Some of the later impressions suggest a person wearing gloves, but that is also inconclusive. Many of the construction workers wear gloves."

"Do you have any idea, Mr. Yichang, of a time frame?" Whitlock asked.

"For planting the bomb? Yes." He referred to his notes. "On July twenty-sixth, the tower underwent its final construction inspection, and those support columns were part of the inspection. On that date, all interior appliances—computers, consoles, furnishings—were already in place, so it would not be someone operating under the cover of a delivery person."

"The bomb was planted between July twenty-sixth and August second," Dowd said.

"Yes."

"And you have naturally examined the records of workers entering and leaving the complex between those dates?"

"Yes, Mr. Dowd, we have. Every worker is accounted for."

"Pardon me," Whitlock said. "More correctly, every identification card is accounted for."

Yichang looked at the American for a long moment, considering the implication he was making.

"Yes, Mr. Whitlock?"

"Late yesterday afternoon, just before we left for the hotel, we viewed the gate on the surface where construction people enter the grounds." Whitlock retrieved a black notebook from his coat pocket, opened it, and flipped through the pages. "We did, in fact, watch the late shift of the Rowd-Smythe-Carrington Civil Engineering Group arriving for work. Each worker produced his ID card, and it was passed through the portable scanner. When the green light came on, the worker was allowed through the gate. Correct?"

"That is correct," Yichang said.

"I assumed at the time that each worker approved for an ID card had undergone a security check before being issued the card."

"That is also correct, sir. Every company with a construction contract presented their employees in person for inspection. Very thorough background examinations were made, and we denied access to approximately three percent of them."

"I realize," Whitlock said, "that you're managing an extremely large group of workers. . . ."

"There were twelve thousand at the peak of construction," Yichang said. "Currently, there are slightly over eight thousand contractor personnel working on the site, in addition to over three thousand people who are now permanent employees of the airport."

"But what you're checking at that gate, as I saw it, is

not the workers. The ID cards were verified by computer, but no one verified that the card was carried by the corresponding employee."

Yichang said nothing.

Yuri Yelchenko observed, "Often, I believe we assume the technology will do everything for us, as it does in your highly secure areas, Mr. Yichang, with the thumbprint verification for the communications and security centers."

"You are saying, Mr. Whitlock," Yichang said, "that I have a headcount for every working day, but not necessarily the correct heads."

"Yes. You have the names, but I don't think we can be certain that the names match the people in every instance."

Whitlock was correct, of course.

"I will immediately see that an adjustment is made in our procedures," Yichang said, but he resented the need to say it.

"Don't get me wrong," Whitlock said. "I don't believe Mr. Bergen, Mr. Yelchenko, Mr. Dowd, or myself intend to be critical. We'd like to help you, and probably for selfish reasons. Helping you helps us."

"Yes. Thank you."

"I wonder if we could skip the control tower tour for now and go take a look at the damaged tower, instead?" Whitlock said.

"The national police are going over the scene at the moment."

"Yes, but I'm certain they would bow to your request."

Sun Chen had quietly arranged it so that Yichang's position, in regard to airport matters, was superior to that of the national police. Whitlock seemed to know this, and

Yichang wondered how he knew. The sources of his intelligence would be interesting to know.

On their way out of the security center, Yichang told one of his assistants to have a van meet them at ground level, and it was waiting when they emerged from the dome. The driver took them directly across the wide tarmac toward Terminal Seven and to the remains of Control Tower Six.

The concrete surrounding it had been swept of glass, exterior skin, and structural fragments, and the operators of several large trucks and a crane stood by patiently, waiting for the signal to begin work dismantling the fallen dome.

Police investigators crawled through the wreckage.

After they left the van, Whitlock led them around the smashed dome to the tower and stopped in front of the door hanging open in its frame.

"As I understand it, Mr. Yichang, there are only two entrances to the tower stairway, this door from ground level and another door from the subterranean tunnel."

"That is true," Yichang said. "Both door locks, in addition to the one at the top of the stairs, leading into the operations rooms, require a magnetically encoded card for access."

"Who has these cards?"

"They are carefully controlled, sir. They are numbered, and there are fifteen cards."

"Fifteen people work each shift?"

"Yes. When the next shift comes on duty, the cards are transferred to the incoming personnel."

"Your card will open these locks, of course," Bergen said.

"Mine is the only card that will open every locked door

on the airport," Yichang said. "Relative to this tower, there are three supervisors whose cards are also encoded for access."

"In addition," Yelchenko said, "there will be some maintenance people with the ability to enter, will there not?"

"No. The cleaning people must ring a bell, and one of the shift workers is required to come down to admit them. The procedures require that the shift supervisor or one of his delegates must stay with the maintenance personnel while they are working in the tower. We have already interrogated everyone in regard to the past month."

"So then," Dowd said, "between July twenty-sixth and August second, only forty-nine people could have entered the tower. Yourself, three supervisors, and the forty-five people working the three shifts."

"In reality, Mr. Dowd, the number is not that high as yet. The airport is not fully operational, and only six people are assigned to the morning work period at the moment. The other nine cards are in the security center's vault."

"Well, good. That narrows the scope of the investigation considerably," Dowd said.

"Let's not go too far, too fast," Whitlock said, stepping through the portal with its broken door.

The others followed him into the foyer at the base of the circular stairway. The sunlight from the exposed top of the tower reflected down the curving stairwell and off the walls. Two men were working in one of the spaces above them. He could hear them talking.

"Off the stairway," Whitlock said, "are a number of doors."

"Yes. They lead into machinery, equipment, and storage rooms in the tower base."

"They are not locked."

"It was assumed that anyone passing beyond the locked doors here would automatically have clearance for those rooms. But you are correct, Mr. Whitlock. We will be installing locks on the doors in the stairwells of all towers."

Whitlock tried moving the panic bar on the door leading to the below-ground tunnel. It did not budge.

Before he could ask, Yichang moved around him and slid his plastic card through the slot of the magnetic code reader. A muted click sounded, and he pushed the door open.

On the other side of the doorway was a small landing, barely large enough to allow for the swinging door, then steps leading down to the maintenance tunnel. Whitlock started down them, and the others followed.

The stairway curved as it descended, until it reached a secondary landing, then it straightened and went down an additional four meters to join the maintenance tunnel. A few meters beyond, it again descended, to bypass the transit level and join the Sublevel Four tunnels. It was well-lit by a hundred-watt bulb in a wire-mesh enclosure every three meters.

When they reached the maintenance level, Whitlock stopped and looked at a solid gray steel door. In the middle of the door was a yellow sign bearing Chinese characters.

"This is the power distribution compartment for the control tower," Yichang explained.

"Could we look?"

This door had a key lock, and Yichang used his master key to release the tumblers.

It was dark inside the room, and he found the switch beside the door and flipped it on.

The compartment was not intended to please the senses. The walls were of poured concrete, with the impressions of their pouring forms apparent, and dozens of gray, steel boxes were fastened to them. A noodlelike maze of conduits emerged from the boxes, ran along the walls, hung from the ceiling, disappeared into tunnels or into the floor, and climbed upward through small access holes toward the tower above.

The blank steel doors of the boxes were identified in Chinese, English, and French, the languages of the contractors who had installed them. Most of them had prominent warnings affixed to them, declaring high voltages. Two walls of boxes were devoted to electrical power routing and emergency power lines. On the third wall were the lines dedicated to communications. Despite the random appearance, the routing of the conduits and the placement of the interface boxes were well-organized and well-planned.

Whitlock wandered around the room as his colleagues watched. He whistled some tune under his breath and read the signs on the panels. He smiled when he found a box with a key lock on it.

"Mr. Yichang, from what I read, this box contains circuit breakers for the facility security system. I wonder if the door locks are part of that?"

With a leaden feeling in the pit of his stomach, Yichang Enlai produced his key ring.

Whitlock waved him off, dug into his pants pocket, and came up with a tool that looked much like a set of automotive thickness gauges for setting spark plug gaps. He swivelled out a pick, then using a separate probe, worked carefully on the lock.

It clicked open within a minute.

On the inside of the door was a label upon which some

contractor had clearly identified each circuit. Number four read: "Tower electrical door locks."

"I think," Whitlock said, "the magnetic cards are superfluous."

"If the breaker opens," Bergen said, "the doors should remain in the locked mode."

"Try opening the breaker," Yelchenko said and turned to climb back up the stairs.

Whitlock flipped the circuit breaker to the off position.

Yelchenko came back a moment later. "It is open."

Yichang silently cursed someone's ancestors.

Stephen Dowd said, "Those circuits should be reprogrammed so that every security door in the airport remains locked in the event of a power failure. And I would strongly recommend that those particular breaker boxes be relocated on the other side of the doors they control."

Whitlock slammed the panel shut, then tried it to be certain it was locked. He leaned a shoulder against the wall.

"I think we can be fairly certain of the route the perp took, and we know what needs to be done to prevent a repeat," he said.

"Also suggested," Yelchenko added, "is the fact that the bomber has seen the plans or the electrical schematic or worked on the installation of the system. He knew where to look."

Yichang Enlai smiled grimly, but he seethed under the surface. His mind devised scathing attacks on the designers, the installation contractors, and the security advisors who had taken Chinese money for their slipshod work. Of graver concern, he had accepted their product as perfection, and that reflected directly on his own competence. He felt as if his inadequacy was stamped indelibly on his forehead.

"I wouldn't worry too much about this, Mr. Yichang,"

Whitlock said. "It happens from time to time. If you had good lawyers working on your contractual arrangements, you can cut off further work and further payments until the designers correct what they've already installed. Don't let them charge you for a plan change or for additional work; they should have been required in the contract to do it right in the first place."

Yichang studied Whitlock's face. He seemed entirely sincere. The man had simply and easily uncovered an obvious defect in the security system, but then had provided Yichang with a way out. This Westerner, like many others he had met, was difficult to decipher.

"This is," Yelchenko said, "as the Americans say, only peanuts?"

"That's right," Whitlock said. "This is only a mechanical problem. We can fix it easy enough. More important, what's the motive?"

"And why this target?" Dowd added.

"What do you mean, Mr. Dowd?" Yichang asked.

"Well, sir, if I were a terrorist, and I had one shot, I certainly wouldn't pick Control Tower Number Six, which is worth, what?"

"Perhaps a hundred million dollars."

"And the main tower? The air control tower?"

"It is probably valued at eight or nine hundred million dollars," Yichang told him.

"If I were a terrorist, concerned only with creating chaos, and I wanted more of a bang for my pound note, I'd have taken out Number One."

Yichang thought this entire scene incongruous. Five men dressed well in Western-styled suits standing in a concrete chamber much like a dungeon, lit with a single hundred-watt bulb, discussing the merits of blowing up one-hundred-million-dollar or nine-hundred-million-dollar installations.

"You are saying, Mr. Dowd, that this terrorist is making a statement."

"Exactly!"

"No group," Whitlock said, "is claiming responsibility or extorting money yet, is it?"

"Not at this time," Yichang said. "But you suggest that this terrorist is saying, 'I can do anything I want, at any time.' "

"If you get a telephone call," Ernst Bergen said, "it could well be from someone who would like a hundred million dollars deposited to his offshore account. Either that or you lose a nine-hundred-million-dollar control tower. He has just proved to you that he can do it."

"Or a large dome, like Terminal One," Yelchenko added.

"And extortion is only one motive," Whitlock said.

Yichang thought that Whitlock had other motives in mind.

And this one was devastating enough.

August 3, 2:55 P.M.

During the afternoon break in the tour, Jacqueline Broussard found a telephone and called the office of the Chairman of the Board, who was also the Managing Director, in Paris. It was almost eight in the morning there, but Henri Dubonnet would have been in the office for two hours or more. He was a morning person, and his seventy-seven years had not changed that habit.

She used the number for his private line, and he answered himself.

"Good morning, Father," she said in French.

Dubonnet was her godfather, but he had very much assumed the paternal role fifteen years before when her biological parent had been killed while practicing for the Grand Prix de Monaco. Her father had been far more interested in high-performance automobiles, purebred horses, skiing in the alps, and cruising in the Mediterranean than he had been in the frailty of life or in earning the money required for his expensive recreational pursuits. For those, her mother, and her mother's family, had provided the resources.

"Ah, Jacqueline. You might have called me before I saw the television reports. I have been worried about you."

"I apologize, Father." She told him briefly what she knew of the explosion in the tower. "You should know that I avoid risk as though it were the plague."

"I know no such thing. How many times have you been bruised, abraded, or fractured as a result of your impetuosity?"

"I fell off a mountain once and broke my arm. Will you hold that against me forever?"

"In addition to mountains, there have been tree houses, horses, and sailboats. You have fallen out of love several times."

Broussard had entered into several affairs, but she did not think her actions could be described as impetuous. Twice, her suitors had refused to acknowledge the end of the affairs when she declared them, and she had found herself hounded for weeks on end. Only visits by agents of Dubonnet had persuaded them to abandon the quest.

"And now," he said, "I have just learned that you browbeat Captain Howard into letting you fly the Concorde II."

Mark Howard was the chief British test pilot for the program.

"It was for but a few minutes," she said.

"It was for one hour and thirteen minutes. I have the cockpit tapes in my office."

She recalled what Kerry had told her about the need to know the airplane. "It is important, Father, that I understand intimately the product I am selling. You must agree with that."

"A takeoff! The most dangerous aspect of flight. I should terminate Howard immediately."

"The landing is the most dangerous, which I did not attempt," she countered. "And Mark merely acceded to my request. Fire me, instead."

"I should, you know."

"But I am good at what I do."

"That remains to be seen. Have you learned anything from this expensive fling in Hong Kong?"

"I had dinner last night with Mr. Kerry."

"*Mister* Kerry? You are in love with him. This is what you are calling me about?"

"That is nonsense, Father. Kerry and I have absolutely nothing in common. He has killed people."

"You have stuck a knife in my heart, how many times?"

"But Kerry said something that causes me to wonder."

His tone immediately became serious. "What did he say?"

"He was talking about Tupolev, but I think he intended for me to read between his lines. I do not believe that Pacific Aerospace considers us to be a competitive threat."

"Tell me."

She related Kerry's observations about the merits of experience versus new technology.

"Nonsense!"

"Is it, Father? I mean, are we trying to give an old dog new tricks and hoping he will perform like a puppy?"

"Of course not. We not only have the safest supersonic aircraft in the world, but one that is reliable and will perform as required well into the middle of the next century."

"I hope so," she said before she hung up.

But hoping was different from believing, and she had come to Hong Kong as a true believer.

Damn you, Daniel Kerry.

August 3, 3:17 P.M.

When Zhao Li called a break, Kerry spotted Mickey Duff, and the two of them went into an unfinished coffee shop in Terminal Seven and sat on stools at the counter.

"Have you heard anything more about the tower blast, Dan?"

"No. Charley should have something more by tonight. What's your take on this place so far?"

Duff was younger than Kerry, but shared much of the same background. He had the same aeronautical engineering degree from the Air Force Academy in Colorado Springs, and he had flown for the Air Force for four years, though his logged hours were in F-15 Eagles and his combat time was over the Persian Gulf rather than Southeast Asia.

Michael Duff was a green-eyed, dark-haired half-Irishman who had grown up in, or survived, as he put it, Brooklyn. He was five-ten, in fighting trim, and had a quirky sense of humor that sometimes got out of hand.

"No doubt about it, Dan. This is the finest setup I've ever seen, and Ric will back me up on that. World-class."

Ric Alvarez was a specialist on physical plant planning.

"What they've done," Duff went on, "is made it much easier for us—for whomever wins the contract—to center the worldwide maintenance program right here at China Dome. Ten of those hangars are designated for SSTs only, and we'll handle the maintenance for every lessee right here. Except for major airframe overhauls, which we'd have to do in California, everything else, from avionics to major power plant overhauls, can be accomplished at China Dome."

Kerry liked the way Duff thought in terms of a contract *fait accompli,* probably a result of his own attitude.

"Have you talked to Alyce?"

"Yeah, but only briefly. You know how those computer people get wrapped up in the machines. Don't tell her I said so, but she looks entirely captivated by the hardware and software these people have assembled. She says they've looked briefly at security systems and facilities monitoring systems, and they had just started going over the aircraft programs. The emphasis seems to be on safety."

"There's another emphasis, Mickey. It just isn't stated in the clear."

Duff's eyes closed halfway as he looked at Kerry. He knew about communications that were coded or in the clear.

"I'm not sure what you're getting at, chief."

"Control," Kerry said.

As he thought about it, Duff's head started nodding affirmatively.

"Yeah, I think you're right. It does smack of Big Brother."

"With the size of China's population, it's understandable that the seats of power have always been interested in control," Kerry said. "And it wasn't always simply crowd control, but mind control as well."

Duff appeared a bit alarmed, and his eyes swept the walls and back counter of the coffee shop.

"You don't think? . . ."

"That we're bugged, Mickey? It's possible, but I doubt it. Charley brought along a pocket-sized bug detector, but he hasn't said anything yet about any listening devices. I think they rely heavily on the cameras." Kerry nodded his head toward a black glass panel in the wall above the entrance doorway. A single row of black glass, offset by rows of red ceramic tiles, circled the upper walls of the restaurant. The darkened glass was a perfect hiding place for television cameras.

"I feel itchy all over," Duff said.

"It's not much different from other airports or large department stores. Still, I get the impression that the need for control will extend to the SST contractor. They want to determine who gets to lease the planes they buy, and who gets to fly in here. They want to make certain the heavy-duty maintenance is taken care of under their eyes."

"Have we ever seen a copy of what the final contract will look like, Dan?"

"No. I'm sure there will be some room for negotiation in terms of price, delivery schedules, and even equipment. But I think the management aspects are going to be tight as hell."

"Can P.J. work under that heavy a thumb?"

"He may not have a choice, Mickey. It may come down to, 'Do it our way, or step aside and let one of the other companies have it.' "

"Hell, I was hoping to get a seat here. Now, I'm not sure I'm up for it."

"Anything can happen between now and October first,"

Kerry said. "But keep your eyes open, will you? We may need some ammunition in our bandolier."

August 3, 5:45 P.M.

Sun Chen and four of his chief aides arrived at Deng Xiaoping International Superport aboard an Ilyushin Il-14 twin-engined, propeller-driven transport that belonged to the Air Force of the People's Liberation Army, but which was on loan to the Committee for Airport Construction.

It was almost an embarrassment.

Not even almost, Sun thought. It *was* an embarrassment.

Until Sun's appointment to the committee, when he had first become involved in modern aviation, he had not realized that China's air force, the third largest in the world in terms of numbers, stood so close to the brink of obsolescence. They relied heavily on squadrons of Shenyang F-6 fighters that were modified designs of the MiG-19. Even later versions of MiG designs, such as the Shenyang F-8 (MiG-23F) were outdated in addition to being in short supply. The inventories contained hundreds of dilapidated aircraft, many of them no longer flying.

As they taxied in toward the terminal, Sun peered through the window at the line of Boeing and Aerospatiale airliners and smaller corporate aircraft ringing the dome. The people he was courting—merchants, really—were flying in aircraft far superior to the Il-14 that had been loaned to him. The Il-14 was known to NATO as "Crate," and the design had first flown in 1946. It looked something like the Douglas DC-3.

But it was reliable, he told himself.

Still, he felt somewhat silly, landing in a fifty-year-old

propeller aircraft at this world-class airport, which was designed for airplanes that flew at twice the speed of sound. He saw his situation as a microcosm of the entire nation. Struggling to catch up.

And they would catch up, he knew in his heart.

The airplane engines died, and he stood up after taking one quick glance in the direction of Control Tower Six. It was a disaster, and he quickly looked away. He did not want to see more of it.

A ground party rolled a staircase up to the side of the airplane and opened the door. Zhao Li was waiting at the bottom of the stairs as Sun Chen descended.

"Welcome, Chairman Sun!"

Zhao was given to hyperbole and silk suits with a Chinese flavor. This one was cream-colored and set off with a brilliant red tie. He had an ultrasmooth complexion, eyes of an almond color, enhanced by his spectacles, and a huge, white smile that appeared to be permanently stamped on his face. The welcoming, open face disguised a shrewd and calculating mind that retained facts like a magnet. He was a computer dressed in the livery of a clownish public relations man. He was, Sun thought, a perfect combination for the administrator of the vast complex of Deng Xiaoping International Superport, and he often congratulated himself on his superb choice.

"Good evening, Administrator," Sun replied.

"I trust that you had a wonderful flight."

"It was a tolerable flight," Sun told the man as he reached solid ground. In fact, the heated air of afternoon had presented them with a bumpy traverse of the nineteen hundred kilometers from Beijing, and Sun's stomach was still unsettled. The overheated air rising off the tarmac did nothing to improve his condition.

With an expansive wave of his arm, Zhao gestured toward the dome and the party from Beijing crossed the pavement and entered the structure through the airlock-style portal. Two of Zhao's minions held the doors for them.

It was blessedly cool inside, and Zhao's route to the upper floors included a stop at a men's restroom where Sun took some time to change his shirt and freshen up.

When they emerged from the elevator on the top floor, Sun found that Zhao had set up the banquet on the southern side of the dome, where the view of the destroyed tower would not distract either Sun or his guests.

A half-dozen waiters with trays of drinks were passing through a well-dispersed crowd that was truly international. The Europeans were distinctive, Sun thought, and the Americans could mostly be discerned by their casual attitudes. Also present were Japanese, Indians, Pakistanis, Filipinos, South Americans, a number of Russians, and several representatives of Islamic states. The louder, distinctive tones of several Australians could be distinguished above other conversations.

Sun had, of course, reviewed the application forms submitted by each of the companies, and he had scanned the accompanying photographs of the representatives. He was not good with names, though, and he was forced to rely on Zhao's excellent memory for introductions.

The four major attendees—Broussard, Kerry, Stuttmann, and Zemenek—were familiar to him because he had met with them in individual meetings in Beijing several times over the last year.

Sun crossed the bridge from the elevator core and stood looking at the people standing in small conversational groups. The Frenchwoman, Broussard, was with a dozen people next to one of the round, linen-covered tables. He saw the BBK Enterprises Deputy Director for Sales, Wilhelm Stuttmann, talking with a man he vaguely remembered as being a Saudi sheik. Pyotr Illivich Zemenek, Chief Engineer for the Tupolev Design Bureau, was in an animated conversation with a young American that Sun thought belonged to Pacific Aerospace. And the PAI agent, Kerry, with a knot of people from the Lufthansa, Quantas, and United air carriers near the dome wall, looked up, saw Sun, and smiled.

Sun returned the smile.

Zhao Li led him into the throng, easily introducing him to the participants, with whom he engaged in small talk for a few minutes before moving on to meet another of the airline hopefuls. The general atmosphere was jovial and vibrant—which Sun had hoped for—but there was an undercurrent of tension present also. These people were vying for the honor of spending a large amount of money in China. If selected as a primary air carrier at Deng Xiaoping International Superport, they would be required to lease facilities along with the supersonic transports supplied by one of the contenders for that honor. It would be a very expensive proposition, but in return, the profits would also be considerable.

Of course, there were others in contention for secondary contracts, primarily regional carriers who would operate conventional aircraft. Sun, who had always been sheltered in the communist and socialist state, was amazed at the congeniality produced by those with greed in their hearts.

Zhao invaded the next group, all smiles, and said, "Chairman Sun, you remember Miss Broussard."

"Of course. It is a pleasure to see you, again, Mademoiselle Broussard." He offered a short bow.

Which she returned. "And you, Chairman. I am very impressed with what you have accomplished here."

"Thank you."

Broussard was radiant in a shimmering pale blue dress that reflected the lighting and featured a high, Chinese collar. Her dark hair swung like heavy cream when she moved her head. If Sun were not a happily married man, he might have entertained inappropriate thoughts about her.

He might do that, anyway.

She took a step closer to him, but not close enough to invade his personal space.

"You did not bring your beautiful wife with you," she accused.

He had forgotten their dinner a year before. Unaccustomed to dealing with Western women in high positions, Sun had arranged their meeting around a dinner with Qing as hostess.

"She was, unfortunately, previously scheduled for a benefit."

"I know she is heavily involved with children's causes," Broussard said, "but please tell her that I missed seeing her."

"I will," he promised, though he probably would not. His wife had not been as impressed with Jacqueline Broussard as Sun himself had been.

Zhao moved him on to meet others, one of whom was memorable, a man named Contrarez, the front man for a new group based in Rio de Janeiro. The organization apparently had a great deal of fiscal resources behind it—Sun hesitated to suggest that it would be cocaine and marijuana money—and hoped to make an international splash by jumping directly into the aviation industry with supersonic transports.

Contrarez, standing much too close to him, said, "I saw you arrive, Chairman Sun."

Sun smiled. "I believe we were more or less on time."

"I must tell you that *Avio S.A.* has several aircraft that are currently classified as surplus. We would be more than happy to present the committee with, I admit, a slightly used Boeing 707." He smiled hugely. "It would make your business trips much more enjoyable."

"I am afraid I must decline," Sun said, turning to Zhao and locking eyes with him.

The airport administrator gave him a slight nod and said, "This way, please, Chairman."

Contrarez would not be invited back. *Avio S.A.*'s applications would not reach the final stages of consideration. Sun had made clear to everyone in the Committee's sphere of control that bribery, or any hint of corruption, would not be tolerated in his regime. The Committee for Airport Construction was operating in the world arena, and Sun intended to be especially sensitive to the world's view of the committee and its employees.

Zhao introduced him to the airline representatives from Lufthansa, Quantas, and United. Kerry stood by, waiting while Sun attempted to commit their faces and names to his memory and talked briefly with them. They were important men, almost assured of receiving contracts, and he could expect some subtle pressure from their chief executive officers when it came time to make the decision on the SSTs. Those airline chieftains would want to feel that they had had some influence in selecting the aircraft they would be flying. Kerry, intelligent man that he was, understood that part of the equation, and he was understandably devoting time to pressing his case with them. Sun Chen had also read reports from informants about Pacific Aerospace lobbyists meeting with airline executives and government leaders in America and Europe. Their campaign was essentially a battle plan, with warriors attacking all fronts. The other supersonic transport vendors, particularly BBK Enterprises, were doing some of the same things, but not on as grand a scale as PAI.

Sun turned to Kerry and extended his hand to the man. Kerry liked the Western gesture.

"Mr. Kerry, I am glad you could be with us."

Kerry's hand was free—he was not drinking, and it was firm and dry; he did not attempt to exert his will in a handshake.

"I am pleased to have received the invitation, Chairman Sun. And I am even more pleased with what I have seen at Deng Xiaoping."

"Not China Dome?" Sun grinned, as he revealed some of his own intelligence-gathering.

"Only in closed quarters," Kerry said. "But please bear in mind that a good nickname can do wonders for an enterprise."

"Such as?"

"Look what 'The King' did for Elvis Presley, or what 'Big Mac' does for McDonald's."

"I will study those concepts," Sun said.

He could be fairly certain that within the week a comprehensive study of public relations campaigns conducted by American advertising agencies and promotional firms would be on his desk. Kerry always followed up on the most minor of details, and Sun had been impressed in the past with the fact that Kerry did not always use such occasions to further PAI's own cause. It was simply a passing-on of interesting information.

Sun Chen might have liked to know Daniel Kerry better,

but he was forever cognizant of the requirement to treat the SST vendors equally. He said, "Why is it, Mr. Kerry, that you, as an aeronautics engineer, have such an inventory of nonaeronautic facts at hand?"

"My mind is a trap for trivia, Chairman. Normally useless trivia."

"I suspect that you would give a much more interesting speech tonight than the one I have in store for you."

"Nonsense. I have been looking forward to this."

"Well, please be forewarned."

Zhao led him up the other side of the group, meeting others, aimed in the direction of the head table. His speech for after dinner was, in fact, a brief one, and he was certain his guests would find it blessed in that regard.

August 3, 08:50 P.M.

Charley Whitlock enjoyed Sun's speech, which mainly welcomed the visitors, contained a few aviation jokes, and outlined the procedures involved in the contractor selection process. He spoke in English, the language shared by most of the people in the room. There were a few interpreters present for those who did not get along very well in English.

Whitlock did not enjoy Rafael Contrarez, who sat across his table from him, and bragged about his money. If he were still in the FBI, he'd have tagged Contrarez for future surveillance. When he thought about it, Whitlock decided he might make a call or two to some old buddies in the Bureau.

His next-door companion for the meal was an enchanting young lady from El Al Airlines named Karen Meyer, who was based in Tel Aviv. They avoided talking politics, but she seemed to be an old hand at security concerns, and they had that in common.

Some of the conversations dribbled onward after the speech and the dessert, but Whitlock kept his eyes roaming, and he saw Yichang Enlai leave the head table, headed for the elevators.

He turned in his chair until he spotted Kerry and caught his eye. Whitlock inclined his head in the direction of Yichang, and Kerry nodded and started making his excuses.

Whitlock told Karen, "My dear, I'm afraid I have to rush off and leave you defenseless."

"I don't think I'm entirely defenseless, Charley," she smiled.

"I suspect that's probably very true."

"Are you leaving tonight?"

"That's what the boss's schedule says. I go by his schedule, or I walk."

"That's too bad. I had hoped we could get to know each other better."

Ah, Christ!

Whitlock's daughter might be younger than Karen Meyer, but he didn't think it was by more than three years. He was too old for this.

Being optimistic, he said, "You'll be getting some airplanes from us. We're bound to run into each other again."

"I hope so," she said, squeezing his hand.

He got away from the table and joined up with Kerry. The two of them tried to look as if they weren't in a hurry as they departed, but by the time they reached the elevators, Yichang was no longer in sight.

Kerry punched the down button.

Whitlock watched the numbers blinking on the left elevator.

"Looks like he's headed for the transport level."

"Trains every ten minutes," Kerry said. "If we're lucky, he's got a nine-minute wait."

The doors of the second elevator parted, and they stepped aboard.

As the car started downward, Kerry said, "Attractive lady you were with, Charley."

"You keeping an eye on me?"

"I might have met her yesterday. She's with EL Al, right?"

"Right. I think she wants to pump me for industrial secrets."

"That what they call it these days?"

"Shit, Dan. . . ."

"Industrial secrets go both ways."

"We're leaving," Whitlock reminded him.

"I think I'll leave you here. Do you mind?"

"I don't mind," he said, but Whitlock wasn't entirely sure what Kerry's intent was.

When the glass doors opened, they found Yichang on the platform waiting for a train.

He turned at the sound of the doors.

"Ah, gentlemen. I understood you were flying back to Tokyo."

"I wonder if we could have a word with you, Mr. Yichang?" Kerry said.

Yichang looked upward, toward a concealed camera, no doubt, then down the tunnel toward an approaching people mover.

"Let us take the train, gentlemen," he said.

Once they were aboard, Yichang waved them toward seats

while he used a key to turn a switch partially hidden below the forward bulkhead.

"That controls the onboard cameras," he explained as he sat on a bench across from them. "I should explain, Mr. Kerry, that all officers and supervisors of the Committee for Airport Construction have been advised to show no favoritism toward any one potential contractor. I should not be meeting with you."

"I understand your position," Kerry said, "and I would not do anything to jeopardize it. We will not try to sell the airplanes to you."

Yichang smiled, the first smile that Whitlock could remember seeing on the man.

"The train can go around as many times as we need to have it do so," the Chinese man said.

Kerry had briefed Whitlock and the rest of his party before they left Tokyo that they were to observe the Chinese desire to maintain formality in all discussions. The arm's length distance created by formal address was intended to make the bidding of contracts and the negotiations surrounding them less awkward. Kerry did not abandon that instruction even among the three of them.

"Mr. Yichang, Mr. Whitlock and I discussed the event at Control Tower Six in some detail before dinner. We think it is a red herring."

"A red herring? I do not know the idiom."

Whitlock said, "We don't think you, or Deng Xiaoping International, is the target."

"If I am not the target," Yichang said, "why do I feel the pain?"

Kerry said, "We'd like to help you find out. Toward that end, I would like to leave Mr. Whitlock here as an advisor to your security section."

Yichang considered that proposal for several long minutes.

The train whirred along the lit tunnel. Terminal One flashed past.

"Mr. Whitlock had been helpful to us already, Mr. Kerry. I would have no objection to his continued assistance."

Whitlock smiled and wondered if Karen Meyer was staying at the President Hotel.

"If I am not the target," Yichang said again, "who is?"

"Me," Kerry told him.

SNIPING

SIX

The Boehm-Bussmeier-Kraft Enterprises prototype assembly and test facilities were located at Tempelhof Airport on the southern edge of Berlin. The former air base was not in impeccable condition, and the facilities were ancient. It was not the best situation for developing a 21st Century aviation enterprise, but Gerhard Ebbing understood the rationale behind Tempelhof's selection.

With the reunification of the nation, the German Federal Republic had assumed the assets and deficits of the German Democratic Republic, and the GDR's deficits outweighed its assets considerably. The communist regime had allowed the country to deteriorate badly, channeling almost no funding into maintenance. The factories that were still operational were decades out of date, and their environmental pollution had forced most of them to close. The old East Germany required substantial rehabilitation of its infrastructure—highways, bridges, public works—and its economic base. Unemployment was rampant. The people were in need, and BBK Enterprises represented a promise to fulfill that need, so the prototype plant had been located in the East as a visible symbol of what was coming.

When the contract with the Chinese was finalized, BBK Enterprises would establish several factories in the East. Refurbished plants in Rostock would manufacture the jet engines. Interior components would be fabricated in Leipzig. Magdeburg would be the site of the avionics production, and new facilities in Dresden would house the airframe production lines. The millions and millions of deutsche marks generated by those facilities and jobs meant salvation for thousands of people. That one contract would percolate through the economy, creating indirect ripples in educational training for factory workers, clothing establishments, restaurants, housing.

BBK Enterprises was a symbol of future prosperity, and its logo and name were prominently displayed throughout the eastern sector of Germany. Germans who wanted meat in their kitchens cheered the name, and Ebbing had personally witnessed the effects of the publicity campaign. In northeastern Germany, where some of the test flights were conducted, he had seen bystanders and pedestrians and motorists standing outside their cars cheer as a low-flying AeroSwift flashed above their heads on its way to the Baltic Sea. They did not care that it was noisy, that its screaming passage stung their eardrums. They viewed the SST as new motorcars, furniture, apartments, and wardrobes.

Gerhard Ebbing himself viewed the East as almost medieval in its backwardness and poverty. The countryside was still pretty, but it was also primitive. He viewed himself as a member of the team of saviors who would tug the backward populace into a thriving economy. He could do no less for his countrymen.

Ebbing had worked for Fokker-VFW for many years, then had joined the design team of the consortium of British Aerospace-Messerschmitt-Bolkow-Blohm-Aeritalia to work on the Panavia Tornado fighter bomber. He was sixty-four years old, and he had been fifty-eight when he was selected to head the development and production of the AeroSwift. At the time, he had seriously been considering retirement. He and Ingrid, his wife of thirty-two years, owned a small house on the East Frissian Island of Wangerooge, and Ebbing had thought highly of a lifestyle centered around sitting on his front porch sipping lager and watching the shipping inbound from the North Sea to Bremerhaven.

Matthew Kraft, the Managing Director of BBK, had talked him out of it. Kraft, whom Ebbing had peripherally known as a large stockholder in both Fokker-VFW and Messerschmidt, had had astounding success as a financial oracle, and Kraft's vision of a regenerated Germany had become Ebbing's own. For the first time, he considered his life's work of designing airplanes as having a profound impact on someone beyond himself, his employer, and some air force or air carrier. What he accomplished could mean revitalization for an entire nation.

Ebbing and Kraft leaned against the front fender of Kraft's Mercedes 560SEL which was parked in front of the operations tower near the main runway. The morning was overcast and gray, a seeming German constant, and rain was predicted for late afternoon. It was needed, for the grass plots in front of the old military barracks and administration buildings were dry and yellow.

Matthew Kraft was not a stereotypical German in appearance. The top of his gray-fringed bald head barely reached the level of Gerhard Ebbing's elbow, though Ebbing was considerably taller than average. The Director's face was thin to the point of emaciation, and his heavy gray eyebrows made his dark brown eyes appear deep and brooding. His thin lips were tightly compressed in his standard, straight-line smile.

Behind the miniaturized Draculan facade, however, was a sly mind. Kraft might not have been brilliant, but he was shrewd. He could read people, interpret their motives, and forecast their responses to a variety of stimuli.

By contrast, Ebbing knew that he was himself above average in intelligence as well as height. His area of excellence was confined to mathematics, and he relied on people like Kraft to pilot him through social seas. He estimated that, in thirty-two years, Ingrid had complained at least 1,014 times about his lack of sensitivity to superiors, co-workers, subordinates, and the wives of all. He had promised her at least as many times that he would attempt to alter his personality and do much better in the future.

His love of good *bratwurst* and dark ales was reflected in his protruding stomach, the weight of which appeared to stoop his shoulders. Ebbing did not care much about what he looked like, and Ingrid took it upon herself to select his clothing for him. If she had not, he would have been wearing a ragged cardigan sweater over a frayed, discardible dress shirt tucked into corduroy trousers. For a visit by Matthew Kraft, who spent uncountable amounts on his dark blue and charcoal gray tailored suits and imported ties, Ingrid had selected a pin-striped beige suit, a shirt of a paler hue, and a tie multistriped in shades of brown. She thought it went well with his blond hair.

Kraft said, "The Arabs will be here next week, Gerhard. They would like to ride in the airplane."

"It is not yet certified for passengers, Matthew. There are no seats in the cabin. We have not allowed anyone, other than the test pilots, aboard."

"Nonetheless, Hakim al-Qatar himself makes the demand. It is his money that has woven this magic carpet, as he tells me, and he wishes to ride on it. See to it that he does."

"Of course, Matthew."

There was so much power in wealth, Ebbing thought. He had always been well-paid, and he was comfortable, but he was not an extravagant man. In a restaurant, he always double-checked the calculation of his waiter. People like Kraft and al-Qatar whisked through life without a thought of such minutiae. Others took care of it for them. Perhaps it was because they owned most of where they walked. They assumed so many things as their just due.

"There she is," Ebbing said.

"Where?"

"To the right, just above the horizon."

The AeroSwift, finished in a light gray, was difficult to pick out against the overcast. It was simply a darker speck superimposed on the face of a cloud, but it quickly enlarged. Ebbing knew that it was subsonic at this point in its flight, but the approach was still rapid.

The pilot lined up on the runway as he neared, and within minutes, Ebbing could detect the bright yellow stripe that ran the length of the fuselage. Above it, in elongated, yellow capital letters, was the logo, "BBK ENTERPRISES."

The nose cone did not droop for landing and takeoff. As he understood of the American transport designers, Ebbing had utilized video cameras for pilot visibility during the critical elements of flight.

The flare of the landing profile was pronounced, with the nose held high and the area of the delta wing at a high angle of attack to maintain lift. The intake ramps of the four jet engines in the twin nacelles was at the extreme declination, to prevent a lack of airflow from stalling the engines. The landing speed, at 155 knots, was higher than that of the Concorde, a result of the wing sweep angle which provided slightly less lift at maximum takeoff weight, but which allowed the top speed to reach Mach 2.45 in comparison with the Concorde's Mach 2.075.

The eight massive wheels of the main gear landing trucks touched the runway briefly, spewed blue smoke, rose, then settled smoothly. Seconds later, the nose wheels touched down.

"Beautiful!" Kraft exclaimed.

Ebbing watched the rollout carefully. Typically, 3,300 meters of runway were required for landing. The maximum load takeoff configuration, as a result of the wing design, utilized nearly all of the runway length available at Tempelhof. If the pilots rotated on takeoff at 3,900 meters, it was considered an excellent day. A number of times, however, the pilots of the AeroSwift had transgressed the overrun at the end of the runway—not designed for the weight limits of the airplane, and had suffered from Ebbing's command of verbal abuse.

The AeroSwift went by them at high speed, her engines screaming in reverse thrust. It was music to Ebbing's ears, though not to those who lived in close proximity to an airport.

Over the cacophony, Kraft yelled, "She is still too loud, Gerhard!"

He waited until the airliner was farther down the runway with her brakes on and the engines decelerating to reply.

"We have a measured sideline noise level at thirty-five nautical miles from the runway centerline of ninety-four decibels, Matthew. That is seventeen less than the Concorde. Plus, on an international runway of around five thousand meters length, extreme reverse thrust will be unnecessary. We anticipate a noise reduction of another ten decibels."

Kraft shook his head, but apparently accepted the explanation.

"I want every characteristic of this airplane to exceed those of the Astroliner, Gerhard."

"I know," Ebbing told him.

He just did not know what the Astroliner's characteristics were. If Kraft had had a better intelligence arm, Ebbing would have a much better idea of his adversary's capabilities. Ebbing was certain that the Americans were delaying the Federal Aviation Administration certification of their aircraft simply to keep the airplane from the public eye— and his own—for as long as possible. The AeroSwift had been photographed repeatedly, and the aviation analysts had made surprisingly accurate guesses about her performance characteristics.

He did not know as much about the Astroliner.

When the SST reached the end of the runway and turned back, the two of them got in the car, and Kraft's driver started the engine, then swung around in a broad turn and went to meet the AeroSwift.

Edwards Air Force Base, California
August 9, 8:25 A.M.

Dan Kerry had slept like a neatly sawed log. There had once been a time when jet lag didn't bother him in the least, but that time had passed without his really noticing it.

He was in one of the guest rooms in the converted Bachelor Officer's Quarters barracks leased by PAI, and he was awakened by a thunderous banging on the thin door of his room.

He opened one eye.

The door flew open, and Terry Carroll barged in, carrying

two large Styrofoam cups of coffee. He was dressed in a flight suit and draped over his arm was another suit.

"C'mon, Air Force puke, get it out of the sack! The good guys have been up for hours." He tossed the spare flight suit on the bed.

Kerry sighed. "You include yourself in that definition?"

"Damned right. If you'd picked the right service, you'd now be fit, bushy-tailed, and bright-eyed. Problem with you, Kerry, you have no discipline."

Kerry threw back the covers, swung his legs out of the narrow bed, and sat up. He was wearing his shorts.

Carroll swung a desk chair around and straddled it backwards, handing one of the cups to Kerry.

"This is Navy coffee, I suppose?"

"Grow hair on a frog's legs."

He tasted it and immediately understood the frog's problem.

"If you want an evaluation. . . ."

"I don't."

"This is a typical baldness remedy for frogs. It won't grow hair. The hair is already in it."

"You aren't dressed yet."

"I'm not awake yet."

"You shouldn't have stopped over in Hawaii. Mai Tais will do that to you."

Kerry placed the coffee carefully on the nightstand, as if it might detonate at any moment, grabbed his Dopp kit, and went down the hall to the bathroom. When he came back freshly shaven and with his teeth feeling less gritty, he was ready for the coffee.

He drank it as he dressed.

"Tell me about it," Kerry said.

Carroll explained the uncontrolled roll he had experienced. "The eggheads have been working on it for five days, and they've come up with zilch. We took the Astrofreighter up, and we couldn't recreate the incident with her. But Aikens is getting all dewy-eyed about the Astroliner."

"So P.J. called me back to the States," Kerry said. "Does he think I'm going to find it?"

"What do you think?"

"I think P.J. wants me to overrule you on the grounding."

Kerry couldn't actually overrule Carroll, but he could be counted on to be persuasive if it was needed.

"Nah. The chief nerd wants that; it was Dennis who talked P.J. into getting you back here."

"What do you really think about the airplane, Terry?"

"Shit, Dan, it's got me baffled. But it scares me, and I don't like to be scared of my airplanes. I bought into the risk, but I don't want to push Matthews and Dormund into an early demise."

"So let's you and me go fly her."

"Just the two of us?"

"See if we can recreate the problem."

"Why not?"

As they went down the stairs to the first floor, Kerry said, "I've got to phone Whitlock. Why don't you call ahead and have someone mount a couple video cameras in the cabin windows?"

"Ah. Aimed back at the elevons?"

"Right on. You Navy guys catch on after a while."

"We just act slow, so we don't embarrass the Air Force."

They stopped in the BOQ office and commandeered telephones. Whitlock was expecting his call, and it went right through to the China Dome communications center.

"Grand Central Station," Whitlock answered the phone. "Station speaking."

"Good morning, Station."

"For you, maybe. You're at Edwards, Julie told me."

Julie Macon was Kerry's secretary.

"We're going to take a joyride."

"Good luck. Or break a leg, or whatever it's supposed to be."

"Anything new on your end?" Kerry asked.

"We've pared a list of five thousand suspects down to just two or three thousand."

"Jesus."

"I'd like His help, Dan."

"Any particular traits showing up?"

"Yichang is still convinced that China Dome is the target. His psychological profile shows guys that don't like the thought of losing international business, and we've got a long list of North Koreans, North Vietnamese, Japanese, Filipinos, and a few Indians and Pakistanis. There's another list of known or suspected Chinese nationalists and possible revolutionaries who don't like the thought of China being jerked into the economic 21st Century. There's a sublist of outright anarchists who just don't like anything. Or anybody, probably. He's got the national cops and his friends in foreign police departments checking on the whereabouts of the prime suspects."

Both Kerry and Whitlock had thought that there was a strong possibility that the bombing of Control Tower Six was a message directed outside of China Dome. Someone was suggesting that it was dangerous for outsiders to visit the airport. If no one, particularly the SST vendors, came to the party, there wouldn't be a party. Yichang didn't think much of the scenario.

"I guess we can't do much more than make suggestions to him," Kerry said. "What have you been doing?"

"I'm learning a lot about subversives I didn't know existed, and I'm making up my own little list."

"Anything else?"

"I'm getting a feel for the politics."

Kerry waited.

"I've discovered there's a hell of a lot going on underground. That's a long, long tunnel, boss."

Kerry waited.

"And I think Karen Meyer might be helpful."

Kerry grinned.

"She's still there?"

"She told me she'd decided to take some vacation time while she was in Hong Kong."

"There's more to this, Charley."

"I'm a gentleman, Dan, but yeah, I think she's Mossad. Or at minimum, a Mossad asset."

The Mossad was the Israeli intelligence service, often acclaimed as being one of the best in the world. They had suffered some public relations face loss with the publication of *By Way of Deception,* an insider's account by Victor Ostrovsky who had been a Mossad agent for four years, but the revelations probably wouldn't affect their effectiveness.

"Don't take this the wrong way, Charley, but why would the Mossad be interested in you?"

"I wondered about that myself, but then, we've got some ultrahigh-tech, ultrasecret security systems on the Astroliner, right?"

"That you would know about."

"That I would know about. The Israelis are always curious about security systems."

"Is Karen Meyer concerned about security?"

"She is."

"Be tender, Charley."

"That's me."

Kerry hung up, and he and Carroll left the building and found Carroll's two-year-old Corvette in its parking place. Carroll liked being a jet pilot on the ground, also.

He drove rather sedately to the hangar, though, and they were met by a beaming Dennis Aikens.

He pulled open the door for Kerry and let him out into the early morning heat wave. "You've ungrounded her!"

"Not permanently, Dennis. Just for a short ride."

Aikens's face fell, but he tried to hold his smile. "There is no factual basis for the event, Dan. It was an anomaly."

"But what if it reoccurs with a hundred and sixty people on board, Dennis? The lawyers will go on safari, and we'll be big game."

Aikens frowned; he didn't like having Kerry get off the fence on Terry Carroll's side.

As they stood by the sports car, the hangar doors rolled back, and a tractor towed the Astroliner from the interior. The tractor braked the airplane to a stop just outside the monstrous doors. Kerry saw the Astrofreighter sitting in the cool shadows inside. Ground crewmen milled about below the airliner, making final adjustments, and a fuel tanker pulled in close to top off the fuel cells.

Kerry and Carroll, with Aikens in trail, made their exterior visual inspection, then climbed the stairway that had been rolled into place. Don Matthews and Jeff Dormund pleaded with Carroll for the right to go along, but the test pilot was adamant.

Inside the doorway, in the unfinished foyer, they found a pair of parachutes and pulled them on. After the first few flights of the Astroliner, the pilots had shunned the parachutes, but the last trip seemed to indicate a need to be prepared for the worst.

While Carroll secured the door, Kerry marched down the long and vacant cabin to where two video cameras had been mounted to the fuselage sides, their lenses aimed obliquely through the portholes toward the rear. He turned on the portside camera and peered through the viewfinder. The wide-angle lens captured the outboard pair of elevons and the outside elevon of the inboard pair. He made sure the locknuts on the mount were tight, then crossed to the other side and checked the camera there.

By the time he reached the flight deck, Carroll was in his seat with the preengine start checklist up on one of his multifunction screens. Kerry pulled the cushions out of the seat to make room for his parachute, then settled into the right-hand seat, powered up his panels, and brought the checklist up on the right screen. He started calling it off, and the two of them aligned circuit breakers and switches and checked the readouts for communications, electronics, and hydraulic systems.

Twenty minutes later, Kerry ran the throttles forward for a full-power check at the end of the runway.

"We've got greens everywhere I look, Terry."

"The power doesn't worry me," Carroll said, rolling the yoke and cycling the control surfaces.

Kerry found one of the transmit buttons with his toe and spoke into the small microphone cantilevered in front of his mouth. "Edwards Ground Control, PA Zero-One is on Runway 27 and requesting takeoff clearance."

Since this particular runway was leased solely to Pacific Aerospace, they weren't required to submit to Ground Control for surface movement to the runway.

"Ah, roger, PA One. You've got a crosswind at three-five-five, gusting to six knots. Barometric at two-niner-point-one-five. There's a pair of FB-111s six miles west at two-zero thousand. You are cleared for takeoff and climb to seven thousand. Go to Air Control."

"Let her roll, Terry."

He dialed the air control frequency into his primary radio and waited for Carroll's commands.

"Full throttles."

"Full throttles coming up."

Kerry advanced the power levers and kept his eyes on the readouts. Without a flight engineer on board, he assumed those responsibilities.

The center screen on both of their panels displayed the runway ahead of them. As the nose came up, the cameras automatically adjusted, pivoting downward to maintain their view of the runway.

Carroll released the brakes, and the lightly loaded Astroliner picked up speed immediately. The runway's centerline unrolled in his screen.

Kerry switched the right multifunction screen to Auxiliary One and found that he had a view of the right wingtip from the temporary camera in the cabin. Auxiliary Two on the center screen gave him the left wing.

He checked the velocity readout.

"One-two-zero knots."

"Roger."

At 170 knots, Carroll rotated, and Kerry studied his screen. He saw nothing alarming. The three elevons he could see reacted exactly as they were supposed to behave and appeared as steady as the hands of the Rock of Gibraltar, if the Rock had hands.

They spent forty minutes getting to their test altitude and sixty miles off the coast of California. Carroll let Kerry fly the plane during the transition to supersonic speed. He couldn't find a single fault in the feel of the controls or the operation of the autopilot, but he reserved his opinion for later discussions.

The skies were brilliant and clear this morning, and the morning sun lit the California coast with bright emerald greens in the hills behind the tan shoreline. The Pacific was deep blue, and far below he could see the tiny triangles of a dozen white sails. Several large commercial ships left long wakes behind them.

"Looks like fishing time to me," Kerry said.

"I haven't even had my boat out in ten months," Carroll complained. "Aikens would have made a good taskmaster on a Roman galley."

Kerry had a thirty-two-foot Scarab running four 200-horsepower Mercury outboards—a drug boat Carroll called it, but it had been in storage in San Pedro for nearly two years.

"When I get stuck in China Dome," Kerry said, "I'll want you to fly my boat to Hong Kong."

"First cargo job for the Astrofreighter? The bill will run you just about the cost of the boat."

"Damn. You'd think I'd get a perk or two after all my loyal years."

Kerry and Carroll had both been with the company for six years, since shortly after its start-up. Prior to that, Kerry had been teaching as a civilian at the Air Force Academy in Colorado Springs and was bored to death. And before that, he had flown as a test pilot for McDonnell Douglas until he slammed an Apache helicopter into the ground when a rotor failed and Marian decided she couldn't take the stress any longer. In the attempt to save the marriage, he had moved to teaching, but she was lost to him by then.

P.J. Jackson's phone call to Kerry's office at the Academy

six years before had been a trumpet sounding, bringing him back to the real world.

After a quick radar check of the area, to be certain they had no unwanted aircraft at 36,000 feet, Kerry put the checklist for Test Sequence One up on Carroll's right screen. He kept the engine monitors on his left screen, and switched in the two wing-view cameras on the other two screens.

The indicated airspeed was Mach 2.6.

"Can you handle the sequence by yourself, Terry? I want to watch the monitors."

"I've got it. Shall we clue in the lab?"

"They can see it in the postmortem."

"Don't talk like that. Disengage autopilot."

Kerry switched off the autopilot and reported it aloud for the benefit of the cockpit recorder. He tightened his harness, aware of how uncomfortable the parachute on which he was seated felt.

"Entering the sequence."

"Roger," Kerry said, leaning forward without touching the yoke to study the center and right monitors.

"Two degrees up."

He saw the top halves of the elevons raise slightly in both monitors. The angle allowed him to see that the bottom halves remained locked in place. Everything looked solid.

"Feel anything, Terry?"

"Three degrees. There! A slight tremble, Dan."

"Can't see anything happening," Kerry said. The wide-angle lenses of the cameras, used so he had a view of at least three elevons on each wing, made the apparent distance between the cameras and the control surfaces about thirty feet, and it was difficult to see minute changes in position.

"Four degrees. I've got a flutter."

Kerry leaned forward and focused on the center screen.

The pair of outboard elevons on the left wing were shaking slightly.

"I see it, Terry."

"Good. I'm coming—"

Abruptly, both elevons collapsed.

The Astroliner lurched and went into a hard left roll.

Kerry grabbed the yoke with his right hand to help Carroll and the power assist fight the roll. With his left, he eased back the power levers.

"Throttles coming off, Terry."

"Roger that."

They were inverted, holding steady.

Slowly, careful to not nudge the nose out of alignment with the aircraft's forward flight, the two of them rolled her upright.

Dennis Aikens broke in on the radio, "PA One, are you all right?"

Kerry clicked the transmit button with his toe. "Later, Dennis."

"He's going to get tired of being told to shut up," Carroll said.

The speed came off slowly. When the indicator showed them below Mach 1, Kerry said, "Let's do it again."

"Hell, Dan. I'm just starting to breathe again."

"Yeah, but let's do it at four hundred and fifty knots."

"Well, as long as we're here."

At the lower speed, they didn't lose control until the readouts showed sixteen degrees of elevator upward pitch, then the left outboard elevons collapsed again, and the airplane again went inverted.

"Got it," Kerry said, hanging upside down in his harness.

Carroll was struggling to right the aircraft, but he said, "I'm damned happy for you."

Sacramento, California
August 9, 1:45 P.M.

Peter James Jackson had never been an aviator, and in fact, he didn't even enjoy flying, but he had commanded a destroyer and achieved the rank of captain before he was passed over twice for promotion to flag rank. He attributed the lack of recognition for his abilities to his sometimes uncontrollable mouth and promptly got out of the Navy.

He was comfortable in the corridors of power, though, and he had served on the boards of several large corporations as well as at executive levels at GE and Ford after retiring from the Navy. The echoing halls and stern, protective secretaries of the California State Capitol didn't intimidate him in the least. He plowed through them as if he had the *Elliot* at flank speed in a Force Three gale with a hostile sub on his sonars.

He plowed his way into the second-floor office of state senator Paul Jason Jackson, bulling his way past a number of impatient constituents to reach the secretary's desk.

She looked up and frowned. "Oh, Mr. Jackson. I'm afraid the senator's tied up for—"

"Get him untied, Gracie. This won't wait."

Gracie did her best, but all of five minutes elapsed before P.J. Jackson was alone with his twin brother.

Though they were identical twins, at age fifty-six, the years had wrought some distinguishing marks. Peter Jackson was as flat-bellied as he had been as a lieutenant (junior grade) on board the *Ranger;* Paul had the comfortable physique of a man who enjoyed his cigars and bourbon to possible excess. P.J.'s hair was styled and short, naturally gray, and his twin fought to retain his youth through dye and flowing locks. The green eyes, the straight, chopped-off noses, and the short-lobed ears were dead ringers for each other, but Paul Jason's jowls were a bit looser.

If they had ever known, they had forgotten which of them was born first, so neither knew who the senior brother was, but P.J. had always acted as if the honor belonged to him. P.J. knew, also, that it was he who had enrolled for Vietnam while Paul shouted slogans in the streets and eventually rode his antiwar sentiment into a San Francisco Board of Supervisors seat. From 1965 on, these twins had been easily separable. Only in the last few years, after their father died and they began to think about termination points for families, had they begun to reacquaint themselves with each other, and that process had been tentative at best.

"Paul, do you know Alan Wicker?"

"Alan? Of course, he's Green's chief aide."

"I just talked to Alan Wicker, and he told me that you have not yet spoken to Senator Green."

Green headed the Transportation Committee.

"Now, P.J., I didn't promise. . . ."

"The hell you didn't!"

"Well, I don't recall. . . ."

"You've still got the draft bill?" Jackson asked.

"I've got it."

P.J. pulled one of the old wooden straight-backed chairs over in front of the desk and sat down facing his brother across the paper-littered desktop.

He tried to keep his voice level and his volume down. "Let me go over this one more time, Paul. I've spent *beaucoup* dollars having my lawyers draft that bill, just to save the California taxpayers some bucks. That bill has to be introduced, and passed, in this coming session so that the SST restrictions at L.A. International and San Francisco International will be lifted by the time the Astroliner has to start using them."

"I know, but—"

Jackson held up his hand to stifle the protest. "And with California leading the way, we'll be in Seattle, Fort Worth-Dallas, O'Hare, Miami, and anywhere else we need to go within the following year. You still with me on this?"

"P.J., the noise. We pass that bill, and we won't be in office for long. The environmentalists will—"

"Bullshit! Have you heard it?"

"No, but—"

"I gave you the studies out of Kennedy and Dulles. Anybody been bitching about the Concorde? And the Astroliner is twenty decibels quieter. You've got all the specifications."

"This is definitely going to look like a conflict of interest issue," Paul Jason complained.

"That's bullshit, too. I didn't ask you to front it. I asked you to take it to Green and let him handle it."

"But he'll see me using my influence. . . ."

P.J. wasn't too certain about the extent of his sibling's influence. "Brother, this isn't a war of missiles and bullets. Goddamn it, this is survival. Tell me your tax base isn't eroding. Tell me that California's scientists and engineers are not immigrating to Oregon and Colorado. Where's the money going? Where are the jobs? You ask Green if he wouldn't like to see a fifteen-billion-dollar infusion into the economy. That bill will fly through the committee at Mach 2 if Southern Cal sees jobs in it."

"Well, I guess I can at least talk to him."

"I've got that on tape, Paul."

Kowloon
August 10, 9:50 P.M.

Kurt Wehmeier took a table at the Golden Phoenix in time for the floor show. Featured were a French female torch singer, who did "Fever" in her native language, a Thai magician, an Australian comic, and a loud and unruly American rock band named Bandito.

He ordered Perrier and waited, listening to the torch singer.

James Lee arrived at five after ten. He was a bulky man, thick-torsoed, with long arms. He wore long-sleeved shirts to shield the public from the ornately obscene tattoos that spiraled up his arms. Over his right eye was an especially ugly scar which Wehmeier knew was the consequence of a dull knife. The little finger of his left hand was missing, not as some gang ritual, but as the result of an encounter with a sharper knife.

Lee was born in Hong Kong, the misbegotten child of a Chinese prostitute and a Victoria District Chinese civil servant. He did not care for the Victoria District, civil servants, or authority in general.

Wehmeier asked him, "Do you have the materials?"

"They are already on-site."

That was alarming. Wehmeier did not like associates who thought for themselves. Most often, they thought wrong.

"I did not tell you to move them, yet."

"It was easy."

"Give me back the money."

The man's eyes enlarged. "I do not have the money."

"Then you must pay with blood."

"But. . . ."

Wehmeier cast a look at the tables near them. He and

Lee spoke softly, but it would not be in their interests to be overheard. "Or you must do exactly as I say, and not until I say it. If you want more money."

"Yes, but—"

"I am asking you if you understand me and our agreement." Wehmeier let his eyes go hard. He knew his eyes could intimidate.

"Yes, Mr. Bern, I understand."

Wehmeier was known only as Bern to most of his associates.

"All right, then, just so we know where we stand. You have the materials in place?"

"Not in the final position, no," Lee said. "But they have passed through the security point."

"All right, then. I want you to complete the installation either tomorrow or the next day. We must be ready by the twelfth."

"It should not be a problem. It will depend upon the police. They are everywhere."

"I will call you tomorrow night."

"Very well."

Wehmeier reached inside his coat pocket and withdrew a manila envelope. In it were six thousand dollars Hong Kong and a miniature transceiver. Though another associate had constructed the transceiver, Wehmeier had personally verified its correct operation.

"There is one more thing, Mr. Bern."

"That is?"

"Did you know that the Pacific Aerospace airplane has top secret security devices installed?"

Wehmeier did not ask Lee how he knew. He reached into his pocket and peeled off another thousand dollars HK and passed them across the table.

SEVEN

Deng Xiaoping International Superport
August 12, 9:22 P.M.

The maintenance tunnels of China Dome were becoming entirely too familiar to Charley Whitlock. For the most part, they were four levels—sixty feet—below the surface, and they didn't make a nice, circular route like the people mover tunnel did. There were alleys and cul-de-sacs and dead ends extending from streets and avenues and boulevards. There were long stretches of half a mile and more where the tunnel was as straight as William Tell's arrow with only tall stacks of conduits racked against either wall.

The main tunnels were about ten feet wide, seven to eight feet when the space for the bundles of cabling and piping were deducted. The remaining space allowed ample room for the electric golf carts that were used as the primary mode of transportation. Unless one met another golf cart coming from the other direction, then caution was indicated. The Chinese drivers, though, tended to be less cautious than the single American. He'd had some close brushes.

Despite the substantial lighting system that prevented the maze from becoming a blind labyrinth, it was dank and clammy. Moisture seeped along the walls at many locations.

Spiders and insects were frequent companions to those who worked in or traversed the tunnels.

Whitlock had to admit that the tunnel system would eventually be about as secure as it could be made. Aware that it would be an expected route of infiltration, the architects had located steel doors with magnetically encoded locks at every entrance point. The problem at the current time was that many of these doors had been propped open to facilitate the movement of engineers, electricians, and plumbers. Some of them were clearly identified by their uniforms. Full-time employees of the airport wore dark blue uniform pants and matching shirts. They also wore short-waisted jackets color-coded to the department for which they worked. Those in fluorescent orange were aircraft service personnel, usually found at ground level. Yellow was reserved for fire control workers, green for maintenance people, red for food service employees. There were other colors, but Whitlock hadn't memorized them all.

With Yichang's blessing, in addition to a newly encoded ID card and a semi-master key which gave him access to a large number of areas within the airport, Whitlock had spent several days exploring the tunnels. He had investigated over three hundred storage and equipment closets opening on the tunnel without finding anything that pricked his curiosity. He had examined the tunnels from the transport facility area to the terminals, to the maintenance and commercial areas. Creeping along at five miles per hour in his cart, he had surveyed the wide tunnel between the maintenance facilities and the subsurface tank farm where jet fuel was stored. The corridor there was much wider to allow for the six-inch fuel mains that transferred jet fuel to the hangars. The tanks which had a capacity of ten million gallons were fed by tank cars wheeled in by electric locomotives on rails from an adjacent tunnel. Buried piping, not accessible by tunnel, carried fuel directly to the terminals so that aircraft could be refueled without the need for tanker trucks. He had taken the single, narrower tunnel that passed under the runways and drove straight to the antenna complex in the northwest corner of the complex. It was an interesting drive, but he hadn't seen anything but concrete.

He hadn't found one thing that appeared lethal or needed correction.

If he had accomplished anything at all in ten days, beyond accumulating his own database of names, he thought that it was his increased rapport with Yichang Enlai. The Chinese security chief had come to trust him more, evidenced by his allowing Whitlock to explore the tunnels on his own.

Conversely, Yichang might think that Whitlock's hands-on detecting served primarily as a way to keep Whitlock out of his way.

Whitlock had been sitting in the security center, about to call it a day around seven o'clock, when a new thought struck him. He immediately called Karen Meyer at the hotel and put off their dinner for a couple hours, then left the center and took one of the employee-only authorized elevators to Sublevel Four.

With his photocopied versions of the tunnel map and the wiring and piping schematics, he had taken a cart and headed for the central switching station. It was south of the main terminal.

He found it full of workers, and flagged down a foreman in a yellow hard hat. He had been here a few times before, and the man knew him.

"Yes, Mr. Whitlock?"

He unfolded the wiring schematic. It was nearly indecipherable to him because his copy didn't have the color-coding of the original. The solid lines and dotted lines and paired lines were difficult to follow, but he did have one of the English language versions, and the lines were at least identified.

"Mr. Yichang told me that there were millions of unused fiber-optic circuits in the primary and backup trunk lines."

"Yes, that is true."

"Can you show where those appear on here?"

The man frowned. "It would all be part of the fiber-optic bundle, Mr. Whitlock. You see, one fiber-optic strand might carry as many as five hundred circuits, all digitally encoded differently. It depends on how the transmitters and receivers are programmed at each end of the circuit."

"Oh. Damn. So a visual inspection wouldn't reveal if an unused circuit were being utilized illegally?"

The frown deepened. "On a continuous basis?"

"Probably not."

"The computer which monitors usage would flag a circuit that was in use if it were not supposed to be in use. However, if the circuit were activated only momentarily, the computer might, well, not miss it, but not remark it."

"I see."

Whitlock was not entirely certain that he understood, or even sure that he wanted to understand.

"Well, look," he said. "I've been wondering how that control tower explosion was set off. It was probably by remote control, rather than by timer, and I wondered if someone could tap into the airport's unused circuits and use one as the transmission device."

Impossibly, the frown spread further on the man's face, but his eyes got larger as he thought about it.

"It might be possible, Mr. Whitlock. What I could do, I could examine the computer reports for the day involved. They are not kept on hard copy, and I will have to go into the storage base."

"I'd appreciate that. And could you tell me what the . . . whatever they are—interfaces?—look like?"

"Data transfer interfaces? Certainly, come this way."

The foreman led him down a corridor to a room full of gray metal cabinets with louvered doors that looked like oversized gymnasium lockers. He selected one and opened the door.

All Whitlock saw were stacks of black boxes with strands of colorful tubing going in and out of them.

"Doesn't look like much, does it?" he asked.

"It would require a specialist to know if one had been tampered with," the foreman said.

"And these things are all over the airport?"

"Yes, sir, though there are a number of major intersection points."

The foreman took his map and marked the locations for him. There were several under each of the terminals, the hangar area, the commercial section, and the transportation transfer domes.

Whitlock thanked the man for his help and went back to his golf cart. He turned it around, stomped the accelerator pedal, and listened to the moan of the electric motor.

Since it was easy to become confused in the tunnel system, signs were suspended from the curved ceiling every fifty yards or so. They provided the number of the tunnel and the direction being travelled.

He made his first stop at Room 3162B, below Terminal One, a place he had been before. With the master key Yichang had given him, Whitlock unlocked the door, turned on the light, and stepped inside. His days were beginning to look the same—concrete, unshaded lightbulbs, gray boxes, and aluminum conduit. A view of the sun would have been nice.

He found the locker with the same prefix, "CC," as the one the foreman had shown him and opened the door. The same row of black boxes, and they all looked the same. Nothing out of place.

He locked up, got back in the cart, and headed for Room 3177C.

And found the same thing.

He continued west in the tunnel, stopping to check on every communications compartment marked on his map. He met many others in the tunnel, most of them on foot, but some in carts. When he met another cart, he slowed down, and passed the other gingerly. The Chinese drivers grinned broadly at him and raced by like an Andretti on his way to the flag.

Most of those he met were dressed in the green jackets of maintenance personnel, though there were a few light blue jackets belonging to security personnel and a few dark blue-coated supervisors among them. It was usually the supervisors who were driving carts. The rest of them walked.

Whitlock had just left the last compartment under Terminal Six when he remembered to look at his watch.

Nine-twenty.

Damn. Where'd the time go?

He'd have to call Karen and beg off again when he reached a phone in one of the hangars.

He passed the entrance of the tunnel leading to the antenna compound and decided he would check it later.

A couple minutes later, he slowed for the left turn into the tunnel between the hangars and the tank farm.

He was back up to ten miles an hour when the muted *whoosh* sounded behind him.

Surprised, he started to turn his head to the rear . . .

And the concussion wave blew him right out of his cart.

Lo Wu, New Territories
August 12, 9:26 P.M.

Darkness was his friend, and Wehmeier always gravitated toward it. He stood in the darkness on the western side of the railway station, five meters from the light over the public telephone he had just used.

The commuter train was in the station preparing to make its return journey to Kowloon.

Wehmeier glanced at his watch. Six minutes until departure.

There was a large number of people on the platform, mostly Chinese, who had been about to board the train when they heard the faraway explosion. Now they were all staring toward the northwest.

It was about twelve kilometers away, but Wehmeier had seen the brief, bright flash, like a red flare on the horizon. It had died away to a dull glow now, but he still felt the satisfaction deep in his belly, like a fine meal composed of roast beef and potatoes.

He waited until the train was about to pull out, then crossed the platform and boarded a second-class car.

Edwards Air Force Base, California
August 12, 8:44 A.M.

Because there was the equivalent of a small city's wiring in the Astroliner, and because much of it was behind bonded skin that no one wanted to cut open, it took three days to locate the fault. They attempted to test each circuit independently, but that didn't work. When the Astroliner was at rest, every circuit tested as perfectly as it was designed.

Just as they had in the previous testing.

"It would be one of the few goddamned connectors not close to an access panel," Don Matthews said.

"There's a Murphy's Law relative to connectors, isn't there?" Terry Carroll asked him.

"Probably."

The two of them stood near the left wingtip and watched as one of the techs on a scaffolding cut into the carbon-reinforced plastic of the lower wing panel with a high-speed, air-powered cutting disk. He braced his wrists against the wing and moved the tool with excessive care since, just a few inches beyond the skin, was a fuel bladder. It had been drained and air pumped through it, but fumes in the bladder were more highly explosive than the JP-7 that normally filled it.

Zip, zip, zip, zip. They were slow zips, performed with care, but then the section of skin finally fell away.

Carroll moved over next to the scaffolding and looked up into the cavity in the wing. Beneath the fuel bladder, and between two wing spars, he saw the connector immediately. A thirty-two-strand ribbon wire coming from the fuselage terminated in a wide and narrow connector. Plugged into it were two sixteen-wire connectors, each set transmitting the signals for the primary and backup solenoids which activated the elevon hydraulic jacks.

"For Christ's sake!" Carroll said with disgust.

Matthews and Dennis Aikens had moved up beside him.

Aikens didn't say anything, but Matthews asked, "That's it?"

"That's it, just what Dan figured. That connector is floating free, and when we put enough G-force on it—five degrees up-elevon at Mach two-point-six and sixteen degrees under Mach one—it came down about an inch and shorted out on the ground wire for the fuel bladder. See it, there?"

"I see it," Matthews said.

"What's worse," Carroll said for the benefit of the chief engineer, "some asshole decided to put the primary and backup systems in the same goddamned wire set. When it shorted, we lost electrical impulse to the solenoids on both the standard and the backup systems. The jacks collapsed, the left side elevons went to neutral, and we rolled."

An electrician was crawling up the scaffolding, and Aikens said to him, "Make certain that fitting is secured very tightly."

"Not good enough, Dennis," Carroll said. "I want it ripped out and two separate ribbon cables threaded through that wing to replace it. One cable for each system. No connectors, unless they're moved aft to the W-4 Access Panel."

"Now just a damned minute, Terry—"

"The right wing has to be rewired also."

"Terry."

"What are we talking about, Dennis? A couple hundred bucks for wire? A few man-hours?" He jerked his head toward the fuselage. "We're also talking about a hundred and sixty-eight full seats."

Aikens stared at him for a moment, then nodded. "Okay. We replace it."

"The Astrofreighter, too."

Carroll and Matthews turned and headed for the door.

He ought to feel better, but he found himself wondering if any other shortcuts had been taken.

Deng Xiaoping International Superport
August 13, 5:21 A.M.

"I want the responsible person put to death within the month," Sun Chen yelled over the phone.

"Chairman Sun," Yichang said in a placating tone, "we

will have to catch him first, and that may take more than a month. There are over two thousand—"

"A month, Director! We must have this resolved to the satisfaction of the international community prior to the opening day ceremonies."

"I will do my best," Yichang sighed.

"The fires are out?"

"The fires are extinguished. It took most of the night to accomplish it. We were fortunate in that only one hundred thousand gallons of fuel was currently in storage."

"And the extent of the damages?"

"Three men were burned to death."

"That is terrible!" Sun exclaimed.

"It is. And we lost but two of the fifty underground tanks. We will have to excavate again, to replace them."

Sun Chen was quiet for a long time, then said, "I want to know how this was accomplished, even if you never locate the perpetrator."

Yichang did not know if he was receiving a reprieve on his deadline, but thought it prudent not to ask. He thought that determining the method might be even more difficult than finding the culprit.

Encino, California
August 12, 1:20 P.M.

"Jesus Christ! Is he all right?"

Mickey Duff, who was holding down the Tokyo office, said, "From what Yichang told me, Dan, he's fine. He got himself knocked down the tunnel about twenty feet, and he slapped his head against the concrete. There was a lot of smoke in the tunnel, but no fire. He's got a mild concussion, and he's checked himself out of the airport dispensary and into the hotel."

"I'll call him there."

"I tried, but he's put a 'do not disturb' on his phone. If I were him, I'd be gobbling aspirin by the handful and trying to get to sleep. Charley will call you when he's ready."

"Okay, Mickey, thanks."

Kerry hung up the phone, looked at the boxes scattered around the living room, then went into the kitchen and got himself a bottle of Michelob from the refrigerator. He took it back to the living room, turned on the TV, found CNN news, and flopped in the Barcalounger.

After forty minutes, when they went to sports, he was finished with the beer and there had been no mention of the event at China Dome.

Somebody was trying to contain the news, and whoever it was was doing a pretty good job of it.

He left the set on and went back to his packing.

Kerry's house in Encino was rented from a man named Chavez with whom he had gone to high school in Clovis, New Mexico. Chavez had made a fair name for himself as an assistant director, then a director in the film industry, and Kerry had rented the house when he went to Saudi Arabia to film a documentary. A month before, Chavez had called Kerry to see if he wanted to buy the house. Chavez had contracted AIDS and needed the money.

Kerry had nearly bought it, just on the forlorn appeal in the man's voice. But, more reasonably, he had thought that he might be in the Far East for quite some time and had declined.

In any event, it had sold quickly, and he had to be out of it in two weeks. When P.J. called him back to the States, he had decided to take advantage of the trip to get his accumulated belongings into storage.

He was trying to organize what went into the boxes, in case he wanted to ship only part of them to Japan.

Or maybe to China.

He thought about going out and having a rubber stamp made. On the bottom of his vases and china, he would imprint in red, "Made in the United States of America."

Some things still were, though not many.

It was a warm day, but Kerry had all of the windows open, trying to air the place out. He had been paying rent on an empty house for a long time, and it was pretty damned stale inside.

Using single sheets from a stack of newspapers he had gotten from a neighbor, Kerry wrapped the items from the small trophy case in one corner of the living room. There were old tennis trophies, pictures of his high-school football team, pictures and relics from his squadron during his first tour in Vietnam. On the second tour, when he had been assigned to the 8th Tactical Fighter Wing, he had collected only one picture of "Jigs" Malone, his bombardier/navigator, and himself standing in front of their F-4 at Ubon Royal Thai Air Force Base, Kingdom of Thailand. He'd also collected a few surgical scars.

Eight thousand feet below, the F-111 bombers streaked across the dark water toward their Haiphong Harbor targets. Thick and random bursts of flak from the ZSU-23 quad-barreled antiaircraft guns were Rorschach blots against the dawn sun. The Fan Song radars were coming alive. Four, five, six surface-to-air missiles took to the sky.

The radio crackled in confusion with calls among the eight F-4s flying High Combat Air Patrol.

"Bandits! Bandits!" screamed "Chick" Saunders, his wingman.

Kerry scanned the skies while arming his Sidewinder air-to-air missiles. He found three MiG-21 silhouettes.

Wrong shape for the silhouettes.

They were coming dead-on.

They wanted the bombers, and Kerry shoved the nose down, calculating the intercept point and the lead.

"Four MiGs on our six, Dan!" Malone called.

Wham!

The canopy disintegrated, the right fuselage side caved in on him. The whole right side of his face erupted in unbelievable pain. Malone yelped over the intercom. Saunders's flame-engulfed Phantom cartwheeled through the morning.

Automatically, Kerry threw the right wing down and rolled hard to the right, diving inverted below the debris of his wingman's destroyed F-4. The wind howled through the jagged openings in the fuselage and canopy. He glimpsed fleeting images of Phantoms scattering in all directions.

"Jigs!" he yelled on the Internal Communications System.

No answer.

Blood filled his eyes beneath the visor. He was aware that his oxygen mask was gone.

Rolled level, halfway knowing he'd come out on a westward heading.

Tried to wipe the blood from his eyes, levered the visor out of the way, discovered his helmet was shattered.

As was his jaw.

The right side of his face was a mass of blood and torn

flesh. His left hand probed but couldn't find any of his teeth on the right side. Crenelated stumps.

He didn't even know what they'd been hit with, but it was probably a dud missile that hadn't detonated.

What luck.

His crippled F-4 had lost speed to 300 knots and altitude to 4,500 feet AGL, but he still had power and flight control. Pieces of the canopy and fuselage kept peeling away, whipping off into the slipstream. Dirt, paper, and other small debris fluttered around in the cockpit. Ahead of him, he saw two MiGs closing on the flight leader's Phantom.

Keying the transmit button, Kerry shouted, "Bronco, break! Break!"

No radio.

He hauled the stick left and triggered a Sidewinder without aiming.

Come on, come on.

The missile streaked away.

Right stick, another missile.

No time to aim and lock on.

The first missile slammed into the left MiG, and the explosion sheared off the right wing. The enemy aircraft began to tumble immediately.

The second missile missed because the pilot scrambled as soon as his comrade was hit. Another F-4 coming out of nowhere pounced on him and sent a Sidewinder up the MiG's tailpipe.

Burst of yellow fire.

And then Kerry was on the deck, straining for the Laotian border, trying to staunch the blood flowing down his face, worried about the JP-4 streaming from his punctured fuel cells, escorted by Chris "Bronco" Davidson. He couldn't get Jigs Malone to respond to him. He had to belly land

*in a field in Laos since he couldn't get Malone's seat to
eject.*

*The Jolly Green Giants were on the ball, and had them
off the ground in less than twenty minutes.*

*That morning cost Malone a leg and an arm. Kerry got
new teeth, months of plastic surgery, a Purple Heart, and
a Distinguished Flying Cross.*

Kerry had never displayed any of the medals. They were
still in their flat blue boxes, stored among the memorabilia
from the academy. He didn't know why he kept all of the
old crap; it just collected dust.

Sealing the box with tape, he marked it with a felt pen,
stacked it on top of another box, and carried the two of them
to the garage. He had a fair stack of boxes building against
the far wall of the empty stall, most of them heavy with books.
Kerry still had every book he had ever owned, from the Hardy
Boys to John D. MacDonald to Winston Churchill to Clive
Cussler. He had often thought that a good book was about
the only constant left in the world. He could always look back
on them and find what he expected to find. Everything else
shifted and changed on him.

In the near bay was his fourteen-year-old, bright red Ferrari 308GT, with its hood up and a battery charger connected to the battery. As soon as he could get it started, he
would make a run to Goodwill with an amazing mound of
clothing and household paraphernalia he no longer needed.

Kerry wasn't going to give up the Ferrari, but he hated
to put it in storage. At one time, he had considered shipping
it to Japan, but Tokyo suffered from more gridlock than
L.A. did. Parking places cost as much as an L.A. apartment.
He would wait and see what developed in China. He could

picture himself sailing through the New Territories on the way to work.

At about forty miles per hour, given the traffic.

Opening the door to the backyard, Kerry stepped outside to get his barbecue grille. His neighbor was washing her car in her driveway, a chore she accomplished once a day, and she waved at him, "Hello, Dan!"

"Hi, Janner. When are you going to get to mine?"

"Bring it over."

"If I ever get it started, I might do that."

He wheeled the grille inside, then disconnected the propane bottle and removed it. He would leave the bottle for the new owners.

The furniture in the house and on the patio all belonged to Chavez, and Kerry was grateful that he didn't have to worry about it.

He went back inside and started emptying kitchen cabinets, remembering why he hated moving. It was always easier to pay rent on an empty house than pack it up for moving.

When he was younger, Kerry had pictured himself in a life of adventure, travelling light, never putting down roots. Part of that was a legacy from his father, who had been an Air Force colonel. Kerry had gone through a succession of hometowns as he was growing up, picking Clovis, New Mexico, as his home of record simply because Colonel Robert Kerry was stationed at Cannon Air Force Base when Kerry left the family cluster for the Air Force Academy.

He had never owned a home, even when he and Marian were married; Kerry always figured he would be moving on shortly.

As he wrapped glasses in white butcher paper, Kerry's litany of regrets came to mind. It seemed as if he had missed part of the American Dream. He wasn't likely to ever have children, a fact frequently hammered home by his mother, who now lived in Sarasota, Florida. Alyce Williams often echoed her.

Sometimes, in morose moments, Kerry had wondered how differently his life might have been if he'd had to run to Little League games and PTA meetings instead of grasping for Mach 3 or buying elaborate dinners for businessmen and government officials who could influence the future of PAI.

And sometimes, Kerry thought that a life of norms might have interfered with his evolution. As a military brat, a military academy graduate, and an Air Force pilot, he had been deeply immersed in inbred nationalism. When P.J. Jackson, whom he had met the first time at an interservice strategies workshop and the second time at an aerospace industries conference before hiring on with the man, asked him to work with the Chinese, Kerry had been extremely reluctant. He had had to force himself to recognize that the old political barriers were falling faster than his ability to keep up with them. Outside of deeply entrenched cultural and religious antagonisms still present in Ireland, the Middle East, and some Commonwealth of Independent States' republics, the world was putting on a new face. Economic survival was the current priority, and that was where nations were flexing whatever muscles they could still flex.

Kerry had finally taken on the job as a result of his concern for rebuilding an American aerospace industry, first, and as an exercise in acclimating himself to a new global perspective, secondly. When he dealt with Chinese, Japanese, and Korean nationals, he often found himself burying old slogans he had learned from his father, who had fought in both the Pacific theater of World War II and in Korea. They died hard, and they struggled all the way, but he thought he was overcoming his trained-in prejudices.

He had six additional boxes piled on the kitchen floor and was opening his second Michelob of the day when the phone rang. He grabbed it from the wall mount above the counter.

"Kerry."

"Charley, here, Dan."

"Hey, Hoss. How are you?"

"I still have the parts with which I started, but some of them are a little sore," Whitlock said. "Must be age that keeps me from bouncing back."

"No sweat. Stay in bed for a week. Find a friend."

"I've got a friend, in fact."

"Ah. You may not have full freedom of speech, in that case?"

"That's right. I just wanted to check in with you."

"I'm damned glad you did, pal. Mickey gave me a rather skimpy report. Concussion?"

"Mild, I'm told, though the headache's still with me. Bruised shoulder. Otherwise, I'm fit enough to find this bastard, and I will."

"Take it easy for now, Charley."

"Yeah, well, I'll try."

"I'll call you when I get back to Tokyo. Couple days. Unless you've got something really new?"

"It'll keep."

Kerry hung up, picked up another box, and reached for his beer.

The phone rang again.

He'd been home for most of one day in a year, and everyone seemed to be finding him.

Paris, France
August 12, 10:35 P.M.

On the Rue de Renaudes, around the corner from the Boulevard de Courcelles, was a spacious three-story granite block house that had been built in 1881 by Jacqueline Broussard's maternal great-grandfather. The grounds were not large, but the house was distinctive with its tall and arched, leaded glass windows. After World War II, it had been subdivided into three apartments, one on each floor, and each apartment was composed of nine comfortable rooms with three-meter-high ceilings. The first floor apartment was just right for Jacqueline Broussard, who had assumed ownership of the house after her mother moved permanently to the family villa in the south of France.

She could have lived well on just the revenue from the rental of the second and third floor luxury apartments, but she would probably have gone mad from inactivity. From her earliest schooling onward, Broussard had always been *involved* in something—a cause, a career, an escapade. Stagnation was one of her fears, and she did not have many fears.

This afternoon, after hearing of the second terrorist attack at China Dome, she had come home early, carrying the briefcase that contained the files relative to the China Dome project. After changing to jeans and a baggy, long-sleeved shirt that had been her father's, she put on a large pot of coffee and sat in the kitchen at the chopping block center island, beneath the copper pots and pans suspended from the ceiling on wrought-iron hooks.

It was one of her favorite spots—a thinking place—in the house. From the stool on which she sat, she could survey the overgrown backyard through the paired glass doors.

The four-car garage, which had once been a stable, at the back of the lot blocked her view of the house across the alley, but it was an architectural wonder of its own—granite blocks framed in century-old oak timbers, arched doors, leaded windows, a sloping roof of gray slate, and ivy creeping up the east wall. Winter was the best time, she had always thought, with the entire scene frosted in white, and the air hushed.

She had devoted several hours to reviewing her files, and they were spread around the surface of the counter in front of her. The remnants of her dinner, a bowl of vegetable soup and a croissant, were pushed to one side.

On the back of a file folder, Broussard listed her concerns with the stub of a pencil. The contents of her folders were a montage of varisized scraps of paper with numbers and half-composed notes on them, and the exteriors of the folders were littered with the graffiti of doodles and reminders. Broussard thought the wonders of the computer age were terrific for supersonic airplanes, but thought that adapting herself to computers would be a waste of time.

She looked over the list and then wrote the numeral "1" next to the entry she had generalized as "Desire." The word encompassed a number of subtopics in her mind.

Despite Henri's protestations to the contrary, she was beginning to believe that Aerospatiale-BAC did not want the China contract badly enough. The germ of that idea had been planned by Kerry, of course, and she was positive that it had been deliberately planted. And yet, there was truth in it. If Henri Dubonnet and his board of directors had had enough desire early-on in the design process, the Concorde II would not look like an extended-fuselage Concorde. Which it was.

She understood that the board was under the constraint

of budgetary limits. The current operations had never been entirely profitable, and the British and French governments subsidized the airline operations. That condition was a consequence of the limited number of destinations imposed on the Concorde by foreign governments. Kennedy Airport, Dulles International, Heathrow, and Charles de Gaulle were an insufficient number of ports of call if the operations were to be profitable. With Deng Xiaoping's opening, however, Henri anticipated that many more airports in the world would become available to them, to their base operations with the original Concorde, and the governmental subsidies would no longer be necessary.

With a conservative view of the Concorde's history, though, the British and French treasuries had been reluctant to open their vaults to the underwriting of an entirely new design, and the Concorde II had been under tight restrictions from the beginning.

Then, too, Broussard had reread the Tupolev, BBK, and Pacific Aerospace files in the light of the broad scope of the Russian, German, and American economies, which were badly depressed. Those three projects were being conducted under the intense pressure of economic *need,* which they had recognized and acknowledged. It was the foundation of their desire to succeed.

The Russians, like the French-British consortium, were attempting to get by with the least amount of up-front expenditures, but the American and German endeavors, driven by desire she thought, had concluded that high risk was worth the end result. They had poured billions of dollars and deutsche marks into the development of new technologies and manufacturing techniques.

Broussard was no longer as optimistic about her chances of securing the contract.

The second item on her list of concerns was the terrorist activity at China Dome. The targets seemed misdirected—a secondary control tower and fueling facilities. Did terrorists not seek out loss of life by which to make their statements? And then make proud boasts of their accomplishments? They could have killed many by selecting sites under construction or areas of the airport which were more populated. These acts, Broussard thought, were intended to suggest the power of threat. She was not an expert, but it seemed to her as if the two explosions were meant to deter outsiders from coming to China Dome for fears of reprisal. If the major air carriers refused to fly into southern China, Deng Xiaoping International would wither and die.

As would her opportunity to secure the contract.

As would her opportunity to obtain the fat commission Henri had promised her. Not that she needed the money, but the recognition of her ability and a reward for her effort was always gratifying.

The third concern on her list was, inexplicably, Dan Kerry.

The Lord knew she did not have to go halfway around the world to find a man, especially a man she felt she could easily despise. He was too self-assured, too confident when he had nothing in which to be confident. Or did he? He had an aura of danger surrounding him. He had been a fighter pilot in a disgusting and unnecessary war, killing others in a random and careless manner. She was certain of that.

His entire manner was a facade for the dangerous character within. He had false teeth, for God's sake.

Broussard knew that she had frequently been drawn to men who risked their lives unduly. The mountain climber, for instance. The deep-sea diver from Nice, for another.

Was that her attraction to Kerry? The danger? She knew herself well enough to know the attraction was present. It had been almost overpowering on the Kowloon ferry, but she had fought it successfully. She could not possibly become entangled with Dan Kerry.

He was her competitor, and if nothing else, that fact should provide the deterrent.

She pulled the coffeepot to her and refilled her cup.

She reached for the remote telephone and placed it beside the cup.

Sitting at the counter in her kitchen, leaning forward on her elbows with her hands folded under her chin, Broussard let all of the images of her concerns blend, flow, and churn in her mind. And after fifteen minutes of free association, she thought she might have a solution to at least two of her concerns.

Disadvantages had to be turned into advantages.

One could not sit in a kitchen, feeling defensive; one had to assume an attack stance. One might have to go into the den of the tiger in order to take what the tiger coveted.

Rifling through the papers spread out before her, she found the listing of Pacific Aerospace executives, picked up the telephone and dialed the international number for PAI's Tokyo office.

The woman there told her that Kerry was in the United States.

She tried the California headquarters.

And from them, she got his home telephone number.

Kerry answered the telephone on the fourth ring.

"Hello, Dan."

"Hold on, I know the accent. Jacqueline?"

"I'm surprised you remembered."

"No, you're not," he said.

He was correct, of course. She was aware that he had felt the same allure as she. She chose not to follow that line of discussion.

"I have been thinking about the latest incident at Deng Xiaoping."

"And what do you think about it?"

"I am thinking that the Chinese are not the direct target."

"That's what I told Yichang," Kerry said. "I said I was the target, but I was speaking generically. My feeling is that someone wants to keep us—you, me, everyone—out of China."

"What are you doing right now?" she asked.

"Doing? I'm packing up my house."

"Stay there. I will come and visit you in California, and we can talk more about this."

She could almost hear him smile.

"You'll take the Concorde, naturally?"

"Naturally."

EIGHT

Jacqueline Broussard was treated as a VIP, of course. Her status might have been considered ultra-VIP, in fact, since almost every passenger on a Concorde was very important. The cost of a one-way ticket, nearly four thousand dollars American, assured that those who purchased a seat were well-off, had a very nice expense account, or were in a great hurry.

She chatted casually with a number of well-dressed passengers in the lounge until the flight was called, then was ushered aboard by one of the stewards. Her seat was in the first row, and she was no more in it than the steward was offering her champagne. She declined for the time being.

Everything about a Concorde flight was first-class, from the deference paid by employees to passengers to the meals. Only French cuisine of the highest grade was offered, and it was prepared by expert chefs.

By ten-twenty, they were on the end of the runway, and almost without hesitation, into the takeoff. The Concorde pilots had many hours of experience, and the takeoff was smooth and flawless. The company retained thirty well-paid and well-trained crews for the fourteen aircraft flying the Atlantic, and it was estimated that transition for any crew into the Concorde II could be accomplished in a week. That was one of the pluses on Broussard's proposal to the Chinese. Another was that, should the Chinese wish to initiate flights early, some of the existing Concordes could be pressed into service until the new aircraft were completed.

By ten-fifty, with the French countryside a pleasant set of matte green squares far below, the large indicator on the bulkhead in front of her registered Mach 2.0. On the ground, the noise of their passage was far behind them, and she was entirely comfortable in the soft cushions of her seat.

The woman seated next to her wanted to chat about pedigreed dog shows, and Broussard attempted to be interested, but it was a difficult facade. She much preferred the conversation of men. Their topics, whether sports or politics or business, were always more substantial and certainly more active.

She had been very much the tomboy as a youngster, and frequently, both her mother and Henri suggested that she had never outgrown that phase of her life.

After fifteen minutes of polite affirmatives, she rested her head to one side and feigned sleep.

To think about Dan Kerry.

And wonder why she was really chasing off to America.

Edwards Air Force Base, California
August 13, 9:00 A.M.

By eleven o'clock of the previous night, Kerry had achieved his objectives. The GT's battery was charged, he had had the car serviced and washed, he had made his stop at Goodwill to drop off his donations, and he had most of his domestic life stacked in boxes in the garage. The storage company wouldn't pick them up until the following morning.

With most of a full day free, he had driven up to Edwards early and had breakfast with Aikens and Carroll, both of whom assured him that the Astroliner was now airworthy. The airplane would go through an additional week of intensive testing, then undergo its examination by the FAA in order to shed the experimental tag and gain a full-fledged airworthiness certificate. That was scheduled for August 22.

"So what's on tap for today, Terry?" he asked.

"We'll try out the ECM for the first time," Carroll said.

With an uncertain world that contained unstable people who had access to lethal toys like Redeye and Stinger shoulder-fired, surface-to-air missiles, Pacific Aerospace had decided to go beyond the specifications of the Chinese request for proposals and outfit the SSTs with Electronic Countermeasures systems. Variants of radar, infrared, and launch detection systems used in the F-15 Eagle and the F-18 Hornet had been incorporated into the structure of the Astroliner. Flare and chaff ejectors were also available to the pilot, to decoy radar and infrared homing missiles away from the airplane. With those defenses in place, the Korean Airlines 747 might not have gone down in the northern Pacific when it was attacked by Soviet missiles. PAI wasn't doing much more in self-defense for its civilian airliners than many corporate aircraft were doing. A million-dollar-a-year chief executive officer was a prime target for terrorists, and his three-million-dollar Cessna Citation II or Grumman Gulfstream II business jet could be shot out of the sky by a twelve-year-old with a Stinger.

And some twelve-year-olds were getting pretty scary.

"I can tell by the dreamy look in your eye that you want to be the bad guy," Carroll said.

"What have you got?"

"An F-16 we leased from General Dynamics."

"Damn."

"I'll take Cliff Coker out of it, and you can have the first shot at me," Carroll said.

"Hold on," Aikens broke in. "I thought P.J. said you weren't supposed to be flying test anymore, Dan."

"He didn't complain when Terry and I took the Astroliner out last."

"Yeah, but. . . ."

"He won't complain about a couple hours in a tiny Falcon, either," Kerry said. "Let's go."

Carroll took off first in the Astroliner. He intended to spend an hour double-checking the modifications made to the elevon electrical system.

Kerry's personal flight gear was packed in the third carton, first stack, second row in the second stall of his garage, so he borrowed a helmet, oxygen mask, and G-suit from Cliff Coker.

"You owe me big, Mr. VP."

"I'll buy you dinner in Hong Kong."

"I'll be there."

"Damned right, you will."

Cliff Coker, also an Astroliner test pilot, spent an hour with Kerry, checking him out on the F-16 since it had been over ninety days since Kerry had flown the model.

The aircraft they had was a General Dynamics demonstration model, an F-16B with two seats, clearly marked on the fuselage sides with the General Dynamics corporate logo. It carried no weapons pylons but was equipped with drop tanks on inboard pylons in order to give it a 2,300-mile ferry range. In place of AIM-9L Sidewinder missiles on the wingtips were infrared and radar emitters, one on each wingtip.

Kerry had always liked the airplane for its agility with the side-stick (fly-by-wire) controls, and it took him less than twenty minutes to regain his familiarity. He made a quick landing at Edwards, dropped off Coker, and took to the skies on his own.

At 30,000 feet, headed for the Pacific, Kerry did a few rolls, just to alleviate his exhilaration. If he had had any regrets about abandoning the Air Force as a career, it was the loss of his access to an aircraft like the F-16. He thought highly of the Astroliner, of course, but there was nothing in the world to compare with being alone in a combat aircraft. The speed, the sleekness, the element of danger all combined to make him think he was in control of his destiny.

So much of his world was out of his control. He worked with people who had their own objectives, which were not necessarily his own, and the results of most relationships were compromises. Probably, if he had one wish out of the genie's lamp, he would ask for the ability to have his word treated as law. With that, everything else was possible.

Kerry had a friend who was an avid model railroader, and Kerry had often thought the hobby was an effective antidote for the standard frustrations of life. The man got to not only design his own miniature world, but to build and operate it as he deemed fit. If one's own world was not perfect enough, one could construct one that was perfect.

Try as he might to make his own life approach perfection, Kerry had learned that it probably wasn't going to happen. Other people were going to stumble into his path.

Like Jacqueline Broussard.

On the purely physical level, he could generate some fantasies that were pretty ideal. On an intellectual level, he understood they were economic enemies and he knew that, given the circumstances, there weren't likely to be any satisfactory compromises. He suspected, too, that she could be highly manipulative. Men would trip over themselves in their rush to do her bidding. When he was near her, he found his defenses heightened, alert to sudden mental moves on her part.

The battle was enjoyable in its own way, but it didn't compare to an F-16 at 30,000 feet of altitude going feet wet over the Pacific Ocean.

He checked in with his air controller and notified him that he was departing the Air Defense Identification Zone (ADIZ).

Then he activated the Westinghouse multimode pulse-Doppler radar and rotated the scanner for look-up search. It had a range of 46 miles, but he couldn't find anything in his path except for one inbound airliner. Its speed put it out of the Astroliner class.

He went passive with the radar for five minutes, then activated it again for one scan cycle.

There.

His target was steady at 34,000 feet, thirty miles to the north, on a northerly heading.

Rolling into a right bank, Kerry came on to the new heading as he advanced the throttle into afterburner and started to climb.

The airspeed indicator quickly went through the numbers until he was holding Mach 1.8. Carroll was supposed to be cruising at around Mach 1.5, otherwise Kerry didn't have a chance in hell of catching him.

"Chase One, this is PA One."

Kerry ignored the call.

"Chase One, PA One. Are you out here yet?"

If Carroll thought that Kerry was going to give away his position by returning the call or activating his radar, Carroll had attended the wrong Navy.

The Astroliner's radar would be scanning ahead of the airplane's track, and the onboard radar threat receiver, which had a range of forty miles, wouldn't alert the crew as long as Kerry kept his own radar passive.

Since they were both headed in the same direction, it took Kerry a few minutes to catch up, but he soon had a visual contact with the airliner. The morning sun to Kerry's right reflected off the silvery surface of the bonded skin.

On the armaments panel, he selected the infrared emitter mounted on the left wingtip. When he keyed the launch button on the control stick, the emitter would activate its supercooled infrared seeker eye, simulating an attack by a heat-seeking missile.

Kerry watched the feedback monitor from the emitter, which was fastened to the bottom edge of the instrument panel with Velcro tape.

At about five miles distance, he depressed the launch stud.

Within seconds, the monitor reported that he had a lock-on. If the emitter had been a live heat-seeking missile, the Astroliner would have been in a tumble five seconds later.

Two seconds after he initiated the emitter, the Astroliner went hard to the left, raising her right wing quickly, coming about so as to get the heat of her exhaust nozzles out of the heat-seeker's eye. Kerry saw the airliner's four turbofan nozzle exhausts dim as the throttles were retarded in the attempt to reduce the heat signature.

Simultaneously, the flare ejector on the right side of the fuselage ejected two magnesium flares, their bright white heat causing spots to blink in Kerry's eyes even in daylight.

A glance at the monitor suggested that the flares had

done their job. The infrared eye was tracking the flares rather than the airliner.

On the radio, Kerry said, "Good show, PA One. You dodged it."

"I knew you were going to sneak up on me, you SOB."

"You've got passengers filling out complaint forms."

"Given the alternative, the passengers are writing letters of recommendation for the hot aviator," Carroll insisted.

Unlike an air battle in which attacking aircraft might fire more than one missile, the evasive tactics Kerry and Carroll had devised, and which Carroll would be teaching to all Astroliner pilots, were designed to accommodate a terrorist who would get only one chance with a missile. They also assumed that the SST would be relatively safe at a cruise speed of Mach 2.4. The periods of greatest danger would occur during approaches and departures from airports, when the airplane was close enough to the earth for some degree of accuracy with a Stinger.

"All right, PA One. Go find a new path, and we'll try you on radar. Or maybe infrared again."

"Roger that, PA One. Give it your best shot, but expect to fail."

Kerry hoped that wasn't a comment on his career.

Kowloon
August 14, 06:40 A.M.

Karen Meyer was petite and dark, but her dark eyes had bright, amused glints in them, and her short, bobbed hair shone, reflecting light like moonbeams on a mysterious lake.

Charley Whitlock was one of that generation that could remember the George Gobel show on early television, along with the blonde female singer that George called pretty, perky Peggy King. The photo negative image of King would have been Karen Meyer. In a silver cocktail dress on the night he had met her, she had radiated energy and amicable charm.

She radiated something completely different as she stepped from the bathroom into his large hotel room wearing a big white towel.

Whitlock was sitting up in bed, leaning back against a pair of pillows, watching her as she shook her head violently, shaking droplets of water from her hair. They flashed in the morning light streaming in the window.

She saw him watching and smiled. Lots of white teeth.

"You like?"

"I like."

Crossing to the bed, she stood beside it and dropped the towel. Her small breasts stood proud and pert, her tiny waist flared into lush hips.

"I like even better," Whitlock said.

She lifted the covers and slipped into the bed beside him, pulling his arm over her shoulders and resting her damp head against his chest. Her skin was still heated from her shower, and the warmth spread along his side.

"How's the headache?" she asked.

"Tolerable."

In fact, the dull throb in the left front of his skull made concentration difficult. Last night, he had looked in the mirror and seen the discoloring that stained his forehead and left temple. In addition to that large bruise, his left eye was blackened like that of a new kid on the block who had just been introduced to the neighborhood bully.

"Karen . . ."

"Uh huh?"

"How did this happen?"

"A big bomb went off."

"Not that. Us."

She rolled her head so that she could look into his eyes. "It happened. Are you worried about it?"

"I'm a fifty-six-year-old broken-down and broke ex-cop. What the hell would you see in me?"

"You're not so broke. You make a hundred and ten thousand a year."

He raised an eyebrow.

"You left your paycheck stub for July on the dresser. I learned to multiply by twelve."

Whitlock lowered the eyebrow. As a snoop himself, he had taken a look at her wallet when she was out of the room, discovering only from her driver's license that she was thirty-seven years old, five more than he had estimated and seven more than his daughter Angela. He still felt like a cradle robber. He was a freshman at UCLA when she was born.

"I'm a gold digger, don't you see?" Her left arm slid across his chest, resting lightly on it.

"You don't look like one," he said.

"What do I look like?"

"My daughter's thirty years old, with two kids. . . ."

"That's it? You're worried about the age difference? We seem to fit together all right," she grinned.

"Are you Mossad?"

Her grin shifted into a slight frown. She rolled onto her stomach and rested on her elbows, studying his face.

After a long pause, she said, "I know some people in Mossad."

"Are they underwriting your sudden desire for a vacation in Hong Kong?"

"Charley. You're questioning my motives."

He nodded and kept watching her eyes.

Which went a little far away from where they were as she wrestled with some decision.

"My country," she said, "has a long history of living with terrorism. And sometimes not living so well with it."

"I know."

"I came here with three objectives, assigned to me by El Al, my employer. I was to evaluate the airport, learn the application procedures, and discover what I could about the four supersonic transports, one of which my airline would be required to lease."

"And then," he prompted, "on the morning of your arrival, there was a big bang."

"Yes. When I reported it to my superior, who is in charge of marketing, I was asked to learn more about it. We do not like subjecting our nationals to the dangers of terrorism. And the next night, I met you."

She still hadn't told him just who asked her to investigate, but Whitlock let it slide.

"I don't see myself as the answer to your prayers," Whitlock said.

"Oh, but you are. You're an insider, as far as security goes. You know more about what's taking place with the investigation of the bombing than the Chinese are telling anyone else. Plus, you probably know something about the Astroliner, about which I am also trying to learn."

Whitlock thought about the past nine days in which he and Karen spent their evenings together, exploring restaurants, sight-seeing, window-shopping. He couldn't recall one instance when she had probed him for information.

"You're a lousy spy," he told her.

"I know."

"You haven't tried to worm any information out of me on either of those topics."

"I was afraid you'd think my motive was impure."

"But it was."

"True, but I changed my mind after I'd known you for about six hours and just hoped you'd volunteer something that would make my boss happy."

"I'm going to get confused," Whitlock said.

"I doubt that."

He shifted position, sliding down in the bed and rolling onto his side, resting his head on his hand. The movement brought a new pounding to his head, and he winced.

Karen watched him, concern in her eyes—he was pretty sure—then moved onto her side to face him in the same position.

"What do you want to know?" he asked.

Her eyes widened. "The Astroliner?"

"It's the greatest thing to come down the pike since Ben Hur and his chariot. Other than that, you'll have to wait for the grand opening on October first. That's when all the air carriers get to look at her."

She pouted, wrinkling her nose at him. "That won't get me the promotion I deserve."

"Sorry, but that's why I get a check stub."

"How about the control tower?"

Whitlock told her just about everything he knew, though he did not reveal some of the security lapses that he thought Yichang Enlai would like to keep to himself.

"And I have a theory about method," he added.

"Will you tell me?"

"If you promise not to pass it on to your friends in the Mossad until I've had time to verify it."

"That's not fair!"

He just looked at her.

"Okay. Promise."

Whitlock explained the unused circuits in the fiber-optic network. "Most remote control devices use radio to transmit the ignition signal, but those radios aren't very powerful and typically have a range that doesn't exceed two miles. Someone outside the fence on the western end of the field would have been in range for the fuel tanks, but Control Tower Number Six is too damned far from the fences for someone outside. Either it was set off by someone inside the airport, or they made use of the installed communication system."

"Which you think they did."

"Yes. I think it would be easy to tap the detonator into the circuit, then use some sort of transmitter on the same circuit to set it off."

"It would be a complex piece of equipment," she said.

"How so?"

"On the receiving end, they would have to have a device that translated the signal coming over the fiber-optic line into an electrical impulse. It would probably be digitally encoded, also, to prevent stray signals from causing a premature explosion. There might even be some sort of safety circuit built into the device."

Whitlock kept his grin to himself. She knew about these things.

"And on the transmitting end, there would also be a device to encode and translate the signal," she said, almost to herself as she mused. "You should let me out of my promise, Charley."

"Why?"

"If your theory holds up, it makes these terrorists much more sophisticated than the norm. I know some people who might be able to tell us if a similar method had been used before."

"A signature?"

"It could be."

"We can keep it in-house?"

"Of course."

"Forget the promise. But damn, I need to call Yichang."

He started to roll over, enraging his head, but she stopped him.

"Charley?"

"Yeah?"

"Call him later."

Whitlock's focus abandoned his headache and moved to other parts of his, and her, anatomy.

Berlin, Germany
August 13, 8:45 P.M.

"Gerhard, that tie must be twenty years old. I have seen it on you fifty times."

"I like this tie, Ernst."

"If Ingrid will not force you to burn it, then I must," Ernst Bergen told him.

"Ingrid has thrown it into the trash at least ten times. Fortunately, I have been able to retrieve it," Ebbing said. "Ernst, you did not come here to complain about my tie."

The Director of Security for BBK Enterprises was a man of impeccable taste in his clothing, and as a forty-five-year-old committed to bachelorhood, must have learned it on his own. He wore his tailored suits on a blocky frame that suggested daily workouts with weights. His hair was styled casually, and Ebbing suspected that he treated it in order to retain its youthful honey-brown color. His eyes were steady and direct, probing those with whom he talked as if they were suspects in a particularly dreadful homicide case. It was likely a trait he had picked up as an investigator for the Bonn police, for whom he had once worked.

"No, your tie is beyond complaint. I have just spent an hour on the telephone with Yichang Enlai."

"The fuel depot bombing?"

"Apparently the signs point to the same perpetrator as the control tower blast. C-4 *plastique* was used, as was remote detonation. Again, the location was one that was difficult to reach, though not as difficult as was the control tower. Still, it was underground, and the bomber had to come through either the tunnel from the airport or through the subterranean rail tunnel from the outside."

"Would that not be easier?" Ebbing asked.

"Not necessarily. There is a wall of steel mesh separated by concrete piers that prevents access into the airport tunnels from the rail tunnel. Yichang thinks the barrier was not penetrated, and that the man who placed the bomb came from within the complex."

"You do not suppose, do you, Ernst, that all of these bombs were placed during construction? Perhaps they are being set off at the will of the bomber."

"Yichang swears that his people found no bombs on that fuel tank when it was inspected ten days ago."

"Very well. What does it mean to us?" Ebbing asked.

Bergen got up from his chair next to Ebbing's blueprint-cluttered desk and went to stand at the window, looking out at the grounds surrounding the administration building.

"I called Yuri Yelchenko and discussed that very point with him," Bergen said. "On the face of it, the two of us might suggest that some very disenchanted communists are voicing their disenchantment against a Chinese regime that is forgetting its socialist background and aligning itself with worldly capitalists."

"I could understand that, I believe."

"It puts us at risk, Gerhard."

"In what way?"

"Taken literally, the Tupolev Design Bureau has also forsaken its communist roots. Yelchenko fears that the Tupolev 2000 could be a target when it lands at Deng Xiaoping in October."

Ebbing considered the implication. "Yes, but us?"

"We intend to manufacture the AeroSwift in the East, Gerhard."

"But I am not a Communist! I never have been. Nor you, I think, Ernst."

"No, but does the bomber know that?"

"I suppose not. What are we doing about all of this?"

Bergen turned away from the window. "I have made inquiries to every national and international data base, seeking information about similar incidents, the location of prime suspects, whether or not explosives are missing from inventories. But, still I wonder about the motive. And I wonder about one other thing."

"What is that?"

Bergen came back and sat in the chair.

"Charles Whitlock was injured in this latest bombing."

"Whitlock?"

"The security specialist for Pacific Aerospace."

"What was he doing there?" Ebbing demanded.

"I have no idea. I had assumed that everyone had returned to wherever they were to return."

"Perhaps Whitlock placed the bomb," Ebbing said hopefully. "If Pacific Aerospace is behind schedule, and they may be with no certification as yet, they might be attempting to delay the October demonstrations."

Bergen made a face. "I do not believe that for a moment, Gerhard. I read Whitlock as a true professional. What I distrust is that Whitlock may be gaining some favorable influence with the Chinese if he is helping them."

Ebbing did not like that. He said, "Take a drive in the country, Ernst, and tell me who needs this contract the most. Our countrymen are suffering."

"I am aware of it, Gerhard."

"You must go to China," Ebbing decided.

"That is what I came to see you about," Bergen said.

Los Angeles, California
August 13, 4:20 P.M.

Dan Kerry tromped the accelerator, heard the tires bark on the hot asphalt, and whipped the wheel to the right.

The Ferrari leaped forward, cut in front of a BMW, and zipped into an open spot in front of the United terminal. Jacqueline Broussard stood at the curb, fifteen feet in front of him, and her eyes caught Kerry's. She shook her head in negative swings.

The BMW squealed to a stop next to him, and the electric passenger window rolled down as the driver prepared to lodge his complaint.

Kerry looked at him and smiled.

The driver changed his mind. The window rolled up rapidly, and the BMW shot away.

Levering himself out of the low driver's seat, Kerry reached the pavement and went around the front of the car to meet her. She was wearing tailored slacks that clung to her hips and calves and a scoop-necked, sky blue blouse that had probably cost a couple hundred bucks. Draped over her arm was the matching jacket that had proved to be too much for L.A. in August. She was carrying another of her five-gallon purses, this one in burgundy leather. The skycap had three pieces of exotically patterned luggage on his cart, and Kerry gave him a five-dollar bill and aimed him toward the Ferrari's trunk.

"Do you always arrive at your destination with such flourish?" Broussard asked him.

"I'm afraid it's a hangover from my job."

"You flew the SST today?"

"No, it was an F-16."

He saw a flicker in her eyes.

"I would like to do that sometime."

"Sometime, maybe I can arrange it."

People meeting at airports should kiss, he thought, as he extended his hand. She took it for a quick grasp and then released it.

The electricity was still there. Or maybe it was in his mind.

He turned and led her back to the car, opening the passenger door for her.

She didn't get in, but stood on the sidewalk surveying the car.

"Sorry it's so old," he told her.

"My father was killed in a Ferrari."

"Like this?"

"No. It was a much faster one. He was driving practice laps for a grand prix race."

He was about to offer something in the way of condolences when she said, "May I drive?"

"Be my guest. Have you been to L.A. before?"

"No. You will give me directions."

She didn't go around, but dumped her purse and jacket on the floor of the passenger side, then slid across the seats. The skycap slammed the trunk lid, and Kerry dropped into the right bucket seat, rearranging the purse so he could find room for his feet.

Releasing the parking brake, she slapped the gear shift into first, came off the clutch, and accelerated smoothly into the traffic lane. A smooth click and she was in second gear.

Kerry directed her onto Manchester Avenue and got her into the right lane for the northbound on-ramp for the San Diego Freeway. With the top down, the speed-induced wind took some of the edge off the hot day. He watched a Boeing 767 taking off as she found an opening in the center lane of traffic. She adapted easily to the flow, which was considerably above the speed limit, but didn't try to outrace any of the neighbors.

He settled back in his seat and watched her. She kept an eye on the cars around her, but also took in the city nestled up to the freeway. He thought she was memorizing the highway signs that passed over them.

"Will we stay on this road long?"

"I don't know. Where are we going?" he asked.

"Do you have a house?"

"More or less."

"Let us go there."

"All right. We'll stay on the freeway."

But they didn't. She asked questions about the signs they passed, and he tried to explain Venice and Santa Monica and Hollywood.

"Do you want to see Hollywood?"

"I do not think so. Where is Beverly Hills?"

Kerry got her off the freeway at Bel Air and let her wander through the Santa Monica Mountains, taking Beverly Glen Boulevard up to Mulholland Drive, then west to Topanga Canyon Boulevard. He thought she was impressed by some of the multimillion-dollar houses hanging on the sides of the hills. She was less impressed when he couldn't point out the home of a single movie star.

Off Topanga Canyon, they took the Ventura Freeway back east to Encino. When she parked in his driveway, he said, "You drive very well."

"I like to drive."

"Come on."

She retrieved her purse, and they went inside the house. Her first comment was, "It does not look very lived-in."

"I'm a Tokyo resident, remember?" But Kerry explained his rental situation. "The only thing I haven't packed yet is the booze and a couple glasses. Would you like a drink?"

"I would, yes. Anything you are having."

She wandered around the living room, which was at the back of the house, looking out on the patio and the big backyard, while he dug out ice and scotch. When he finished, he found her out on the patio. With the shrubs and bougainvillea surrounding the perimeter and the fruit trees scattered about, it was a private patio and sheltered from the sun.

She took her drink and a chair at the glass-topped table. Kerry sat down across from her.

"I am sorry you have already packed your belongings."

"Why is that?"

"I had hoped to learn more about you."

He smiled. "You don't need to see the pictures hanging on the wall. I'm pretty much what you see."

"I do not think so."

She was sitting rather rigidly in the wrought-iron chair, her shoulders held taut, and Kerry wondered if she ever relaxed.

"Ah, come on, Jacqueline. I'm a straightforward guy."

"Henri thinks you seek to undermine my confidence. By what you told me in Hong Kong."

"Henri? That's Dubonnet?"

"My godfather. He helped my mother to raise me after Father died."

So much for the innuendos of private investigators hired to perform background checks, Kerry thought.

The afternoon sun slipped through the leaves of an orange tree and dappled the skin of her cheeks, emphasizing her high cheekbones. The violet eyes studied him, but Kerry thought they were much more guarded than they had been in Hong Kong. She was in a state of high alert, and conversely, Kerry felt more relaxed than he had in Hong Kong. A morning alone with an F-16 did that to him.

"Is Henri correct?" she asked.

"Of course he is. Part of the job, you know."

"Yes, the job. Do you want to discuss what I have been thinking about the bombings at Deng Xiaoping?"

"We can do that in the morning, Jacqueline. First, we need to take you to dinner."

"Do you know what I would like? Americans always cook barbecue."

Kerry tried to remember where he had packed a pair of pliers. He would have to reassemble the grille. And he would have to call Jan next door and see if he could buy a couple steaks and some potatoes from her.

"And I want to go see an American supermarket."

Which settled the food problem.

"We can do that, and we'll have to find a hotel for you."

She didn't respond to that, so he said, "Tell me, Jacqueline, are you as reserved around everyone as you are with me?"

She sipped from her drink, then said, "I am frightened of you, Dan."

"Frightened? Why?"

"We are competitors."

"That's a given. We can still be friends."

"I do not think so. I am frightened, not of you, but of you and me together."

"Oh." And that explained a large portion of his magnetic field problems.

"Which is why I will not need a hotel."

NINE

In the New Territories and Kowloon, Yichang Enlai was not yet recognized as a person with influence. His committee-provided gray Honda Accord with the name of Deng Xiaoping International Superport printed on the doors did not open parking spaces for him, and it took him fifteen minutes to find a space a block away from the President Hotel.

He walked through the thick throng of people to the hotel, eyeing the pedestrians with professional curiosity, went directly to the elevators, and rode to the twelfth floor where he found Room 1215 easily.

Whitlock responded to his knock, opening the door and saying, "Good evening, Mr. Yichang."

He was dressed casually in denim pants and a sport shirt.

"I am sorry to arrive so late," Yichang told him. "The day has been particularly hectic."

"Doesn't bother me a bit. I've been sleeping so much in the past couple of days, I won't need a bed for a week."

Yichang followed Whitlock's gesture and entered the spacious room. "How are you feeling?" he asked.

"The headache's down to the irritant classification. How about you? Have you eaten yet?"

"As I said, it has been a long day."

"Hamburgers all right? We'll go American."

Yichang Enlai had never eaten a hamburger, and did not think that he wanted to, but courtesy prevailed, and he nodded.

While Whitlock called room service and ordered hamburgers with the works—whatever the works were—French fries, coffee, and apple pie, Yichang moved to the small table by the window and sat in one of the two chairs. The curtains were drawn wide, and the lights of the city intruded almost violently into the room. Chinese cities did not rely on neon advertising to the overwhelming extent that Kowloon did. His eyes were accustomed to posters, more of them of a political nature than a commercial one.

Placing the single-piece, upright telephone back on the bedside stand, Whitlock came over to the table and took the other chair. He tended to slouch in it, compared to Yichang's rigid-back posture, but perhaps the posture was necessitated by his injuries.

"Any progress on your suspect list?"

"The responses to our inquiries continue to mount, but the progress does not impress my superiors," Yichang said. He was beginning to feel better about sharing information with Whitlock. "There are still over eight hundred names on the primary listing, those whom we have been unable to locate."

The American nodded. "Percentage-wise, you're moving fast. If I had ever had that many suspects in a case, I think I'd still be looking at a couple thousand possibles."

Yichang acknowledged the comment with a slight dip of his head.

"Now, then," Whitlock said, "you're wondering why I asked you to come by?"

"I am curious why you did not wish to discuss your theory on the telephone, yes."

"I have what might be considered a low-grade fear that your communications system could be compromised."

Yichang had thought that would be the basis of Whitlock's reluctance. He did not give much credence to the concern, but then, Whitlock had been helpful in the past, and he was now willing to listen. Part of that willingness, he admitted to himself, resulted from Whitlock's apparent disdain for claiming credit for his insights. Yichang could probably have gained favor with Sun Chen by assuming ownership for the discovery of the design flaws in the control tower lock system, but he had not. Sun was aware that Whitlock was the source of that revelation, though Whitlock had apparently not mentioned his involvement to anyone else.

He also noted that he and Whitlock refrained from using each other's names so as to avoid some of the distance of formality and yet adhere to the Chairman's policy of utilizing proper forms of address.

"I suspected as much," he said.

"Please understand that I am trying to be diplomatic."

"It is not required."

"All right, then. It goes this way." Whitlock outlined a fantasy scenario where the terrorists made use of Deng Xiaoping International Superport's very own and very secure fiber-optic system to communicate the detonation signals to their explosive devices.

"Are you still with me?" Whitlock asked.

"I understand the concept."

"This supposes some high-level technical expertise. I understand that the connection points between the fiber-optic strands and the translator devices are unusually critical."

"Yes. I have been told that a slight twist in the connector, so that it does not align precisely with the optical cable, will produce gibberish, if it produces anything at all."

"Then, beyond the connections, there is the matter of the transmitter, the receiver, and the—"

"Transceiver," Yichang interrupted.

"Transceiver?"

"That is correct. We have a warehouse full of them, so as to be prepared for customer installations."

"Under lock and key?"

"Naturally. However, you have already proven to me that locks may be a figment of my imagination."

"Ummm . . . okay. So we've got a potential source. Beyond the transmitting device, then, I would suspect that there's some little black box that plugs into it somehow. There would be a code, I think, to prevent premature or accidental detonation."

"How would this be accomplished?" Yichang asked.

"The guy gets on a phone anywhere in the world, dials the number, and when the device answers, punches out the code on the telephone keypad."

"It is that simple?"

"User-friendly, as they say. Getting it to be that way, of course, takes an electronics assembler who knows what he's doing."

"There are many of those in the Hong Kong Dependency."

"Yeah, I was afraid of that. But what do you think?"

Yichang feared that the theory held at least the promise of merit. He was beginning to think that the effort to draw the international community into China's sphere was a tremendous mistake. It also attracted devious and murderous individuals he would just as soon not meet.

"You are presupposing that there is an inside man," he

said. "Someone on the permanent cadre of employees, rather than a construction worker."

"Yeah," Whitlock told him, "I am. This is where I run short of diplomatic charm."

"Since it would be someone with electronic, and perhaps computing, skills, it would be someone among the technical maintenance staff."

"Or someone right inside your shop."

"My shop?"

"The communications center or the security center. You have people cleared to work in those areas, right?"

The roster of those cleared for the secure areas was almost indelible in Yichang's mind. He raced through it, remembering most of the names and faces. He had cleared them personally, over his own signature. Not one name stood out with a question mark behind it.

Straying from an answer just now, Yichang said, "Still, the explosive had to be imported, brought past the gates."

"I think its been on the site all along, maybe six months or a year. Who knows? I'd bet there's a stash somewhere in the airport, and our Mr. X just grabs what he needs whenever he needs it."

"But we have searched everywhere."

"Every Cheerios box?"

"Cheerios?"

"A breakfast cereal. Every can of almonds?"

It really was impossible for any search of a complex as vast as the Superport to be one-hundred-percent conclusive, especially with a commodity appearing as innocuous as pliable, shapable plastic explosive which did not even register on metal detectors.

Yichang sighed. "Very well. I will begin interrogations immediately."

"Oh, no! We don't want to do that just yet."

"We do not?"

"Nope. The hamburgers will be here any minute."

Honolulu, Hawaii
August 14, 6:12 A.M.

With his hair neatly cut and trimmed and the shaggy ends of his mustache shaven back to the corners of his mouth and snipped to a toothbrush depth, Kurt Wehmeier was an entirely different person from the man whose grainy likeness filled the dossiers of Interpol and the police organizations of several European nations. Normally blond, his hair today was a dark brown. He might have been a regimental British officer on holiday in his nicely fitting blue suit, light blue shirt, and dark blue figured tie. His broad-shouldered physique also supported that image; he was a man who took care of himself.

The customs officer asked him if he wished to declare anything, which he did not. The officer rifled through the two suitcases.

"What is all this?" he asked of the contents of the second bag.

"Demonstration samples. Integrated circuits on microchips."

"But not for sale?"

"No, not for sale," Wehmeier smiled. "I wish that they were. Perhaps then I would be a millionaire, like my employer."

The man studied the British passport issued to Cecil MacMillan briefly, then wished him a good day. Wehmeier returned the greeting and walked briskly onward, into the terminal, carrying his pigskin attaché case and his teal and black, nylon-covered carry-on.

The first thing he did was to locate the British Airways ticketing counter and buy himself a ticket to Hong Kong, using cash. The flight departed Hawaii at 3:25 in the afternoon, allowing him ample time.

He strolled through the terminal until he found a restaurant and treated himself to sausage and potato pancakes. He followed that with several cups of coffee and two cigarettes while he read the newspaper.

At a quarter of nine, Wehmeier walked down to the United concourse and stood to the side of the corridor out of the way of incoming and outgoing passengers while he waited for the flight to arrive. Anxious people lined up before the desk, hoping to obtain seats on the aisle, or next to the window, or near the tail, wherever they thought it was safest. The more complacent travellers, having obtained seat assignments from their travel agents, were already spread around the lounge seats. Wehmeier counted eleven people in dire need of a cigarette. Smoking was not allowed in the waiting area.

The Boeing 747 parked next to the jetway six minutes behind schedule, and a few minutes later, the interior door opened and the passengers began to emerge. Wehmeier watched their shoes. Twice, when he saw white Nike running shoes with blue swoops, he looked up into the face of, first, a skinny blonde woman, and next, an overweight black man. The third pair of shoes was accompanied by the expected University of Colorado T-shirt, hung outside well-worn jeans.

The man he was expecting had nothing to do with the University of Colorado or even the State of Colorado. He had been educated in Teheran before taking an advanced degree at the Massachusetts Institute of Technology. He was in his midforties, with dark curly hair and full lips that appeared to be locked in a permanent sneer.

His name would be Mohammed Dakar in his permanent role. Today, like Wehmeier, he travelled as another.

Wehmeier took two steps to the side, to catch the man's eye and let him see the blue tie he wore, which was the recognition signal.

The movement caught the man's eye; he looked at the tie and then changed his course to approach Wehmeier.

"Mr. MacMillan?"

"And you are Ahmed Heuseini."

"Yes."

"Let us go into the lounge."

They took a table near a window overlooking the flight line and ordered coffee from the waitress. Wehmeier placed his two pieces of luggage on the floor near his feet. Heuseini was not carrying a bag.

They waited silently for the waitress to return.

"You are highly recommended," Wehmeier said after their cups were placed in front of them.

"I have no choice in the matter," the Arab told him.

"No, I do not suppose you do. And you need the money."

The man's nod was barely perceptible. His liquid eyes revealed little. Perhaps a dash of hate, but that could have been directed at nearly anyone.

Withdrawing the envelope from his inside jacket pocket, Wehmeier passed it across the table. "That contains a bearer bond in the amount of twenty thousand dollars."

Heuseini pushed it into his pocket. "It was to be fifty thousand."

"Twenty now, eighty more afterwards. That is how it must be."

"I will not run from this."

"Of course not."

Wehmeier knew the man thought of his wife and his two sons and of stainless steel blades flashing light in the darkness of an alley. He would not run; there was no place remote enough to hide him.

"The materials?"

"In the attaché case," Wehmeier said.

He finished his coffee and stood up as he said, "A good day to you, Mr. Heuseini."

The Arab did not reply, and Wehmeier picked up one of his bags and strolled back onto the concourse. He stopped at a vending machine to pick up a newspaper, and he was disappointed not to have received front-page, or even first-section, attention.

That would change soon.

Encino, California
August 14, 7:20 A.M.

The last time Dan Kerry had slept past six o'clock in the morning, he had been in Letterman General Hospital under sedation.

It took several blinks of one eye, with his watch held two inches in front of his face, to confirm the time. Then he rolled over slowly, so he wouldn't awaken anyone else, but discovered that he was alone in bed.

He sat up.

The house was L-shaped, and the window wall of the master bedroom was perpendicular to the back wall of the living room and also looked out on the patio. The draperies, as always, were wide open, and he saw that Jacqueline

Broussard was out there, sitting at the table, reading a newspaper. She was wearing a short white terry cloth robe that left very little leg hidden from the morning light.

Kerry stood up and pulled on a pair of Levis that had been thrown across the back of a chair. He crossed to the sliding glass door and pulled it aside.

She looked up at him as he stepped out into the warmth of morning. The flagstones were already heated and felt good under his bare feet.

"I take it back," he said. "You aren't reserved at all."

She ignored the start of that conversation by saying, "I stole your neighbor's newspaper."

"Anything in it?"

"They have finally reported the *minor* destruction of a fuel tank at Deng Xiaoping International. There are no other details, not even supposition as to the cause of the explosion."

Kerry walked to the table and peered into the cup in front of her. "You made coffee?"

"And I am making breakfast. You must wait, however, because it is in the oven."

"May I have coffee?"

"Bring me some more, too."

Kerry went inside, got the coffeepot, another cup, and an extension cord. He carried the pot out to the patio and plugged it into an outside outlet, then filled their cups.

He sat opposite her, unsure of her mood this morning.

She did look relaxed.

She smiled at him, but a trifle grimly. "We have done a terrible thing."

"We?"

"I have done a terrible thing."

"I don't recall a single instance of terrible, Jacqueline."

He sipped from his cup and decided she made better coffee than he did.

"I am impulsive."

"I began to realize that around ten o'clock."

"Henri has always told me to never sleep with anyone within the company. It leads to complications."

"I hasten to point out, Jacqueline, that we are not in the same company."

"The same industry. That is too close."

She had a good point. Kerry tried to think of a way around it, but couldn't do it without twisting logic into a helix. He was afraid his hormones had gotten him into trouble.

Again.

He got up and moved to the chair next to her. She leaned forward and kissed him softly and quickly on the lips.

"I was only satisfying a curiosity," she said.

"I admit to having the same curiosity."

"It was to be that, and then done with."

Kerry took her hands in his own, tugged a little, and when her head came forward, kissed her.

"Not that easy for me, Jacqueline."

"There is a magic to us, Dan Kerry."

"Could be."

"It should not be."

He slipped his hands inside her robe and felt the heat of her skin. A flush moved slowly up her throat.

"How long until our breakfast is ready?"

"An hour," she breathed, leaning into him. "We must talk about the airport. That is why I came here."

"We'd be better off trying to get over this silly obsession of ours, don't you think?"

"Yes," she said.

Beijing, China
August 15, 8:45 A.M.

Sun Chen left the meeting with the Minister of Transportation in the company of General Chou Sen of the Air Force of the People's Liberation Army (PLA). Chou was Commander of the Southern China Defense Sector, and he maintained his headquarters at the large air base in Guangzhou.

A tall and thin man, with a nearly emaciated face, Chou's spine appeared to be inflexible as he walked. His backbone was quite similar to his mind in its rigidity Sun Chen had often thought. The general had been vocally reluctant to any interaction with Westerners for as long as the Deng Xiaoping International Superport had been under discussion or construction. Sun recalled many committee and ministerial meetings where the general had stood tall and straight in his immaculate uniform and denounced any scheme that would allow a nonChinese freedom of entry and exit to the country. Chou had been voted down firmly by the politicians at each of his appearances.

Yet, he was a capable commander, and Sun had heard many flattering descriptions of his tactical and strategic adeptness. Sun held no sense of personal animosity toward the man, but he had hinted several times to the minister that Chou's posting to another command within the country might prove beneficial in the long run.

The general had not been transferred, and Sun had not pursued the issue. Either the minister did not wish to act upon the recommendation or the military did not wish to accept the suggestion, and it was probably the latter. The Chinese military machine was a considerable one, with three million persons on active duty and ten million in the civilian militia. The machine was powerful, and not many politicians attempted to circumvent it.

The meeting this morning, beginning at seven o'clock, had been conducted according to a short agenda: economic development and public relations.

Several years before, the leadership had allowed local authorities to proclaim economic development zones to entice investments, particularly from foreign sources. The local governments had been lax—some said criminal—in the manner in which they offered tax incentives, and a cauldron of real estate enterprises had begun to boil, leasing land from the state for development, but then reselling the lease rights in order to obtain unimaginable profits before any development at all took place. Luxury hotels, golf courses, country clubs, high-rise office buildings, and villas had begun to appear almost overnight. Fledgling realtors had become millionaires in the same time span.

The real estate speculation had driven the economy upward more quickly than the leadership approved. Fearing rampant inflation and preferring stagnation or mild recession, the national government had reacted sternly, banning new golf courses and halting work on hotels and high-rises in midconstruction. Many of the latter had been converted to apartment complexes to help alleviate the always critical shortage of personal accommodations. Real estate companies had been threatened with prosecution should they again become involved in quick-profit schemes rather than long-term investment strategies.

Now, the Minister of Transportation had just told Sun Chen that he was responsible for five thousand acres of land south of Deng Xiaoping International Superport which had just been declared an economic development zone. He was to develop the policies and guidelines for the area which would allow foreign and domestic entities to create tax-producing properties such as hotels, and he was to ensure that no foreigner or Chinese national became a millionaire as a result of their involvement.

Sun Chen was not enchanted with those new prospects. His plate was already full with the airport nearing completion, especially in light of the recent attacks against it.

Which was the import of the balance of the meeting. The minister felt himself strained to the maximum in his efforts to downplay the death toll and the property destruction for the foreign media. Even *The People's Daily,* feeling free speech confidence, was pressing him about the investigation and its results. He had told both Sun and Chou that further tarnished images in the foreign media could not, and would not, be tolerated, and he had taken a giant step toward ensuring that course.

In seeking assistance from the Party Chairman for his burden, the minister had compounded his own, Sun's, and General Chou's problems. The Chairman had decided that an overt military presence at the Superport would preclude additional terrorist attacks.

And that was the reason for General Chou's presence at the meeting. He had been ordered to dispatch a squadron of six fighter aircraft for temporary assignment to the airport. Sun's protest that the foreign media would react with ceaseless questions about the international airport's mission went unanswered. In perhaps the first time that Sun and Chou had agreed about anything, Chou's response was similar, but for different reasons.

Civilian ministers did not order air force generals to do anything, of course, and Chou had politely refused to submit to civilian authority.

That resulted in a telephone call to PLA headquarters,

with General Chou subsequently retreating from his defiant position. Sun knew that the general's demeanor was not a happy one, and the storms were displayed in his dark eyes as the two of them approached their chauffeur-driven automobiles.

"I am certain we will be able to make this situation work smoothly, General," Sun said, stopping beside the opened rear door of his car.

"The fool is attempting to involve the air force in what should be a law enforcement matter, Chairman. It is strictly against policy, and after I have discussed it with the general staff, I am sure the decision will be reversed."

Sun courteously did not inquire as to which of two possible persons might be a fool—the Chairman of the Communist Party or the Minister of Transportation. "It is not a request of mine, I am sure you realize, General. But if this is what must be done, we will do our best to accommodate you."

"Do not plan on seeing me soon, Chairman," Chou said as he continued on to his automobile, the heels of his shoes clicking loudly and leaving black marks on the concrete of the sidewalk.

Sun Chen stood there for a moment, looking at the black heel marks and thinking of tarnished images and hoping the transportation minister knew what he was doing.

Korea Bay, North Korea
August 15, 10:56 A.M.

The transfer required less than four minutes.

Ku Chi drove the rubber Zodiak boat with the 50-horsepower Yamaha outboard motor directly into the rust-streaked hull of the *Jade Merchant.* The boat bounded away from the steel hull, then pressed back, snuggling against it like a puppy to its bitch.

Ku looked back at the shore and saw some activity in the village of Chungsan, but nothing that he could define, and certainly nothing threatening. It was over six kilometers away.

The waters of the bay were choppy, and the Zodiak rose and fell by a meter, rubbing hard against the scraped black paint of the freighter. The motion created small geysers of cold water which splashed into the bottom of the boat and against Ku's face.

He looked up to see the block and tackle from the midship's crane lowering toward him. Leaving the motor in gear and idling, Ku waddled forward, balancing himself against the bob and sway of the boat. He grasped the hook on the line, and attached it to the steel O-ring of the cargo netting which contained his twelve crates. Each crate was one and a half meters long, forty-five centimeters on a side, and weighed fifteen kilograms.

When he was certain the hook was secure, he signalled upward, and a deckman relayed the signal to the crane operator. The line reversed direction and began to lift the loose upper section of the cargo net.

Ku reached into his boot and withdrew a razor-sharp stiletto. Quickly, he bent to slash several holes in the air bladders of the boat, then stuck his toes into the cargo net and wrapped his hands tightly in the woven hemp.

The weighted net rose quickly from the Zodiak, and Ku rode with it. As the crane swung him over the lifeline at deck level, he looked down to see that the rubber boat was already awash in the gray-green sea.

His journey had begun.

And he was proud of his participation in it.

The voice of the people would be much stronger, now, and it would carry a barb.

Century City, California
August 14, 2:17 P.M.

The executive offices of Pacific Aerospace Incorporated were located on the seventeenth floor of a tower which gave P.J. Jackson a panoramic view of Los Angeles. On some days, he would just as soon not see it. Today, for example, the shit-brown layer of contaminated air hung low over the city, trapped by some atmospheric inversion. Los Angeles was almost obliterated by it, as were the lungs of anyone out and about in it, he was sure.

His big teak desk was aimed toward the windows, but as often as not, he found himself turned the other way, his feet up on the matching computer credenza placed against the wall, studying the oversized color portrait of the USS *Elliot* (DDG-967) that hung on the burlap-textured wall. The sparkling, crisp image of the destroyer always brought back torturous memories of sweaty, overheated interior spaces, freezing wind and sleet in twenty-foot seas that crashed over the forepeak and sluiced down the decks, and the often agonizing snap decisions required of her captain.

The memories of those days were positively idyllic when compared with some of the crap he had to put up with at Pacific Aerospace Incorporated. Today's fiasco was a case in—

His office door whipped open, bringing him out of his trance, if not his blue funk. He dropped his feet to the carpet and swung the chair around.

Kerry stood in the doorway, grinning at him.

"The Air Force teach you to ignore doors?"

"No, but I usually did, anyway."

"Get rid of the grin, would you? This is not a grin day."

Kerry strolled to the side of the desk and dropped into one of the leather-covered visitor chairs. He leaned back and put his feet up on the credenza, shoving a pile of legal documents aside as he did so.

Jackson rotated his chair back to face the wall and propped his Gucci loafers next to the computer, which was displaying the mid-month P&L statement. It was not a good statement, was not expected to be just yet, but was still driving the directors crazy.

The two of them sat there, side by side, feet up, staring at the destroyer. They had done this before.

"You first, or me first?" Kerry asked.

"I'll go," Jackson said. "You know, once when I was on that tin can, I had an engineering officer give me a bunch of shit. I fired him on the spot and dropped him off in Subic Bay two days later. Never heard another thing about it."

"Fired someone today, did you?"

"Cresswell."

"No lie? Christ, P.J., he's one of the leading aerodynamics scientists in the world."

"I learned by accident from some headhunter outfit out of New York that he's been talking to Rockwell and a couple others. He was going to jump ship, anyway."

"He know something we don't know?"

"I hope to hell not."

Kerry didn't say anything. He was good at that, letting others talk themselves into revelations or into a corner.

"You can't just fire a guy anymore, Dan. It takes twelve lawyers, a judge, two accountants, and a bank. I've got the in-house legal-beagles working overtime to figure out what the severance pay is going to be. I've got one attorney sitting over at Superior Court, waiting for a judge to get free enough to issue a temporary restraining order, preventing Cresswell from removing any of his notes from his office. We're also going to have to get an order stopping him from using proprietary information wherever he goes. Had to put a security cop on his office. Got the computer whiz downstairs to freeze his computer files. Shit."

"He was tough to get along with, anyway," Kerry said.

"Real prima donna."

"Yeah."

"You here to bitch about something? What are you doing here, anyway?"

"Had to pack my house up."

"That's right. I forgot. Thanks for the help on the elevon thing, by the way. I'm glad I called you back."

"Always glad to fly, P.J. You know that."

"Stay out of the F-16."

"You don't know about that," Kerry insisted.

"Goddamned insurance doesn't cover you, and the premium's out of sight as it is."

"I wouldn't have filed a claim."

"Not dead, you wouldn't," Jackson said.

"I talked to Broussard this morning."

Jackson swung his head around to look at Kerry. "Still the same cold bitch?"

"She came up, independently, with the same theory I've been pushing on you."

"Which one is that?"

"That the attacks on China Dome are meant to scare us off, that if we pursue this thing, we get to be the target."

"And Jackie-babe has the same worry?"

"She tells me she does."

"What's she want to do about it?" Jackson asked.

"Dubonnet isn't as concerned as she is, is my guess. She wants to work with us to see if we can't fashion some kind of prevention program."

"Think you can work with her?"

"It might be tough, but I'll work it out."

"Is this some kind of scenario you're pitching so that I treat you to a free ride to France?"

"P.J., you know me better than that."

"That's the trouble. I know you."

"Besides, she's already in L.A."

Jackson studied Kerry's face, but the stoicism didn't give anything away. And that was answer enough. Kerry put on his poker face to hide his thoughts now and then, but the poker face gave him away every time. At least to P.J. Jackson.

"Where's she staying?" he asked. "I'll give her a call and welcome her to America."

"I already welcomed her."

"I'll bet."

Kerry raised an eyebrow.

"You've got Charley in the China camp, right?"

"Right."

"And you think we need to be doing more?"

"How many bigwigs are we going to have on that ceremonial flight to China, P.J.?"

"Oh, Jesus! Don't talk like that."

"Tell me," Kerry said.

"Fifty governors or lieutenant governors. Secretaries of State, Commerce, and Transportation. The Vice President might come along; I don't know about that, yet. I think nine or ten movie stars are committed. We've got a few rock and country singers. Three networks have committed their news anchors. Seventeen CEOs that I know personally. There'll be more."

"One Stinger, P.J."

Jackson looked back at the *Elliot*. Goddamn it, his war effort was supposed to be over.

"Go get the son of a bitch, Dan."

Encino, California
August 14, 5:25 P.M.

For almost the entire day, Jacqueline Broussard had lolled on the patio of Kerry's rented house. With her telephone credit card, she had made over a dozen telephone calls around the world. She did not adapt to inactivity *that* well, and she had to keep up with her other responsibilities.

Between telephone calls, she reflected upon the foolish trap into which she had inserted herself. Damn him, Henri was always correct, and because she had slipped—as she might have done once or twice in the past—her immediate future was going to be somewhat more complicated.

The surface of her skin tingled when she thought of Kerry. When she allowed free associations to race through her mind, the Concorde II and Aerospatiale-BAC's grand promise and her sizable commission had drifted out of the forefront, to be replaced by soft touches, smooth caresses, demanding lips. A silver forelock hanging over his forehead, suspended above her. Sardonic smile.

She had touched his teeth with her forefinger, and he had told her, "The best money can buy."

"How did it happen?"

"Poor quality control."

"What does that mean?"

"A Soviet air-to-air Atoll missile didn't detonate when it hit me. When it hit my plane."

She felt the skin around his mouth, his cheek. It felt stiff.

"Soviet?"

"They supplied it. Some NVA pilot fired it."

"It was a terrible war," she said.

"Yes. It was."

The buzz of the telephone startled her out of her reverie, and Broussard picked it up.

"Yes?"

"Mademoiselle Broussard, it is Gerhard Ebbing."

"Herr Ebbing, you have talked to Kraft?"

"I have. He is reluctant to have me leave at this point of development, as am I. However, what you and Mr. Kerry suggest is disturbing enough that I will make myself free."

"That is well," she said. "And Pyotr Zemenek will also be available."

"I know. I have just talked to him. How will we proceed?"

"I will call you back with the details as soon as the arrangements are made."

"Very well. I await your call."

Ebbing hung up just as Broussard heard the garage door opening and the sound of Kerry's automobile driving into it.

She stood up and smoothed the linen of her skirt. She was dressed as severely as was possible in a medium blue suit with a masculine cut. It was time now to concentrate on her purpose and not on romantic interludes that could never sustain themselves.

Crossing to the patio door, she slid it aside and traversed the living room to the kitchen as the garage door opened and Kerry entered.

"Gorgeous," he said, and she did not know if he really meant it. The suit was selected to put him off.

"Am I supposed to say, 'Daddy's home'?"

"God, I hope not. Not yet."

Kerry dropped his attaché case on the kitchen counter. He turned to her, put his hands on her shoulders, and gently pulled her forward. She allowed him to kiss her, but with strength of will, resisted an ardent response.

He backed away a step, and his eyes searched her own. "Something wrong?"

"Of course not."

"I'm getting confusing signals," he said.

"We must accomplish what we set out to do."

He studied her face a moment longer, shrugged, and moved to the liquor cabinet. "Scotch?"

"Please."

"Did you reach Ebbing and Zemenek?"

"I did, and they will work with us."

Broussard had given into Kerry's suggestion that their counterparts at BBK and Tupolev had to be involved in their endeavor. Otherwise, it would appear as if the British-French and American companies were forming a syndicate to oppose them. The problem, even with them all working together, was that no one could trust another. One of her conclusions today, made during her daydreaming intermissions, was that, despite her physical willingness to share with Kerry, she could not trust him in the least on an intellectual level.

"The trick then," Kerry said, "is getting the Chinese to agree."

"I assume you have thought about that," she said, accepting her glass.

Kerry led her into the living room and sat on the couch. She sat at the opposite end.

She could not tell by his expression if he was bemused or confused by her change of heart. A tiny smile played across his lips.

"I think we'll approach Yichang," he said. "If we go directly to Sun, then Yichang will feel as if we're being imposed on him. I'd rather have Yichang convince his boss."

"I agree. And if we're successful, then what?"

"You have any friends in Surete?"

That was the French secret service. "I am acquainted with several people, though not well."

"How about MI-5 or MI-6?"

"I believe Stephen Dowd is friendly with the British Secret Service."

"They're being reorganized, I think," Kerry said.

"Yes, but not disbanded."

"All right. We'll see if we can't get something from those sources."

"And you?"

"Some guys I once served with are now in Defense Intelligence and Central Intelligence. I'll hit them up."

Kerry took a long drink from his glass.

"Are you about ready for dinner? We'll go out somewhere tonight."

"Call Yichang, first," she said.

"I should do that. We're all business, right?"

"That is correct."

Deng Xiaoping International Superport
August 15, 3:19 P.M.

James Lee was given twenty minutes for his mid-shift break, and he used his magnetically encoded identification card to let himself through the pair of locked doors and into the corridor. The restricted-use elevator was already on the tenth floor, and he took it to Sublevel Two, stepped out, and scanned the tunnel. Two hundred meters away, an orange-jacketed man was walking away from him.

Lee turned the other way and hurried down the tunnel. He wanted to run, but he also did not want to attract attention.

When he reached the 933 storage room, he used his master key on the lock and slipped inside.

Going directly to the steel shelves which made several rows at the back of the room, he slipped into an alleyway. The shelving blocked the overhead lights, and he had to hunt in the shadows for the box marked, "Detergent, Tile."

It was a large cardboard box, holding two kilos of material, and he opened the top carefully. Reaching inside, he found the first of two blocks of what felt like pliable putty. He placed one block in the right pocket of his light blue jacket, then added a second block to the left pocket. Folding the flaps of the boxtop back together, he replaced the box on the shelf.

By the time he shut off the light and stepped back into the vacant tunnel, he still had sixteen minutes of his break left.

It would be enough time.

TEN

"China is a very large place, Chairman."

"Director Yichang, I *know* how large China is," Sun Chen told him.

"Yes, Chairman. . . ."

"You have told me of the massive man-hours you are devoting to narrowing, winnowing, this massive list of yours. Is that all that you are doing? Or should I now be selecting your replacement?"

Yichang's hand felt slippery on the telephone receiver. "We have, naturally, a short list of the most probable. . . ."

"Ah. Give me one name on this elusive short list."

The listing was entirely in Yichang's mind, with perhaps twenty-five names on it, if he had bothered to count. He did not want to mislead his superior, to provide the man with false trails leading toward a phantom solution.

"Chairman. . . ."

"I will replace you, you know?"

"I am the best at what I do," Yichang said, amazed that he would extol his own virtues.

After a long silence, Sun Chen said, "One name."

"James Lee."

"Who is James Lee? From Hong Kong?"

"He is from Kowloon, Chairman. He has connections with the Red Dragon Tong."

"Tell me more."

"I do not wish to. . . ."

"Why is he a prime suspect?"

Yichang sighed. "Simply, he fits the profile we have drawn. There are several like him on the roster, men with electronics and demolitions abilities, with philosophical leanings toward the anarchist. Lee learned his trade during his second term in prison."

"For what crime?"

"Extortion and murder, Chairman. He and an accomplice trussed the wife of a bank president and wired her with explosives. They then demanded a large payment—I do not know the amount—from the president, but were apprehended during the transfer of cash."

"And the woman?"

"The explosive was booby-trapped. It exploded when the police tried to remove it."

"She died?"

Yichang found himself nodding, even though Sun could not see him. "Along with the police demolitions man."

"And he is out of prison? How can this be?"

"I am told it is because of the overcrowded prisons. He escaped prior to his execution date during some disturbance. That was two years ago."

Sun lapsed again into silence.

Yichang waited.

"Very well, Director. Go on with what you are doing. But, please, for the sake of us all, keep your eye on the clock. Our time is growing short."

The chairman was about to hang up before responding to the question for which Yichang had called him.

"Chairman?"

"Oh. Yes. The aircraft people. They may come to Deng Xiaoping International, but you are to keep close watch on their activities."

After Sun hung up, Yichang settled back into his desk chair in relief. For the entire night, he had worried that he had been precipitous, giving Daniel Kerry permission to bring the SST representatives back to the airport before he had cleared it with Sun.

They were already en route, and he would have lost a great deal of face if he had had to turn them back on his doorstep.

Yichang had begun to worry that his lack of progress and the pressure coming from Beijing were forcing him to take slippery steps. He had allowed Whitlock to stay, and while that decision had proven useful, he had been dressed down by both Sun and the national police commander for not consulting them about it.

He would have to be more careful in the future, or he would be accused of adopting Western ways.

Kai Tak Airport
August 16, 11:16 A.M.

On the long flight from Moscow aboard the Aeroflot Ilyushin Il-76, Gerhard Ebbing and Pyotr Zemenek had agreed that Broussard's hypothesis had some merit. Deng Xiaoping International Superport was conceived around the massive utilization of supersonic transports. Some person with a maniacal bent could well have decided that elimination of the SSTs would result in the Superport failing to achieve its touted goal of becoming the commercial center of the globe. It was the same argument in essence that Ernst Bergen had raised with Ebbing only two days before. Bergen put the possible blame on disenchanted communists, and Broussard had mentioned the possibility of disenchanted capitalists.

Soon, Ebbing thought, he must become paranoid. Everyone in the world would be after his head.

Ebbing could even imagine a few of his countrymen who, distressed by the migration of industrial might to the East, would consider schemes to undermine China Dome's success. He could imagine them thinking about it, but he did not for a minute believe that any one of them would advance to the point of action. He himself was not enamored of China's rising promise, but conversely, he saw Germany's salvation in it.

As the airliner made its approach to Kai Tak, Ebbing leaned against the window and studied the long runway jutting into Hong Kong Harbor. It was constructed on landfill, and it appeared puny against the cityscape behind it. More than once, a departing or arriving airliner had missed its mark and gone into the bay. The events did not give him comfort, and he would have preferred wider and longer runways. Of course, he was now comparing every airport in the world against what he had seen of Deng Xiaoping International, and not many airports compared favorably.

Beside him, Zemenek began to rouse himself from his nap. They had crossed five time zones since leaving Moscow, which would induce an elevated sense of jet lag, and Zemenek had the enviable ability to sleep on aircraft. As he straightened up in his seat, he asked, "We are there?"

Zemenek, who was not a large man, had removed the

jacket of his suit, rolled it, and placed it next to him in his seat. Now, he shook it out and pulled it on. Ebbing watched him from the corner of his eyes. The Lord knew that Ebbing would look like a street bum if it was not for Ingrid, but he felt that a man of Zemenek's rank might have done better for himself in the matter of wardrobe. The untailored, square-cut suit hung on him as it would on a scarecrow. The man had a fine mind, but it was well-hidden behind the bulbous nose and splotchy, reddened skin of his face. He wore a sparse goatee that only seemed to draw attention to his bad complexion and his washed-out brown eyes. He was probably in his midsixties, but he might have been eighty years old from his appearance. The asset in Zemenek was that he made Ebbing feel young.

"We are about to land, Pyotr."

"Good. I am tired of flying."

Zemenek settled back in his seat and pulled the belt tight. "Tell me, Gerhard, how is it that you came to be the spokesperson with the Chinese? BBK does have a marketing department."

"Matthew Kraft felt that someone with technical knowledge should be present, to answer questions that might arise."

"It is the same with me," the Russian said, "though in my case, it had to be someone from my design bureau. We do not have salesmen."

"And now, we seem to be designated as security specialists. I am afraid, Pyotr, that I am far out of my league."

"I would prefer to be back with my computers, also."

The landing was uneventful, and Ebbing watched the bay during the process. A large number of commercial vessels and junks were underway, their wakes trailing after them, like ducklings in a row behind their mother.

The airliner parked at the terminal, and the skyway snaked out to make contact with the fuselage. Ebbing and Zemenek were in no hurry, and they gathered their carry-on luggage as the other passengers jammed themselves into the aisle. The two of them were the last off the airplane and the last to pass through the customs inspection.

A beaming Ernst Bergen, who had arrived the day before, was waiting for them patiently on the other side of the customs barrier. Ebbing thought the man had probably spent the day before at some prominent and rapid tailor shop; he did not recognize the suit.

Ingrid's lectures were getting to him, he thought. He was beginning to take notice of the fashions of other men. He could not imagine a more worthless utilization of his time.

"Good morning, Gerhard, Mr. Zemenek."

"You look too pleased, Ernst," Ebbing said. "There has been some development?"

"We have a note."

"A note?"

"From the terrorists. It is a great breakthrough, and it will be their downfall."

Pacific Aerospace Cessna Citation
August 16, 1:45 P.M.

A copy of the note, which had been mailed to Superport Administrator Zhao Li, was faxed to Kerry aboard the Citation, which was an hour out of Tokyo and en route to China Dome.

Kerry hadn't bothered checking in at his office. He and Broussard had deplaned from their United flight at Tokyo International and taken off in the business jet within an hour. Jim Dearborn had had the plane fueled and stocked with sandwiches and coffee.

Jacqueline Broussard was in the copilot's seat, and doing quite well with the instructions Kerry was giving her, when Dearborn stuck his head into the flight compartment from the cabin.

"Fax just came in, boss."

Kerry finished chewing his chunk of ham sandwich, took the single sheet of paper, and said, "Thanks, Jim."

They were flying at 18,000 feet, seaward of the island chain. Shikoku Island was an emerald off the starboard side of the Cessna, and Kyushu Island was just becoming visible in the mist ahead. Low-altitude streams of scud blotted out large sections of the Pacific Ocean on his left.

He took his eyes off the view and scanned the note.

"I'll be damned."

"What? What is it?" Broussard asked.

Because of her unfamiliarity with the airplane, her concentration on the instruments and controls was a bit intense. She was enjoying herself, Kerry thought, but at the expense of some tension.

"This is from Charley Whitlock. It's a translation from Chinese characters of a letter Zhao Li received. Some outfit calling itself the People's People is claiming to be behind the bombings at China Dome."

"Read it to me."

"According to the interpreter, it goes like this: 'The People's People decry the disastrous turn the leaders have taken in steering China toward her destiny. Let them be warned: the people will not tolerate the intrusion of Western ideology into the fabric of Chinese culture. Should our warnings go unheeded, we will be forced to provide more of them. We have ample supplies of plastic explosive, and our will is as strong as that of the ox. Turn away the Westerners now!' That's it."

"Is it authentic?"

"Charley seems to think so. The fact that the explosives were plastic hasn't been released to the press."

"What do you think?" she asked.

"I suddenly don't feel very welcome."

She didn't respond to that, and Kerry folded the paper and stuck it in his shirt pocket.

He didn't feel very welcome where Broussard was concerned, either. Since leaving California, she had been civil and conversational, but the ten or eleven hours that they had spent in each other's arms seemed to have vanished from her memory. She didn't allude to their lovemaking at all, and the two times he had tried to bring the topic up, she had immediately changed the subject.

It was a subject he definitely felt was worthy of discussion. Kerry hadn't been as captivated by a woman ever before. Since the collapse of his marriage to Marian, Kerry hadn't again tried to define what love was. He didn't know. This Frenchwoman, though, had started those wheels turning.

Then slammed on the brakes.

Kerry didn't know what to make of her. Maybe she had decided to heed Henri Dubonnet's warning. Maybe she had found Kerry a turnoff, though that thought was ego-busting. Maybe this was a new twist on seduction.

He definitely felt seduced, though he could also admit to himself that he had looked forward to it. If this was a new, nineties-woman tactic to get him hooked, he was hooked. Kerry had never met a woman as sensual, as impulsive, and as unreadable as Jacqueline Broussard. One corner of his mind—the larger corner—had been dwelling on the sensory memories of the night she had come into his rented house.

The scent of her perfume in the cockpit triggered the recall of other aromas—the crisp, clean smell of her hair, the musky traces of desire. His fingertips seemed to vibrate when he thought of other tactile recollections.

Before he voiced what he was thinking about mile-high clubs, Kerry turned slightly sideways in his seat, as far as the armrest would allow, and leaned across the throttle pedestal toward her.

"Jacqueline."

"I'm busy."

"I'll put it on the autopilot. I want to talk."

"I do not want to talk."

"My airplane," he pointed out.

With a slight downturn of the corner of her mouth, she shrugged.

Kerry checked the speed and heading settings, then engaged the autopilot. She had been off-course by three degrees for the past twenty minutes, but he thought he wouldn't mention it.

She sat back in the seat, loosened her harness, and looked at him.

"I want to talk about us," he said.

"I do not."

"Would you believe I'm a very confused man?"

"That will have to be your problem. I made a mistake, and I said as much. That is all there is to it."

Kerry couldn't quite believe that, unless she was a hell of an actor. "Look, Jacqueline—"

"No, there is more. I told Henri about us. He is very upset, and he threatens to go to your president to complain."

"Complain? Complain about what?"

"That you attempt to influence me in regard to our pursuit of the China contract. He mentioned a lawsuit."

When Kerry studied her face, he decided she didn't look very contrite. A little smug, maybe. Had she been trying to set him up? Gain some degree of control over him? He didn't think so, but it was certainly a possibility.

"I don't think your Henri knows my P.J. Jackson very well. P.J. laughs at the absurdities of life."

Sometimes, he did. He might not laugh at the prospect of a very public legal skirmish, especially one in which the ethics of businessmen were aired. The public and the shareholders were damned tired of hearing about the lax morals and ethics of corporate executives.

Christ, he was over twenty-one and single.

She was a competitor.

He didn't want to be on any page of the *Wall Street Journal*.

"It is best if we simply forget it," she said.

"Do you actually believe this line Dubonnet is giving you?"

"I know where my butter comes from."

Kerry had to think that one over for a second. "The expression is 'where your bread is buttered.' "

"What?"

"Forget it. Jacqueline, I have a proposal."

Her eyes grew larger than he thought possible. He would liked to have kissed her. "Look, I want to be honest with you."

"You do? That is refreshing. Are you asking me—"

"I'm telling you that Aerospatiale-BAC doesn't have a chance at this contract. And while I haven't mentioned this to P.J., I think we might be able to come up with some arrangement where we could offer Aerospatiale-BAC a subcontract to provide maintenance services and, perhaps, pilot and crew training for PAI Astroliners."

"What? What are you saying?"

"I'm trying to suggest a backup position for you, if things don't go your way. It's just occurred to me—"

She was unbuckled and out of her seat in a flash.

Her eyes radiated darts at him as she slipped between the seats and through the curtain at the back of the flight deck.

About five minutes later, Dearborn came into the cockpit and settled into the copilot's seat.

"What's she doing, Jim?"

"She's drinking orange juice and staring at the ocean. The ocean's going to lose."

"I think maybe I pissed her off."

"That right? I didn't have a clue."

For the next couple of hours, Kerry and Dearborn talked aviation. Kerry promised, if things went right, to get Dearborn upgraded into the Astroliner. As they approached the coast of China, Dearborn contacted the Chinese Air Defense controller and received permission for an overflight into Deng Xiaoping International. He was reminded that he must stay in the defined air corridor. There was to be no sightseeing.

Kerry bled off altitude as he crossed the coastline.

"I want to land the airplane."

He looked back and up to find Broussard standing in the doorway. She had brushed her hair out. It shone like black diamonds. She wasn't scowling, but her smile wouldn't win many contests.

"Have you ever landed a plane before?" he asked.

"No, but I need to learn sometime."

Kerry looked over at Dearborn, who started shrugging out of his harness. "Be my guest, mademoiselle."

They changed positions, then Dearborn went on back into the cabin to buckle in.

Broussard was barely settled into her seat when Kerry looked beyond her, through the side window, and was shocked to see a jet fighter.

He hadn't been paying close enough attention.

It looked like a MiG-23. He had shot down a MiG-21. He flashed back momentarily to a time he didn't often revisit.

Then he noted the red star and bar outlined in yellow on the fuselage side and decided it had to be a near copy of the MiG-23F, designated the Shenyang F-12 by the Chinese.

"Jesus! I'm glad we're not at war. We'd be digging up weeds by now."

Broussard glanced out her window, gasped once, but then smiled and waved her hand at the fighter pilot. His oxygen mask was hanging to one side of his face, and he grinned broadly and waved back.

Seconds later, he peeled off and disappeared.

"Now," she said, "what do I do?"

"Let me get a clearance first."

Kerry contacted Deng Xiaoping Air Control and received a VFR clearance for landing, right behind a pair of Shenyang F-12s.

"Looks like they've moved the air force in," he told her.

"Is that bad?"

"I don't know. It probably means that someone in Beijing is starting to get serious about terrorists. I don't think, however, that they're going to lock an air-to-surface missile on some guy with a suitcase full of dynamite."

"It is overkill?"

"That's the word. Look, for your first time, I'm going to fly the landing. I want you to keep your right hand lightly on the yoke and your feet on the pedals. Put your left hand on top of mine on the throttles. You feel what I do, and I'll talk us through it, okay?"

Kerry gripped the throttles with his right hand, and Broussard placed her hand on top of his. It felt warm and tremendously soft.

"But I get to do the next one?"

"Is there going to be a next one?"

"Of course."

Damn. I'm going to have to go back to graduate school, if I can find a program on overcoming the female language barrier.

Newport Beach, California
August 15, 8:50 P.M.

After dinner, Valerie took the women off to the family room, and P.J. Jackson fixed after-dinner drinks for his two guests. They carried them out onto the patio and sat next to the pool. A light breeze working up the bay from the Pacific left ripples on the surface of the water.

His brother Paul appeared relaxed in P.J.'s presence for the first time in years, though this was the first time Paul and his wife, Margaret, had consented to be overnight guests at Jackson's house.

Paul and Ken Stephenson were engaged in a lively discussion of thoroughbred horseflesh, and Jackson let them engage away. He didn't know the first, or last, thing about horses.

Stephenson was an amiable people-person. He might not know anything about horses, either, but he was always willing to talk to anyone on any subject. His conversants always walked away feeling good about themselves. And that was why Stephenson, a Minnesota native with a Norwegian ancestry, blondish hair, and blue eyes, was Chairman of the

Board and President of Pacific Aerospace incorporated. It was a decent arrangement, from Jackson's point of view. Stephenson handled the public relations, the national lobbying, and the hand-pumping for the company. Jackson, as the vice president and chief operating officer, took care of the detail work and the day-to-day decisions.

Jackson realized he'd lost track of the conversation, which must have shifted to horse racing, when Stephenson said, "Speaking of races, Paul, have I been hearing rumors that you're considering a gubernatorial challenge?"

"I don't know what you've heard," Paul Jackson said, "but that contest is a couple of years away. And I think Senator Green might take it on for the Democrats. He's certainly senior to me."

The Chairman of the Transportation Committee and his staffer, Alan Wicker, would be flying into LAX in the morning, and Jackson and Stephenson would haul the legislative contingent up to Edwards so they could listen in person to the Astroliner. Green wanted some personal assurances about the noise factor beyond what he had read in the scientific study.

"Green's too damned old," P.J. Jackson said.

"Oh, now . . . ," his twin started to protest.

"P.J.'s right, you know," Stephenson said. "Look around at the nation. The taxpayer today likes the thought of young guys in office. The status quo has cost them bucks and sunk the nation deep into debt. On both the state and national levels, John Doe is looking for fresh faces."

"You'd be good, Paul," Jackson said.

"I don't mind saying that I've thought about it, but Green would have to bow out first."

"That could probably be arranged," Stephenson said.

Paul Jackson just looked at him.

"But it would take someone committed to the State of California to unhorse him," Stephenson went on. "It would take someone who has demonstrated the ability to halt the erosion of minds and intellect and dollars that is taking place every day of every year."

The senator considered this. "What you're talking about, Ken, is my shepherding your bill through the legislature."

"That's right. Through both houses. You've got to get up front, show your face so people remember it, and talk about jobs and the need for new tax dollars. That's what it will take. That and a belief that PAI can save those jobs and create those tax dollars."

"P.J. and I have talked about it. I can see where the China contract could be beneficial."

"And that contract's out the door if we can't fly the airplanes out of, at minimum, L.A. and San Francisco."

Paul Jackson mulled it over for a few minutes, then said, "A run at the governor's mansion is an expensive proposition."

"I think you'll find you have a lot of support from your party," Stephenson told him, "and I think you'd be surprised how fast a campaign fund can fill up."

Jackson watched his brother weighing the pros and cons. The pros were winning, according to the contortions of his face. Paul Jackson liked the national limelight in which the governor of California found himself. There was so much political potential beyond the statehouse. That was a con, as far as P.J. Jackson was concerned.

"You know, Ken," the senator said, "I don't have any qualms about becoming more active with your bill."

He bought it, Jackson thought, and in doing so, was himself bought.

There, you son of a bitch. Two years from now, when

you're hung out to dry, go march in the street and yell about inequity.

Deng Xiaoping International Superport
August 16, 8:30 P.M.

The security center was jam-packed with people who probably shouldn't be there, Charley Whitlock thought.

Kerry and the Frenchwoman had arrived in midafternoon, and Ebbing and Zemenek had joined them shortly after. They met in a conference room for half an hour, and at five o'clock, Yichang, Whitlock, and Bergen had briefed them. Over hamburgers ordered in by Yichang, who had discovered he liked them, Whitlock had explained his suspicion that the terrorists—now the People's People—were using the fiber-optic system to activate their bombs. Like Ernst Bergen the day before, Kerry had bought it right away, but Whitlock thought the others were skeptical.

Yichang had detailed his reinvestigation of the people working in the communications center, but admitted he had as yet discovered nothing that would discredit any of the people working there.

At six o'clock, as the work shift changed, the group had moved to the security center, and had been there since.

Extra chairs had been brought in, but Whitlock tended to wander, stopping often by the four video monitors that had, for the last four days, been tracking the unused circuits in the fiber-optic system which ringed the airport. The gibberish on the screens didn't mean much to him, just lines of numerals and letters scrolling up the screen. Each line designated an available circuit, and at the end of the line was the cryptic notation, "Inactive."

The four new arrivals also found the monitors fascinating, glancing over at them from time to time.

Yichang's cousin, Wu Yhat, an assistant director for security personnel who was taking his turn at the console, had explained to him that the computer had been programmed to sound an alert and pinpoint the interception point if any interference occurred in the unused circuits.

Whitlock leaned against a console next to the monitors and surveyed the room. He figured most of them would bail out in the next couple hours and head for their hotels. They weren't accustomed to police work, which was mostly drudgery. Wait, wait, wait.

Kerry would hang around.

He didn't know about the Broussard woman. There was something strange going on between her and Kerry. Like two lions circling each other, they knew they belonged to the same species, but they figured one or the other of them ought to be king.

Whitlock respected his boss, but he wondered if Kerry hadn't finally met his match. The French lady was a knockout, but from the little he had talked to her, Whitlock also thought she could be hard-edged.

Moving down the row of consoles, he found a vacant one, sat in the chair, and picked up the phone. He dialed his own room at the President.

Karen answered on the first ring.

"Hello, lady."

"Charley. I hoped you'd call. No, I hoped you'd come back early."

"I'm afraid it's going to be a long night."

"All night?"

"Maybe. I can't leave before the boss does," he alibied.

"I had a telephone call from my friend," Meyer told him cautiously.

"An interesting call, was it?"

"It may have been. I have some names for you."

Curiosity reared its head. "Look, if nothing happens before midnight, I'll try to get away."

"I'll look forward to it."

Whitlock hung up, then found his bottle of Tylenol in his pocket and popped two caplets.

"Still got a headache?" Kerry asked him from the other side of the desks in the center of the room.

"It's getting to be a good friend," Whitlock told him.

"Why don't you scoot?"

"I might, after a while."

Whitlock wasn't going to mention the names Meyer had acquired until he had a chance to look at them.

BEEP! BEEP! BEEP!

Everyone in the room swung toward the console where Wu Yhat sat. A red symbol was flashing in the upper right corner of one of the monitors.

"Sublevel Two, Room 1121," Wu called out.

"That is below the main terminal," Yichang said. "Alert the nearest security officers. They are to assume surveillance, but not approach the room."

Whitlock had already started toward the door, and he got there just behind Yichang.

The security director stopped and turned to the bunch of people assembling at the door, holding up his hand.

"Just Mr. Whitlock and Mr. Bergen will accompany me, if you please."

The three of them made their way through the double set of doors and started running down the corridor.

Whitlock heard an extra pair of leather soles slapping the

tile, and looked back to see Kerry taking long strides behind him.

"You don't hear so well, chief?"

"Been a problem all my life, Charley."

The elevator was on the floor, its door propped open to keep it there. Yichang was the first one in, kicking the wooden wedge from the door as he entered. When he saw Kerry, he frowned but didn't order him out.

It was an express elevator, but it seemed to take the milk run getting to Sublevel Two.

When the car reached the tunnel and the doors opened, Yichang led them out, turning to the right.

"This way, but please be quiet."

He followed a floor plan in his head, taking several turns to the left and right, moving swiftly down long alleyways. Whitlock stayed next to him, becoming aware of an increasing hum.

Yichang slowed down before taking the next turn, to the left.

As they came around the corner, Whitlock saw two men dressed in the light blue jackets of the security detail huddled at the next intersection. The humming noise had increased to a level where it could be irritating after a while.

Yichang moved up the corridor to the security guards and spoke softly in Chinese.

The three Westerners edged their way along the hall.

Yichang came back a few steps and whispered to them. "The room is immediately around the corner to the right and on the other side of the corridor. My men say the door is closed and they have seen no one nearby."

"Let us open it," Bergen said.

"What's in it?" Whitlock asked.

"In the room? Ah, I will check."

Yichang used a walkie-talkie to call someone, then told them, "It holds the transformers for the Terminal One mechanical systems. That is, for the air conditioning and ventilation systems."

"Okay, I'm game," Whitlock said.

The two guards had automatic pistols, and Yichang ordered them around the corner, up against the wall on the other side of the room.

"I'll go with you," Whitlock offered.

"You men are guests of my country. Please wait here."

Kerry, Bergen, and Whitlock moved up to the intersection of the tunnels and watched as Yichang crossed the hall and approached the door, holding his master key in front of him.

It was a steel door, like any other along the corridor, and distinguished only by its room number.

Yichang inserted the key, then twisted it.

The door flew open.

A steel blade flashed in the light from a hundred-watt bulb.

Yichang slid sideways. His feet went out from under him.

One of the guards fired.

The bullet *whanged* off the door and went ricocheting down the tunnel. The shot seemed to echo forever.

Several people yelled, but Whitlock wasn't sure who.

A man in a tan jacket—communications?—shot out of the room, skidded to his right, and came running toward them. He held a vicious-looking knife in his right hand, and Whitlock noted the repugnant scar slashed across his forehead.

He stepped out into the intersection.

"Charley!" Kerry called.

The tan jacket saw his course blocked and slid to a stop, waving the knife back and forth horizontally in front of him. His eyes appeared enlarged, and Whitlock would swear they were mostly whites.

Crazy bastard.

With his feet spread wide for balance, Whitlock feinted with his right hand, and when the man went for it, reached out for the knife hand with his left.

Got him around the wrist.

Slipped.

Lost the grip.

And then felt the most incredible pain as the stainless steel blade ripped him open from the groin to the breastbone.

Whitlock thought he saw Karen Meyer's face shining in the dark gray clouds that came out of nowhere.

Then the darkness engulfed him.

ELEVEN

Men yelled and another shot rang out, the concussion slamming back and forth loudly in the concrete confinement of the tunnel.

With the fighter pilot's ingrained reflex, Kerry didn't consciously think about the next few seconds; he reacted instinctively. His mind barely registered the spray of blood that had erupted from Whitlock.

He took one step into the cross corridor, landing on the ball of his left foot, and swung his right leg in a sweeping arc that reached up and connected with the attacker's right wrist. He heard a bone snap as the knife spun away, clacking into the concrete wall of the tunnel.

The assailant yelped in anguish, crashed into the wall, rebounded, and began running.

Kerry's follow-through spun him around counterclockwise, but he glimpsed the Chinese darting to his left, and propelled himself into a diving tackle. He slammed shoulder first into the back of the man's knees and wrapped his arms around the man's legs. The two of them smashed to the cement floor, sliding along it. Kerry felt concrete grinding at the backs of his hands. The Chinese was wiry and strong.

He began thrashing his legs, twisting his body inside Kerry's grip, rolling onto his back, banging his good fist into Kerry's head and neck.

Kerry started to lose, then tightened his grip, felt a toe gouge him in the ribs, tried to roll the man over, hit the wall, and rolled back. The wild kicking threatened his grasp.

Then Ernst Bergen landed with both knees on the man's chest, driving the air from his lungs in an audible whoosh. Kerry released his left hand and drove his right fist into the terrorist's groin, eliciting a scream and killing the last shreds of resistance.

Bergen pinned the attacker's arms against the floor, yelling, "Let's not kill him, Mr. Kerry!"

One of the security guards slid to a stop next to them, bending to slap handcuffs to the broken wrist.

Kerry rolled off the man's legs, got to his feet, and ran back to where Whitlock lay on his back. Blood was everywhere. It spread in a heavy, bright pool from the long gash across Whitlock's stomach, drenching the ripped clothing. Sliced intestines were visible.

Kerry dropped to his knees next to Whitlock's head, got his left hand under the head to cushion it, and felt with his right fingers for any hint of a pulse in the carotid artery.

There was none.

"Ah, Jesus, Charley!" he said aloud as his head drooped forward.

Yichang Enlai squatted next to him, holding his bloody left arm with his right hand.

"He is gone?"

"Yes."

Yichang mumbled something in Chinese.

Kerry looked up at him, saw the blood.

"Are you all right?"

"I will live."

More men were arriving, the soles of their shoes rapping against the concrete as they ran. Kerry's ears rang with the aftereffects of the two shots that had been fired. The smell of cordite and the acrid tang of blood permeated the air.

He let Whitlock's head down gently, stood up, shed his coat, and draped it over his friend's head and torso.

"I want that son of a bitch, Mr. Yichang."

"I understand your feeling completely, Mr. Kerry. I admired Charles Whitlock a great deal."

Kerry looked down the tunnel toward the killer. The guards had him on his face on the floor, his hands cuffed behind him. One guard held him down with his foot pressed into the man's neck, grinding his face into the floor.

They were being too gentle.

Kerry turned to go back, but Yichang touched his forearm lightly. "Mr. Kerry. Please."

Kerry put his hand over his eyes and sighed. "All right, Mr. Yichang."

He noticed blood on the backs of his hands, oozing from abrasions caused by contact with the concrete floor. He pulled his handkerchief from his pocket and dabbed at the blood. Portable radios were babbling everywhere.

A Chinese man in a white jacket showed up. He dropped a case on the floor and went to work on Yichang's arm. After he cut away the sleeves of Yichang's coat and shirt, Kerry saw a long slice along the outer arm.

A short round of Chinese dialogue ensued, but the medic apparently lost the short argument. He sprinkled an antiseptic on the wound, then began to bind it with gauze.

"What did he say?"

Yichang's face did not betray his pain, but Kerry guessed

that it must be fierce. He simply said, "It will require stitches, but I will get them later."

Kerry saw two more white-coated attendants approaching with a gurney, and he stepped to one side to give them room to lift Whitlock's body.

After a short order from Yichang in Chinese, the security guards rolled the assailant over, and Yichang, with the medic trailing along still working on his arm, walked over to look down on the man.

Kerry followed them.

Ernst Bergen, standing against the wall, asked, "Do you know him, Mr. Yichang?"

He would have been easy to remember, Kerry thought. Beneath the lank black hair resting on his forehead, an ugly, puckered scar was etched across his skin like a zipper.

"His name is Hu Ziyang," Yichang told them. "He has a Classification Four clearance, and he works in the communications center as a computer maintenance specialist."

Hu's face didn't demonstrate any fear whatsoever. He lay on the floor with his eyes wide open and his mouth held in a tight, straight line. The eyes showed defiance, if they showed anything.

Kerry remembered the strength Hu had shown, and he studied the man's shoulders and arms which, despite the tan jacket, appeared to be thick and muscled. The jacket sleeves were pulled up a couple inches by his posture, stretched out on the floor partly on his side with his wrists shackled together, his arms along his side. He noticed a blue-green splotch emerging from the right sleeve.

He pointed to it with the toe of his shoe. "What's that, Mr. Yichang?"

Yichang said something to the guards in Chinese, and

one of them bent down, grabbed the seams of the sleeve, and ripped it apart.

The right arm did indeed ripple with highly conditioned muscle, and was painted almost totally in an intricate tattoo. The splotch Kerry had noticed was the tip of a serpent's tail. It wound around the forearm, rising to the biceps, where the head of the huge snake was buried in the crotch of an abundantly proportioned figure of a Caucasian female. The expression on her face was at once ecstatic and filled with repugnance and pain.

Yichang said something to one of the other security people who had shown up and got a "Hai!" in response.

"This man is not Hu Ziyang," Yichang said in English for Kerry and Bergen. "His name is James Lee, a gang member from Kowloon."

"You know the tattoo?" Bergen asked.

"It is in his dossier, from his prison record. He was on my short list since he is a known anarchist and an electronics expert."

"But the scar?" Kerry asked.

"Hu Ziyang had the scar, the result of an accident between his bicycle and an automobile. I presume Lee was scarred to match in order to assume Hu's identity. Look at the hands. The missing joint of the small finger is also an identification of Hu."

That a man would undergo disfigurement in his pursuit of ideology was an alarming concept for Kerry. The adversary's will was certainly not to be underestimated.

The tunnel felt suddenly cold.

Bergen asked, "When was the substitution made?"

"At least two months ago," Yichang replied, finally shaking off the medical technician bandaging his arm. "That was when permanent staff for the communications center began their duties."

Yet another of the security men approached from behind them and spoke to Yichang.

He responded to the man, then spoke to the two guards standing over James Lee. They lifted him from the floor, and holding him tightly, shuffled him down the corridor.

Kerry and Bergen followed along as Yichang explained, "The demolitions team has found the bomb and defused it."

The gurney with Whitlock's body on it trundled slowly down the corridor toward the elevators.

Kerry felt his rage building. His vision seemed to be tinged in red. It was all he could do not to rush forward and grab Hu, or Lee, by the throat and throttle him. He figured he could have a dead man before the guards pulled him free.

The group turned into Room 1121, the guards shoving James Lee ahead of them. Kerry smelled the odor of ozone, and the temperature level was higher than in the hallway.

It was a long, narrow space, with fifteen large transformers mounted to one wall. Dozens of signs spelled out, "Danger! High Voltage!" Heavy copper wire clad in black, white, and red insulating jackets was neatly aligned along the walls, dropping off their runs in pairs and triplets to be secured to the transformer terminals by large clips and bolts.

Halfway down the room, the demolitions man stopped and pointed out four blocks of plastic explosive adhered to four of the transformers. Kerry noted that the detonators had been removed from the blocks.

The explosives expert moved along the wall, his finger

indicating a thin black cable as Yichang translated his explanation.

"The cable leads down here, to the communications panel. As Charles suspected, it has been connected, through a translator device, into the fiber-optic system. The computer monitoring the system detected the change in the electrical load as soon as Lee tapped into it."

"Any chance we could trace it to the transmitter?" Kerry asked.

"I doubt it, Mr. Kerry. We will examine the electronics, but I anticipate that, in addition to the transceiver, there is a decoder which accepts a signal tapped out on the keypad of a telephone. It is very simple in operation. Charles Whitlock told me that."

Kerry thought about it for a minute. "We have another option, Mr. Yichang. If we leave the transceiver in place and put a trace on the line, we might learn something when someone calls the number and attempts to set off the explosives."

Yichang's eyes brightened. "You and Mr. Whitlock thought very much alike, did you not? We will do as you suggest."

Yichang spun around toward his prisoner, his shoulders held in the tight grasp of two security guards. "James Lee, you speak English. I want to know the name of the person who employs you."

Lee spoke for the first time. "You will suffer the agonies of the damned before I say anything to the traitors of my country."

Yichang shrugged and said to Kerry, "He will disgorge the total content of his scummy mind before we are through with him."

Lee exploded into instant action. His right leg whipped

out and sawed the legs of one guard out from under him. He dropped into a squat, pulling the second guard after him, twisted out of the man's grasp, and rolled away to the right, leaping over the first guard.

As he rolled across the floor, he pulled his legs through the loop made of his manacled hands, finally rising to his feet with his hands in front of him.

Half a dozen guards leaped after him, but not before Lee reached a transformer on the wall.

He pressed his forearms into a pair of the high voltage terminals.

A bright blue flash lit him up.

And the odor of fried meat immediately spread through the stale air of the room.

August 16, 9:21 P.M.

For Jacqueline Broussard, too many minutes had passed. The security personnel manning communications consoles were babbling away on the telephones and radio circuits, but it was all in Chinese, and no one was translating for Ebbing, Zemenek, or herself, not even when she finally requested it.

It was obvious that something was happening, somewhere, and her feeling that at any moment she would be propelled upward through the ceiling as some monstrous bomb exploded below made her uneasy.

She grabbed her purse from a console and headed for the door.

Ebbing called after her, "Mademoiselle Broussard, should we not wait here?"

"You may wait, but I will find out what is going on."

Ebbing started after her, and Pyotr Zemenek lurched out of his chair to trail along.

At the door, she was confronted by a large Chinese man in a light blue security coat.

He moved in front of her to stand before the door. His face was immobile, but his expression attempted to be intimidating.

She stopped a few inches from him and let the full blast of her frustration and anger show in her eyes.

He shrugged and stepped aside. Why should he keep her inside the security center? Most people were kept out.

Marching resolutely down the corridor with the German and Russian engineers hurrying to keep up with her, her mind flipped through images of Daniel Kerry. He was dead. He was gravely wounded. He was collapsed in the corner of a descriptionless compartment, the blood streaming from dozens of wounds. She was unable to help him.

The imagery almost made her gag with remorse. Never before had she used her body to manipulate men. What had she done to him?

Reaching the elevator that was authorized to access the sublevels, she stretched her arm out to press the button, but found only the slot for a key.

"Damn it!"

"We had best wait," Zemenek said.

They were only engineers. What could they know?

She looked up to the floor-level indicator and saw that the car was stopped on the second sublevel.

He was dying; she knew it.

As she watched, the lights began to change. The car was coming up.

When the doors slid aside, Kerry was the first one out. She immediately saw that his suit jacket was missing and his hands were streaked with dried blood. There was blood on the knees of his suit pants.

He was hurt badly.

Bergen, Yichang, and several security people were right behind him. Yichang's sleeve was ripped apart, and his arm was wrapped in white bandages beginning to stain with his own blood.

They were alive.

Broussard almost chastised Kerry for making her worry so, but the grim look on his face stopped her.

"What is it? What happened?"

They formed a circle in the corridor, and Yichang briefly related the battle that had taken place in the tunnel. She could tell that he was fighting the pain in his arm. Broussard had not known Whitlock, but Kerry's demeanor suggested that his grief was close to the surface. The security director's description of Kerry's actions were laudatory, but Kerry merely shook his head negatively.

"Now," Yichang said, "there is much to be done, but that is for my office to handle. I will call for an automobile to take you all to your hotels."

"Mr. Yichang," Kerry said, "I would like to make arrangements to send Charley's body back to the United States."

"First, there must be an autop—no, it will not be necessary. I will make those arrangements, Mr. Kerry."

"We will use the Citation. I'll have my pilot prepare the airplane."

"Very well. Now, please, if you would go to the main floor, I will have a driver meet you."

Yichang and his retinue continued on down the hallway toward the security center, and Pyotr Zemenek pressed the call button for one of the standard service elevators.

It was almost ten o'clock by the time their van let them

out at the hotel. Broussard had been seated in the middle seat with Ernst Bergen, and Kerry had been in the front seat with the driver, so she did not get a chance to press him for details. Judging by the self-imposed silences Bergen and Kerry were wearing, though, she did not believe she would have learned much.

As they entered the hotel behind the luggage the driver had stacked on a bellhop's cart, she took his arm.

"Daniel, are you all right?"

"I'll be fine, Jacqueline."

"Do you want a drink?"

"Maybe when I get to my room. I have a lot of calls to make. Charley's daughter, for one."

She let it go for the moment, while they all registered. Kerry moved to the side of the registration desk with an assistant manager and arranged for Whitlock's belongings to be packed and shipped.

"And attach his bill to mine, will you?" Kerry asked the assistant.

"Ah, Mr. Kerry . . . there is the matter of the young lady."

"Young lady?"

"Staying in Mr. Whitlock's room."

"Oh, damn. I'll go up and talk to her. Don't kick her out tonight."

"Of course not, sir."

Kerry gave some Hong Kong bills to the bellhop and sent his luggage to the fourteenth floor.

"I will go with you," Broussard said.

"It's not necessary, Jacqueline."

"It is," she insisted.

While the rest of their group headed for the dining room, Kerry and Broussard took the elevator to the twelfth floor. Broussard could not help feeling that their walk down the thickly carpeted and hushed hallway was much the same as a walk through a mortuary.

Kerry stopped before 1215 and knocked on the door.

A few seconds later, it was opened by a dark and pretty woman. "Charley . . . oh?"

"Karen?"

"Yes?"

"I'm Dan Kerry. This is Mademoiselle Broussard."

"Charley has told me about you, Mr. Kerry. Come in, please, both of you."

They stepped inside the room and stood self-consciously for a moment, until Karen Meyer noticed Kerry's blood-stained hands and slacks, then anxiously asked, "Where's Charley?"

"Karen, this is difficult. . . ."

"Oh, no! He's dead!"

"I'm afraid. . . ."

"Oh, my God!"

She spun around, groped for the bed, and sat on the edge of it. Tears streamed down her face, streaking her mascara. A low groan issued from her throat.

Broussard did not know how to handle this. The thought that she had been on the brink of the same gulf of grief rose unbidden in her mind.

Kerry sat down next to Meyer and put his arm around her shoulders. The woman nestled her head into the hollow of his neck and wept unashamedly.

Kerry murmured in her ear.

Was that jealousy she felt?

Or envy that he knew how to help the woman with her sorrow?

She moved over to the table, placed her purse on it, and sat in one of the chairs. She found herself seeing patterns in the bloodstains on his knees and forced herself to look away.

Kerry held the woman close for several minutes, then searched in his hip pocket and came up with his handkerchief.

It was brownish with caked blood. He stuffed it back in his pocket.

Broussard got up and went to the bathroom. She found the tissue dispenser and pulled out a handful, then took them into Kerry.

He dabbed at the woman's face with a tissue, drying the tears.

"How . . . how did it happen?"

"A man we think is a terrorist killed him." Kerry mercifully did not go into details.

"Oh, God. He was the nicest man I've ever met, Mr. Kerry."

"Dan. And I know. He was my friend, too."

"I loved him."

"I know."

"I don't think he knew."

"He knew," Kerry insisted.

"He told you about . . . about us."

"He told me."

"Ohh. . . ." She began to wail again.

Kerry waited her out. Broussard did not understand how he had the patience; she would not have.

After a while, Meyer regained some degree of composure, pulled away from Kerry, and used tissues to dry her eyes.

"There will be a service?"

"Yes, in San Francisco, I imagine. That's where Angela lives."

"His daughter?"

"Yes."

"She will hate me."

"I don't think so. I'll tell her you're coming."

Meyer stood up abruptly, crossed the room, and picked up a purse resting on an easy chair. She rifled through it, found a folded sheet of paper, and brought it back to Kerry.

"What's this?" he asked.

"Names. I got them for Charley. One of them may be his killer, and I want you to be certain that he dies horribly."

"I'll do my damnedest, Karen."

They left her alone then, and took the elevator to the fourteenth floor. Their rooms were across the hall from one another.

Kerry unlocked his door and pushed it open.

She said, "I want to be with you for a while, Dan."

He turned and stood in the doorway.

"I have to make some phone calls, Jacqueline."

"Please." She had never said, "please," to a man before in her life.

"No more games, Jacqueline. From here on out, it gets very serious."

He took a step back, then closed the door softly in her face.

August 16, 10:40 P.M.

Yichang called Sun Chen at his home. He was not in bed, but it was several minutes before he came on the line. Yichang waited, sitting at his desk with his anesthetized arm resting on a towel and watching dispassionately as the doctor deftly stitched the severed edges of skin together.

"Director Yichang?"

"We have located one of the men, Chairman Sun."

He told the story with excruciating detail, much of which he knew Sun would as soon not hear.

"There was no damage?"

"Not to the facility, no. Two men are dead."

"One of whom is an American," Sun said. "That will displease the leadership greatly."

"For the sake of public relations, it is all right to kill a Chinese, but not a foreigner," Yichang thought, but did not say.

He grunted instead.

"And the other dead man. He was not working alone?"

"I do not believe so, Chairman."

"But you will be able to trace the telephone call when it happens?"

"As a result of the short connection time required, I estimate a fifty percent chance of tracing the call, and even then, it will be to a public telephone. Possibly, we will learn from what part of the world the call is made."

"One of the dead men is James Lee. That is the name you gave me earlier."

"It is, Chairman."

"Why had he not been apprehended before this time?"

"We could not find him, and we could not find him because he was living the persona of Hu Ziyang."

"What course are you now taking?"

"We continue to cull our lists of prominent suspects, and we will now, in conjunction with the Hong Kong police, attempt to pinpoint the people with whom James Lee had contact. Our security remains at high alert."

"General Chou is there?"

"Not personally, Chairman, but there is a squadron of fighter aircraft present. They are under the command of

Major Hua Peng. They have set up living quarters and head-quarters in Maintenance Hangar Two."

"Good."

Yichang did not think it was good; he thought it was use-less. Jet fighters were not the proper response weapons to terrorists. Did they think that terrorists would appear on their radars and be obliterated by their missiles? And as a deterrent, the fighters might as well be invisible. Terrorists sneaking through the subterranean tunnels of the airport would not even see the aircraft much less be impressed by their fire-power. If anything, the aircraft made a delicious target, and with that thought, he wrote a note to himself with his good hand to call Hua. The presence of the squadron at the airport only heightened his own security concerns.

"What of the SST representatives?" Sun asked.

"They are currently at their hotels."

"I do not know what they hope to achieve."

Yichang had not yet shared with his superior the theory proposed by Daniel Kerry that the supersonic transports were the eventual targets of the terrorists. He had not shared it because he had not yet found it entirely feasible.

"Perhaps they will be useful, Chairman. Mr. Kerry cer-tainly demonstrated an ability I had not suspected."

"Perhaps. But do not let them run too far afield, Director."

"Of course not," Yichang replied.

"Continue with your work," Sun told him and hung up.

He replaced his own telephone in its cradle and watched the doctor wrapping his neatly stitched arm in a white ban-dage.

His work, he thought, was beginning to contain entirely too many surprises. The fact that his communications sec-tion had been penetrated by a spy angered him immensely, and he had already ordered a thorough reexamination of all employees. Further, he had come to like Charles Whitlock, and he knew that he would miss the man.

And lastly, he knew that when the anaesthetic wore off, his arm would ache, interfering with his concentration.

Kowloon
August 16, 11:00 P.M.

After providing them with the bare details of what they needed to know, along with three envelopes containing thousands of Hong Kong dollars, Kurt Wehmeier dismissed his three associates, and they left the restaurant while he finished his coffee. He paid his bill, then strolled out onto Granville Road.

The rainbow of colors from the neon lights etched his face like a kaleidoscope as he walked eastward. Taxi horns honked and people laughed aloud as they emerged from nightclubs and restaurants. Ahead, at the intersection with Chatham Road, he saw double-decker buses passing.

When he found a public telephone, he dropped coins into it and dialed the telephone number at Deng Xiaoping International Superport. When the connection was made, he heard only a low chime note, the signal that the decoder was on-line and the safety switch was in the armed position. James Lee had insisted on the safety switch which armed the system five minutes after the microswitch on the circuit board was closed. He did not want to be anywhere close to the location when the explosive was detonated.

Though he thought the additional circuit unnecessary, Wehmeier had ordered his electronics specialist to include it. He must keep Lee satisfied since the man's presence in the communications center was priceless. How else would he have learned about the security systems in the American supersonic transport?

Dakar had confirmed Jeremy Smith's guess that the Astroliner carried missile countermeasures, but for Smith, that was only a challenge. He had laughed off any potential difficulty.

Wehmeier could only assume that, by now, Lee had closed the microswitch and returned to his job at the airport.

Wehmeier held the telephone in front of his face and tapped out 9, 6, 3, 7, 2.

He pressed the receiver to his ear in time to hear the *click.*

That was all he ever heard since the decoder did not have a microphone with which to pick up the sound of the detonation.

He would like to have heard the detonation.

Technology was taking much of the fun out of his work.

Taya Wan, *China*
August 18, 4:22 A.M.

The freighter was already out of sight in the darkness of the sea, on its way to Hong Kong Harbor, when Ku Chi beached his rubber boat on the rocky shore of the bay which, in English, was known as Bias Bay.

The boat had barely scraped ashore when he was surrounded by three men, hopefully the ones who had responded correctly with their flashlights to the signals he had made with his own flashlight.

The taller of the three men leaned forward to peer into the boat at the cargo netting and the crates.

"Those are the missiles?"

"The Grail missile, yes."

"Excellent. Come, we must hurry."

The four of them quickly unloaded the rubber boat, and Ku Chi punctured its air chambers, then shoved it back into the bay and waited to make certain that it sank.

The cliff face backing the beach was not high, but its rocky projections and crevices were treacherous, and it took them twenty minutes to carry all of the boxes to its summit, then a kilometer inland to where a truck was hidden in the trees, several meters away from a gravel road. He was sweating profusely by the time they were finished.

After the truck bed was loaded with the crates, then topped off with a scattering of hay, two of the men crawled on top, and Ku climbed into the cab with the tall man whose name was Hyun Oh.

He started the truck, turned on the headlights, and bounced through a ditch onto the road. It was fifty kilometers to Deng Xiaoping International Superport.

TWELVE

The Hong Kong policeman's name was Maynard Wing, and he carried the rank of inspector. As he led the way into the apartment, he apologized, "Director Yichang, we had no idea that Hu Ziyang rented two apartments. This landlord called us after seeing Hu's name in the newspaper."

The first apartment, the address of which was listed in Hu's personnel record, had proven to be a disappointment. It had obviously belonged to the real Hu, and it had contained only clothing and some items related to the hobby of electronics—a home-crafted stereo and television, some test equipment, a personal computer. The data on the computer's hard drive and floppy disks was under examination by police experts, but Yichang did not expect to learn much from it.

This apartment, rented for only the last four months under Hu's name, was located in the back reaches of Kowloon, accessed through a maze of stairways and hallways, and was differently appointed. The single room held only a futon shoved into one corner, with a low table placed in front of it. The kitchenette along one wall was a garbage dump of filthy cooking utensils, food wrappers, paper plates, and dried and rotting food. Cockroaches scampered as they entered. The floor was ankle-deep in paper, clothing, and dirt. From the odor, Yichang knew that James Lee had not always gone down the hall to the communal bathroom. The walls were papered with frayed posters.

Yichang noted a large poster of Mao and another with a drawing of Che Guevera.

Wing said, "I did not know that Che was still a hero."

"For some, perhaps."

Wrinkling his nose at the aroma, Yichang waded into the room, shifting trash aside with his feet, looking for he knew not what.

Wing and two of his detectives began to go through the cabinets over the sink and the two-burner hot plate on a cabinet.

In half an hour, they came up with three items of interest: a copy of Hu's identification card, two thousand Hong Kong dollars, and a small red notebook containing four pages of numbers.

Yichang looked over the ID card with interest.

"Is that of concern, Director?" Wing asked.

"It may be, Inspector. Hu Ziyang's card was recovered from Lee's body. If he has managed to duplicate the card and the magnetic strip, we will certainly be concerned."

"And the book?"

Yichang studied the pages, then began to see a pattern.

"These numbers may be related to the communications system at Deng Xiaoping International. I believe some of them may be associated with unused telephone circuits."

"I will have the pages copied for you."

"Thank you."

Yichang would rather have had the book, so as to prevent the numbers, if they had any importance, from receiving wider distribution. Unfortunately, the law enforcement relationship between China and the Hong Kong Dependency was still tenuous. While, in anticipation of the resumption of Chinese control, the colony had entered into agreements which gradually transferred administrative functions to China prior to the end of the treaty, there was ample opportunity for stepping on toes and bruising bureaucratic feelings.

He would not press the issue.

Inspector Wing was also cognizant of the tender spots. He said, "As to the card, I imagine you will need it in order to test its effectiveness."

"That would be helpful, yes."

"I will have my photographer take a photograph of it and let you have the original."

Yichang smiled his appreciation, then took another look around the room. "I suspect we will not find Hu Ziyang. Or his body."

"I sincerely doubt it. Too much time has passed."

And the oceans were very deep.

"Yes. The switch was made before James Lee, as Hu, made application for his job at the airport. The fingerprints in his file and on the computer database are those of Lee."

"It suggests long-term planning for the sabotage occurring at the airport," Wing said.

"That does worry me, Inspector."

Yichang wondered how many of the current two thousand-plus permanent employees of Deng Xiaoping International Superport were dragons in the disguise of mere mortals.

Beijing, China
August 22, 1:00 P.M.

Sun Chen had once enjoyed meeting his salvation—the world's media representatives—in the conference room on the first floor of the ministry. Now, he was apt to view them as his nemesis.

As he entered the large and brightly lit room, his eyes swept from right to left, and he estimated that over thirty television and newspaper reporters were present. Many of them were familiar, and he pinpointed the men and women he dreaded. Their questions tended to be simplistic and repetitive, as if previous answers to the same questions could not penetrate their minds.

Walking directly to the cluster of microphones at the podium, trailed by his aide carrying a folder of the hard data— if it proved to be necessary, he smiled and nodded at the people who thought they knew him.

They smiled back, as if they thought he knew them.

It took him six minutes to read the statement he had prepared. In writing it, Sun had utilized a generous sprinkling of details. One thing he had learned about the Western correspondents was that they would not accept slogans and platitudes as substitutes for concrete information. This was not a preference of the leaders, who preferred simple statements in *The People's Daily,* without the illumination of tiresome minutia, as in the court trials of dissidents. Sun Chen walked a fine line between what the reporters demanded in the way of particulars and what the leadership considered trivia best kept from the light of day.

The hands went up, and he nodded toward the closest, a woman from the *Washington Post.*

"This man James Lee, Chairman. You described him as an anarchist. Was he working alone?"

He had said as much in his statement. "He was alone when captured by security personnel."

"You're certain he had no accomplices?"

"It is an uncertain world, madam. However, the national police and the law enforcement people from the Hong Kong Dependency are currently examining Lee's background and associates. If there were others involved, I am sure they will uncover the fact."

Sun Chen would not point his finger at people, not even reporters. He nodded his head toward a man in the back of the room who represented a Canadian newspaper.

"Lee was caught in the act of placing a bomb. Can you describe the bomb, Mr. Sun?"

These people had no respect for titles.

"Only that it would have caused considerable damage. All other information is to be confidential for the present, as an aid to the investigation."

Another hand. The *Baltimore Sun?* "Who captured Lee?"

"Men from the airport security detail." Once again.

"I mean, who exactly?"

"Director Yichang Enlai was present."

"Yeah, but I heard there were Americans involved. The rumor mill says an American was killed."

The confounded rumors always disrupted his press conferences. People with wagging tongues could not resist wagging them in the direction of reporters. He sighed.

"Mr. Charles Whitlock, a security expert employed by Pacific Aerospace Incorporated, died as the result of a knife wound inflicted by Lee. Mr. Daniel Kerry, a vice president of PAI, assisted in the capture of James Lee."

"Did Kerry also assist in the death of James Lee?"

"Once again, Lee slipped from the grasp of two security personnel and purposely electrocuted himself."

"Suggesting," the woman from the Washington newspaper said, without being recognized, "that Lee had information that he did not want to divulge."

"That is one interpretation, yes."

"About his friends, do you think, Chairman Sun?"

"I suppose that is possible, madam."

"So there's still a chance that these terrorist attacks against the airport could continue?"

"I think we have curtailed the terrorist activities directed against Deng Xiaoping International Superport," Sun said.

He knew he sounded positive in that statement, and he did not believe a word of it.

Astroliner 01
August 21, 9:20 P.M.

"Edwards Air Control, PA Zero-One."

"Go ahead, One."

"PA One requesting final landing clearance."

"PA One, final clearance for landing is approved. You have a seven-knot wind from two-five-five gusting to twelve knots. Barometric thirty-point-zero-five. Current temperature seven-eight."

"Roger, Edwards," Carroll said.

"I don't like this fully automatic shit," Don Matthews said from the right seat.

"We get used to it, Don, we can play bridge and slug back Bloody Marys for the whole trip," Carroll told him.

"What if we don't like Bloody Marys, Terry?" Jeff Dormund asked from his flight engineer's seat.

"You'll just have to get used to them. Hardship duty."

"What if we don't like bridge?" Matthews said.

"No one dislikes bridge."

"Bullshit."

At 300 knots, the flight deck was noisier than at cruise speeds. The monster turbofans were barely idling as the Astroliner lost altitude rapidly.

Matthews called out the altitude, reading from the orange-colored digital readouts on his eyebrow panel: "Fifteen hundred . . . twelve hundred . . . nine-five-zero feet. . . ."

The computer, preprogrammed for the approach patterns available at Edwards Air Force Base, guided the SST into a smooth left turn, utilizing the autopilot for its control.

Carroll, who didn't like the fully automatic shit, either, instinctively reached out with both hands as the aircraft went into the bank. He managed to keep his hands off the yoke, but it was a struggle.

"I saw you," Matthews said, his own hands perched above the wheel, ready to intervene when the computer gave out.

"You're not supposed to be watching me."

Dormund read off the now-routine numbers for engine functions—oil and fuel pressures, exhaust temperatures, revolutions per minute, synchronization.

This was their first test of the interface of the aircraft avionics with the Instrument Landing System (ILS) at Edwards. They were under simulated blackout conditions, though the stars were bright and obscured by only a low rise of clouds in the west.

Ahead on his left, Carroll could clearly see the runway lights of 27R, the runway designated for them.

He had to keep telling himself that he couldn't see the damned thing. They could have draped the cockpit windows, and would for the next trial, but for this first simulation, they would only pretend that the airfield was fogged in.

"Eight hundred . . . seven hundred. . . ."

The long nose eased up as the Astroliner's computer decided to flatten the glide, then the left wing dropped as she went into another left bank.

"You're right on the track, PA One," the air controller told him. "This is letter-perfect."

Carroll didn't like hearing that, either. The damned machines were always perfect. If it wasn't for probability—the odds of an engine giving up the ghost or a servomotor sticking—humans would be unnecessary.

"Deploying landing gear."

The damned computer talked, too. The voice was mechanical, devised from recordings of a Glynnis Johns-type voice, deep and throaty and definitely feminine. There were sexy overtones.

Carroll sometimes fantasized about the lady behind the voice. It wasn't anything he told his wife about.

"Deploying flaps," the computer said softly into his earphones. Soothing, seducing.

Though the computer was directing the action, Carroll kept a studious eye on the instrument readouts, verifying for himself that green LEDs confirmed the gear down and locked and the flap portion of the flaperons properly sequenced.

Indicated air speed displayed as 280 knots.

Carroll had been in the Navy when carrier landings were still mostly accomplished with eyeballs and nerves, the aviators dancing their aircraft into the glide path based on the position of the carrier's "meatball." And he had missed the wires once and taken an F-14 over the side, managing to eject himself and his backseater just before the Tomcat slammed into the sea. He would be the first to admit that technology had done more to increase the safety and reliability of aircraft traps aboard carriers, yet he still resisted the impulse to rely totally on silicon chips and gold-plated terminals.

The Astroliner aligned herself with the runway and leveled her wings. All by her lonesome.

"You're on glide path and centerline," the air controller told him.

"We're going to get rid of air controllers, too," Matthews said. "They're even more useless than we are."

"Just the numbers, please, Don."

Matthews went back to his chant of altitude and speed changes.

Carroll began to lose his view of the runway as the nose blocked it, and he switched his attention to the image on his center screen.

"Outer markers," Matthews said.

The runway was perfectly lined up on his screen. The white dashes of the centerline were soon distinguishable.

When the tone of the turbofans abruptly abated, he almost slammed the throttles forward, which would induce manual override of the computer.

They touched down slightly harder than he expected, and the airplane bounced high for one long leap before settling.

Even then, the computer didn't give up. With input from airspeed, engine rpm's, and sensors detecting wing lift and wind direction, the computer gently applied reverse thrust, then began to apply pressure to the brakes.

Carroll took command again halfway down the strip. Grudgingly, he had to admit that, had they been in the middle of a raging snowstorm with no view of the airport, the high-tech avionics would have been a lifesaver. The passengers would appreciate the system, even if the pilots did not.

"On the debrief," he said, "we're only giving the machine five points for landings."

"That was quite a bounce. I wasn't going to rate her that high," Don Matthews said.

Deng Xiaoping International Superport
August 22, 4:33 P.M.

On the sixth floor of Terminal One, one floor above the security center, in a large drywalled room that had not yet been subdivided or decorated into a tenant's plan for space, Dan Kerry and his colleagues were entrenched.

At Yichang's request, Superport Administrator Zhao Li had provided the space for them at no charge, and Kerry suspected the largesse was primarily an attempt to keep them out of Yichang's hair. Zhao apologized profusely for his inability to provide them with living quarters, since the terminal's hotel was a year away from completion, but he did have a half-dozen desks, chairs, and telephones installed. In addition, there was a large coffeepot, and Pyotr Zemenek, who was developing a habit for strong coffee, spent a lot of time in front of it.

In front of Zemenek, Ebbing, Bergen, and Yuri Yelchenko—who had arrived two days before, Kerry and Broussard maintained professional correctness. If they ever found themselves alone together, which wasn't often, Kerry was treated to a chill that threatened to overcome the magnetic field surrounding her. He had no plans for penetrating the field, though. In another time and another place, Kerry would have succumbed to his infatuation and increased the intensity of his pursuit of Broussard, no matter how illogical her response. With Charley Whitlock's death, Kerry had rearranged his priorities.

At the moment, the six of them were gathered around Kerry's desk for lack of a conference table. He had shared with them the list of eleven names that Karen Meyer had provided to him, and which he assumed had originated with Israel's Mossad. He couldn't verify the assumption since Meyer had disappeared, apparently returned to Tel Aviv.

All they had known about the listing, from the page heading, was that the names were associated with terrorist organizations, and they had been known to utilize sophisticated technology. One other filter had been applied; the people attached to the names were also known to have rented themselves out to other organizations.

For the past four days, they had been on the telephones pressing friends and acquaintances, and friends of acquaintances, for information about the names. Kerry's left ear felt flattened to his skull; he thought there would be a permanent impression of the phone on the side of his face. He had not only tried to run the names down through people he knew in the Central Intelligence Agency and the Defense Intelligence Agency, but he was staying in contact with Mickey Duff at the Tokyo office, with P.J. Jackson, and with Terry Carroll and Dennis Aikens at Edwards. He also had to maintain the contacts he had made with officials and with businessmen in Japan, Korea, the Philippines, and the subcontinent. There seemed to be minor but irritating glitches everywhere, the closer they got to what P.J. was starting to call D-Day. Kerry preferred to think of the first of October as V-C Day, Victory in China.

Terry Carroll was antsy since he would take the Astroliner and the Astrofreighter through their trials for FAA certification the next day, which was the twenty-second of August on Carroll's side of the International Dateline. China was a day later than California.

All of the other supersonic transports—the Tupolev 2000, the Concorde II, and the AeroSwift—had already been certified.

P.J. Jackson was also worried. "What if we got this far, avoiding the press by postponing certification," he had asked, "and then didn't pass?"

So Kerry was a little worried, too.

Kerry stacked the notes from his phone calls to one side, then took one copy of the listing and printed "Master List" at the top of it. He looked up at the others surrounding his desk. They had all pulled their chairs over, and Zemenek had a mug of coffee in his hand. Broussard, directly opposite him, kept her gaze level and cool. She appeared to have an unlimited wardrobe with her. He hadn't seen her in the same outfit twice, and today, she was wearing a teal dress made of something that looked like silk, but wasn't. All the right curves were accented, and Kerry was forced to suppress his desire. Recalling how she had tried to set him up helped. Tried? He had no idea of where that tactic was at the moment. For all he knew, Henri Dubonnet was talking to his lawyers.

He thought she also resented the evolution of this group; Kerry seemed to have become its chair and its spokesperson. He hadn't sought the distinction, and didn't think of it as one, but it was he who summarized their progress and reported it to Yichang and Sun.

"Okay," he said. "From what I've been hearing, a lot of responses to our inquiries came in today. I got a few myself. Let's start by crossing out some names on Charley's list, if we can."

It had come to be known as Charley's list.

Ernst Bergen said, "Adid. He's been in a jail in Greece for three months."

Kerry drew a line through the name and made a note next to it. "Ten to go."

Yelchenko said, "I have two, the Pole Davidoff and the Iraqi al-Badri. You may eliminate them."

"Why?" Ebbing asked.

Yelchenko obviously didn't want to go into it, but finally said, "Both of them have, at one time or another—how do you say it?—contracted with the old *Komitet Gosudarstvennoy Bezopasnosti,* the Committee for State Security under the USSR, and their locations have been tracked. Davidoff was killed in July during some incident in Lithuania, and al-Badri attempted to . . . betray a group he was working with. He was, ah, terminated almost eighteen months ago."

Kerry saw Broussard's eyes squinch at the revelation. She wasn't very adaptive when it came to realities in the shadow world.

He added notes to his list and crossed out the two names. He thought that, if he could find her, he'd give the revised list to Meyer.

"I've got a couple," Kerry said. "Ramon Enriquez, the Columbian, has been working undercover for the U.S. Drug Enforcement Agency—"

"Your government uses terrorists?" Broussard interrupted.

"I don't make the rules, Jacqueline. It happens."

"If I were you, Jacqueline, I wouldn't ask the same question around Paris," Bergen told her.

"And the Syrian Seef Omar is enrolled under an assumed

name in a doctoral program in electronic technology at the Massachusetts Institute of Technology," he added.

"What!" she blurted.

"Hey, they're watching him."

"He's accused of twelve murders."

"Accused," Kerry said. "They don't have any hard evidence. So they're watching him."

He looked around the desk. "Anyone else?"

There were no further additions, or rather, deletions to be made.

"That leaves us with six. We're getting there. Did we pick up any rumors about any of them?"

"Kurt Wehmeier," Ebbing said, "was seen six months ago in a cafe in Baghdad, in the company of an Arab and an Asian."

"For sure?"

"The source is generally reliable."

"Any names?"

"For the other two? No."

"How about you, Yuri?"

"There may have been sightings of Rahman and Cooksey, but the reports are insubstantial. I am pursuing them."

"Jacqueline?"

"No. I am not very good at this. Stephen will arrive tonight, and he may have additional information."

"Ernst?"

"We have a line on Josef Imel, but I am awaiting further word."

"How about the Red Guard character, Meoshi Yakamata?" Kerry asked.

Nothing yet.

"And the Chinese Ku Chi?"

Again, there had been no contacts.

On a fresh sheet of paper, Kerry made out a new list:

Ibrahim Rahman
Ku Chi
Ned Cooksey
Kurt Wehmeier
Meoshi Yakamata
Josef Imel

"I think we're making some headway," he told them.

"You have shared these names with Yichang Enlai already?" Gerhard Ebbing asked.

"I have. He had a couple of them on one or the other of his lists, and he's got them all on his short list, now."

"And where are we philosophically?" Ebbing asked.

Kerry grinned. "Well, Yichang still believes that the airport is the target of some group—perhaps the People's People—which opposes the capitalistic development of China. And perhaps he's right. In any event, that has to be his concern.

"He's being tolerant of our hypothesis that the SSTs will be the true objective of this group of misfits. The end result is about the same; China Dome is relying on supersonic travel as its keynote. It wouldn't be the same, and might not survive, with conventional air transport."

"Are we belittling the airport by calling it China Dome?" Broussard asked.

"I sent Sun Chen some information about nicknames and advertising. The last time I talked to him, he called it China Dome. And then told me his reference wasn't official, of course."

There was another possible scenario, and while Kerry was sure everyone had considered it, no one here was going to bring it up. Ebbing, Zemenek, Broussard, and, least of all, Kerry wanted to mention that one of their companies could be seeking a simplistic method for outperforming their competition.

He closed the meeting on that happy note of distrust.

Six Kilometers East of Deng Xiaoping International Superport
August 22, 8:21 P.M.

A warm wind disturbed the soil and lifted a slight haze of dust into the air. It gave the evening dusk a reddish tint. Beyond the flat ground to the west, the major domes of the airport were lit, but the smoked glass diminished the power of the lighting, and the domes appeared to be dull gray marbles, half sunk into their playing field.

A slight rise of low hills between Ku Chi and the Superport prevented him from seeing the dual strips of runway lights on the single lit runway, but the brighter cast of the horizon assured him that they were illuminated. Closer to him by about a half-kilometer were two towers on which were mounted lights designating the outer markers of the runway approach.

He had been here the night before, but the airport had suffered from a lack of air traffic, a fact that the German seemed to have overlooked.

Behind him, nestled in a grove of low trees was the twenty-year-old Renault sedan that Hyun Oh had stolen two days before. Oh was a North Korean recruited by Bern, the tallest of the three men who had met Ku at Bias Bay. Oh was very susceptible, Ku thought. He had rapidly assimilated the cause for which the German was providing leadership. Ku would not have embraced it—and Bern—so thoroughly himself had it not been for the German's bottomless supply of money. But then, Ku thought of himself as a pragmatist. If the German had the funds, then he would use the German. As soon as the money ran out, he would kill the German.

It was that simple.

The Korean sat in the front seat of the Renault with the door propped open and his feet resting on the ground. He had removed the lightbulb from the car's courtesy fixture, and in the darkness, Ku placed him solely by the bright red glow of his cigarette.

Ku was himself seated on a flat boulder, as he had been for two hours, surrounded by shoulder-high shrubs with thorny spikes that had punctured the skin of his arms in several places. Flies fluttered about him, attracted by the smell of his blood. Beside him on the rock was one of the crates he had so carefully transported from North Korea, and for which the German had paid. The lid was pried off and the assembled missile launcher rested across the crate. Still tamped into its protective foam rubber in the crate was a second missile, but Ku did not think he would have the time to reload the launch tube and use it.

He was about to light another cigarette for himself when he heard the aircraft. It was distinctively a jet engine, or a pair of them, and after a few moments, he decided it was a single multiengined airplane.

He hoped that it was not too large. The SA-7 Grail was not very effective against large aircraft unless several missiles were launched simultaneously.

A few minutes later, he decided the airplane was approaching Deng Xiaoping International and not just overflying it. Seconds after arriving at that decision, he located the navigation lights. It was low and flying east, parallel to the airport, as it made a left-hand approach. It would circle behind him and come in from the east. The wind came from out of the west and made that determination, as he had expected. As he watched, the airplane's lights disappeared behind the hills to the south.

Ku pursed his lips and gave a low whistle to alert Oh. He heard the car start and settle into an idle.

Picking up the missile launcher, Ku swung around until he was facing east, then lifted the launcher, resting the tube on his shoulder. This was an older model of the SA-7, without the infrared filter to screen out errant heat signals, but with only one target in the sky, he did not anticipate problems.

The sound of the jet engines died away as the airplane changed course, then strengthened as it came around onto a westerly heading.

With his left hand, Ku gripped the frame supporting the launch tube and raised it in the general direction of the approaching aircraft. It was heavy; in addition to the launcher, the missile itself weighed nine kilograms, including the 2.5 kilogram warhead. The sights were open on the weapon, and he could not use them very well in the dark.

Not until he saw the navigation lights again.

Several heartbeats later, the red and green lights appeared, followed suddenly by a bright new glare as the landing lights were switched on.

He placed the lights in the open circle of the lead sight.

Applied pressure on the trigger.

Saw the red light appear, assuring that the missile's heat-seeking head was active.

Since the Grail almost always required a hot exhaust pipe for lock-on, he would follow the airplane as it passed overhead, and as soon as the jet engines provided the heat he needed, indicated by a green light, he would fully compress the trigger. From experience, he knew that the initial boost charge would kick the missile out of the launch tube and far enough away from him to prevent harm to him before the sustaining rocket fired. It would accelerate to over Mach 1.5 in a very short time, and it had a range of slightly over six kilometers. He reminded himself that he had plenty of time.

Ku Chi waited for the airplane and the green light.

He idly wondered who was on board the aircraft, and how many people there might be.

It did not seem to matter much, however.

August 22, 8:22 P.M.

Stephen Dowd had slept for most of the leg of his flight out of New Delhi, awakened when the pilot spoke over the public address system, warning everyone to raise their seat backs and tighten their seat belts.

The Dassault Falcon 20 owned by Aerospatiale-BAC was very definitely a VIP transport. Its luxurious interior was fitted in teak wood and gray leather, and the sumptuous chairs moved in every direction but up or down. Small teak tables could be folded up from the fuselage wall between facing chairs. In the rear was a small galley and a smaller bar, but both were well-stocked. Dowd and his two companions, British and French engineers that Broussard was trying to sneak into China Dome under the authorization for Dowd, had sampled some superb wines during the journey.

Dowd could not help but feel guilty. In his time with the secret service, he had flown a great deal, but never in an airplane dedicated solely to himself. He thought it not only ostentatious, but extremely cost-inefficient. All there was to salve his conscience was the fact that Broussard had ordered it. She had apparently decided rather abruptly that, with the death of Charles Whitlock, Dowd should present himself to Yichang as a replacement.

Thereby ingratiating Aerospatiale-BAC in Chinese minds, he assumed.

Andre Premaris, the Aerospatiale engineer, had refilled their stemmed glasses shortly before the pilot's announcement, and Dowd was still holding a half-full goblet of excellent dark red burgundy. He sipped at it as he peered through the porthole next to his seat. There was not much to see as he was on the right side of the cabin and the domes were on the left. A few water-drenched rice paddies reflected a bit of starlight. It was a moonless night.

He sensed more than saw their loss of altitude.

The outer markers flashed underneath the wings.

When he leaned against the porthole, he could see the runway lights ahead, coming toward them quickly.

Then, an instantaneous white flash in the periphery of his right eye.

The airplane whipped sideways.

Dowd was slammed into his right seat arm. His head banged against the fuselage wall.

Premaris yelled.

Alarms wailed.

The airplane went over on its side.

Dowd saw a flash of earth and light.

And the Falcon dove toward the earth.

THIRTEEN

Deng Xiaoping International Superport
August 22, 8:27 P.M.

Yichang Enlai was at his desk, spooning well-spiced Szechuan beef over a steaming mound of white rice, when the airplane crashed on the runway.

His office was darkened, illuminated only by the security center lights washing through the side window, so that he could survey the dark night outside as he ate his dinner. He ate with his right hand, his left arm resting in his lap. The arm ached fiercely.

Though the insulated walls and triple-paned glass of the dome did not allow him to hear it, he had seen the landing lights of the approaching airplane in his peripheral vision, and he knew from an earlier examination of flight schedules that it would be the Aerospatiale-BAC corporate airplane bringing Stephen Dowd back to China.

The flash of white light near the plane caught his attention.

Then the pair of landing lights, which had been horizontal, went vertical as the plane rolled to the right. Immediately thereafter, the lights dimmed and went out. In the back of his mind, he thought it was because they had lost their electrical source, but the front of his mind told him that something else entirely had happened.

By then, he was on his feet, spilling his dinner over his desktop. He banged his hip on the corner of the desk as he went around it, racing for the wall of triangular windows.

He leaned against the glass, straining to see the east end of the runway, which was two kilometers away. Some flaming object hit the ground as he watched. An engine?

And then, in the light reflected off the concrete from the runway lights, he saw the airplane. It seemed to be skidding sideways through the air, fighting to stay upright.

Though he knew it might be duplicative of orders coming from the control tower, Yichang called through his open office door, "Wu! Emergency landing! Alert the crash trucks!"

The closer it came to the ground, and the closer to the terminal, the easier the airplane was to see. It was still flying like a crab, almost sideways with the right wing rising and falling. From his vantage point, Yichang could not see any damage to the aircraft, but his eyes and his intellect told him it was in mortal danger.

It touched down nearly in front of the terminal, a half-kilometer away. Canted to the right from its line of flight, the wheels skimmed the concrete for a second, then the entire landing gear collapsed and it smashed to its belly. A tremendous rush of sparks spewed from beneath the fuselage.

The left wing went down, and the airplane began spinning counterclockwise on the pavement. Smoke, then flames, boiled from the left engine. Yichang did not see a right engine.

The airplane ground to a stop off the left side of the runway, nearly two kilometers away. Its movement had barely ceased when the first of the yellow crash trucks raced away from Terminal Six, where one of the fire departments was maintained.

Yichang spun around and charged into the security center. Wu Yhat had just hung up his telephone.

"Get the helicopters airborne. I want a search of the grounds north of the airport."

The Superport's security unit included two helicopters, and though the detachment was not yet designated as operational, for the past two weeks, Yichang had ordered the aircrews to be available.

"It will take some time," Wu said.

"Do it."

Grabbing a portable radio from the recharging station near the door, Yichang stormed out of the center and took an elevator to ground level. He ran down the corridor to the outer doors and found his gray Honda just outside.

By the time he reached the crash site, the blue strobe lights mounted above his front and rear bumpers flashing his authority, four crash trucks were on the scene, and the fire had been dampened by foam.

He slid the car to a stop in the dirt, out of the way of the firemen, and climbed out. A group of men in yellow protective gear was gathered thirty meters away, and he started toward them.

An ambulance siren wailed, the moan rising quickly in volume as it approached at high speed.

The airplane was a mess, but he saw that the cabin door was open.

There were two figures stretched out on the ground at the feet of the people milling about. As he neared them, one dark figure broke away to meet him.

In the confusing flash of multicolored lights, it took a

moment for Yichang to recognize him. He looked as if he had been crawling in the dirt.

"Hello, Mr. Dowd."

"Mr. Yichang."

Dowd stopped in front of him, shaking his head, and Yichang asked, "Are you all right?"

"I'm a bit shaken up, a few bruises. My faith in flight is disturbed."

"Do you have any idea what happened?"

"Indeed I do. It was a missile."

"That is what I feared. Who are the injured? The pilots?"

"The pilots are all right. They're brave men, got us on the ground. There's a Brit engineer; he's dead. The Frenchman is badly hurt, I'm afraid."

Yichang sighed. "There was to be only three of you on the flight, including the pilots."

"Is that right? I don't know about that, Mr. Yichang."

He would take it up with Broussard.

The ambulance squealed to a stop, and the medics spilled out of it. Yichang had been seeing far too many white-coated employees of Deng Xiaoping International in the last weeks.

He turned and looked past the wreckage of the Falcon toward the east. Beyond the runway lights, it was dark as a tomb.

Twelve minutes more elapsed before the first of the helicopters took off from its place near Hangar One.

Hong Kong
August 23, 9:35 A.M.

The view from the thirteen-hundred-foot-high peak was one of the most spectacular in the world. Looking down over the tracks that guided the two funicular cable cars to the peak, one could see the left and right wings of the government buildings, the Governor's Residence, and beyond, the Hong Kong Hilton. They were all pristinely white against the fresh and lush green of the grass and trees. All of the buildings of the Central District were spread in a panorama of industry and commerce, backed by the silver blue of the bay and harbor. On the far side of the bay, Kowloon rested in a light haze that obscured detail. And beyond Kowloon, the mountains in the New Territories were blue-gray in the morning, backed up by purple sky. Eight of the peaks in the New Territories, in addition to a young emperor, gave Kowloon its name, which means "Nine Dragons."

Looking the other way, to the south from the observation point, the view was of the tree and shrub-shaded residential area of Aberdeen along the southern coast, and to the southwest, the far reaches of Deep Water Bay and Repulse Bay were visible. There was a great deal of beauty packed into the twenty-nine square miles of Hong Kong Island.

Kurt Wehmeier did not care for, nor about, the view. He would not bother, as the tourists around him did, putting coins into the telescopes for a more detailed examination of the island. He leaned against a low stone wall, pretended interest in the southern half of the island, and smoked a cigarette while he waited.

When he heard the next cable car arrive and squeak into its dock at the station, he turned around and pressed his hips against the wall. The Chinese and the North Korean, Ku and Oh, descended from the tram.

There were only the two of them.

Wehmeier cursed under his breath, then turned and

walked ten meters to where a vacant bench was located. He sat on it, and eventually, Oh and Ku joined him.

"Where is Angelo?" he asked.

Angelo Malgretto, an Italian with former ties to the Red Brigade, had a mercurial temper and an impetuous personality. He could as well have been in a barroom fight or changed his mind and gone back to Milan; nothing would surprise Wehmeier.

"He went to find another car for us, and he has not yet returned," Hyun Oh said.

"And Saldam?"

After a long moment, Ku said, "He is ill."

"The bloody damned fool," Wehmeier said. "If he jeopardizes any of us, kill him."

Ibn Saldam, like a few others of the Islamic faith that Wehmeier knew, revealed a fatal streak when he strayed far from the regions where Allah might be watching over him. He completely abandoned the teachings of the Koran and indulged a latent appetite for liquor and drugs.

Neither of the Asians responded to Wehmeier's comment.

"What is it, this time?"

"Heroin, I think," Oh said.

"Kill him."

Oh simply nodded.

"Tell me about last night."

Ku grinned broadly. "It was a business jet of some kind; I did not get a sufficient look at it in the dark to tell what kind it was."

"But you hit it?"

"Very much so. It crashed on the runway and burned."

"Excellent," Wehmeier said. "There will be a bonus."

Ku shrugged. He and Oh were less driven by the money than by the desire to have the airport fail to open and to kill as many as possible in achieving that end. Wehmeier wished that he had more like them. Malgretto professed an ideology that he did not often live; he needed his money for wining and dining as many women as he could. His goal was to fuck himself to death.

Mohammed Dakar, in California, was not an idealist at all, but he would perform his tasks out of fear for his family and for the money. He wanted the toys with which Americans played.

Jeremy Smith, an Englishman whose real name Wehmeier did not know, was the other member of his team, but the others did not know of his existence, and never would. Wehmeier kept Smith out of sight, in a rented house in Aberdeen. Smith had aristocratic tastes, and Wehmeier indulged them because Smith also had superb talents.

"What of James Lee?" Oh asked.

"I assume the papers are correct. He is dead."

"And the last bomb did not explode?"

"I have no way of knowing," Wehmeier said.

"Lee could have given away our names, Mr. Bern," Ku said.

"I think not."

"The newspaper said only that he died during his capture. It did not say when he died."

"You must read something other than *The People's Daily,* Ku. The Western papers all reported that Lee electrocuted himself. To protect us."

"Ah."

"And what is next?" Oh asked.

"We will step up the attacks. You must position yourselves and wait for another airplane to arrive."

"They had helicopters, two of them. We were able to

elude them this time, but I suspect that they will be quicker next time."

Wehmeier considered the development. He had not known about the helicopters.

"Do this," he said. "Take two, no, three launchers with you. After you have shot down the airplane, wait before running. When the helicopters arrive, shoot them down."

"Will they not shoot back?"

"I suspect these are not military helicopters. They will belong to the airport security department and will not be armed."

"There are military fighter aircraft at the airport."

"Yes," Wehmeier said, as if he had known about them. "But not helicopters. In fact, your best target would be one of the fighters."

Oh bobbed his head affirmatively. "I like it."

"Good."

Wehmeier gave them each an envelope packed with cash, then leaned against the back of the bench as they wandered away, waiting for the next cable car to descend.

He waited forty minutes, absorbing the sun, then took a cable car to the foot of the mountain. Precisely at eleven o'clock, he was at the correct public telephone in the lobby of the Hong Kong Hilton when the phone rang.

"Yes?" he said.

"Doctor?"

"Disease," he replied to the code.

"Report."

Wehmeier briefly provided the details of the airplane that was shot down and what he knew of James Lee's debacle.

"This is quite inadequate. You will see that something more newsworthy happens."

"I will see to it," Wehmeier said, but he was speaking to a dial tone.

He replaced the receiver and turned to cross the lobby. He assumed that, with the loss of James Lee, he had also lost use of the airport's communication system. But he also thought that Jeremy Smith would have some more brilliant ideas.

Wehmeier went out into the bright sun and aimed himself at the corner of the block, where he would wait for a bus.

Edwards Air Force Base
August 22, 4:15 P.M.

P.J. Jackson was as nervous as a brand-new ensign on his first watch as JOD, Junior Officer of the Deck. In a Force Seven gale.

He had tried sitting in the laboratory, listening to the radio reports, but the reporting from the aircraft was almost nil, and the frantic pacing of Dennis Aikens drove him out. So he sat in his Lincoln Town Car which was parked outside the lab. With all the doors open, a semblance of a breeze moved the hot air through the car. It didn't cool him, but at least, it moved.

He had a Thermos of lemonade with him, and he had been working at it steadily.

The cellular phone buzzed, and he picked it up.

"Jackson."

"P.J., what's happening?" Stephenson asked.

"I wish to hell I knew, Ken."

"They aren't done yet?"

The Federal Aviation Administration team had started at six in the morning. Jackson had been on hand to meet them, but aside from fifteen minutes over coffee and doughnuts, he hadn't seen much of them all day.

Through the windshield, he could see the Astroliner sitting on the tarmac in front of the hangar. A few technicians worked around it.

"It doesn't look like they're done," Jackson said. "They came back around two o'clock, left the Astroliner, and took off in the Astrofreighter. I haven't seen them since."

"No hints at all?"

"Carroll wasn't smiling."

"Shit. What if they find something wrong?"

"If they do, it's got to be something damned minor, Ken. Maybe a couple days' delay."

Jackson was trying his best to be optimistic.

"I just talked to Senator Green," Stephenson said.

"And?"

"He's got all of his committee in line."

"My brother help at all?"

"I think he did, yes. Only thing is, P.J., they're not buying our version of the bill."

"What!"

"Essentially, it's in the same form, but they want to make it provisional. A year's trial would be approved, just to see whether or not the good people living next to the runways at L.A. and San Francisco raise a lot of hell."

"Damn it!"

"Can we live with it?" Stephenson asked.

"I don't know that we have a choice. Yeah, let's take what we can get."

"I'll call Green back, then. He'll get it introduced, through committee, and onto the floor the first thing in the next session."

Jackson tapped the keypad to shut off the phone and

looked up at the sky. The damned sun wouldn't go down for hours. He hoped he got to see his airplane again before it got dark.

Kowloon
August 23, 2:28 P.M.

"Mademoiselle, I am going to ask you to leave the country," Yichang Enlai told her.

"But, whatever for?" Broussard asked. She was seated across his desk from him in his office in the security center. She smiled at him and held his eyes with her own, but inside, she quivered. If she were ejected from China, losing whatever gains she had made on the contract, Henri would disown her.

"After interviewing Monsieur Premaris, I have determined that you ordered he and his British counterpart, David Volstead, to enter China without obtaining the proper permissions."

She was already devastated by the death of Volstead and the injuries—fractured leg and hip—to Premaris. Henri Dubonnet had lamented those casualties, as well as that of his personal Falcon 20. It was all she could do to face Yichang.

"Director Yichang, I am guilty. I apologize deeply for overlooking the formalities."

"Overlooking, mademoiselle?"

"Flaunting, then," she admitted.

"What did you hope to gain?"

"Presence."

Yichang sighed visibly. She could tell that his arm hurt him. He was wearing a short-sleeved khaki shirt, and the white bandage wrapped around his forearm appeared especially prominent. He held it gingerly, and he placed it flat on the desk with care.

He said, "Mademoiselle Broussard, I wish you would understand that you do not have to impress me, nor most of the people resident at Deng Xiaoping International. I will not select an airplane; that will be accomplished in Beijing. My single objective is to protect the people and the facility, following the law as I do so. I cannot do that when you insist upon circumventing it."

"It will absolutely never happen again," she said.

"Your presence here is allowed simply as yet another course of action in overcoming our current problem," the director told her. "If you cannot adhere to what, I admit, is a tenuous agreement, I will be forced to take action."

"You will have no more trouble from me, Director."

"That is your promise?"

"It is."

"Very well. We will put this behind us."

Broussard's legs had been shaky when she left the security center, and she bypassed the elevators after crossing the bridge to the dome's core. She found a lounge seat nestled under potted palm trees in the atrium and lowered herself into it. Looking up, she could see, seven stories above her, the top of the dome. The smoked glass filtered the strong sun and bathed the core in soft light.

She was making mistakes.

And they would be fatal mistakes, not only for her, but also for Henri Dubonnet and Aerospatiale-BAC.

She had completely misjudged Daniel Kerry. Her lapse of judgment, guided by her glands, had been horrendous. In her row of mistakes, it was the first domino to fall. She could not understand how she could be so attracted to him physically and yet so disenchanted with him personally. They were so perfectly suited to each other on an intimate level, and yet on any other level, she did not see him and herself as the perfect couple. She had nearly panicked, back in California, when she thought she might have actually fallen in love with him. And after that first domino tumbled, she had made the mistake of trying to manipulate a man who, she should have seen, was not to be manipulated.

Then, to have him turn away from her so abruptly had hurt her deeply. In most of her waking moments, which were many since she was not sleeping well, Dan Kerry was the object of her attention. She thought about him constantly.

It was ridiculous.

He was not an obsession, could not be one; she had never been obsessed with anyone in her life.

Her focus was affected. She was ignoring telephone calls and not responding to messages. She tried her best to immerse herself in her work.

And yet, her thoughts kept turning to him, seeking a touch of the hand, one of the soft words he was capable of uttering.

Damn him! He has turned my own tactics back on me.

She was certain he was acting deliberately. Her mistake with Dan Kerry was being compounded, and it would not disappear.

And this last error had led to the death of David Volstead. She felt directly responsible.

She would never correct them, and she knew her only option was to refocus. Her job must become her first priority. That was selling the Concorde II to the Chinese.

Her second priority was assisting the group on the floor above in overcoming the obstacles to any of them selling their airplanes. China Dome must be safe enough for the demonstration flights on October 1.

Broussard stood up, feeling herself invigorated with new resolve. She would ignore her history with Dan Kerry—never bring up the sexual blackmail she had attempted, though never mentioned to Henri—and concentrate on the future, which could be very bright.

She strode back to the elevators with new confidence and new determination a part of her soul.

Deng Xiaoping International Superport
August 23, 3:50 P.M.

As one of his first acts upon returning to the Orient, Stephen Dowd had put a hand-lettered sign on the door to their spartan office, calling it, "The Provisional Offices Of The Provisional Group."

Superport Administrator Zhao Li had loaned them another desk and one of his secretaries, a pretty little woman with a winning smile and a magical way of cutting through red tape on the telephone. Since their desks were randomly placed around the room, without barriers between them, Sung Min didn't bother with an intercom they didn't have, anyway.

And besides, he wasn't in the provisional office.

She came to the doorway and called out, "Mr. Kerry! Line Six!"

Kerry was standing by the atrium of the central core, watching meticulous gardeners planting exotic greenery in red-and-black-tiled planters. He walked back and entered the office.

"Thank you, Miss Sung."

She smiled and answered another line.

Stephen Dowd and Yuri Yelchenko had gone somewhere, but the rest of the group was present, most of them on their phones. Broussard's eyes followed him as he crossed to his desk, which was next to hers. He thought she was talking to Dubonnet.

Punching the button, Kerry picked up.

"We got it, Dan!"

"P.J.? Got what?"

"The certification, damn it! Both planes."

"Well, hot damn! Congratulations, P.J."

"To all of us, brother. Jesus! What a relief! Shit, this has been the longest day of my life."

"They wring them out pretty good, did they?"

"Terry says they did. Have you been nervous?"

"Tell you the truth, P.J., I forgot all about it."

"What!"

"You forget you're a day earlier than I am. I thought it was yesterday, and no one had bothered to call me."

Kerry had worried about the certification, but he liked to flummox Jackson now and then.

"You jerk!" Jackson said.

"Are we getting the word out?"

"Damn betcha. I've had interviews with *Aviation Week* and *The New York Times* already."

"So now the world knows about the Astrofreighter?"

"Couldn't very well hold it back, Dan. Most of the magazines have called, and we'll set up a photo shoot for them next week sometime."

Kerry leaned back in his chair and put his feet on the desktop. He saw that Broussard was watching him, and he put his hand over the mouthpiece.

"We got our certifications, Jacqueline."

"Certifications?"

"Yep, both aircraft."

"You have *two* SSTs?"

"Right. Didn't you know?"

She hadn't been smiling, but her mouth turned down even more, and she spun her back to him in the swivel chair and made her report to her boss.

He thought she was still trying to listen in, so he uncovered the phone and spoke loud enough for her to hear, as if he had a bad connection.

"P.J., I've got a couple items we need to go over."

"Shoot, Dan."

"First, the Chinese want to put their aviation examiners on the airplanes for the opening day flight into China Dome."

"Everybody's planes?"

"Right, except they don't yet know we've got two."

"How many people?"

"Four examiners per plane."

"Damn it. I've filled every seat for this flight."

"So kick four people off."

"I can't do that, Dan. These are influential people."

"Move Madonna to the freighter."

"Madonna's not invited, to begin with."

"Good choice. But if she were, I'd put her on the other plane."

"No one can see out of the Astrofreighter."

"Well, look, P.J., I'll be staying here, so that frees up one seat."

"I can move Aikens to the freighter," Jackson said.

"Good. I'll let you wrestle with the last two. Next point, I want those investigators we hired to do a little more work."

"The outfit that did the background checks on the opposition?"

"Right. Tell them to take another look at all of the principals at Aerospatiale-BAC, BBK, and Tupolev. Say for about the last year. I want to know if there's been any contact with people of a suspicious nature."

"Jesus Christ, Dan!"

"It's the next step."

"Ah, hell. This is going to cost a bundle."

"Will you do it?"

"I'll do it," Jackson said.

Kerry had his head tilted back, studying the ceiling, but Broussard was visible in his peripheral vision, and he was sure she was taking in his half of the conversation.

"Then, P.J., this one's just a little sensitive. You know Mademoiselle Broussard?"

"Of course I know her. Know about her."

Broussard's chair spun around until she was facing him, still clutching her telephone to her ear. "Hold on, Henri," she said into the phone.

"Well, it seems that she and I, ah. . . ."

Broussard shook her head at him.

"You son of a bitch!" Jackson said. "You did."

"The thing is, P.J., you might expect a phone call from Dubonnet's—"

Broussard's heavy hair was flying in all directions as she shook her head in violent negation. "Dan!"

"She's there?" Jackson asked.

Kerry put his hand over the mouthpiece again.

"Don't, Dan," she said. "Please."

"Cancel the last item, P.J."

"What the hell's going on?"

"I might tell you about it, sometime. Tell Dennis and Terry congrats, for me, will you?"

Kerry hung up.

Broussard said, "You are a bastard, aren't you?"

"Call your bluff, Jacqueline?"

She went back to the phone, told Dubonnet she would call him later, then said, "Let us go somewhere to talk."

"By all means."

Kerry dropped his feet to the floor and stood up. He gestured toward the door, and let her lead him through it.

They didn't get very far.

Zhao Li approached them, coming from the elevator stack, accompanied by two men in uniform. Kerry read the insignia on their uniforms as that of a general and a major. The major was wearing wings over his left breast pocket.

"Mr. Kerry, Mademoiselle Broussard, I should like to introduce General Chou Sen and Major Hua Peng of the air force."

They shook hands all around, and Kerry was aware of Chou's reluctant grasp. The general was a man not enamored of Americans, he decided. Or of Frenchwomen, for that matter, judging by the lightning speed with which he grasped and released Broussard's hand. His pinched face tried to remain neutral, but wasn't very successful.

Major Hua Peng was less reluctant. Of medium height, he was built with chunks of solid flesh. His chest was broad, and his arms and hands were substantial. His hair was trimmed so short that he appeared almost bald, but he had an easy smile, and he used it on Broussard. When he looked into Kerry's eyes, he probably saw the same eyes looking back at him. At least, Kerry recognized the quick, clear lenses of a fighter pilot.

"We have met once before," Hua said.

"We have?" Kerry asked him.

"When you were flying the Citation."

"Yes, that's right. I was being particularly inattentive that day."

"I can see how you might have been distracted," Hua smiled.

They went back into the office, with the general showing some distaste as he read Stephen Dowd's sign. Zhao introduced the air force officers to the rest of the group.

The general turned to Kerry and said, "Chairman Sun has explained to me the task you have taken on. I wonder if you would be so good as to brief Major Hua and myself relative to what you have learned."

Kerry supposed, now that surface-to-air missiles had become part of the equation, the Chinese military felt obliged to intervene.

"Of course, General. Why don't you and Major Hua take those chairs?" He gestured to the desk chairs at his and Broussard's desks. "Mademoiselle Broussard and I have a previous appointment, but I'm sure Herr Ebbing can give you the complete rundown. If you'll excuse us?"

Ebbing gave him a dirty look.

Broussard spun on her three-inch heel and headed for the door.

Kerry smiled at everyone, then followed her, wondering if his private war was about to escalate.

FOURTEEN

Kowloon
September 2, 6:00 A.M.

The treaty formulated by Kerry and Broussard even made allowances for breakfast, and they had been meeting in the President Hotel's coffee shop, usually in the company of the others, daily. The group had evolved somewhat strangely, as groups go, Kerry thought. Each of the members spent about half their time on a long-distance telephone line, or microwave link, taking care of the things for which they had been hired. The rest of the time was spent tracing down their individual leads, usually by phone, and sharing their progress with each other. The task had brought them all closer together, despite the divisions of competition and suspicion.

Kerry reached the coffee shop first this morning and ordered his standard fare, thinking about Charley Whitlock as he did so. Charley's funeral had been two days before, and he was sorry he had missed it. He had spent some time on the phone with Angela. This morning, he also thought about what he was calling the Deng Xiaoping Accord.

They had left Gerhard Ebbing trying to deliver an extemporaneous briefing for the Chinese air force officers and crossed the bridge to the dome core. Broussard sat on a couch next to a palm tree, and Kerry sat down next to her.

"I do not wish to continue this . . . this antagonism," she said.

Kerry could swear he wasn't the original source of antagonism, but he didn't belabor it. "Fine by me, Jacqueline."

"I must tell you that I did not mention to Henri anything of the, of the. . . ."

"I didn't think that you had."

"But, you were about to. . . ."

"End the stalemate."

They were each sitting sideways on the couch, facing each other, and Kerry saw the fire come up in her eyes for a moment, before she suppressed it. She was awfully sensitive to nuance, and her moods could shift on a dime.

When he tried to extend that observation to others, though, he had some difficulty. From what he had seen, her attitude with Zemenek, Ebbing, Sun, Yichang, anyone, was more or less constant. Only with Kerry did she blow hot and cold.

Did that tell him anything?

"There is something I don't understand about you, Jacqueline."

"And what is that?"

"Why you think you have to go through some kind of subterfuge with men, or maybe it's just me. I don't know."

She started to bristle, but he went on, "I guess I'm guilty of some of that, too, but I view you as a strong and intelligent woman who should not have to resort to manipulation."

"Intelligent."

"You're smart, but damn it, I'm just as smart. Not more,

not less. Let's come at each other head-on from now on, huh?"

"But there is something between us, Dan, that we cannot ignore."

"We'll set it aside until October fifth, and then we'll talk about it."

"On October fifth?"

"Right. That's the day you buy me the most expensive dinner I can find, if Aerospatiale-BAC comes up a winner. If any of the rest of us win, I buy you the same dinner."

She stared into his eyes for a long moment, then apparently decided she could live with whatever was there. "Very well."

"Shake on it?"

He held out his hand, and when she took it, the sparks still flew.

For him, at least.

Ebbing was the next to arrive for breakfast, and broke up Kerry's vision of history. They talked about the sports headlines—the Broncos were playing the Redskins—and Ebbing, who had seen an NFL exhibition game in Berlin, followed American football, favoring the Washington team. Because of his time in Colorado Springs, Kerry had become a Broncos fan. They settled on a ten-dollar bet, with no point spread.

When Broussard appeared in the coffee shop, radiant as usual, she took the chair next to Kerry and ordered a fruit plate from the waitress.

"I have been thinking," she said.

"About what?"

"The airplanes do not fly at night."

Kerry thought about her statement for a full minute before he figured out where she was going. Sometimes, it took some time to deduce just what steps had been left out of her declarations. He had to narrow it down to China Dome, then the aircraft in residence at the airport.

"You're right," he said. "They don't."

Ebbing said he thought they were both crazy.

Deng Xiaoping International Superport
September 2, 8:25 A.M.

Gerhard Ebbing called Matthew Kraft every other day to report on progress, of which there was very little, relative to the People's People and their still vague aims. In return, Kraft kept him apprised of the status of the AeroSwift, about which Kraft worried. Except for a few small problems, the airliner was responding superbly to her flight trials. Suspicious, Ebbing feared that Kraft was keeping important information from him, but knew that, as one of the fathers of the aircraft, he was probably just demonstrating a parental paranoia.

"Have you talked to Sun?" Kraft asked.

"Not directly, no. Kerry summarizes our reports for the Chairman."

"I was wondering how he is bearing up under the media pressure."

"It is a bit strange here, Matthew. In the morning, I read one or the other of the major world newspapers over breakfast in the Kowloon hotel, and I see that the People's People articles have not been pushed very far back from the first page. But, after we cross the border and come to the airport, there is **very little of world news.** *The People's Daily* is the only paper I see around here."

"That will change," Kraft said, "when they finally open the place up to the world. They cannot very well stop travellers from bringing in newspapers."

"Yes. I wonder if they understand that? In any event, I do not know what Sun Chen reads, or how he is reacting to the stories. I would suspect that he, and others in the governmental hierarchy, have access to any of the media they want. Kerry, however, has not mentioned whether or not Sun is displeased."

"See what you can find out, will you?"

"Certainly, Matthew," Ebbing said, wondering why it was important. "Did al-Qatar get his airplane ride?"

"He did. I talked to some people, and we got him a waiver. And I tell you, Gerhard, he was truly impressed."

"That is good."

"Yes, it is. He will reassure his fellow investors, and that is good for us," Kraft said before hanging up.

Hakim al-Qatar was Director of the Arab Investment Group, Ltd. He carried a great deal of influence with the board of BBK Enterprises since AIG owned forty-five percent of the stock in the aviation company.

Ebbing had not thought that, ever in his life, he would be required to impress Middle Eastern sultans and sheiks and whatever else they were. It was but another example of how the world was changing so swiftly around him, and not taking him with it.

Now that the AeroSwift had obtained her airworthiness certificate and was soon to have her final flight trials completed, Ebbing found himself losing some of his earnest interest in the project. He would do whatever it was possible for him to do to see that BBK received the contract, but his intent in that was to see the rewards spread across eastern Germany.

For himself, he was thinking more and more of that front porch on his Frissian Island home. He had told Ingrid as much in his last telephone call to her, and he thought that she was as pleased as he with the image.

East of Deng Xiaoping International Superport
September 2, 11:17 A.M.

The 1st Squadron of the 479th Tactical Air Wing was the responsibility of Major Hua Peng, and he took his role as a leader quite soberly. He demanded discipline, and he demanded respect, and he gave respect and just reward to his subordinates in return.

The squadron was currently composed of seven pilots, one of whom served as his executive officer and did not often fly, and fifty-one support personnel, ranging from aircraft mechanics to cooks. Hua was proud of the ability of every pilot and of every cook.

The ground personnel and their equipment had been transported to Deng Xiaoping International Superport by seven trucks, and though they were housed in relative comfort in Hangar Two, Hua treated the deployment as an exercise in forward base staging.

The squadron's mission, assigned by General Chou, was simply to demonstrate a presence. They were to be visible, the grounded aircraft clearly armed and in evidence, and the airborne fighters remaining in close proximity to the airport. In supporting that mission, Hua had set up a schedule of training flights, two aircraft at a time, one flight a day per pair. He varied the routes, but generally each flight was to patrol the border between the People's Republic and the Hong Kong Dependency as well as the eastern coast in several passes. He limited the ceiling to 4,000 meters so that the fighters were heard, in addition to being seen. Occasionally, he ordered dummy bombs mounted on the ordnance pylons, and the pilots trained in attack mode by delivering their bomb loads of white powder against an old target barge anchored off the coast. The 1st Squadron, which had a normal mission in air defense, did not often have the opportunity to serve in the attack role, and Hua took advantage of the temporary duty to improve their skills in that regard.

The Shenyang F-12, a variant of the MiG-23 designed by the OKB (Design Bureau) named for A. I. Mikoyan and M. I. Gurevich and manufactured by the Chinese, was a multirole fighter and attack aircraft. Though the original design had first flown in 1966 and entered service in 1970, Hua thought it still a capable airplane. The high-winged, single-engined (Chengdu Wopen afterburning turbojet) fighter could achieve Mach 1.1 (1,352 kilometers per hour) flying clean at sea level and Mach 2.3 (2,443 kilometers per hour) at eleven kilometers of altitude. Outfitted in its defense role, the F-12 mounted a 23-millimeter cannon with two hundred rounds in a centerline pod along with two medium-range and two long-range air-to-air missiles. When Hua ordered the aircraft configured for attack, they carried AA-2 Atoll close-range air-to-air missiles for self-defense, AS-8 air-to-surface missiles, and six-hundred-kilo practice bombs. The combat range was 900 kilometers, but in the present assignment, fuel loads were not a concern.

Hua was fond of the airplane, and though he knew it would have performance shortcomings when matched against the American F-15 Eagle or F-14 Tomcat, he did not believe that that particular contest would come to pass. And while he did not have access to the musings of the general staff, the rumor mill prevalent in any military organization suggested that the general staff was more concerned with the northeastern and southern borders than with the United States or with the scattered and disrupted republics of the Commonwealth of Independent States. The fact—which he knew for certain—that air defense units had been bolstered along the borders with Vietnam and North Korea hinted at the government's concern that China's move toward a cozier relationship with the West may have disenchanted those two sister communist states.

Hua Peng no longer knew who the enemy was, but he intended to be prepared, and to have his squadron prepared, whenever the leadership identified the enemy for him.

He and his wingman, Captain Jiang Guofeng, had not seen any enemy at all during their flight. Off the coast, when they made their practice bomb runs against the barge, Hua had noted several airliners on his search radar, all of them headed to, or away from, Kai Tak Airport. When he deflected his antenna and searched the surface of the sea, he had been rewarded with uncountable radar returns from the hundreds of commercial and fishing vessels that peppered the coastal shipping lanes. As was typical in an examination of shipping, he looked primarily for the dim returns of wooden junks which were underway without their required radar reflectors. Whenever such a craft was encountered, the naval defenses were to be alerted since a junk avoiding radar contact was quite often engaged in illegal trafficking, quite often of cigarettes or liquor.

Hua and Jiang had not even had their morning enlivened by the sighting of a contraband-carrying vessel, and they were now nearing the new airport.

A military air controller had been installed in the airport's control tower, and it was with that controller that Hua made contact, utilizing a frequency set aside for the purpose.

"Deng Xiaoping Air Control, this is Blue Dragon One."

"Blue Dragon, Deng Xiaoping. Identify with all modes and codes."

The F-12's Identify Friend or Foe transponder was already transmitting the coded signal which identified the aircraft on other radars as a Chinese air force airplane. Using the thumbwheel, Hua selected the code which also provided his altitude, currently 3,300 meters AGL.

"Blue Dragon, I have you."

"Deng Xiaoping Air, Blue Dragon, with a flight of two, requests landing clearance."

"Blue Dragon, maintain your current altitude and make one three-hundred-and-sixty degree orbit. There is an Ilyushin Il-18 currently on approach."

"Blue Dragon copies, Deng Xiaoping."

On his secondary radio, tuned to the squadron frequency, he asked Jiang if he had heard the transmission.

"Affirmative, One."

Hua knew that the Ilyushin, a four-engined turboprop airliner, belonged to the aviation bureau of the Ministry of Transportation and was engaged in calibrating and testing the instrument landing system and air control radars for the airport. The airplane had been making takeoffs and landings dozens of times a day for the past five days, moving from one runway to another. He assumed the pilot would soon go berserk.

Four minutes later, Hua's flight was given permission to land on Runway 27 Left, still the only operational runway for most aircraft. In the next week, Runway 27 Center and 27 Right were to be opened for testing, as well as the four north-south runways in the commercial sector known, in the southerly direction, as Commercial 18 Left, Commercial 18 Left Center, Commercial 18 Right Center, and Commercial 18 Right. As soon as the latter were declared operational, the military flights would move to 18 Right Center.

The landing, as a pair, went smoothly, and Hua switched to ground control and was directed by a controller in Control Tower Four onto a taxiway that took them past Terminal Six and south down a taxiway two kilometers long connecting the main airport section with the commercial section. Small signs close to the ground identified parking areas and taxiways. The red, amber, and green lenses of traffic signals, also low to the ground, were utilized to direct taxiing airplanes, also.

At Taxiway 17, which crossed the four north-south runways of the commercial section on a diagonal, he was ordered into a right turn. Even though the runways were not yet used, and the traffic signals was green, Hua slowed and carefully scanned the skies to the right and left before crossing each runway. He saw that one of the security helicopters was aloft, patrolling the western airport boundary.

On the far side of the runways, they paused while two crewmen moved under the wings and safed the live ordnance with pins on yellow streamers. When the technicians signalled him, he continued taxiing, increasing speed to forty kilometers per hour as the two fighters bypassed Hangar One, then slowed and pulled off onto the tarmac in front of Hangar Two. They parked in line with the other four F-12s and shut down the turbojets.

Hua's crew chief was ready with the ladder, and he placed it against the fuselage and climbed up as Hua raised his canopy. The chief inserted the safety pins in the ejection seat, then helped him disengage his communications, oxygen, and pressure suit fittings. Hua unclipped his oxygen mask, removed his helmet and handed it to the chief, then stood up, edged his way over the cockpit coaming, and followed the man down the ladder.

He reached the roughened, antiskid surface of the concrete, which appeared far too clean and whitewashed for a real airfield, and looked around. Twenty meters away, standing near the pedestrian door to the hangar, was the American who had been introduced to him as Daniel Kerry.

Hua retrieved his helmet from the crew chief, then began to walk toward the hangar.

Kerry came out to meet him.

"Good morning, Major Hua."

"Good morning, Mr. Kerry. Is there something I can do for you?"

Kerry smiled, perhaps disarmingly, and said, "I'm taking my lunch break, Major, and I thought I'd come over and peek at your airplanes."

Hua had been told nothing about Kerry, except that he was an executive of Pacific Aerospace Incorporated and was assisting the airport's security forces with the identification of terrorists. At the moment of their meeting, however, Hua had sensed a military bearing in the man. He remembered wondering at the time if Kerry was an aviator. He did not think the man was spying on the airplanes, and if he was, he would learn nothing that had not been long reported in aviation magazines.

"Come, I will show them to you."

Despite the age of the fighters, Hua had nothing for which he was embarrassed. His ground crews maintained the aircraft well. The paint was fresh, the insignia crisp, and very few leaks dripped hydraulic fluid onto the ground.

The two of them spent twenty minutes on the tour, and

Kerry's questions were informed. He did not ask anything that might have required an answer that could have been deemed as classified information.

As they walked back toward the hangar, Hua said, "I think you are a pilot, Mr. Kerry."

"I fly a little," he said.

"In your military? Are you a reservist?"

"No reserve duty, Major, but I did fly for the Air Force for a while. In F-4s, mainly."

"Ah, the Phantom."

"It was a good airplane."

Hua thought Kerry would be the right age for Vietnam, but he did not ask. Instead, he said, "Would you join me for lunch?"

"I'd be happy to do that."

Hua led the way through the door into the hangar. This quarter of the domed facility was being utilized for aircraft maintenance, and the unit's workbenches and tools had been lined up against one wall. Next to the far wall were parked several of the trucks and vehicles assigned to the squadron. They crossed the huge space and passed through a door into the next quarter. Here, the space had been divided by canvas partitions into living, recreational, and office spaces. Immediately to the right was the dining area, backed up by portable kitchen facilities.

The long tables were already crowded with members of the squadron, and Hua skirted them to reach the steam tables.

"Today, Mr. Kerry, we are having steamed rice with shrimp. The sweet-and-sour sauce is a concoction of the squadron's cook, but I assure you that it ranks with that of any of the country's best restaurants."

"The aroma alone has increased my appetite, Major."

In *putonghua,* Hua passed the comment on to the cook,

who only spoke Chinese, and Kerry was rewarded with a plate containing a double ration of rice and large, succulent shrimp. They carried their plates, chopsticks, and teacups to a table reserved for officers, and Hua introduced the American to his executive officer and pilots.

It was a congenial meal, with the conversation centered around aviation topics after Hua explained to his officers that Kerry had been a fighter pilot. In the course of the dialogue, he learned that Kerry had limited experience in the F-15 and F-16. Kerry appeared very open, without revealing anything confidential, in discussing the flying characteristics of the two advanced fighters.

The group finally broke up, leaving Hua with Kerry and his executive officer, Major Yang, at the table with a second pouring of the hot, aromatic tea.

"Has your group made progress in identifying our terrorists, the People's People, Mr. Kerry?"

"We have several lists of names, Major, but the lists don't seem to get much shorter."

"Perhaps you have frightened them away from the airport? There have been no recent attacks."

"I sincerely doubt they are frightened," Kerry said. "I think the answer is much simpler."

"How so?"

"Their man inside the airport has been eliminated, for one. Also, there have been no night flights since the Falcon was hit and crashed."

The wreckage of the Falcon 20 was laid out carefully in one of the bays of Hangar One, where aviation investigators pored over it. Though Hua could tell them in a minute that the crash was the result of losing an engine to a missile, bureaucrats frequently devised their own make-work. If they did not have voluminous reports to fill in, they were lost.

"No night flights?" he asked.

"I don't think our terrorists would try anything in daylight. And about the only thing flying in the last week has been the Ilyushin test platform and your fighters. That all takes place during the day."

Kerry was grinning at him.

Hua looked at Yang, who offered a faint smile.

He turned his eyes back to Kerry. "Do I detect a challenge in your statement, Mr. Kerry?"

"Not a challenge, Major. After the possibility occurred to me, I came over here to make a suggestion. Excellent meal, by the way."

"I will pass your compliment to the cook. What is the suggestion you wish to make?"

"I've been watching your training flights, and I wonder if you might consider moving one of those flights to after dark."

Hua considered the implications.

"You would have us perform as decoys."

"Your pilots could enter the approach with flare and chaff dispensers armed and ready. If you drew a missile, I think you could shake it off and accelerate out of the approach."

"And if we drew a missile?"

"We could pinpoint the launch site and pounce on it with the security helicopters."

"If this is true. . . ."

"I give it about a thirty, maybe a forty percent chance of coming off. It might take several nights."

"I would be placing my pilots in extreme danger."

"I'll fly it."

Hua smiled. "Now, you are challenging me. You would want one of my aircraft?"

"My Citation is back in Tokyo at the moment, or I'd use it."

"The Cessna incorporates countermeasures?"

"It does."

"I find that surprising," Hua said.

"It's a brave new world."

Hua looked at Yang again.

The executive officer shrugged and said, "The plan has possibilities."

Hua, in concert with General Chou, was of the opinion that the presence of the squadron at the airport would have little or no impact on the search for, and the apprehension of, the terrorist perpetrators. But here was an American with an idea that would give the 1st Squadron of the 479th Tactical Fighter Wing a much more active role in the capture of the people responsible for a half-dozen deaths. They were murderers and thugs, and Hua had no use whatever for them.

"Have you mentioned this to anyone else, Mr. Kerry?"

"No, Major. I don't want to step on any toes, and I thought speaking to you first was the best course to follow."

"Let me discuss your idea with some others," Hua said.

"It's all the same to me if you make it your idea, Major. Mademoiselle Broussard came up with the concept, but neither of us is looking for any credit here."

"Nor am I," Hua said. "Would you have anything else to add?"

"Just that, tactically, the best bait would probably be one fighter. If there are two in the air, the missile man might think twice. One of the fighters could turn on him."

"Yes, I agree. I will speak to my superiors."

Beijing, China
September 2, 2:20 P.M.

Sun Chen and his aide sat on opposite sides of the table on the two couches in front of his desk, and Sun examined each piece of paper the aide handed him.

"We have now received copies of the airworthiness certificates for each of the supersonic transports, Chairman."

He studied the last two documents carefully. Everything appeared to be in order.

Except that Pacific Aerospace intended to send two airplanes to the grand opening of the Superport. One appeared to be a passenger liner and the other a freighter configuration of the same airplane. Daniel Kerry had not mentioned this to him.

Sun smiled inwardly. It was like the Americans, he thought, grasping for the idiom. Like having an ace up the sleeve. When he thought about the seven men on his committee who would serve as judges for the competition, he could not think of one who would not be impressed by the American foresight of including a cargo airplane in their presentation.

The judging procedure was not yet known to the vendors, and would not be announced until October 1. If they had known, perhaps they would be pressing for the names of the judges, rather than courting Sun himself. From the very beginning of the endeavor, Sun had determined that he himself would not be involved in the final decision.

He might have some preferences, but he would not voice them. Anything could happen.

And probably would.

"Make a note," he told his assistant. "We will have to create a fifth team of examiners and send them to the United States for the inaugural flight."

"You will allow the second airplane to participate?"

"Why not? If Pacific Aerospace went to the trouble to build it, we will take a look at it."

"Of course, Chairman. It shall be done."

Each of the examination teams that would accompany the supersonic transports from their point of origin to Deng Xiaoping International was composed of three aviation experts and one of the judges from the committee. The aircraft would depart their home countries at predetermined times, so that they would all arrive at China Dome . . . at Deng Xiaoping International Superport very close to one o'clock in the afternoon of October 1.

On October 2, the aircraft would be subject to intense inspections on the ground, and on October 3, each of the contenders would undergo extensive flight trials, attempting to perform according to a set routine developed by the committee and its aviation experts.

On October 4, the Committee for Airport Construction would announce the winning vendor. It would be a day of great jubilation and perhaps even greater disappointment for some. Additionally, the leading twenty air carriers selected by the committee would be announced, and there would be reason for rejoicing in their hospitality suites, he was certain.

Sun thought of the entire week as one of jubilation. The grand opening ceremonies would draw the world's attention, even though the grand opening preceded the official opening of the airport by one year. Much consideration and discussion had gone into the evolution of the timetable, but there were valuable aspects involved in it. The grand opening day would serve, first, to entice the world with a glimpse of the most magnificent aviation facility in history. The celebration would attract, not only political and commerce leaders, but also publicity of a wondrous nature. Secondly, it would finalize the agreement between the People's Republic and one of the transport vendors.

And a year later, with the official opening, would come another round of publicity, along with the closing of Kai Tak Airport which would be converted to some commercial enterprise. Property in the crowded confines of Kowloon was very valuable, and the People's Republic expected to recoup a great deal of its investment in the new airport with the sale of the Kai Tak land.

The intervening year would be one of great industry. The successful SST vendor was expected to produce at least twenty aircraft for lessee airlines by the date of the official opening. All of the airport's electronic and mechanical systems would have undergone extensive testing, and unfinished lease space would have to be prepared for tenants, at the direction of the tenants. The committee had set as their goal that sixty percent of the leasable space would be under contract to tenants in the first year, and those tenants would be spending the time available in determining the finished appearance of their spaces and moving into them. Sun Chen had a staff of ten people organizing and prioritizing the requests for commercial space at the airport.

A year from now, Sun Chen expected to be in great good humor or in one of the people's hospitals, suffering from exhaustion. Since the latter was a distinct possibility, he intended to fully enjoy the grand opening, which was now less than a month away.

He placed the two certificates carefully on the table and asked his aide, "Do you have the passenger manifests?"

"I do, Chairman. First, here is that of Pacific Aerospace."

The listing was numbered, and when Sun looked at the bottom of the third page, he understood why. There would be 168 passengers on board, a first hint that the Astroliner exceeded the specifications by eight seats. Again, he found himself smiling.

The listing was also impressive. He knew less than ninety percent of the names, but someone at Pacific Aerospace had kindly placed a title after each name. There were governors and lieutenant governors, United States senators and representatives—some of whom he knew by name, members of the cabinet, the Vice President of the United States, perhaps fifteen chief executives or board chairmen from the nation's largest corporations, and a broad selection of celebrities. He was aware of many of the names—cinema actors and actresses, musicians, entertainers, and television personalities. All three of the major American network-news anchors would be flying the Astroliner to South China on its first trip.

"What do you think?" he asked of his aide.

"I believe, Chairman, that the paparazzi and the celebrity . . . what do they call them . . . hounds will be out in force. When the dignitaries deplane at Terminal One, they will be inundated in admirers."

"And?"

"And we, that is, the Superport will be on every front page and every television news show."

"Wonderful, is it not?"

"Absolutely, Chairman."

Sun looked over the other manifests. The French and British were to be well-represented, also, in the same manner as the Americans. The listing included entertainment, industrial, and political dignitaries representing European countries from Spain to the Netherlands. The BBK Enterprises' manifest leaned more toward bankers and industrialists than to those in the political and celebrity worlds. And the Russians appeared to be at a disadvantage. Their listing included many politicians, a few ballerinas and cinema persons, and a few names of complete ignominy. Sun assumed they were persons owed a favor or two by the politicians.

The latter three manifests did not number the names, and Sun patiently counted each sheet. The Concorde II, the AeroSwift, and the Tupolev 2000 apparently matched the specifications and seated only 160 passengers.

Score one point, or perhaps two points, for the Americans, he thought, though he had carefully removed himself from the judging process. Others of his committee would determine whether or not these new revelations were worthy of point assignments.

"The reservations?" he asked.

"We have secured seven hundred hotel rooms in Kowloon for the period of October first to October fifth."

The People's Republic of China was generously assuming the cost of meals and accommodations for their guests. Sun had argued for it, pressing the point that the cost of advertising in the amount of coverage that they would receive for free would amount to millions of yuan.

"And the other activities?"

"All arranged, Chairman. There are tours scheduled throughout Hong Kong and southern China. We will keep them active and involved for the three days of the evaluation."

On the fifth of October, when the SSTs returned to their homelands, only one of the airplanes would contain passengers still in a celebratory mood, but that was not to be his problem.

"This," he told his assistant, "will be an event to surpass any in this century's history of China."

The assistant did not look happy.

"What is it?"

"I worry, Chairman, that something might happen."

"Something? What?"

"Well, if an airplane crashed. Or something. . . ."

Oh, blessed fortune. Now, I will not sleep for a month.

Deng Xiaoping International Superport
September 2, 3:45 P.M.

Director of Security Yichang Enlai took a walk by himself on the top floor of Terminal One. It was a magnificent place. The glass dome above encircled him like the sky itself, stretching from one shortened horizon to the next. The complete top of the floor below the dome was open, with the movable floor partitions only reaching four meters high. The partitions themselves were now extended and divided the monstrous space into four quarters, suitable for extravagant banquets or lounging. The central core, on the other side of the connecting bridges, contained the elevators, storage rooms, and kitchens for serving those banquets. Currently, the floor was finished with acres of carpeting in an earthy teal color, hundreds of leather couches and chairs in a variety of complementing colors—gray, blue, taupe, and a miniature rain forest of tropical plants and flowers. At several places on the perimeter, near the escalators, nearly hidden by palms, sugar cane plants, and Chinese fans, were located havens for the parched travellers. The lounges would serve beverages and food originating from a dozen cultures.

The lounges were already stocked, and the floor finished, since the dignitaries expected for the grand opening would gather here. It was to be the centerpiece of Deng Xiaoping

International Superport, and it was. This, the major dome, was precisely in the center of the airport's property.

Until the floor was overrun by thousands of visitors, Yichang would treat it as his private park, as he had for several months, even before the carpeting and plantings had been installed. It was almost templelike in its stillness. The thick carpets hushed the air and provided a solemn environment for meditation. He strolled slowly along the outer wall, not looking at the outside world, but turning his thoughts inward.

He had never married, though during his twenty-two years of service as a policeman, steadily rising to positions of greater responsibility, he had been offered a large number of marriage proposals. Infrequently, he would lament the fact that he had never followed through on one of them. He did not know what marriage would be like, but he thought he might have found some comfort in sharing with someone else the doubts and fears that sometimes nagged him.

Yichang had never had a close confidant. He had never known his parents, and he had been raised by a grandmother who would not speak of them other than to say that they had died in the great war. His grandmother, too, was more given to issuing commands than to listening to the complaints of a little boy.

For all of his life, Yichang had found that his closest allies were solitude and his inner self, and so it was to areas of privacy, like the top floor of Terminal One, that he went to wrestle with his demons.

His demons seemed many at the moment. Sun Chen was under great pressure to resolve the issue of the People's People, and he naturally transferred much of that pressure to Yichang. Should he not respond well, Yichang would find himself retired and facing solitude with no respite. He did not think he would handle it well. His professional life had been a constant turmoil of problems, criminal cases, and solutions. He had reveled in it, knowing that his successful performance resulted in convictions and exemplary service to the state.

He had no illusions about himself; he *was* a servant of the state, and he saw no greater reward for himself than to be remembered as one who had served his country well.

He had many reservations about the encroachment of the West into China, through the Superport. Yichang did not accept their ideals for himself, and he found it difficult, if not for his direct orders from Sun, to work openly with the people like Kerry, Broussard, Ebbing, and Bergen. For Yichang, the two Russians Yelchenko and Zemenek represented the exact image of the socialist state that had crashed in flames after admitting Western doctrine.

Entering a lounge on the eastern side of the terminal, Yichang went behind the bar, found a sparkling glass, and filled it with water from the tap. He went back around the bar and sat on one of the mauve-tinted, leather-topped stools.

His concentration had been marred all day long by the irritating itch of the flesh on his left forearm as it attempted to reknit itself. Ignoring it took some willpower.

He sipped from the glass and thought of his lists. He had all but abandoned the major list. It had been culled to about three hundred names after Interpol had consented to reviewing it, but it was still cumbersome. It also contained the names that were singled out on his short list, which also included the names Kerry and his group had identified. It was now twelve names long, but all twelve of the persons identified were nowhere to be found.

Nothing had come of the items found in James Lee's apartment, except that the forged identification card had been determined to have an exact copy of the magnetic strip. Every identification card associated with the airport was now being replaced with a new card, and the magnetic strips included a coding that prevented copying. The technology for that process had been provided, at a high, but understandable cost, by Kerry's company. Kerry himself had said that China would be billed for the technology simply as a demonstration of their desire to avoid the appearance of favoritism.

It was one more instance in which Yichang felt indebted to Kerry, and he did not like the feeling.

One of Yichang's demons had a split personality, due to the division between Yichang and Kerry as to the nature of the motive involved in the attacks on the airport. Yichang, supported by the note from the People's People, was certain that the decision of the leaders to invite the West into China had prompted the attacks against the symbol of that move— the airport. Kerry continued to insist, though not forcefully, that the SSTs were intended to be the ultimate target.

The end result was the same, Yichang thought. Kill the airport, or kill the aircraft, and China's movement into the global arena would be arrested.

And then again, the result was perhaps not the same.

He sipped from his water glass and churned the image crowding the edge of his mind.

There it was!

Kerry did not see the same terrorists as he himself saw. Though Kerry had never voiced the possibility, he was painting the perpetrators with an entirely different coat of paint. Kerry's concern was not that of the Superport, but of his own capitalistic nature. He—

The portable radio clipped to his belt buzzed.

Yichang jerked it loose and depressed the activation switch.

"Director Yichang, this is Major Hua."

He had left instructions in the center to not call him unless it was urgent.

"Yes, Major?"

"I have a proposal to make to you. May we meet somewhere?"

Yichang sighed and told the pilot to come to the top floor.

Already, his private spaces were being invaded.

September 2, 8:41 P.M.

The two helicopters assigned to the China Dome security division were all-purpose, lightweight SA.342 Gazelles manufactured in France by Sud Aviation, a partnership of Aerospatiale and Westland. They were five-seat utility choppers, and in their white paint, were reminiscent of the Bell JetRanger, Kerry thought. There was a little more Plexiglas area up front, and the tail rotor was encased in a rudderlike shroud called a fenestron.

A military version of the same helicopter would carry a couple of 7.62-millimeter machine guns, a couple pods of Matra 2.75-inch rockets, or perhaps some wire-guided anti-tank missiles. The scariest thing about these helicopters was the red "Division of Security" insignia emplaced below the "Deng Xiaoping International Superport" lettering on the side of the fuselage.

And that wasn't very scary.

After Major Hua had made some plea to General Chou, the general had ordered a couple of military helicopters dispatched to the airport, but they wouldn't arrive for a couple of days, and the animated Hua had become impatient. He didn't want to wait for them.

For that matter, Kerry was also impatient. He, Hua, and Yichang had spent several hours together, debating the pros and cons of the plan, and weighing the risks. Hua had insisted that he would be the sole pilot of the F-12 decoy plane. Yichang would lead the assault by the helicopters, and he had denied Kerry's request to be present.

Kerry had given him a hurt look and a reminder that the idea had come from him and Broussard.

"Very well," Yichang had relented with a sigh, "but Mademoiselle Broussard is not to be included, simply because the concept was hers. I will not put a woman at risk, no matter the current disposition of the Western world toward femininity."

"As a matter of fact," Kerry had told him, "I didn't mention to her the details of my talk with Major Hua."

So now they stood around on the darkened tarmac near Hangar One and waited to hear from Hua, who had taken off an hour before.

A quarter-mile away, the five remaining F-12s of the 1st Squadron were parked in front of the next hangar, their presence obvious from the bright lights shining from the hangar. A few technicians walked among them.

Here, the two security helicopters were more obscure. The lights of the hangar had been extinguished in order to mask the movement of men around the helicopters. Two pilots sat in each of them with the doors propped open to admit the night air. Four security guards armed with Kalashnikov AK-74 automatic assault rifles smoked cigarettes fifty feet away, but were ready to leap aboard when called.

Kerry and Yichang stood together near the first helicopter, operating under the call sign of Guard One, so they could hear any traffic on the radio.

"This will very likely be an inconclusive night, Mr. Kerry."

"Perhaps, Director Yichang. But then, I've been thinking about this guy. What if he's been sitting out there somewhere, every night, waiting for some airplane to come along? And none has. I'd bet he's as impatient as you and I are."

"Perhaps."

The radio inside the helicopter crackled with static, then cleared. Kerry leaned against the fuselage and stuck his head in the doorway.

"Guard One, Blue Dragon."

The copilot responded, "Blue Dragon, this is Guard One."

"I am making my approach now, twenty-five kilometers out."

"Copied, Blue Dragon."

Yichang barked an order in Chinese, and the four guards field-stripped their cigarettes, stomped the glowing embers into the concrete, and moved to the helicopters.

Kerry turned and headed for Guard Two. As a certified rotary-wing pilot and a former test pilot on the AH-64 Apache attack helicopter, he was reluctant to climb into the back. Most combat pilots, rotary- or fixed-wing, distrusted any other pilot controlling their destinies, and he would have felt much more satisfied if he were taking the right seat of the Gazelle. Or even the left seat, as copilot. To be relegated to the back was the worst possible scenario.

He crawled in along with the two armed guards and strapped himself into his seat on the left side.

They waited.

The pilot switched frequency to air control, and they listened to the dialogue as Hua made his approach.

And waited.

Hua was either taking his time or time had slowed down.

"Contact!" Hua yelled over the radio. "Missile fired!"

Chaff! Flares! Come on, Major!

The 590 shaft horsepower turboshaft engine above Kerry whined as the pilot coaxed it into life.

RETURN FIRE

FIFTEEN

Major Hua Peng had had his threat receivers active and his forefinger poised near the chaff and flare ejector buttons. The wing sweep was in full-forward position and the flaps deployed for slow-speed lift, but he had not lowered the landing gear. In the darkness, he had thought that any potential sniper would note his slow speed, even though it was twenty knots faster than the normal landing speed, but not the absence of the landing gear extension.

The instant the infrared threat receiver blinked its message on the Head-Up Display (HUD) and the warning chime sounded in his earphones, he had punched the flare button, then slammed the throttle past its detent into afterburner. Since he was in a nose-down semiglide and already moving at 190 knots, the acceleration came quickly. He was slammed back into his seat by the 11,500-kilogram thrust of the turbofan, and the indicated airspeed began to climb abruptly.

"Contact! Missile fired!" he called into his microphone.

His adrenaline level climbed faster than the airspeed, and he was amazed by his excitation. He had never before been in combat. The dark night suddenly seemed lighter, and the runway lights stretched out ahead of him were far crisper. The illuminated domes on his left appeared to be . . . tombstones?

No.

Counting.

One . . . two . . .

Airspeed coming up.

Hard turn to the right.

The fighter lost altitude, the lift slipping away in his steep bank; he felt as if his right wing would soon scrape the ground.

The near end of the runway, turning away from it. Get the exhaust away from the missile.

Punch more flares.

Speed still climbing, lift returning as he leveled the wings, starting to sweep them back.

A white flash in his peripheral vision.

The missile had found a flare and detonated.

Speed 245 knots. Altitude 215 meters AGL.

The airport was now in his rearview mirror, several kilometers back. Hua banked into a right turn, coming back on the east end of the airport. He saw the helicopters launching from the hangar area.

Now, you verifiable son of a rabid dog, we will see how you like being on the receiving end.

Hua knew that he did not like it.

September 3, 8:59 P.M.

Guard Two was first off the ground, its pilot so eager he did not wait for an appropriate warm-up of the turbine engine.

Kerry didn't give a damn. He thought about Charley Whitlock, and he thought about getting his hands on more of these bastards. He silently urged the pilot to even greater speed while he pulled on the headset which allowed the passengers to converse on the intercom over the thundering roar of the turbine.

He could hear the radio transmissions.

Hua: "Missile detonated. No damage."

Kerry was relieved; he liked the major.

Yichang: "Have you determined the launch point, Blue Dragon?"

Air Control: "What is happening! Someone tell me what is happening!"

They hadn't bothered to include the tower in their planning.

Hua: "Coming around now. Launch point. I think it must be about five kilometers due east of 27 Left."

Kerry's pilot dropped the nose and shot past the terminals at over 300 kilometers per hour according to the airspeed indicator. Kerry translated that to 190 miles an hour. The ground clearance was less than a hundred feet, and the lit domes went by so fast he barely noted the dozens of faces pressed to the glass in the area of the communications and security centers.

Air control demanded information.

The guard next to him shot the bolt on his AK-74, priming the automatic weapon. He hoped the guy knew what he was doing with it.

They sped over the end of the runway and into the darkened countryside with Guard One a quarter-mile behind. The loss of the lighting around the airport didn't help Kerry's night vision. He waited for his eyes to adjust and wished he'd been consuming more Vitamin C.

Ahead, he saw the navigation lights of Hua's F-12 as it raced across their line of flight. The airplane abruptly went into a left turn.

"Guard One, I have spotted him," Hua called. "It is a small car speeding eastward on the dirt road."

"Do not lose him," Yichang warned. "We will soon be there."

"I am going to use an anti-tank missile."

"No! We need to have him alive!" Yichang begged.

"Blue Dragon!" the controller called. "What are you shooting? *Who* are you shooting?"

"I will use the missile on the road."

The Gazelle climbed a few feet as the pilot gave himself some more clearance over low hills, and when Kerry leaned forward to peer past the copilot, he could pick out the lighter line of a road wavering through the dark contours of the countryside. Above and to his right, he saw the lights of the fighter as Hua circled back to the right in preparation for his attack run.

He could not see the target.

The helicopter pilot tracked on the road, and a minute later, Kerry saw the brake lights of a car flare as the driver slowed for a curve. He wasn't using his headlights. Kerry kept his eyes trained on the spot, and when the red lights disappeared, he found he could still track a dark spot moving down the lighter background of the road.

It was moving fast, but it was getting closer by the second.

The Shenyang F-12 was still a couple miles to the right when it launched its missile. Kerry saw the streak of rocket exhaust cut through the dark sky, and seconds later, it slammed into the ground a quarter-mile ahead of the car.

A bright flash of detonation was accompanied by a geyser of dirt and gravel.

Then there were brake lights.

The obviously shocked driver locked up his brakes, and the car slewed from side to side between the ditches lining the road as it slid on the gravel, clutching its way to a stop.

The helicopter, now with its landing lights on, bringing out detail in sharp relief, was on top of the car by the time the doors flew open on its left and right sides. Two figures bolted out of it and headed for both sides of the road.

"Two of them," Kerry said into the intercom.

The copilot relayed the information on the radio.

The pilot swung the nose of the Gazelle around, hovering for a second, then set it down in the middle of the road, ahead of the car.

Kerry released the door latch and beat the copilot out of the chopper. He had leapt over the ditch at the side of the road and was running to the south, pursuing that fugitive, by the time Guard One landed.

One of the guards behind him fired several bursts from his Kalashnikov, and Kerry hoped it was into the air. They weren't to fire on the suspects unless they were shot at first.

As the whine of the helicopters died away with turbine engines idled, he heard the beat of boots pounding behind him. The ground was rough and dry. He tasted dust in the air.

Kerry couldn't see his adversary in the dark, but he heard his passage through dry brush and shrubs. Prickly thorns grabbed at him as he pushed his way through thickets of shrubbery.

More shots to his rear.

He tripped on a hummock of dirt, regained his balance,

and kept running. His breathing picked up the pace faster than his legs.

The angle of the ground changed, and he realized he was running uphill on a slight slope. He searched the night ahead of him, tracking the sound of footfalls and tearing shrubs, which were becoming more distinct.

Then, against the starlit sky at the summit of the hill, he saw a dark figure.

He increased his speed, or thought that he did.

Caromed off the trunk of a dead tree he hadn't seen.

Pounded ahead on the balls of his feet, slipping in loose crusts of dirt.

Legs not in the best shape.

Closer.

Thirty feet?

Twenty.

The figure topped the hill, abruptly slid to a stop, reversed, and came back at him.

He saw the glint of metal in the man's hand.

Remembered Charley.

Two shots cracked from behind him, not aimed. The slugs whistled and compressed the air as they went overhead.

The figure jumped at the sound of the shots.

And Kerry, still at full speed, slammed into the man like a free safety gleefully finds a running back. Dennis Smith leveling Marcus Allen.

The impact knocked the breath out of Kerry, but sent the smaller Asian tumbling backwards, his arms flailing. He landed flat on his back, now without his weapon.

Kerry recovered his balance, spinning around to face the man.

The assailant rolled onto his stomach, rose to his hands and knees.

And Kerry kicked him full in the face.

He heard facial bones snap.

Good damned deal, he thought. He was long past the point of fighting fair.

September 3, 1:42 A.M.

Wu Yhat came into Yichang's brightly lit office and said, "We have located the launch site."

Yichang asked his cousin, "You found the launcher?"

"Yes, the launch tube as well as a second missile for it. Major Hua identified it as a Soviet-made Grail. An SA-7, he said."

"And the car?"

"A Lada. It was stolen in Kowloon."

"It would be. Very well, thank you."

Yichang rose from behind his desk and went out into the security center. He was tired, but too keyed up to sleep. The small night shift of men monitoring the security cameras was a vibrant group. They grinned at him as he walked through the center. He was certain they all thought that their trial by fire was concluded, but Yichang did not think so.

Five hours of interrogation of their two detainees had failed to elicit one bit of useful information. Yichang thought they were but soldiers in the army of the People's People. The general of that army remained elusive.

He left the center through the paired security doors and went down the corridor to the conference room. His domain did not include jail or interrogation rooms, and he had commandeered this conference room for the first criminal. The second was in a previously empty office across the corridor.

Opening the door, he stepped inside. The prisoner, a tall

Asian man they were certain was Korean, was strapped into a steel chair near one wall. In three chairs facing him, three of Yichang's assistants were firing questions at him, one after the other.

One of the assistants looked up as Yichang entered, then shook his head negatively.

He went back into the corridor and crossed it to enter the office. A single bare bulb in the ceiling provided the illumination, revealing walls of unfinished gypsum board, their joints filled and smoothed, but as yet unpainted. The floor was of bare concrete.

Kerry leaned against the wall next to the door, watching the three security officers questioning Ku Chi, who was tied to a chair. While they had yet to identify the Korean across the hall, Ku Chi's face had been quickly located on both the computer database and in his dossier on Yichang's desk. He had also been on the list of suspects Kerry's group had compiled.

His face did not closely resemble his picture at the moment. The left side of it was swollen to twice its size. His upper jaw was broken, as was his nose, and most of the teeth on the left side had been left on a hill in the dark. Blood from lacerations and bleeding gums was caked on his face and lips. Yet, his face was stoic, and he had not uttered a word since Kerry had captured him.

Yichang had not seen fit to bring in a doctor just yet. The pain might be helpful.

Yichang closed the door and moved to stand next to Kerry.

Speaking softly, he said, "He has revealed nothing?"

"Not a damned thing, Director. All we've got is that flyer we found in his pocket."

It was a treatise in Chinese characters, extolling the doctrine of the People's People. It was, in Yichang's view, further support for his opinion that the People's People was a simplistic group with the sole aim of preventing Deng Xiaoping International from opening its doors to the world.

"I wouldn't mind spending a few moments alone with this guy," Kerry told Yichang.

There were interrogation methods which would elicit confessions to crimes real and imagined, but Yichang was astute enough to know, without Sun Chen's urging, that they were no longer appropriate. The world's eyes were upon them, and Ku Chi and his ally might well have to be paraded before the cameras. For that reason, Yichang had already written a short statement, to be released through the office of the committee, regarding the capture of the two men, and the injury suffered by Ku Chi during the capture.

Yichang turned slightly to face Kerry and studied his eyes, which seemed cold and flat. There was a repressed fury that was very close to the surface, and he thought that Ku Chi was probably fortunate to have suffered only the damage that he had.

"Mr. Kerry, you have done much to assist the People's Republic, much more than I probably should have allowed. Still, I thank you."

"You know damned well that I'm less interested in serving the Republic than I am in seeing Charley's killers run through a meat grinder."

Yichang nodded. "Still, we must observe the courtesies."

"Protocol. Yes, you're correct, Mr. Yichang. My apologies."

"They are not necessary. However, this is now a matter of my jurisdiction, and I suggest that you return to your hotel for the present."

With apparent reluctance, Kerry nodded, then left the office.

Yichang dismissed his three subordinates, then went to sit in the chair directly in front of Ku Chi.

The man's hostility was apparent, despite the wreckage of his face. It was in his dark eyes, like sparks flashing off flint. His shoulders were held rigidly in tension, and Yichang thought that after five hours of insistent, unending questions, he was likely close to fatigue, if not total exhaustion. There was probably some infection in his jaw by now, and the aching pain would be gnawing at him.

Yichang's arm still ached, and the pain did not improve his temper. He forced himself to maintain a neutral tone.

"Let us speak of the future," Yichang said in Chinese. "Your future."

There was no change in his posture or his glare.

"The trial will be quite public, I imagine, and you will be represented well by legal counsel. There will be television cameras, and the world will be watching you. You will not, however, be allowed to speak. I suspect that, if anyone fears that you might speak out in an inopportune fashion, your vocal cords will be cut prior to the trial."

A change in the cast of the eyes?

"Despite the best efforts of your counsel, of course, you will be convicted. You know this."

Naturally, he knew this.

"What is important, then, is the charges you will face. It will not be attempted murder against the pilot of the airplane. It will be treason against the state since you attempted to shoot down a military airplane. That is punishable by death. Then, too, with the evidence provided by your colleague, you will also face the complaint of murder. That complaint, as you know, results from the death of the Englishman who was aboard the Falcon aircraft."

Ku Chi finally spoke, though not to deny the Korean's fictitious betrayal. Through his broken teeth, he croaked, "The people will not allow that to happen. The state abandons them, and the people will free me."

For some reason, Yichang took up the theory espoused by Kerry. "The people are a figment of your imagination. It is simply a story concocted by someone to appeal to your mind and your idealism. The people, as you think you know them, do not exist."

"Untrue!"

Fine. Now they were talking.

"Why don't you tell me about your people," Yichang said softly, his voice full of silk and curiosity.

Edwards Air Force Base
September 2, 11:50 A.M.

Terry Carroll and Cliff Coker—who would fly as captain of the Astrofreighter—carried open cans of Coca-Cola and wandered through the passenger cabin of the Astroliner.

In the entrance foyer, just behind the flight deck and ahead of the cabin, plumbers and electricians were completing the fittings of the two restrooms and the galley. In the cabin itself, the telemetry boxes had been removed from the deck, and a rich, thick, burgundy carpet had been laid the full length of the cabin. Nice neat rows of holes peppered the carpet where the seats were to be bolted in place. The fuselage sides, between ribs and stringers, were packed with yellow insulation, and for half the length of the cabin from the rear, sculptured plastic panels had been installed, along with the overhead compartments. The carpeting and insulation had effectively reduced the echo quality of the cabin, though it was tough to detect the difference at the moment because of the noise created by the men working in the cabin. Technicians were finalizing the connections of oxygen lines, air flow ducts, and the wiring for overhead lighting.

At the aft bulkhead, in front of the rear restrooms and the emergency access to the rear cargo compartment, four of the luxurious passenger seats had been bolted to the deck. The upholstery was a blue-gray tweed fabric, soft and pliable.

The two captains sidestepped the workers and settled themselves into the seats.

"Damn," Coker said, "this is the life. I could ride back here, all right."

"If you can afford it."

"What do you think they're going to run?"

"It's anybody's guess. The Chinese will own the aircraft, and they'll want to show a little profit, or a lot of profit, off the leases. The air carriers will have to cover the lease cost and the maintenance, as well as a profit margin. The Arctic route from L.A. to Hong Kong is sixty-five hundred miles, compared to a Paris-Washington distance of forty-two hundred miles. I'd make a wild guess of six thousand bucks, one way."

"Jesus, Terry!"

"Time is money, Cliff. It's about eleven hours for the flight, now. With this bird, the time is cut to about four hours. The last time I talked to Kerry, he wanted to come back for Charley's funeral, but couldn't get away for the two days it would take. A just-over-eight-hour round trip, he'd have been able to do it. Hell, the Astroliner's flight time barely allows enough time to get in a movie and a few phone calls."

The right armrest of every seat in the Astroliner cabin was an electronic console. At the outside end of the armrest, a four-inch color television screen rested on a flexible stalk, and the passenger had a library of forty movies or documentaries from which to choose. Ten channels provided a wide selection of news summaries or music—Garth Brooks to Andre Previn. A voltage selector and a connector provided power for laptop computers—rentable, if the passenger didn't have his own. Inset into the armrest was a telephone, and thirty microwave, satellite-relayed telephonic channels were available.

PAI would recommend to the Chinese and the lessee air carriers that all of the above, except telephone charges, be priced with the ticket. The cuisine would be determined by the air carrier, but could be guaranteed to be the finest available, given the ticket price.

Coker tapped the armrest. "Do you think any of the others are going to have this?"

"The Concorde II might have upgraded seats, since it doesn't have much else that's upgraded, but I see the Germans and Russians as being pretty austere. Dan thinks their philosophies run along the lines of air travel as a method of getting from one place to another."

"Not so for PAI," Coker said.

"Hell, no. We want it to be an experience to be remembered for a lifetime. Like Disneyland."

They were speaking above the cacophony of grinders, power drills, power screwdrivers, and swearing and joking men, so it was difficult for Carroll to place himself entirely in the mind-set of a passenger. Still, he thought that, given a relatively smooth ride by the pilot, a passenger would alight at China Dome fresh and ready to tackle his or her day. If he or she had ever been a Concorde passenger, Carroll knew the Astroliner would forever be the new choice.

He took a long drag at his Coke can, thought of it as a Mai Tai, and leaned his head back against the headrest.

"You're going to go to sleep on me," Coker complained.

"If you'd kindly get the power tools out of here, I might."

"We going to get around to Kerry's fax?"

Carroll raised his head. "I suppose we ought to."

Kerry's message had explained the capture of two terrorists, along with an SA-7 Grail shoulder-fired missile launcher. Kerry also thought, based purely on instinct, that there were a few more terrorists and Grails around.

"If I'm reading him right," Coker said, "the approach to China Dome could be similar to taking a C-130 into An Khe or Khe San. I'm talking about your generation, of course."

Coker had spent four years in the Air Force, but he hadn't accumulated any combat time.

"I didn't fly the Hercules," Carroll told him, "but the aviators who did learned to avoid potential ground fire by coming in steep as hell and flaring out at the last minute."

"Makes for a rough landing. I'll bet the passengers didn't like it."

"The passengers didn't have a choice, Cliff. And if they had, I'll bet they'd have opted for alive, rather than dead."

"I don't see those tactics working here, Terry."

"Nope. I don't want to worry the bigwigs. Got to be smooth as satin."

"But you're worried?"

"Yeah, I am. I'd hate to lose all those celebrities."

"Especially Julia and Reba," Coker reminded him.

"Reba, especially. Then, too, I've got P.J. and Stephenson

on board. Sure as hell, they'd cut off my paychecks if I killed us all."

"So what have you been thinking about?"

"You sure I've been thinking?"

"Damned right. You're always thinking."

"I'll tell you what I think, Cliff. I think that most of these terrorists have shit for brains."

"Agreed."

"And these intellectuals would look at a wind sock, if they had a wind sock. Since they don't, they hold a wet finger in the air."

"To see which way the wind is blowing."

"Right. And that's our answer." Carroll closed his eyes and laid his head back against the headrest.

"Now, wait! You're going to leave me hanging?"

"Think about it."

"Okay, they test the wind."

"What for?"

"To see which way it's coming from . . . ah, which determines which direction the airplanes will land."

"Right."

"That's so they can set up their firing points at the approach end of the runway."

"So. Now, think about the layout of China Dome." In the package they had received from Kerry a month before was a full schematic of the airport and its approach patterns.

"Shit. You're going to land downwind."

"Damned right. I'll have to come in a little hot, but hell, I've got eighteen thousand feet of runway. Those assholes with the missiles can sit out there on the normal approach end and play with themselves, or with the missiles. Which aren't going to shoot down anything."

"Don't slow down, and don't look back," Coker told him. "I'll be right behind you."

Kowloon
September 3, 6:20 A.M.

"This is not the sensational news that I wanted to see on the television," the voice told him.

The press releases out of Beijing had gone worldwide during the night, and the bravery of an air force pilot, along with the capture of two terrorists, dominated the media outlets. Kurt Wehmeier had first seen the report on television, and a more extensive version was on the front pages of both morning newspapers, the *South China Morning Post* and the *Hong Kong Standard.* The *China Mail,* with afternoon editions and a more tabloid format, could be expected to also blare the failure of the People's People.

Wehmeier did not care about the People's People; he did care about the voice on the other end of the telephone connection.

"Do you think I am happy with it?" he asked. He was, in fact, highly enraged at the incompetence of Ku and Oh, but there seemed at the moment to be no release for his towering rage. The release would come in the future, and the very near future, at that.

"Will those two talk?"

"Under the right kinds of pressure, anyone will talk. In this case, they will have nothing to say, other than what they believe."

"And what do they believe, Herr Wehmeier?"

He took a full minute before answering. Wehmeier had been absolutely certain that the man he was talking to did not know his true identity. He was less than subtly adding a new component to the equation. Where X had once equalled dollars, there was now a Y involved. Wehmeier was being told that, now, he not only stood to lose dollars, he also chanced the loss of his freedom or of his life.

"Ku and Oh believed they worked for the People's People. That is all they can reveal."

"Names?"

"Of Mr. Bern, only."

"You're certain of this?"

"Or of James Lee, now a matter of inconsequence."

Or of Ibn Saldam, also inconsequential, though he did not mention it. Saldam had died of a drug overdose, helped along by Hyun Oh. And Oh would not be expected to boast of that accomplishment.

Wehmeier also thought it best not to mention the name of Angelo Malgretto, whom Ku and Oh also knew. He had already sent for Malgretto.

"This is going to drastically affect the terms of our contract," the voice told him.

"Not at all. In fact, it works to our advantage."

"You had better explain that."

"We will allow them to think they have eliminated the People's People campaign."

"Lull them into complacency?"

"Exactly."

After a short consideration, the man said, "Perhaps."

"We have already established the foundation which we envisioned. Now, we will save the great strike for last."

"You still have missiles? They did not lose the missiles?"

"I have twenty missiles."

"And the men to operate them?"

Wehmeier had not planned on losing Ku and Oh. Not

this soon, anyway. At any rate, it did not matter. He had others available, and he had changed the final scenario, though he would not explain the change to the man on the other side of the globe.

"We have the resources necessary."

"If you fail me in this, Herr Wehmeier, you will not rest."

"Be prepared to transfer ten million dollars American to my accounts on the evening of October first," Wehmeier said and replaced the telephone.

That ten million dollars would finance his activities for five years, and Wehmeier did not intend to lose it. This campaign would come to its inevitable and happy conclusion.

He left the public telephone at the back of the restaurant and went back to his table near the front window. He was able to drink another cup of coffee before Malgretto arrived.

Leaving bills on the table, he met Malgretto at the door and turned him back into the street.

"What is happening, Mr. Bern?"

The Italian was dark and wiry, with unkempt, curly black hair that seemed to coil in every direction. He was also tough and amoral. Wehmeier had once walked unannounced into the man's apartment to find him intimately engaged with two women and three men. As a member of the Red Brigade, he had routinely tortured and executed the enemies of the Brigade, which amounted to almost anyone in favor of the governmental administration.

"We must get you off the street."

"But, why?"

"You have not read the papers?"

"Why would I do that?"

Wehmeier was continually amazed that political revolutionaries were so ignorant of current affairs.

"Because the Chinese Nationalist Police have Ku and Oh in custody. They will give you up before long."

"I will leave Hong Kong."

"Yes, but not right away. Come."

Wehmeier flagged a taxi and directed the driver to the Two Moons Marina. He had responded to a classified advertisement in the morning newspaper, and he was expected.

The Chinese man they met at the marina was living aboard the boat, and in anticipation of potential buyers, had cleaned it to perfection. The deck fittings shone with polish and industrious rubbing.

As he took them aboard the forty-four-foot custom-built cruiser and into the salon, the man explained, "It is fifteen years old, but in magnificent condition. It was built by Hiptimco Marine, the boat division of the Hip Shing Timber Company. The power comes from two Chrysler marine diesel engines. The engines were installed less than two years ago."

Wehmeier did not care unduly about the condition, as long as it was seaworthy, but had to admit that the owner had maintained it well. The interior was handfitted with teak, and the bright blue and beige cushions and other upholstery had been replaced recently.

"I will pay for your fuel if you take us for a ride."

The man eyed them suspiciously, but acquiesced, and they spent forty minutes testing the boat in the bay. Wehmeier and Malgretto both learned the controls. When they docked, Wehmeier said, "I will pay you one hundred thousand, U.S."

"She is in very fine shape. I expect to receive more."

"In unreportable cash?"

Century City, California
September 2, 2:16 P.M.

The main conference room was a boardroom today, and none of the sixteen directors had called in with one excuse or another. They were all in attendance, and they were all intent.

P.J. Jackson and Kenneth Stephenson sat at the head of the table, with the other directors arrayed down both sides of the boat-shaped table. Jackson's secretary was at a small table behind him, recording the meeting on a reel-to-reel tape recorder and in shorthand.

The sixteen directors represented a cross section of American enterprise. They all sat on the boards of other large corporations, ranging from the manufacture of automobiles to the production of cereals. Three of them were chief executive officers. Two were executives of major banks. One was the president of a prestigious Ivy League university. They dressed as if Brooks Brothers and Gucci were in-house functions.

Kenneth Stephenson had just provided his monthly report, highlighting the certification of the aircraft and the ninety percent probable passage of legislation allowing the SSTs to operate out of the Los Angeles and San Francisco airports. Both items were highly positive developments, but board directors tended to think black thoughts.

"You're gauging the passage of this legislation at ninety percent?" the banker asked.

"P.J.," Stephenson said, "your call."

Jackson looked directly at the banker and said, "We first attempted to take our bill through the normal steps, but we couldn't even get an audience with the Transportation Committee. Too many of them are scared to death of the environmental impact of noise. So I enlisted the help of my brother, we got to Green, and we've got unofficial passage of the bill through committee. Once it's on the floor, there's likely to be some opposition, but with the committee weight behind it, I don't think it's insurmountable."

"How did you get Senator Jackson to help?"

"By heightening his political expectations."

The banker, who was familiar with California politics, said, "Not in any formal sense?"

"Only in the most abstract of terms."

"That won't come to pass?" the banker asked.

"That won't come to pass."

"Good. Nice job. What else are you doing?"

"We're going to take some of the key people for a little airplane ride as soon as the interior is finished. We'll pass around some wine and crackers."

"That ought to do it," the banker said.

The advertising man from New Jersey stabbed a finger at one of the minor points in the written version of the president's report. "What's this contract with Calesco?"

Jackson, who had secured the agreement, said, "We've signed a contract with them to provide our advanced airline passenger seats, which they will resell to the airlines for first-class passenger cabins. We intend to formalize a number of such agreements in the future with other companies."

"How much is it worth?"

"The initial contract will bring in about twelve million."

"That's like pissing up a rope."

"That's a start in our spin-off operations," Jackson said. "We've developed technology that doesn't have to be limited to the Astroliner. I fully expect to realize over two hundred million a year in off-shoot contracts."

"That only works if we're still in business," the New Jerseyite said.

"Take a worst-case scenario," the CEO from the Midwest said. "We don't get the contract. What happens then?"

Stephenson responded. "As P.J. pointed out, we've got technology that's desirable to other companies, even the successful vendor of SSTs. As another course, we could create an airline and go into competition with the Concorde. We'd have one hundred percent of the market inside a year. We could—"

"You don't have a year," the Midwest CEO pointed out to him. "The cash flow would dry up too damned soon, and you can't plan on the investors dumping more cash into a losing proposition, hoping you sell a hell of a lot of first-class passenger seats."

"How long do you think we have?" Stephenson asked.

The CEO looked around the table at his fellow directors. "I don't think that's changed, Ken. Come October fifteenth, this place is a going enterprise, or we're cutting the losses immediately."

The problem with P.J. Jackson's employment contract, and with the contracts of every other top executive, engineer, or scientist, was that there were no bail-out provisions if the company ceased to exist. No golden parachutes. No nothing. Hit the street and start looking for something new.

SIXTEEN

"You have seen this issue of *Aviation Week,* Henri?"

"I have seen it. So?"

His testy response told Broussard that the managing director was not happy with the cover of the magazine: a crisp and clear portrait of Pacific Aerospace Incorporated's Astroliner and Astrofreighter parked side by side on some runway in a California desert.

"You do not think this poses a threat?"

"A threat? Because they have two versions of the same airplane? Why should it?"

"How would we counter it, Henri, should the Chinese decide that a cargo aircraft is desirable?"

"It is a simple matter, Jacqueline, to make the conversion."

She did not think it was so simple. The matter of the cargo ramp alone required major airframe changes, and since the ribs of the Concorde II—and she assumed those of the competing SSTs also—were components cast in carbon-reinforced plastic, rather than of metallic elements bolted together, the design changes would be extensive, as well as very expensive. With an opening in the fuselage that large, the stresses placed on the airframe and skin of the aircraft were entirely different.

"Do not let this interfere with your concentration, Jacqueline," Dubonnet continued. "Consider the timing. Pacific Aerospace held off on its FAA certification simply to make this last-minute publicity splash in the aviation industry. The rest of the SSTs have been certified and reported in the media for months."

She understood the timing, and thought it well done. The specifications reported in the magazine article were more bothersome than the timing. Switching the telephone to her other hand, she looked around the office. She and Zemenek were the only two present, and she knew that he did not understand French.

"They carry eight additional passengers," she said. That could result in forty to sixty thousand dollars in added revenue per flight.

"Yes," he said, and the tone of his voice suggested to her that he was under heavy pressure from the board of directors as a result of the numbers cited by the magazine.

"And they are faster. We could lose our existing routes."

"I do not see how that would happen, Jacqueline. The new routes will be established between China and specific destinations."

"But what if a New York to Hong Kong flight had a stopover at Heathrow or Charles de Gaulle? That would effectively parallel our routes."

"The competition would not be approved by the authorities in Britain or France," Dubonnet insisted.

"In an atmosphere of deregulation and a philosophy of

market economics? Not right away, Henri, but perhaps two or three years from now."

"Jacqueline, why do you raise these issues now?"

"Because I am worried."

After seeing the cover of the magazine and reading the admittedly brief article inside, Broussard had begun to wonder if Kerry's arrogance was not justified. She had been consumed with feelings of disloyalty when she thought that perhaps, just perhaps, the Concorde II would not fare well in comparison.

Her godfather maintained his silence. He was concerned, also.

"Daniel Kerry made a suggestion some time ago, Father."

"And what would that be?"

"He said that, in the event that Pacific Aerospace secured the contract, there might be avenues to explore with us in terms of subcontracts for air and ground crew training. Perhaps also for contracts to maintain aircraft at European terminals."

"The arrogant son of a bitch!"

"That was my reaction also, Father."

"This is something that has been discussed in Pacific Aerospace executive offices?"

"I don't believe so," she said. "Kerry said he would have to discuss it with Jackson."

"You may tell him from me that he may roll his offer into a tight cylinder and shove—"

"I will tell him."

She hung up in relief.

To have Henri Dubonnet tell her to explore the possibilities with Kerry would have been for him to admit defeat. He would not do so, and therefore, she would not do so.

September 6, 11:38 A.M.

Hua Peng, Major Yang, and Daniel Kerry stood outside Hangar Two and watched the helicopters approach. They were Super Frelons, manufactured by Aerospatiale, and were dressed in the livery of the Air Force of the People's Liberation Army—aluminum skin with the red-and-yellow star and bar insignia painted on the fuselage sides. They were minimally armed with machine guns mounted in the side doors; they lacked a missile launch capability.

For once, Hua felt as if the proper counterattack capability was being applied to the mission at Deng Xiaoping International.

Kerry, who had visited the 1st Squadron several times now, said, "I'll feel better with those birds patrolling the approach lanes."

Hua smiled at him. "We are doing our very best to make you feel better, Mr. Kerry."

The American grinned. "I know you are, Major."

Hua liked the American, though he was not certain whether or not he was supposed to like him. None of his superiors, or those with whom he liaised at the airport, had told him otherwise, so for the time being, they would be friends. Kerry's plan for trapping the terrorists had, after all, vastly improved Hua's standing among his fellow aviators. He had been interviewed by numerous reporters in regard to his narrow escape from the Grail missile, and he had been characteristically modest in his responses to their questions.

He was forced to be modest and to not reveal that the incident had been a planned one. As far as the world knew, the capture of the terrorists had been an accident of time and place; he managed to evade the missile and locate the escaping car; Yichang's security people happened to be airborne and available.

That scenario had been developed because Hua Peng had failed to obtain General Chou's permission for the escapade. After listening to Kerry's suggestion, and after presuming that there was less than a twenty percent chance that the attack would take place, and after considering the general's attitude toward the Superport, Westerners as a group, and probably Kerry's idea in particular, Hua had foregone the chance to clear the mission with Chou. He had proceeded on his own, and while wildly successful, the incident had placed him in a precarious position with his superior.

The helicopters touched down lightly in front of the F-12s, and their rotors began to spin down. Hua held his service cap to his head while he waited for the swirling wind created by the aircraft to subside.

Kerry brushed some dirt from his eyes.

The side door of the lead helicopter slid back.

"Oh, no!" Hua said.

"Problem?" Kerry asked.

"General Chou has come with them."

He led the way across the apron and met the general halfway. He and Yang saluted smartly, and the general returned the salute, then said, "Good morning, Mr. Kerry."

"Good morning, General. I'm pleased to see you again."

Chou did not look pleased, but said, "I understand that you performed a valuable service in apprehending one of the criminals."

"I just happened to be there," Kerry told him.

"Yes. Twice, now, you have happened to be present when needed. You have the gift of prescience, sir."

"You give me qualities I know I don't possess, General," Kerry smiled.

"Perhaps." Chou turned to Hua. "Major, I present you with two helicopters. They are to be attached to your squadron temporarily for administrative and operational purposes. You will be responsible for devising a schedule of patrols. Put them to good use."

"I will, General. Thank you."

"I have also decided to place some sensors in the countryside. We will discuss that momentarily."

"Very good, General."

"I inform you now," Chou said, "that you are to be in Beijing on the ninth of September for a ceremony at which you will be awarded a flying medal."

"Sir!" Hua came to attention and clicked his heels. "I am gratified, but feel that I simply performed my task as expected of my country."

"Quite likely, Major, but you have drawn the attention of Western print and broadcast correspondents, and the leadership believes you should be suitably rewarded."

Hua was disheartened. He knew he had incurred the displeasure of the general, whose name should have appeared in the newspapers, rather than Hua's. His fame would be fleeting, and once it had evaporated, he would be subject to whatever suitable punishment the general was currently formulating. It was perhaps a supreme irony. General Chou did not like having the Western media present, but if they were to be reporting from China, they should be reporting the general's name.

Chou turned back to Kerry.

"Mr. Kerry, Chairman Sun extends his compliments to you, as well as an invitation to attend this ceremony."

"I would be happy to accept, General."

"Very well. Major Hua and Major Yang, we now have operational items to discuss."

"Of course, General Chou."

Effectively dismissed, Kerry headed back toward the hangar for the elevator to the underground to catch the rapid transit train, and Hua and Yang followed an impatient commanding officer into the cool depth of the hangar, where Hua's temporary orderly room was located.

September 6, 1:40 P.M.

Gerhard Ebbing and Ernst Bergen ate a late lunch in the cafeteria on the second floor of Terminal One. It had been open for many months, servicing the needs of the airport workers, and the outside visitors had become accustomed to taking their midday meals there.

On the table beside Bergen's plate of dim sum was the offending issue of *Aviation Week,* given to him by Ebbing. Bergen had just finished reading the article while spinning strands of noodles onto his fork.

"We match it for speed," the security man said.

"True."

"I am not the engineer you are, Gerhard, or the financier Matthew Kraft is, but I suspect I would be concerned about those extra seats."

"You should be on the board of directors, Ernst. When I talked to Kraft this morning, he had already received telephone calls from most of the directors, all related to the same topic."

"Is there a solution?"

"There is, but it is a troublesome one. We could add the seats, but it would be at the expense of leg room, which is already constricted. We would also lose some airspeed as a result of the weight change."

"What of the other airplane, the cargo model?" Bergen asked.

Ebbing managed a smile. "There, we have a slight advantage over the Russians and the British-French, I think. We *do* have a cargo aircraft designed. It is on the computers, and while there is not a prototype, we could have one within seven or eight months. After I talked to Kraft, I think we will be presenting the designs along with our prototype airliner submission."

"Then, it is a horse race?"

"We always thought it would be, with the Americans."

"I hope we have the stronger finish," Bergen said.

Kowloon
September 6, 7:15 P.M.

It had taken one trip by taxi for Kurt Wehmeier to move his belongings from the apartment to the yacht named *Oriental Orchid.* He had paid for two months' rent in advance on his mooring in the marina, and the manager paid no attention to him after that.

In the morning, Wehmeier removed the mattress from the oversized bed in the master stateroom, below the stern deck. With a knife and wire cutters, he cut into the box spring and clipped out several of the springs. He trimmed the opening until his hardshell attaché case would fit into the slot, then replaced the mattress and linen. His most important possessions—several official documents, a half-dozen tape cassettes, and a half-million dollars worth of several different currencies—were contained in the case. He had closed out his Hong Kong accounts, transferring nearly three million dollars to his banks in Switzerland and the Cayman Islands.

In the early afternoon, he and Angelo Malgretto bought $5,000 HK worth of provisions and filled another taxicab. When they reached the marina, it took them both several trips down the long floating dock before the cab was empty and the salon of the boat was stacked with cardboard boxes and sacks.

He then gave Malgretto a roll of bills.

The Italian smiled broadly.

"That is not to be spent on debauchery, Angelo."

The smile faded.

"I want you to find us some weapons. Three handguns, for certain, and three assault rifles, if you can locate them."

"Three?"

"That is what I said."

"This will be simple, Mr. Bern."

"We will need plenty of ammunition. Extra magazines."

"Naturally."

"Rent a car to do this. And go to the cache and retrieve the missile launchers."

"They will be bulky, Mr. Bern."

"Remove them from their crates."

"Very well."

"And bring me the change."

"Of course. *Ciao!*"

Wehmeier had the perishables stored in the refrigerator and half of the canned goods packed into cabinets when Jeremy Smith arrived carrying two oversized suitcases.

He hailed the boat, and Wehmeier climbed the short companionway to meet him on the afterdeck.

Smith was rail thin, almost a caricature of a man, with a bright mop of red hair perched on his elongated and horsey face. His green eyes seemed too large for his face, and they were made more prominent by the thick lenses of the large spectacles he wore. He was dressed in torn denim trousers, a red-and-white-striped polo shirt, and an American army fatigue jacket. His back was hunched by the weight of the suitcases.

He grinned hugely. "Good evening, Mr. Bern!"

Wehmeier glanced around at his neighbors. The marina was packed tightly with craft of every description. In the slip next to them, a sixty-foot-long Chris Craft motor yacht towered above the *Oriental Orchid.* A party seemed to be getting underway on her stern deck.

"Come aboard, Jeremy."

"Take one of these, will you? They're heavy bastards."

Taking one of the cases, which seemed to weigh about fifty kilos, Wehmeier led the way down into the salon. He placed the case on the deck near the banquette.

"Well, now, this is nice! I like it!" Smith said.

"You will share the bow cabin. I am in the master's cabin astern."

"Whatever," Smith said, rummaging through the cardboard boxes. He came up with a bottle of Glenfiddich scotch. "Ah, just what the physician ordered."

Smith had told him earlier that he would not move onto the boat unless certain of his basic needs were met, one of which was first-class Scotch whisky.

Wehmeier watched him while he located a glass, broke the seal on the bottle, and poured the glass full to the rim. He took a long drink, then licked his lips.

"We're going to get along just fine, Mr. Bern."

"Is there more?" he asked.

"Oh, indeed, there is! Out in the car."

"We will get it later. Let me see this, now."

Smith shrugged, placed his glass on the banquette table, then hoisted one of the suitcases onto the tabletop. He pulled a key from his jeans pocket and unlocked the pair of locks. Lifting the lid, he smiled.

The interior of the case contained a puzzle of seemingly unrelated pieces of junk. Wehmeier was dismayed by what he saw.

"This . . . this *exkrement* is what I have paid you two hundred thousand deutsche marks for?"

"Of course! Splendid, is it not?"

"It is incomprehensible."

"To you, perhaps. To me, it is a work of art."

A jungle of wiring in single strands and in flat cables connected spider-legged integrated circuits taped to the lid and base of the case with small bakelite boxes and other IC chips. Glued to the raised lid were apparent digital readouts, but they were uncased. Along one side of the base was a long strip of thin plastic attached to the case by an uneven bead of silicon. Mounted in the plastic were a dozen unlabeled switches and rotary knobs. A large transformer with attached heat sinks was screwed into a block of wood glued to the bottom.

"This thing works?" Wehmeier asked.

"Well, we've still got a few kinks to work out, but it's coming along nicely. I need to pick up a few parts yet."

"Parts? What parts?"

"We need a second video monitor. Also a decent UHF antenna. And the safest thing we could do is get us a filtered two-twenty-volt power supply. I don't want to trust the boat's electric system."

"Is that all?"

"I should think so. The rest of it, I've already got."

"Including the radar?"

"Certainly."

Smith opened the other suitcase on the table next to the first. Its contents were more reassuring. In addition to more wiring and unboxed electronic components, there was a computer. It was the single component that Wehmeier recognized for what it was.

The conglomeration did not inspire confidence in Wehmeier. He only knew that the man came highly recommended and that the circuits he had purchased from him earlier had performed flawlessly.

"Where do you want to work?"

"This table's just dandy," Smith said, taking another long pull from his uniced scotch.

Wehmeier let him set up his equipment on the table and in the settees to either side of it while he went back to storing boxes and cans of food.

Smith turned on the boat's stereo system and found an English language station that played excruciating rock music. He turned it up too loud. The bass tones caused a side window that was loose in its sash to vibrate and rattle. It irritated Wehmeier, but Smith seemed oblivious. He unwrapped tools from a plastic holder and started working on his creation, frequently sipping from his glass of straight Scotch.

It was the price one paid for genius, Wehmeier decided.

A little after nine o'clock, Malgretto came back carrying several wrapped packages. He whistled as he bounced down the steps into the salon, then stopped and eyed Smith suspiciously.

"Well, now," Malgretto said. "Hello, Ned."

Smith looked up from his seat in the booth, holding a soldering iron. "Bloody hell! My cover's blown!"

"A man with telltale hair like that could not hope to hide anywhere in the Orient."

"How are you, Angelo, old chap?"

Wehmeier looked at both of them. "You know each other?"

"We've worked a couple jobs together, haven't we, Angelo?"

"I feel much better about this, Mr. Bern," Malgretto said. "Ned is the best there is."

Given Malgretto's reputation, Wehmeier did not know whether or not he should feel reassured.

September 6, 10:22 P.M.

"Yichang's got an all points bulletin out in China and in the Dependency for three Chinese and a North Vietnamese," Stephen Dowd said.

He had spent the day with Yelchenko, Bergen, and Yichang, then returned to the hotel with Broussard.

Kerry had come into the dining room late and found Broussard and Dowd still at a table, with their dinner finished. He had bought a round of brandies for the three of them.

"Anyone from our list on it?" Kerry asked.

"Nary a one. Yichang's convinced the People's People are the real thing, and all we're offering, now that Ku Chi's crossed off our listing, are two Germans, a Japanese, and a Brit."

Kerry had the list constantly in memory now: Yakamata, Wehmeier, Cooksey, and Imel.

"He is totally convinced that this group is acting alone?" Broussard asked her security director.

"Absolutely. It seems that Yichang and Ku had a long, long talk. Ku's a zealot about his cause, though he won't give up any of his brethren. He and his lot are sure China is headed to hell in a wheelbarrow."

"The Korean hasn't said anything?" Kerry asked.

"No. They've got him trussed up in a straitjacket now because he tried to hang himself."

"Perhaps," Broussard said, "Yichang is correct. Maybe there really is a People's People."

She shook her head, brushing away an errant fly, and her dark hair swished heavily, brushing the tops of her shoulders. Kerry flashed back to when he had had his hands wrapped in that thick, dark mane. He refocused on her violet eyes to avoid the memory, but discovered he might get lost in them, too. He sipped from his snifter.

"I think Ku Chi's been brainwashed," Stephen Dowd said, "but not necessarily by any revolutionary group. If our theory holds out for a while longer, I think Wehmeier's our best shot."

Dowd had learned that afternoon from his friend in the British secret service that Kurt Wehmeier had been seen in Shanghai three months before and that there had been a possible sighting of the German terrorist in Hong Kong in July. That put him in the right place, though not necessarily at the right time. Germans, even fugitive Germans, were not uncommon in Hong Kong.

He tended to agree with Dowd. Wehmeier's dossier, compiled from information provided by the CIA, by Interpol, and by German police, profiled him as a man completely disenchanted with civilized society. His suspected crimes were all directed at establishment targets.

"Why Wehmeier?" Broussard asked.

Kerry replied to the question. "He's supposed to have

been associated with Baader-Meinhof at one time, and he was implicated in bombings attributed to that group. He has served prison time twice, but on minor matters, and his short incarcerations seem to have only fortified his rebellious side. In two instances, Interpol suggests strongly that he has hired himself out as an assassin for other causes. Both the CIA and Interpol suspect him in at least six bombings. And what gives him special status in my mind is that three of those explosions were initiated by remote electronic means, one by telephone for sure."

"And the authorities do not have him under arrest?"

"He's not currently charged with anything, Jacqueline. Only suspected."

"Did you reach Karen Meyer?" Broussard asked him. Her tone of voice with him was more moderated lately; she was living up to their truce.

"I did, finally. Caught her at the El Al offices in Tel Aviv. She had been to Charley's funeral in San Francisco." And had gotten along quite well with Charley's daughter, she'd told him. "As to any more information about Wehmeier, she wasn't very forthcoming. When I mentioned the list, she said, 'What list?' "

Dowd said, "She probably couldn't talk over the phone."

Maybe. Or maybe the powers that be in Israel didn't want to get involved in the Far East. They had enough to worry about at home.

Kerry switched topics. "The Chinese are going to give Major Hua a medal."

"They ought to," Dowd said. "In fact, I ought to be recognized, myself. I went through a missile mishap, if you recall."

"I'll see if I cannot get you a bonus, Stephen," Broussard told him.

"That'll do it."

"I've been invited to the ceremony in Beijing," Kerry said. "Do you two want to ride along with me?"

"Count me in," Dowd said. "I haven't been to Beijing, yet."

"Jim Dearborn will be back with the Citation tomorrow, so we can use that. In fact, I guess we might as well invite everyone to go along."

"Do I get to land it?" Broussard asked, smiling.

"We might give it a try."

"I just changed my mind," Dowd said.

Broussard punched him lightly in the ribs. "Now you have to go along, Stephen, so that you can view my expertise."

"I'm glad these runways are so long," Dowd said.

"Speaking of these runways," Kerry said, "I spoke to PAI's chief pilot this afternoon, and he had a great suggestion."

Kerry told them about Carroll's intention to land downwind in the hope of avoiding any potential sniping with missiles.

"That's a wonderful idea!" Broussard said.

"Why don't you let your pilots know about it, then, and I'll clue in Ebbing and Zemenek. Let's do it quietly, though, just in case there are some more leaks in the China Dome comm center."

"Spring it on the air controller at the last moment?" Dowd asked.

"I think that's the idea."

"Splendid!"

They finished their drinks and left the dining room, headed through the lobby toward the elevators. Broussard walked between the two men.

Kerry caught an elevator door before it closed, they got in, and he punched the buttons for twelve and fourteen. Dowd got off on twelve.

On the fourteenth floor, he and Broussard exited and turned right down the hushed hallway. It was dimly lit with red-shaded fixtures.

He had an overwhelming impulse to take her hand and turn her toward the door to his room. Broussard didn't say anything during the short walk. She fumbled in her purse for her key.

Kerry fought his urge. He knew from experience that it only led to complications that he didn't need.

They both stopped at their own doors on each side of the hall and twisted keys in the locks.

" 'Night, Jacqueline."

"Good night, Dan."

The fifth of October seemed like a time away.

And the first of October seemed like tomorrow.

SEVENTEEN

Hong Kong
September 10, 8:10 A.M.

Dan Kerry and Stephen Dowd met with Avery Baker in the East Wing of the British Government Building. Baker, who appeared to be in his midfifties, was dressed in a summer-weight white suit, a proper diplomat, but wasn't introduced to Kerry with a title. Kerry assumed the man did something innocuous for the overt government and something less innocuous in the way of intelligence gathering. The appointment had been arranged through Dowd's London-based friend in the secret service.

Baker's office was a comfortably aged room—worn and highly polished walnut paneling, heavy gold drapes standing wide of the large windows overlooking the green grass and manicured shrubbery of the grounds. A pair of heavy, brown leather wing-backed chairs faced the desk, which had a green blotter, a marble pen holder, and a single telephone in the middle of its broad mahogany expanse. A pair of matching bookcases against one wall contained historical and sociological tomes. Kerry figured that, if the books belonged to Baker, he was a conservative and dry intellectual.

"How was Beijing?" Baker asked as they took seats.

Kerry had taken a planeload of people up to the capital

for the military ceremony honoring Hua. As a group, they had had a fifteen-minute audience with Sun Chen afterward.

"Keeping tabs on us, are you, Avery?" Dowd asked.

"We find the activities at the new airport interesting."

"It seems as if many people feel the same," Dowd said.

"But you have an additional interest, according to Darrell."

"Mr. Kerry could explain it best, I think."

Kerry said, "There's a distinction between what the Chinese, or possibly just Yichang Enlai, believe and what the SST representatives believe. The Chinese tend to think that the attacks against the airport are the work of a somewhat backward Chinese group."

"I am, naturally, kept aware of the police reports in the Dependency," Baker said.

"A few of us think that the ideological base of this group may be a bit broader, going beyond Chinese borders."

"Please explain that, Mr. Kerry."

"There's a very apparent shift of commercial, industrial, and financial strength to the Orient. And there are those in power centers around the world who do not view that shift optimistically."

"This group is not identified?"

"No. It could be a sizable organization or just a few people. It might never be identified. What's important, in the short term, is that we think they have hired some gunslingers to make certain China Dome doesn't open on time, if at all. That could be accomplished by destroying a few SSTs."

"And setting it up so that it appears to be the work of this, shall we call it fictional, People's People?"

"The foot soldiers," Dowd put in, "might even think that it's a valid organization. Judging by the results of interrogations with Ku Chi and the Korean, that aspect seems likely."

"Shall we be blunt?" Baker asked.

Kerry looked around the wing of his chair at Stephen Dowd, who shrugged, and Kerry said, "Why not?"

"The behind-the-scenes perpetrator could well be one of the SST vendors, correct?"

"The thought has sauntered across my mind," Kerry said.

Dowd added, "No one in the group has voiced the possibility out loud, Avery, but yes, I'm certain we have all considered it. If one of us fears that we might lose the contract, one of us might be targeting the leading candidate."

"And, naturally," Kerry said, "we all consider ourselves to be the leading candidate."

Baker smiled. "All right, I think I understand the dynamics. No one of you is willing to point a finger. . . ."

"I don't know where I'd point it," Kerry interrupted. "So I'm looking at the operational side, rather than the mastermind side."

"And that is Kurt Wehmeier, according to Darrell?"

"After a great deal of culling, we have four prime suspects, but Wehmeier leads the list, as far as I am concerned. That is helped along by the possible sighting made in Hong Kong," Kerry said.

Baker pulled a file folder from his top drawer and opened it. He unclipped, then passed a photograph across the desk, and Kerry and Dowd leaned forward to look at it.

The picture was a blowup from a video surveillance camera, Kerry thought. It showed a man coming through the customs line at Kai Tak Airport. He was tall and broad-shouldered, with a narrow waist and hips. He looked as if he would be a formidable adversary in hand-to-hand combat. Other than that, it didn't look like Wehmeier.

"The pictures we've seen," he said, "show Wehmeier as blond. This guy's got brown hair."

"And blond eyebrows, if you'll notice," Baker said.

"I suppose he trimmed the mustache back," Dowd said, "as well as the hair. I've never seen his ears before. The eyes are green, but he could be wearing tinted contact lenses."

"You cannot see his ring well in the photo," Baker said, "but trust me. It is made of handcuff chain, hammered flat, soldered solid into a circle, then gold-plated. It is the same ring I have seen in an Interpol photograph."

"Hmm," Kerry said, looking at the ring for the first time. "I suppose it's symbolic."

"Undoubtedly, but of what, I would not hazard a guess."

"What name did he come in under?" Dowd asked.

"Walter Bern. It was a German passport."

"And you didn't detain him?" Kerry asked.

"I have no right to do so," Baker told him, "and I am quite certain that such an entry into the Dependency is not an isolated, nor a rare, incident. In any event, the man named Bern did not appear at the hotel where he was registered, and we have not seen him since."

Kerry said, "He's probably a careful man, but this is a big city. Someone had to have seen him."

"Taxi drivers, most likely," Dowd said.

"Would it be possible to get copies of this photo out to airport and taxi people?" Kerry asked.

"That is quite an expensive proposition, even if it were possible for me to arrange it," Baker said.

"Do you know who's going to be on those airplanes, Mr. Baker?" Kerry asked him.

The Brit sighed. "Yes, we do. And we are worried about it. I'll see what I can do."

Deng Xiaoping International Superport
September 10, 10:00 A.M.

In the scheme of things, Daniel Kerry seemed to be hold-ing two jobs. He worked with his counterparts from the other vendors, and he seemed to be filling in for Charley Whitlock in the circle of security men. He attended the meeting Yichang had called for himself, Bergen, Dowd, and Yelchenko.

The five of them sat around a small table near the outer wall of Yichang's office. On the western end of the airport, Yichang saw one of his own helicopters patrolling the outer boundary. Major Hua had scheduled the security helicopters for daytime patrols and was using the army helicopters at night, when the threat seemed to be at its highest point. During the day, too, the fighter aircraft continued to patrol, but they were less obtrusive now for they had moved their operations to Commercial Runway 18 Right Center. All of the east-west runways in front of the terminals and the north-south runways in the commercial section were now open and certified. Yichang had been told that another six weeks would be required before the final runways were opened to traffic.

He kept watching the low-flying helicopter as Stephen Dowd reported his and Kerry's meeting at the British gov-ernment office. As he listened, he felt himself growing dis-tant from these men. The Westerners did not trust him; they were going around him to pursue their own vision of what was taking place in Yichang's jurisdiction.

When Dowd finished, Yichang swung around to face him. "Why is it, Mr. Dowd, that you are so certain of this Wehmeier's involvement?"

"First of all, Mr. Yichang, he is known to have worked

for other organizations. Secondly, he is suspected in incidents in which the same kind of technological methodology was utilized."

"And," Kerry added, "he could even be working for an outfit like your People's People."

"I think you do not understand, Mr. Kerry. The People's People is a fundamentalist group. They would not entertain the idea of allowing outsiders to assist them."

"You are certain of this?" Kerry asked.

"I was the one who spoke for three hours with Ku Chi."

"I never thought I'd say this," Kerry told him, "but maybe we should do more with Ku and the Korean than talk to them."

"*We* will do nothing of the kind. It is my responsibility. Ku and the Korean are scheduled for trial on October ninth."

Yichang felt the hostility developing between him and Kerry, and Yelchenko, perhaps aware of it, interrupted. "Have you made any progress in identifying the other man?"

Yichang let his eyes drift from Kerry slowly, then responded to the Russian. "We have sent a description and a photograph of the Korean to Pyongyang and to Seoul. As yet we have not had a reply."

"And the missile?" Ernst Bergen asked.

"As you know, there is no identifying serial number on the SA-7. They have been manufactured in profusion, and a great many are in the hands of subversive organizations. We cannot trace it by manufacture, and though we have notified law enforcement entities around the world, no one has reported missing inventories. I doubt that they will."

"Let's get back to Wehmeier," Kerry said.

"Let us not," Yichang told him. "I called the meeting, and I have set the agenda."

Kerry's eyes turned to icy slate gray and the planes of his face took on a new surface tension. Yichang had seen the man in action, tackling Whitlock's killer, but he had never seen the transformation that took place before the explosive reaction. He suddenly realized that the American, despite his congenial ways, could be a killer himself.

"I can understand your agenda, Mr. Yichang," Kerry said. "You have the airport to protect, as well as anything that may be on the grounds. In your experience, you have dealt with Chinese revolutionary groups. However, there are some other agendas taking place, which may or may not be more common in the Western world. I believe you should at least allow for their existence."

"Mr. Kerry—" Dowd said.

Kerry held up his hand. "Let me finish, Stephen."

"What agendas are you speaking of?" Yichang asked. With the way Kerry's eyes bored into his own, he was hesitant to divert the man now.

Kerry leaned back in his chair. "You know the one we've been professing, that the SSTs are the target. Behind that is this, Mr. Yichang: I know I've got the best damned airplane in the bunch. And I know that," he slowly pointed his finger at the others as he spoke, "Mr. Bergen, or Mr. Yelchenko, or Mr. Dowd is also aware that I've got the best airplane. There's a hell of a lot of money at stake, in addition to national economies, so Mr. Bergen, or Mr. Yelchenko, or Mr. Dowd figure the only way they're going to land that contract is to eliminate my airplane from the competition. A missile is one way to do that."

Yichang had never before been faced with considerations of pure greed. When he had been a policeman, he had pursued petty thieves, but their motivations had more often been those of hunger rather than material acquisition. Normally, the crimes he had investigated had related to motives of ideology or of family feud. Which meant he understood the People's People.

Yet, when he looked around the table, he saw that the German, the Russian, and the Englishman did not protest Kerry's accusations.

"You are accusing—"

"I am only suggesting, Mr. Yichang. Perhaps it is I who think Mr. Yelchenko's Tupolev 2000 is the front-runner. Maybe I run down Kurt Wehmeier and hire him to make sure the Tupolev never gets its wheels on the ground at Deng Xiaoping International.

"And let me make one more thing clear," Kerry said. "I don't for a minute think that any of the men here are involved. They don't have to be. It could be someone else in their companies. It could be someone else in my company. None of us here like to think of the possibility, but it exists. There's too much at stake to discount the likelihood."

Yichang looked to Ernst Bergen. "Mr. Bergen?"

The man looked back at him without blinking. "You can understand that none of us have spoken openly of this before, Mr. Yichang. However, the scenario is quite possible."

"Mr. Yelchenko?"

The Russian nodded. "I am appalled by the implications, but yes, the prospect exists."

"And Mr. Dowd?"

"If it were someone in my crowd, Mr. Yichang, I would pursue them as diligently as I would some bastard from PAI, BBK, or Tupolev."

Yichang got up and went to the sideboard to pour himself some tea from the ceramic pot resting on a hot plate. He sipped it as he slowly walked around his office, circling the small table. The others watched him.

Sun Chen had warned him, now that he had let himself be surrounded by the Westerners, to not antagonize them, though he should also not allow himself to be guided into uncharted waters by them.

Would someone kill hundreds of people for mere money? He could understand the action if it were committed by someone with deeply held beliefs, like Ku Chi, who saw himself as supporting the foundations of China's modern founding fathers. Ku Chi did not need money to support his zealotry.

He turned abruptly to face Kerry, whose back was toward him.

"Mr. Kerry."

The American turned in his chair.

"You see the economic factor perhaps more clearly than I do. Please explain your thinking further."

"There was a time, Mr. Yichang, when socialism and democracy all around the world divided us and held our attention. Frankly, it just got too damned expensive for governments to maintain elaborate military organizations. Our people rebelled; mine, Mr. Yelchenko's, Mr. Bergen's, Mr. Dowd's, and perhaps your own. The new enemy is not a people; it is poverty, disease, and hunger. We all want what is best for our nations, and we have to expand our economies to support that, to fight the new enemy.

"We are not alone. Your own country is part of the same fight. The money to build this airport, where did it come from?"

"I do not know," Yichang said. "I do not think of such things."

"I don't know, either, but I'll bet it came out of your defense budget."

Kerry was probably correct.

"Very well. I will add the names of Wehmeier, Imel, Cooksey, and Yakamata to the all points bulletin."

Yichang did not believe that it would make a difference in the long term, except to perhaps diffuse the concentration of the police looking for his suspects, but he also thought that Sun would never forgive him if he had ignored the probabilities of Kerry being correct in his assumptions.

Six Miles Above Seattle, Washington
September 9, 7:18 P.M.

The fully finished Astroliner cruised at subsonic speeds as P.J. Jackson hosted his first party aboard it.

He estimated that the party was costing him, or rather the company, about a hundred grand. He also expected the return on investment to be about ten to one, personally.

State senators Green and Jackson were enjoying themselves, he thought, as were the other senators on Green's committee. Some of their staffers were also aboard. The governor was holding court with the political types near the front of the cabin. Their wives were in mid-cabin, probably also talking politics. Four stewards, moonlighting from United Airlines, circulated with trays of hors d'oeuvres and cocktails.

It was a relaxed atmosphere; very few were in their seats. They moved from one conversational grouping to another. Many had their faces pressed to the portholes, to capture the image of Seattle's lights at night.

Senator Paul Jackson was a bit miffed at P.J. for bringing the governor along, and they hadn't spoken much.

In about ten minutes, Carroll would take them out to sea, then ram the throttles forward and show them all what Mach 2 was about as they made the return trip to Edwards.

Jackson winked at Valerie, who was in earnest dialogue with the state's first lady. She was enjoying herself.

The public address system clicked, and he heard the engineer's voice, "Mr. Jackson, please pick up a telephone."

He excused himself from the three senators he was talking to and walked to the back of the plane. Flopping in one of the seats, he lifted the receiver from its niche in the armrest.

"You called, Jeff?"

"Yes, sir. Your connection has been completed."

"Put me through."

"P.J.," Kerry said, "I understand you're partying."

"This is work, Dan."

"I'll trade places with you."

"You wouldn't like it," Jackson told him.

"Probably not."

"What's happening over there?"

Kerry told him about some asshole named Wehmeier and what they were doing to try and track him down.

"This is a German?" Jackson asked.

"He doesn't care who he works for, P.J. I think he just likes blowing up people."

"Damn, I don't like that."

"Until we run him to earth, P.J., you might consider putting off the air trials at China Dome."

"I don't control that," Jackson reminded him.

"But if you and the other CEOs talked to Sun, you could convince him to delay a month or so."

"Not going to happen, Dan, for many reasons. Our board of directors would come unglued, for one."

"Well, it was a thought. You have anything new? You called me."

"Yeah, I got a report from Sunlight."

"What the hell's Sunlight?"

"That's the investigative agency we use."

"Oh. So what did they learn?"

"Nothing you haven't already seen. They took an in-depth look at the board members and top execs of Aerospatiale-BAC and BBK. No one is consorting with shadowy characters, and hasn't, in the past couple of years. As far as they can tell, no one is subject to blackmail. A couple of people in France have some extramarital affairs going. One multimillionaire on the BBK board is a closet gay."

"What about the Russians?"

"That's a different story, since they're not organized the same way. Sunlight went over everyone associated with the design bureau, and only came up with one new item. Pyotr Zemenek has a heart condition we didn't know about. He's had a triple bypass operation. The surgery was done in Norway."

"Beyond the bureau?" Kerry asked.

"For the Tupolev 2000 project, the OKB is supervised by the Ministries of Transportation and Domestic Commerce. What I've got here is some short bios on the chairmen and chief deputies in those ministries."

"And above the ministries?"

"Christ, Dan! You're talking about the president of the country."

"And his flunkies."

"Shit. I'll call Sunlight back."

"Do that. And send me what you've got, will you?"

Jackson hung up, hoping Kerry wasn't going too far with this. The ramifications of a public company in America investigating the political heavies of another country could reach far. Kerry could put both of them out on a limb that the board would be happy to chop off.

Deng Xiaoping International Superport
September 10, 1:35 P.M.

"Thanks for taking the time to see me, General."

"What is it you wish to discuss, Mr. Kerry?" Chou Sen asked him.

Kerry understood, from the general's cold demeanor, that he wasn't exactly in favor of the China Dome enterprise. Maybe he was the mastermind behind the People's People? Still, he tried to be diplomatic, an attitude he had nearly blown this morning in the meeting with Yichang.

General Chou was seated at the desk in Hua's orderly room in Hangar Two. He had his immaculate uniform blouse in place despite the overheated interior. His face gave away absolutely nothing of his thoughts. It could have been cast in bronze, but bronze would have had more movement.

"I appreciate very much the security measures the air force has taken, General. Yet, I am still very concerned about the people who will be on board the SSTs when they arrive on the first of the month."

"The general staff has given me responsibility for their safe arrival, Mr. Kerry. It is not a responsibility I sought or desire to have, but I take it seriously. There will be no attacks completed against the airliners."

"Have you spoken to Mr. Yichang?"

"He did brief me on your meeting this morning," Chou said. "I found the hypothesis interesting, if nothing else."

Interesting? Hell, it should have been more a condemnation of Westerners in general, one you would support, Chou.

"General, I—"

"If you will allow me, Mr. Kerry? I do not agree or disagree with the policies of my country. My life and career are simply dedicated to serving her. I have done so since my youth. I was stationed on the southern border during the time of your conflict with what was then North Vietnam. Did you not serve your country in that arena?"

"I did," Kerry said.

"And did you approve the antiwar sentiment in your homeland? The, what? Peaceniks?"

"No, sir, I did not. I thought it harmful to our efforts."

Chou placed his hands flatly on top of the field desk. "In the same way, I do not relish admitting to the outside world that my country condones the existence of such as the People's People. Still, I must deal with the reality."

"General, I am not absolutely certain that you must put the blame on your nationals. My thought—"

"Your scenario could give me solace," Chou said. "It would reaffirm my ingrained, and perhaps biased, beliefs. Yet, I think the evidence points us in another direction, and to serve my nation honorably and well, I think it best to pursue that direction."

Generals always spoke on levels that perhaps only they understood, Kerry thought.

He was about to protest further when Chou said to him, "If that will be all, Mr. Kerry?"

"Yes, sir," he said, as he had often said when he was a member of the United States Air Force.

Kerry made his way to the elevator stack remembering why he had always disliked generals, no matter their insignia.

They were never wrong.

Beijing, China
September 10, 3:40 P.M.

Sun Chen's aide stuck his head in the door and caught Sun standing at the sidewall, studying the latest aerial photograph of the Superport. All but one of the commercial east-west runways was now completed. The reconstruction of Control Tower Six was substantially under way. By the following week, when the next picture was taken, there would be no trainlike caravan of mobile cement mixers north of the commercial domes.

He turned and waved his assistant into the office.

"I am to remind you, Chairman, of the four o'clock meeting."

"Yes. Would that I could forget it."

He was to meet with a committee formulated to develop policies regarding the development of the enterprise zone south of the airport. He was not looking forward to it.

"And then, Chairman, we have received additional confirmations of attendance at the opening ceremony."

"Tell me, please."

"The Japanese premier will attend, along with his wife."

"Do you have a suitable suite arranged for them?"

"I do."

"Go on."

"We have confirmations, also, for representatives of the executive offices of Vietnam, Laos, Thailand, Burma, the

Philippines, and South Korea. Also, high-ranking representatives from Australia and New Zealand plan to attend."

Sun had not expected all of them to attend the ceremony. That they were coming further demonstrated the tremendous importance the airport was going to play in their political and economic lives. In addition to all of the provincial and municipal officials from mainland China who intended to be present, the guest list was going to be impressive. Sichuan Airlines, Northern Airlines, and China Airways had assigned several aircraft to charter service, sweeping the country to transport the Chinese luminaries to Deng Xiaoping International.

"I have taken it upon myself, Chairman, to reserve an additional one thousand hotel rooms in Kowloon and Hong Kong. These are not reserved at the committee's expense, but at the cost of the visitors."

"I see. A thousand rooms."

"We are now expecting nearly two thousand in attendance, in addition to the media correspondents. My concern was that the correspondents have rooms set aside for them."

"How many have notified us?"

"Six hundred and forty-one, Chairman."

Sun smiled. So many reporters meant that perhaps only a small, dark corner of the African jungles would be unaware of the 21st Century opening its doors in southern China.

"Then, too, Chairman, the Russians have sent us a revised passenger manifest for the Tupolev 2000."

"What?"

The aide shrugged his shoulders.

Sun took the sheet of paper and sat down at his desk. He rifled through the file in his desk drawer and found the original manifest. Placing them side by side on the desktop, he compared the changes.

It appeared that a number of personalities—two actresses, a ballerina, a number of cabinet ministers, including the ministries of transportation and domestic commerce, and two principles in the Tupolev OKB—were bowing out of the trip, to be replaced by persons with names he did not recognize. They were not identified by title, either.

Sun Chen wondered what the changes meant. He also wondered if they were related to the speculation that Daniel Kerry had raised with Yichang Enlai.

He decided that they were unrelated.

Because he did not want them to be.

EIGHTEEN

Kowloon
September 17, 6:10 A.M.

Jacqueline Broussard swore at the alarm clock as it chirped for the second time. Since depressing the snooze button, however, she had not really slept, but merely drifted in and out of semiconsciousness. It seemed as if the last week had been composed of semisleep, ever since Daniel Kerry had made his speech in Yichang's meeting. Stephen Dowd had told her about it.

She turned off the chirping clock, threw the covers back, and sat up on the edge of the bed. She slept in the nude. The air conditioning was turned high, and the chilled air prickled her skin.

Feeling as though she should stay in bed for another few hours, she stood up and went into the bathroom and turned the shower on. When it was running hot, beginning to issue steam, she slipped past the plastic curtain and into the tub. The hot needles of the water took the chill away and made her drowsy.

She did not like what Kerry had done to them, to the people who inhabited the only operating office on the sixth floor of Terminal One. Now, they moved around each other with suspicious eyes, and their conversations were extremely guarded. No one wanted to speak out of turn or allow a slip of the tongue to paint another, or oneself, as a traitor.

Traitor to what? she asked herself. To the industry?

Dowd seemed to accept the conditions with equanimity. He had probably known all along that Kerry suspected one of them as a conspirator intent on killing off the opposition. She had come to studying Zemenek and Ebbing as if she were trying to peer beneath their skulls and uncover their hidden, black souls.

And what of Kerry himself? He knew about things military, about missiles and such. Were his henchmen in hiding, waiting to strike down the Concorde II as it made its approach to China Dome? Had he created the downwind landing solution merely to give them all an illusion of safety?

Or was he simply a supersonic paranoid, seeing in the rest of them his own fear of failure?

When, during her restless nights, she reviewed all that she and Kerry had talked about, almost since they first met each other, she realized that he had thought all along that someone from Aerospatiale-BAC, BBK, or Tupolev was behind the attacks at the airport.

Did Kerry think her extremely naive for not seeing what the others thought was obvious?

Probably.

It was another of his macho, arrogant traits.

She soaped herself viciously, letting her anger escape. And as she stood with her head tilted back, letting the full blast of the water rinse her body, the anger dissipated, as it had numerous times before, and she was forced once again to attempt to objectively weigh both sides of the argument.

Kerry was correct, of course. She gave him a fifty percent chance of being correct.

But who was he correct about?

On the small table in her room were her handwritten notes, gleaned from the pages of the aviation magazines. She had assembled the known specifications for the Astroliner, the Concorde II, the AeroSwift, and the Tupolev 2000, and placed them side by side in columns.

If she were to be truthful with herself. . . .

Broussard had not yet pursued that statement to its conclusion.

Shutting off the water, she stepped out of the tub and lifted one of the fluffy white towels from its rack. She wandered back into the bedroom as she patted at her skin with the towel.

She stood at the table and looked down at the columns of numbers she had written.

The AeroSwift and the Astroliner were superior to the Tupolev and the Concorde. On paper, there was no mistaking that inference, though she had tried every way possible to avoid it.

Dropping the damp towel on the carpet, she settled into the chair and looked at the rows and columns of numbers almost hypnotically.

The Russians, she was certain, were capable of nearly anything, if it achieved their goals, and they badly needed the Chinese contract. Look at their history. The Korean Airlines 747. The KGB atrocities. Zemenek and Yelchenko did not have to be a part of it; there were always others.

And there was her godfather. Henri Dubonnet had never failed at anything he had ever attempted. Would he go to such lengths to prove himself a success?

Of course he would not.

She knew him too well.

She knew him like—better than—her own father.

Or did she?

Without apparent qualm, he had hired thugs to rid her of unwanted suitors. She had known it, had appreciated it, and had given no further thought to it.

She suddenly felt lost. She did not know which way to turn, how she should think.

Broussard lifted the telephone resting on the table and dialed the number of Kerry's room.

One thing the numbers told her; they told her that Kerry had little to fear from his competition.

It rang three times before he picked it up.

"Kerry."

"Dan, come over here, please."

"I'm not dressed yet, Jacqueline."

"Neither am I."

Deng Xiaoping International Superport
September 17, 11:20 A.M.

The problem with having fifteen runways, Hua Peng thought, was that there were thirty approaches to them. It helped that only seven of them were currently operational.

Hua hung in the open side door of the Super Frelon helicopter as it passed over the double fences, then the succeedingly taller towers of the approach markers on the west end of the field. When they reached the outer markers, the helicopter pilot went into a shallow glide, and a hundred meters from the markers, began to hover.

Over the intercom, the pilot asked, "Here, Major Hua?"

With a firm grip on the doorjamb, the squadron commander leaned out and looked back at the runway which was the main Runway 9 Right. They were offset to it by about fifteen meters.

"This is fine, Lieutenant," he replied.

The Super Frelon settled to the ground, raising a whirlwind of dust and dead branches from shrubs. Hua turned back to the interior and gave the technical sergeant a thumbs up.

The sergeant picked up one of the plastic cylinders secured in netting at the back of the cabin and slid out the opposite doorway. Hua watched him as he ran a few meters away, his head rotating back and forth as he searched for a suitable hiding spot. He picked out a stunted pine and went to his knees next to it. With a trenching tool, he dug a shallow hole, settled the cylinder into it, flicked the arming switch, then covered it. He made certain the thin and stiff antenna extending fifteen centimeters from the top of the cylinder was clear, then stood up and looked back to Hua.

Hua nodded, then spoke on the intercom. "Lieutenant, connect me with Thunderfoot."

Hua did not have control over the radio from his position in the back, and the pilot dialed in the frequency for the listening post that had been set up in Hangar Two.

"Thunderfoot, Sparrow One."

"Sparrow One, I read you clearly."

"Sensor One is in place."

"Hold on, Sparrow. We are checking."

After a few moments, the operator reported, "Sensor One is identified and operational."

The major identified the location for the operator, who marked it on his computer map.

Hua signalled the sergeant and he came running back to tumble onto the floor of the helicopter.

"All right, Lieutenant, let us go one kilometer directly west."

The Super Frelon lifted off.

When this day's work was done, they would have twenty-eight of the supersensitive sensors in place at the ends of the operational runways. Each of them could pick up the sound of footfalls for a half-kilometer in any direction and identify the direction and approximate range from the sensor in which the sounds occurred. The data collected by the sensors was transmitted to the base station where a computer unscrambled the digital signals from all sensors, determined whether the sounds were generated by a human, a dog, a tractor, or perhaps an automobile, then pinpointed the location on the monitor screen. The operator, codenamed Thunderfoot, could sit at his console and watch a man walking through the fields at the end of the runways.

From this day forward, Hua knew, no man would get within three or four kilometers of the runways before Sparrow One or Sparrow Two pounced on him.

Hong Kong
September 17, 3:12 P.M.

Ned Cooksey, whom Wehmeier had known as Jeremy Smith, was late getting back to the yacht.

Wehmeier waited restlessly, unable to stay for long on the settee which spanned the transom of the *Oriental Orchid*. He got up and paced the deck.

Angelo Malgretto, on the other hand, was perfectly at ease. He sprawled on the lounge seat, with his feet up on the railing and his bare chest exposed to the sun. He was drinking from a bottle of Philippine beer and talking to a young Chinese girl dressed in a clinging *cheongsam* who had been walking the dock until Malgretto got her attention.

Wehmeier had been just as comfortable as Malgretto until midnight last night, when Malgretto had returned from a date—probably with a half-dozen people. He had come aboard laughing, stumbling half-drunk down the companionway to stand in the salon and grin at Wehmeier.

"You have had a tremendous evening, no doubt," Cooksey had said. "Are you going to share the humor, Angelo?"

Slurring his words only slightly, Malgretto said, "Walter Bern, here, had me believing I was the target of an international manhunt."

"And you're not?"

"Not like the one they have got going for him."

That, plus Malgretto's sudden decision to not address him as Mr. Bern, had brought Wehmeier out of his reclined position on the couch. "What are you talking about?"

The Italian grinned widely, "The cab I came back in? Your picture is taped to the instrument panel. Along with a few others, mind you, but mine is not among them."

Wehmeier could not believe it.

"You asked the driver about it?"

"Of course. I could not resist. He said the police are contacting all of the drivers, passing out photographs. He did not know for what crime you stand accused."

Wehmeier had wanted to cast off and put to sea immediately, but Cooksey had vetoed it since he had not yet accumulated all of the components he needed.

So now they waited for Cooksey . . .

Who might have abandoned them and could well be on

an airplane bound for Australia or India or Pakistan. Who knew?

"Well, now, chaps! Someone give me a hand here!"

Wehmeier turned around to see Cooksey eyeing the Chinese girl as he struggled down the dock with his arms full of packages and a three-meter-long antenna. In his jeans and fatigue jacket, he looked like one of the disaffected American youth of two decades before. Malgretto did not move, so Wehmeier stepped down to the dock, met the Brit, and relieved him of a large cardboard box.

The two of them carried the paraphernalia below, then Wehmeier returned to the afterdeck and climbed the ladder to the flying bridge.

He flipped the switches for the bilge blowers and pumps while calling to the afterdeck, "Angelo! Release the lines."

"Hey, Walter? The girl wants to come along."

"No."

"We could go to Macau, drop her off there."

"Get the lines, Angelo. Now."

"Hey, it is just a little—"

"Would you like to stay, Angelo?"

Malgretto sighed and hoisted himself off the stern bench seat. He crossed to the dock and murmured apologies to the girl as he untied the spring lines holding the boat to the dock.

Wehmeier fired the diesel engines as the former owner had taught him, and as soon as the Italian was back aboard, pulled both transmission gearshifts into reverse. Slowly, the cruiser backed out of the slip, sliding from the shadow cast by the larger Chris Craft. He shifted to neutral when he saw another powerboat coming down the channel. By the time it had passed, the *Oriental Orchid* was far enough back in the channel for him to shift to forward and apply power to the port engine. Spinning the helm, he turned toward the entrance to the Yaumati Typhoon Shelter, inside which the marina was located. He advanced the starboard throttle until he was holding five knots.

The yacht passed through the entrance, and Stonecutters Island appeared off the starboard bow. He added more power as he turned south, staying clear of the mooring where larger ships were placed. The first line of buoys, the B Class buoys secured ships of 300 to 450 feet. Beyond them, the A Class buoys were designated for ships up to 600 feet in length. Most of the buoys were occupied.

After the piers and freight-handling clutter of Tsimshatsui passed to port, Wehmeier turned to the east, cruising the middle of the passage between Kowloon and Hong Kong Island.

Forty minutes later, the *Oriental Orchid* was but one of hundreds of boats plying the Lyemun Pass eastward. Wehmeier called Malgretto up to the bridge and turned the helm over to him.

He went below to the salon to find Cooksey slumped in the banquette with another glass of Scotch. He was gleefully opening packages and examining his purchases.

"Did you get the paint?" he asked.

"Of course I got it, mate."

Deng Xiaoping International Superport
September 17, 4:45 P.M.

The sun was low in the western sky, but was not visible anyway when Gerhard Ebbing and Ernst Bergen went for their afternoon walk. The sedentary nature of their work had encouraged them to find mild exercise, and the crowded condition of their office had encouraged them to find solitude when discussing some issues that Ebbing thought best kept between themselves. It was a ritual they had observed frequently since coming back to China.

All afternoon, the cloud cover had been building up, and now a mottled gray overcast spread from one horizon to the other. The clouds above rolled and shifted in an easterly wind, and on the ground, the breeze was stiff and refreshing. Ebbing expected rain to fall at any moment, and for that reason, they walked a circular course around the main terminal, staying close to it.

To the west of them, over at Terminal Six, a small jet airliner was parked. It was identified as belonging to Sichuan Airlines and, with the PAI Cessna Citation parked next to Terminal One, comprised the entire complement of passenger craft in the terminal area.

"This place is becoming positively overpopulated," Bergen said, pointing to the airplane.

"Terminal Six is dedicated to domestic flights," Ebbing told him. "I think we shall see a few flights from Sichuan and China Airways as their employees are brought in from around the country for orientation tours. Zhao Li took us over there a couple days ago, and I saw that their facilities are all but completed."

The two men strode along briskly. Ebbing enjoyed a good walk, but he was thinking more of walking in the sand of an island beach and not on the hard surface of a concrete island in the middle of southern China.

"How are you doing, Gerhard?" Bergen asked.

"Me? I am fine."

"You have not been so fine."

It was true. Ebbing had been very depressed since Bergen had reported Kerry's suspicions to him. Then, to learn that Bergen had also harbored the same distrust of unknown persons at Pacific Aerospace, Aerospatiale-BAC, and Tupolev had been a trifle unnerving. He was an engineer and a scientist who lived in a fantasy world of numbers and concepts and not in the world of industrial intrigue. It was difficult now to sit in their combined office and look at Kerry, Broussard, and Zemenek and not think that one of them could be a murderer, or at the least, a conspirator.

"I suppose, Ernst, that I am disappointed in mankind."

"Mankind does not have a very good record," Bergen pointed out.

"Of late, though, they have been improving, I think. Or thought."

"The problem with you scientists is that you wish to think the best of everyone. In my line of work, we tend to think the worst."

"You are never surprised, then."

"Rarely, Gerhard, rarely."

"Between you and me, Ernst, do you have a prime suspect?"

Bergen grinned at him. "I have the same suspects as anyone else."

"Beyond that damnable list?"

"There is no hard evidence which compels me to point a finger in any direction."

"But, surely—"

"In police work, Gerhard, we try to keep narrowing the choices. Eventually, there will be only one choice."

"And have you narrowed your choices?"

"By one. The Japanese terrorist, Yakamata, has been discovered in Angeles City, near Manila. He has been hiding out there for over a year."

"Which leaves?"

"Four on Yichang's short list, and three on our own."

"And this Wehmeier? He is your first choice?"

"He is Kerry's first choice," Bergen said, pondered for a moment, then added, "and perhaps my own. I would like to know more about Josef Imel, who has a degree in electronics from Frankfurt."

"These are our countrymen," Ebbing said.

"Do we really want to claim them, Gerhard?"

"I suppose not."

"If it helps you at all," Bergen said, "based on my infallible instincts about the nature of man, I do not believe that anyone in our office on the sixth floor is guilty of anything other than excessive optimism."

Ebbing stopped walking as the first raindrops began to fall.

"Really?"

"Really, Gerhard. Except for Broussard and Kerry, of course."

"What have they done?"

"I suppose we had best call it indiscretion."

"What is your evidence?"

"The way a man walks, or is too careful of implied intimacy. The way a woman looks at a man."

"I did not think she liked Kerry."

"That is the puzzling aspect, but I think she overcame the repugnance," Bergen said and smiled.

The rainfall was increasing, and they turned toward the ground-level doors.

"What do you think of Kerry?" Ebbing asked as they picked up their pace, breaking into a trot.

"I am jealous of him, of course," Bergen said.

Astrofreighter 01
September 17, 1:25 A.M.

"GOTCHA!"

The exclamation roared in Carroll's earphones, and a couple seconds later, the F-16 Falcon shot by, its navigation lights flickering on and clearly visible in the right-side cockpit window.

"Jesus Christ!" Cliff Coker yelped.

As command pilot, he was in the left-hand seat, and his copilot, Norm Mentor, was in the right seat. Terry Carroll was acting as flight engineer and was aft of them on the flight deck.

Don Matthews, who was flying the fighter, did a victory roll far ahead of them.

"PA Zero-Two, that was poorly executed," Matthews said on the interplane frequency.

"Hell, Don, we never saw you," Carroll admitted. "Go away for a while, and then try us again."

The F-16's lights blinked out, and it peeled off to the right. A minute later, as he turned back under them, the glow of its exhaust disappeared.

"What the hell happened, Terry?" Coker asked.

"Never came up on the threat receiver."

Carroll checked each of his settings, then flipped the circuit breaker on and off. He still had a green LED, signifying that the set was working properly.

"Antenna problem, you think?" Mentor asked.

"Shows good," Carroll said.

The radar threat receiver also had green lights, but it had worked perfectly on Matthews's first attack run.

Twelve minutes later, Matthews sneaked up on them from above and behind, and again theoretically blew them out of the sky. Carroll did not pick him up on the forward-facing radar antenna nor on the infrared threat receiver.

Carroll made notes on the pad resting at his elbow.

"What do you think, Terry?"

"This hummer's going to be grounded, unless it's fixed."

"Aikens and Jackson aren't going to be happy."

"Tough."

"Damn, it's only a cargo plane," Coker said. "You don't ground a cargo plane for a busted threat receiver."

"If it's headed for China Dome, you do."

Kowloon
September 17, 11:35 P.M.

The telephone chimed twice before Kerry decided he had better answer it. He snaked an arm out, captured it from the bedside stand, and pulled it close.

"Good night," he said.

"Mr. Kerry, this is Yichang Enlai. I apologize for interrupting your sleep."

Kerry was on his left side, and Broussard was snuggled up tightly against his back. Her right arm was draped around his waist. Her even breathing against the back of his neck told him she was still asleep.

He spoke softly. "That's all right, Mr. Yichang."

"Inspector Wing of the Hong Kong police has located Kurt Wehmeier. I wonder if you would like to go with us."

He was awake now.

"Where are you?"

"In the lobby of your hotel."

"I'll be down in five minutes."

Kerry managed to slip out from under her arm without

waking her, but when he rose from the bed, the mattress shifted.

"Uh? Dan?"

He found his shorts and jeans on the chair and pulled them on, then sat down, fishing for his socks and running shoes.

"Go back to sleep, Jacqueline."

"What are you doing?"

She sat up in the bed. He could see her pale form in the partial light of the city coming through the slanted shades over the window. Rain was spattering against the glass.

"I've got to meet Yichang."

She leaned over to look at the bedside clock. "This late?"

His sport shirt was draped over the back of the chair. Pulling it on, he fumbled with the buttons.

"He just called. They've got Wehmeier pinned down."

She started to get out of the bed.

"I'm coming along."

"Too late, my dear. Go back to sleep."

Grabbing his nylon windbreaker from the chair, Kerry headed for the door, checking the night lock as he closed it on her protest.

Yichang was standing near the front doors when Kerry stepped out of the elevator. He was in a gray suit and wore a tan trench coat.

As Kerry approached him, he said, "Thanks for calling me."

"I was going to get Mr. Dowd or Mr. Bergen, but they are not back in their rooms yet."

Yichang's Honda was parked in front of the hotel, and they climbed into it. The security director slapped the gearshift into first and pulled away. At the end of the block, he turned right and accelerated. The traffic was heavy, and

Kerry noted the deftness with which Yichang drove, shifting lanes to avoid tie-ups. The rain continued to fall in a thick drizzle. The black asphalt gleamed with moisture, and the lights of cars and neon signs reflected off it like an out-of-control kaleidoscope.

"Have they picked up Wehmeier already?" Kerry asked.

"When Inspector Wing called me, he said only that a taxi driver had called with the address, and he was just preparing his team to respond. Other than that, I know nothing."

Yichang made several more turns, then they were moving through sparser traffic along the waterfront. The rain prevented him from seeing anything more than a few hundred yards offshore. A few minutes later, he pulled the car into a no-parking zone next to a police car. Another police car was across the street, on the bay side, but none of their emergency lights were on. Kerry didn't think it looked promising.

They crawled out of the car and crossed the street to a small office with a large sign reading "Two Moons Marina."

A policeman was stationed next to the office, standing in front of an open chain-link gate. Yichang identified himself, and they were allowed to descend the slanting wooden gangplank to the floating dock.

Walking along the dimly lit dock, Kerry noted the lights on in a few of the vessels. Out on the bay, beyond the typhoon barrier, larger ships were moored, their anchor lights sparkling through the rain. The wooden planks were wet and slick under his feet, and the rain drummed on the fiberglass and the wooden decks of the boats crammed into the slips around him. Rivulets of water ran down the front of his windbreaker.

Yichang turned left at an intersection of the dock lit by

a gooseknecked fixture on a short lamppost. The dock ahead
stretched out ahead of them for a quarter-mile, but halfway
down it, they reached a slip that had an obvious vacancy.

"Damn," Kerry said.

"Yes, I think so."

A cop in a yellow slicker stood at the base of a wooden
stairway leading up to the deck of a large cruiser, and
Yichang spoke to him in Chinese. They were ushered
aboard.

Kerry climbed the short flight and stepped onto the stern
deck behind Yichang. The afterdeck was protected from the
rain by a blue-and-white-striped awning. Several men stood
under it in the light of several lanterns, talking.

Kerry figured out right away that the biggest man, about
six-four, with a definitive Texas accent, was the boat's
owner.

". . . naw, hell, Inspector, there was only the three of
them."

"And you are certain the man in the photograph was
one?"

"Damn tootin'. The guy had these crazy eyes, like would
stare you down just 'cause he enjoyed it."

"Could you describe the other two to me?"

"One guy was dark, you know, dark skin, black, oily
hair. He—hey, there, you an American?"

Kerry stepped forward and shook the outstretched hand.
"Kerry, Dan."

"Where you from, Dan?"

"L.A., Mister? . . ."

"Hank Dawson, Houston. You with the cops?"

"Observing, Hank. What did this man look like?"

"Oh, yeah, well like I said, they were only here maybe
ten days, since they took over from the guy used to live

aboard, but the dark guy—I think they called him Angelo, he was a ladies' man. Hustled every gal walked down the dock. My wife had to shoot him down one time."

"Shoot him down?" the inspector asked.

"Verbally, you know?"

"Do you remember anything else about him?"

"Lessee. He's maybe five-seven, five-eight. Built real good, I guess."

"How about the third man?"

"That's the easy one. Skinny as hell, call him five-eleven. Wore an army coat all the time, kind of dirty."

"The coat?"

"That, and the guy. I don't think he took many showers. He'd sit on the stern of the boat and slug back whiskey straight from the bottle, but you know, I never saw him fallin' down drunk. He could handle it."

"Was there anything else about him that you recall?"

"Glasses. Wears glasses thick as Coke bottle bottoms. And he's got bright red hair."

"You ever hear him called by name?"

"The first guy, with the crazy eyes, called him Jeremy."

"Ned Cooksey," Kerry said.

The inspector looked over at Kerry, then at Yichang.

Yichang said, "Inspector Maynard Wing, this is Mr. Daniel Kerry."

"Ah, yes. Director Yichang has mentioned you to me. You say his name is Cooksey?"

"Out at the airport, I have a dossier on him, Inspector. He's English. An expert in electronics."

Wing looked again at Yichang, who only nodded.

The inspector asked Dawson a few more questions, then the contingent of policemen went back down the stairs to the dock.

Dawson said, "Dan, ya'll come back for a drink, anytime. Hell, all of you come back, sometime."

They thanked him as they trooped down the stairs. At the bottom, they grouped together under a couple of umbrellas held by two of the men. Since they were all in civilian clothes, Kerry took them for detectives.

"If the taxi driver had called earlier," Wing said, "we might have had better luck. Mr. Dawson said that the yacht departed in midafternoon, perhaps around three o'clock."

"Mr. Dawson seems to have been very observant," Yichang said. "Did he notice anything else?"

"He said that they had provisioned the boat well. Today, the red-haired one—Cooksey?—brought some large packages aboard just before they left. There was an antenna, as well."

"Any ideas about the dark man, Mr. Kerry?" Yichang asked.

"None," Kerry said. "But putting Wehmeier and Cooksey together reinforces some of the things I've been thinking about."

Yichang appeared thoughtful.

Wing waited patiently.

"Perhaps," Yichang said finally.

Wing asked, "Director, could I ask for a hint?"

"The man Cooksey would have been capable of duplicating the airport identification cards," Yichang said to him. "Including the magnetic strip."

Kerry wasn't sure what that was all about, but it sounded to him as if Yichang didn't want to let Maynard Wing in on all of the details of the investigation at China Dome. Yichang's explanation was a plausible one.

To get off the subject, Kerry asked, "Do we know the name of the boat?"

"Yes," Wing said. "It is a forty-four-foot Hiptimco cruiser, white, with the name *Oriental Orchid* in gold letters across the transom. Mr. Dawson said it was in excellent shape."

The conference broke up then, and Kerry and Yichang walked back to the Honda.

Once he was back in the car, Kerry used his handkerchief to wipe the moisture from his face.

Yichang didn't start the car. He rolled his window down an inch to counter the haze building on the inside of the windshield.

"Mr. Kerry, your theory has more credibility."

"I'd just as soon it didn't have any credibility, Director. They could still be working for the People's People."

"Yes. That is possible, but only just possible."

"What's the next step?"

"I will talk to General Chou in the morning. He could involve the navy in searching for the boat."

Kerry noted the "could." He supposed Yichang wasn't getting much voluntary cooperation from the general.

Checking his watch, Kerry saw that it was after midnight.

"If you want to take a break," he said, "I'll buy you a drink."

"Not a drink, thank you. We could purchase a hamburger."

"Sounds good to me."

"Charley Whitlock liked hamburgers," Yichang said.

"Yes, he did."

NINETEEN

P.J. Jackson's secretary buzzed him on the intercom.

"Yes, Mollie?"

"I have Dennis Aikens and Terry Carroll on the line for you."

"Thanks."

He punched the blinking button and said, "Good morning."

They responded simultaneously.

"Where are we on this goddamned threat receiver?"

Aikens replied. "As you know, P.J., we designed this system specifically for these aircraft, and the linkage between the antenna electronics and the cockpit console is fiber optic."

"Yeah, I've got that."

"The electronics all check out, and the antenna is fine. We had green lights on those components. The problem appears to be in the aft fiber-optic translator. We're going to have to build another one, but we're doing it from scratch, and I don't see us having it ready by October first."

"From scratch? Damn it, we're supposed to have a backup for every piece of new technology."

"This one *is* the backup, P.J. It's the backup for the Astroliner. When we decided to go ahead with the Astrofreighter, we grabbed this translator. Somewhere in the process, someone dropped the ball on restocking."

"Fire that son of a bitch!"

"I suspect it was me," Aikens said.

"Fire yourself later. Fix the damned airplane now."

"I can't guarantee—"

"I don't care what the hell you can guarantee. If it's not ready, we'll go without it."

These guys didn't understand the impact of negative publicity. Pacific Aerospace had already displayed the Astrofreighter to the public. It was certified by the FAA. It was approved by the Chinese for the flight to China. If they backed out now, everyone in aviation was going to wonder why, and worse, wonder if the problem extended to the Astroliner. And an alibi of a defective translator wasn't going to save them. Plus, they didn't want to announce to anyone that a civilian aircraft, much less an airliner, was sporting military-type countermeasures. That wouldn't do much to impress the flying public about the safety of air travel.

Carroll broke in, "P.J., I won't unground the airplane."

"This isn't related in any way to flyability, Terry."

"Given the events at China Dome," Carroll said, "we'd be putting the aircraft at risk."

"Nothing's happened there in weeks. The airplane is flying."

"P.J.—"

"End of fucking conversation." Jackson slammed the phone down.

Deng Xiaoping International Superport
September 24, 2:16 P.M.

The phone rang once in Tokyo before Julie Macon picked it up.

"Pacific Aerospace, Office of Development."

"Hi, Julie."

"Dan! When are you coming back?"

"Lonely, are you?"

"Not lonely, but Mickey makes us work."

"Good man. Is he around?"

"Hold on."

Duff came on the line a minute later. "Hello, boss."

"How would you like to go flying, Mickey?"

"Anything but a blimp."

"F-16?"

"Shit! I'll go dig out my flying gear."

"Here's what I've got," Kerry said and told him about the problem Carroll was having with the Astrofreighter. "What I'd want you to do is fly to the States, get that leased Falcon, and get it back to Tokyo. Then, on the first, you join up with both Astros and fly escort for them into China Dome."

"Piece of cake. I'll get a plane reservation for L.A."

"Hold on, Mickey. You know what I'm asking you to do?"

The response came from a more sober Mickey Duff. "Yeah, I do. If a missile appears, I shake it with chaff and flares. Or I take the hit. I know what's expendable and what's not."

"This rates a hell of a bonus, Mickey."

"The bonus is in flying the airplane."

"I'd do it myself, but I think I'd better be here."

"I like you there, and me in the fighter," Duff said.

"Okay. So far, you and I own this idea. I've got to clear it with P.J."

"Get on it, Dan."

"I'll get back to you."

Kerry depressed the disconnect bar, and when he got another dial tone, pushed the memory button for PAI's Century City headquarters. He got right through to Jackson's office.

"Morning, Mollie. The captain there?"

"He's on another line, Dan."

"I'll wait."

Two minutes later, Jackson came on the line. "Let me guess. Carroll complained to you, and you're going to cry to me."

"Wrong."

"Okay, then, something new blew up at China Dome."

"Nope. I'm solving Carroll's problem and your problem for you."

"If this works, I'm giving you the rest of my problems."

"I'm sending Mickey Duff to Edwards to pick up the Falcon." Kerry said. He outlined the rest of his plan.

"Goddamn. You know, Dan, our insurance doesn't cover this."

"You want to buy a new Falcon or a new prototype SST? And that presupposes that anything happens at all. Weigh the risks, P.J."

"Mickey understands?"

"He knows."

After a long moment, Jackson said. "I can be a son of a bitch."

"We all know that."

"But I haven't asked any of my employees to put their lives on the line. Not for a long time."

"We all did it in the first trials of the Astroliner," Kerry reminded him.

"That's a civilian trade, not a wartime threat."

"Say yes."

Jackson sighed and said, "I'll get Mollie going on getting the clearances."

Kerry replaced the receiver and looked up to find Broussard studying him from the next desk.

She smiled and said, "Have you ever listened to your side of a telephone conversation?"

"It's in code."

"It must be. It's practically unintelligible."

"You want to leave work early today?"

"Yes. But I'm waiting on a call."

Kerry wasn't sure where he and Broussard were going with this relationship, and though she could be expected to do the unexpected from time to time, they'd had a pretty smooth few days. He had found himself thinking beyond October 1 and October 5.

He stood up. "I've got to go down and see Yichang. I keep forgetting I have to clear all my great ideas with him, too."

"When you get back, will you do something for me?"

"Sure."

"Tell me what a threat receiver is?"

September 24, 6:10 P.M.

The photographs of the three Chinese, the Vietnamese, the two Germans, and the Englishman were displayed in the security center now. Yichang had taped the enlarged photos in prominent locations so that none of his men would forget what their primary mission was at the moment.

Five of his security officers were assigned to telephones, continually calling law enforcement agencies around the world to see if any of the suspects had been detected. He had hopes that the constant interrogations of other agencies were creating an international pressure for legal entities to cooperate. And as evidence of his goodwill, Yichang had ordered his staff to provide unlimited information to those who asked for it. It was an unprecedented release of data from Chinese coffers, and Yichang had not actually secured the permissions he should have. He would deal with it later, after the grand opening.

Only in passing had he considered that Western influences appeared to be affecting him; he was making decisions that were normally reserved for other levels of his government.

He had smaller versions of the same photographs taped to the back of the nameplate on his desk, facing him, so that he, too, knew what was to be his focus for the next week.

Yichang's mind was now divided, as were the pictures. On the left side, he had grouped those men he thought possibly connected to the People's People, and on the right, he had placed the three Europeans Kerry favored.

Yichang's experience told him that, too often, China had bred individuals of a rebellious nature. A People's People could well have been nourished by the climate of Western favoritism.

Still, the eyewitness account of Wehmeier and Cooksey in company with one another gave added credence to Kerry's supposition of thugs hired to interfere with the supersonic transport competition.

He would feel better if General Chou, who had returned to his headquarters, would return his telephone call. He desperately wanted to know if the navy had been involved in the search for the yacht, and if they had, whether or not they had yet sighted the *Oriental Orchid*. He almost picked up the telephone to try again, but feared that he might irritate the general. In that event, he would receive very little cooperation.

Wu Yhat knocked once, then opened the door to his office.

"Cousin? There is news."

Yichang looked up hopefully. "Yes?"

"Hanoi finally presented us with information on the criminal Thanh."

"And that is?"

"The man was executed for crimes against the state."

"When?"

"Over a year ago."

"It seems to me," Yichang said, "that if we had better communications with our sister nations, we would not have spent the last weeks chasing a phantom."

"That is so."

Edwards Air Force Base
September 23, 1:20 P.M.

Terry Carroll crossed the warm concrete of the hangar to the Astroliner. The portable stairs were in place against the fuselage, and he climbed them to enter the foyer.

There was a vacuum going in the passenger cabin, and he peeked in to see one of the maintenance men cleaning the cabin. P.J. Jackson's intimate party had resulted in a few cigarette burns and spilled drinks. Fortunately, when the aircraft became the leased property of some airline, cigarettes would be banned. There weren't even ashtrays built into these seats.

He pushed open the door to the flight deck and stepped inside. He was going to download the maintenance computer data to a floppy disk and take it back to the lab to update the lab's database. The Astroliner monitored her own systems and flagged those that needed routine or special attention.

He came to a stop when he saw a white-coated technician seated on the floor between the two pilot's seats. He had the front panel removed from the center control pedestal. His stack of digital test instruments was on the deck beside his knee, and he had his hands inside the equipment bay, using probes to test circuits. Odd numbers in green numerals appeared on the faces of the test instruments as he worked.

The man looked back at him, and he recognized the dark face.

"Hey, Mohammed. What's going on?"

"Hello, Captain Carroll. I was told to check the continuity of the threat receiver circuits."

"How long are you going to be?"

"If all goes well, perhaps another hour. I could delay if you need to do something important."

"It'll wait," Carroll told him.

Kowloon
September 24, 7:35 P.M.

The entire group ate dinner together in a corner of the main dining room of the President Hotel. The meal was hosted by

Pyotr Zemenek and Yuri Yelchenko, both of whom had spent a few hours working with the hotel's chefs.

When they arrived, *zakuski*—hors d'oeuvres of smoked fish, caviar, marinated mushrooms, and pickled cucumbers were spread across the table, along with carafes of white wine and *khorilka spertsem,* a Ukrainian vodka with hot peppers in it. Zemenek detailed the salads, *shchi*—vegetable soup, *pirozhki*—pastries, *kasha*—buckwheat porridge, and *pirog*—cream-filled cake that would be forthcoming.

Broussard told him, "Pyotr, you will make me fat."

"Mademoiselle, a woman should be substantial," he smiled.

"Not that substantial."

She and Stephen Dowd moved over to the table to load small plates with black bread and caviar, pickles and mushrooms. Dowd poured her some Chablis and filled a glass with the pepper vodka for himself. The dining room was not crowded at that hour, but the people at the few tables that were occupied eyed the gathering in the corner with either amusement or perplexity.

They had all agreed that they would use their last week together to promote their own causes with their fellow travellers. She and Dowd had drawn the evening of the twenty-seventh as their night, but they had yet to agree on a menu. Merging dishes from both sides of the Channel into one meal was proving to be an instant provocation for culinary combat. When Dowd suggested that he would provide the beverages, if she provided the meal, she was required to debate the merits of French wine.

Dowd looked around and asked, "Where's your boyfriend?"

She widened her eyes. "My what?"

"Kerry."

"Stephen, I don't know where—"

"Don't argue with an old spy, lassie."

She decided not to do so. "He is meeting Yichang and Zhao."

A few minutes later, Kerry appeared with the two Chinese. They had been invited to each of the dinners.

Zhao was his typical, outgoing self, and with Yelchenko guiding the way interpretively, he dove into the goodies on the table. Yichang was more reserved in filling his plate, and once he had, he and Kerry wandered over to join Broussard and Dowd.

Kerry carried a glass of the vodka, and he smiled at her, and his gray eyes shone in the dim light of the dining room. She could tell now when his smiles were full-fledged. The fine lines at the corners of his eyes crinkled. The way he looked, his attitudes, his actions irritated her less and less.

Even when he had returned from his meeting with Yichang and explained threat receivers to her, she had been unable to get mad at him.

"They are for military airplanes?"

"Usually, yes."

"What is meant by 'usually'?"

"Well, we installed them on the Astros."

She was immediately aware of the implications. Protection against terrorists, for one; but for another, it would be yet another asset for the Astroliner in the Chinese evaluation of the SSTs.

With Kerry listening to her, she had immediately called Dubonnet.

"Henri, we must immediately put radar and infrared threat receivers on the Concorde II."

"Jacqueline, that is ridiculous. Why must we do that?"

"Because they shoot at airplanes here, and because the Pacific Aerospace airplanes have them."

"That is quite interesting, Jacqueline. Why could I not have known this a month ago?"

"I did not know it a month ago."

"It cannot be done in the time that we have. Some of those sensors are placed in the skin of the fuselage and wings."

"Then you must provide the Concorde II with air force airplanes as escorts," she said and hung up.

She looked up at Kerry, who sat on the corner of her desk.

"It cannot be done," she said.

"I know."

She should have been infuriated with him, but she was not.

"Director Yichang," she said, "you look tired. You should have a month for holiday."

He smiled back at her. "You will tell this to my superiors?"

"Of course."

She waited for a moment, and when no one spoke, said to Kerry, "Will I have to beg to find out what determination has been made about the fighter aircraft?"

Kerry said, "I'll let Director Yichang explain it."

"I have spoken with General Chou and Major Hua," the security chief said. "They, in turn, have had discussions with the general staff. What has been decided is that the *unarmed* Pacific Aerospace fighter will be allowed to accompany the supersonic transports since it is already in Tokyo."

She looked at Kerry, who kept his face stoic. He would

tell her later, no doubt, that it was a minor fib, that the F-16 was not yet in Japan.

"However," Yichang continued, "the general staff is apparently uneasy about having French, German, and Russian military craft all converging on the airport. Instead, Major Hua's squadron will be detailed to accompany the SSTs arriving from the east."

She felt a little better about it.

Though, once again, Kerry seemed to have slipped something over on them.

She would chide him about it, of course, but later in the evening.

Beijing, China
September 24, 8:10 P.M.

Without his awareness, Sun Chen's office hours had steadily increased until he was devoting the time from five o'clock in the morning until nearly nine o'clock at night in his office. He had not complained aloud, nor had his staff. He supposed they looked forward to the time after the ceremony when the routine might again return to what was normal.

Tonight, he stayed in his desk chair waiting for General Chou to call. It was not a prearranged telephone call, but he knew that it would happen. Sun had had to go to the Minister of Transportation and make that personage unhappy enough to call in favors from members of the general staff. He did not enjoy doing it, but only a word picture of the thousands of dignitaries that would be present at Deng Xiaoping International Superport during the grand opening was required in order to bring the reluctant minister to action.

When the call finally came on his private line, he lifted the receiver immediately.

"Chairman Sun?"

"Yes, General Chou?"

"I am ordered to respond to your request."

"I am sorry that it must be this way, General. However, you are the commandant of forces devoted to the protection of the airport."

"It is offensive," the general said. "I know nothing of the navy, and the general staff has assigned the southern coastal patrols to my command. All of this to satisfy the curiosity of a foreigner."

"Simply, we must follow all leads that are presented to us," Sun said. "What is the status?"

"I have sent orders to the coastal squadrons to search for this elusive pleasure craft. They are to detain the occupants once they have made contact."

"How did you send the orders?"

It was a ridiculous question, but Sun thought that the general's disdain for his mission could well have resulted in written orders transferred by oxcart.

"By telephone, of course."

"Excellent, General. I thank you, and I trust that I will hear from you as soon as the men are apprehended."

"I would not count heavily on the navy, Chairman."

TWENTY

Hong Kong
September 26, 1:00 P.M.

Gerhard Ebbing entered the quiet elegance of the Hong Kong Hilton's lobby, went directly to the elevators, and rode the car to Kraft's floor.

Until eleven o'clock that morning, when Kraft called him, Ebbing had not known that the Managing Director was coming to Hong Kong early. People with money moved in mysterious ways, but also at mysterious times.

Kraft answered his rap on the wooden door to the suite and swung the door wide.

"Gerhard! Come in, come in."

Ebbing entered the sitting room of the suite to find one of the twin brocaded couches in front of the picture window occupied by a massive man in a silver-gray suit. The suit probably cost five times the daily rate for the suite, which he estimated at five hundred deutsche marks.

The dark-faced, hook-nosed giant did not have to be dressed in flowing robes for Ebbing to identify him as Hakim al-Qatar. Ebbing had never met him before, but the multibillionaire's likeness had been on television many times and had probably appeared in every newspaper in the world. The man stood up as Ebbing approached the couches.

Kraft introduced them.

Al-Qatar extended his hand, saving Ebbing the indecision about a cultural greeting. He shook it firmly. The Arab also had an unexpectedly soft and soothing voice.

"I am very pleased to meet the designer of our airplane. My single, short flight aboard it was immensely rewarding."

"I am but one of twelve who worked on the design," Ebbing protested.

"Ah, but you led it. That is what counts."

"A drink, Gerhard?" Kraft asked.

"Whatever you are having, Matthew."

It was tea, perhaps in deference to the Arab.

They sat on the couches, and at Kraft's prompting, and despite the fact that he had been reporting to Kraft every other day, Ebbing briefed the two men on developments at the airport.

"This man Wehmeier is the chief suspect?" Kraft asked.

"He and an Englishman named Cooksey. But they are only suspects in the collective mind of our group, I think. Yichang Enlai has not yet fully come to grips with the concept."

"You have been told by Yichang, though, that Wehmeier and Cooksey have left Hong Kong."

"Yes. Along with a third man identified only as Angelo."

"The threat to the aircraft has disappeared, do you think, Gerhard?" Kraft asked.

"It is substantially reduced, I believe. With the sound sensors placed at the ends of the runways, it will be difficult for snipers to position themselves without being detected. Then, too, the Chinese will escort the airplanes on approach with fighter aircraft that have countermeasures. Major Hua has already proven that defense to be effective. And finally, we are adopting a suggestion made by Dan Kerry. The SSTs will land downwind, opposite the end of the runway where a sniper might be placed. I do not think there will be any problems, Matthew."

"Can we land the AeroSwift downwind?" al-Qatar asked.

"At Templehof, we would not attempt it, but at China Dome, the runway length is more than adequate."

"Excellent!" Kraft said. "And do you have a feeling for the reception we will have? In the way of judgment?"

"Sun Chen has avoided any contact between any of the principals at the airport and himself, but I am beginning to wonder if there is any value in courting Sun."

"In what way?"

"There are rumors about that some independent panel of judges will perform the evaluations."

"Just rumors?"

"Yes. But there may be some substance in them. On the ninth, we were in Beijing for a military ceremony, and I believe we saw some of the men who might be judges, but were not allowed to meet them. In the newspapers, Sun professes to maintain an open mind."

"And what of the representatives with whom you have been working? Have you impressions of their concerns?" The question came from al-Qatar.

"It is something of a strange and sometimes awkward relationship that we have," Ebbing said. "You are aware of the phenomenon whereby a hostage begins to identify himself with his captor?"

"I have read of it."

"The seven of us are bound by the confines of one office, and we have been working together toward the single goal of identifying terrorists. Despite our competitive stances, we have become closer."

"And in this closeness, you have noted changes in the people?" Kraft asked.

"Yes. Broussard and Zemenek have been somewhat reserved, especially after the specifications of the Astroliner became available." Ebbing did not say that he thought part of Broussard's alteration in behavior resulted from the new relationship with Kerry that Bergen had noted.

"They are worried?" Kraft asked.

"I believe so. The additional seats, the cargo-configured craft, and now, the terrorist countermeasures have come as surprises. Their attitudes could reflect concerns in the home offices in Paris and Moscow."

Hakim al-Qatar leaned forward, placed his elbows on his knees, and looked keenly across the coffee table between the couches at Ebbing. "How about yourself, Herr Ebbing? What do you think of our chances?"

Ebbing considered for a long moment before he answered. "They are still strong, I think. PAI may yet have more surprises for us, but we have a capable craft. We have a slight edge in speed—point-two Mach, which is an all-important aspect. We could produce a cargo—"

"I have brought the plans and specifications along," Kraft interjected.

Ebbing nodded his approval. "And we could easily add the countermeasures in production models."

"What of the seat differential?"

"That is more troubling. I have been thinking about it, and yes, we could extend the fuselage, but we would lose speed and some maneuverability. We might have to redesign the engines to overcome the losses."

"Expensive," al-Qatar said, sitting back.

"Outside of the capacity, the technology of the AeroSwift is equal to, or better than, that of the Astroliner," Ebbing said. "I say that with total conviction. I give us an even chance to win the contract."

Kraft sighed. "I had hoped for better."

"As did I," Ebbing said. "My sleep is troubled by visions of Eastern Germans starving to death."

"Let us keep one thing clear," Kraft told him. "The conditions of ex-communists are not of concern to us. Any improvement is simply a by-product of our success. We must keep our eyes on the only objective, and that objective is pleasing the shareholders."

"Absolutely," Hakim al-Qatar said.

Century City, California
September 25, 9:20 A.M.

P.J. Jackson had his feet up on his credenza, studying his picture of the *Elliot* when Mollie announced his brother on the line. Without changing position, he reached back over his shoulder and grabbed the phone.

"Hey, Paul."

"Good news, P.J. I just came from the governor's office."

"We get it?"

"That's right. One bona fide executive order. It gives you permission to take the Astroliner into L.A. International for one time, on September thirtieth."

"All right! I sure as hell wasn't looking forward to busing all these people out to Edwards."

Jackson dropped his feet to the floor and spun around in his chair, reaching for a memo pad. He had things to do.

Arrange to lease a gate from one of the major airlines. Set up a VIP lounge.

"You know, P.J., after talking to the man this morning, I've finally decided I've got to make the run."

"Sure, Paul. I thought you'd get to that point."

Get hold of Carroll. Make sure Aikens had the airplane in her final configuration.

"Thing is, I've got to start setting up my organization."

"That's probably a good idea," Jackson said. "These things take plenty of planning."

"I wondered if you wanted to run the campaign. You know, serve as the coordinator."

Shit!

"You can imagine, Paul, that I've got my hands full at the moment, and the next year is going to be a bastard as we get the plants tooled up."

"Oh. Yeah."

Jerk thought the world revolved around *his* needs.

"The other thing, P.J., it's going to take some important money to get this thing rolling."

Already?

"I'll send you five grand, Paul."

"That's all?"

"Look, you can imagine where my priorities have to be for the next couple of weeks. I've got to get these celebs on the plane, get the plane to China, and with some deft moves, sell the damned thing. That's what I have to concentrate on."

"Yeah, well, I can understand that. Look, we'll talk next week."

"Sure thing, Paul."

Jackson dropped the phone in its cradle.

Not so sure, asshole.

Over South China Sea
September 26, 5:00 P.M.

From 1,000 meters of altitude and fifteen kilometers of distance, the coast of China had the qualities of an emerald necklace. Hua's wingman, Blue Dragon Two, flying off his left wing, partially blocked his view, but the shoreline did indeed appear to be a deep-green necklace resting on a blue-green cloth. There was not a cloud in the sky, and the backdrop was a crystalline light blue, lit by a sun that was low upon the western horizon.

Ahead of him, and below, was a long line of vessels plying the commercial channel northward. To his left, toward the shore, were several dozen fishing boats. On the right was the naval cutter *Kanchou,* which carried the call sign White Bear on the temporary command frequency.

It was temporary because six vessels of the coastal patrol had been attached to General Chou's Deng Xiaoping International Superport defensive unit, including Hua's squadron of fighters and the two helicopters. It was now called Task Force Ten, for no reason Hua understood. Hua was beginning to believe, as Chou did, that this unit was becoming unwieldy and disunified.

He keyed his microphone on the command frequency.

"White Bear, this is Blue Dragon."

"Blue Dragon, White Bear. We have you in sight."

Hua did not know if the voice belonged to Lieutenant Shi, whom he had been told commanded the cutter.

The fugitive yacht had been given the codename Dagger, and Hua asked, "Have you had contact with Dagger?"

"Negative, Blue Dragon."

"What can we do to help?" Hua fully expected General Chou to be listening to the radio network and to break in with a contradictory order to leave the navy to its task.

"The vessels in our northwest quadrant have not yet been examined."

"We will take a look for you," Hua said.

"That would be much appreciated."

"Blue Dragon out." Switching to the flight frequency, Hua said, "Dragon Two, go to two-seven-zero and five hundred meters altitude. I will continue in this direction, and we will look for Dagger between us."

"Two-seven-zero and five-zero-zero. I will comply."

The F-12 rolled away and headed west.

Hua reduced his throttle setting, bringing his speed back to three hundred knots, then put the nose down and lost altitude rapidly. He went into a slight left turn as he descended, lining up on a white-hulled cruiser.

He passed over it to its starboard side and noted the name on the stern: *Bali Paradise*. It was at least twenty meters long, and much too large to be the missing vessel.

He made a note on his kneepad, then banked into a right turn and headed for the next target. Long before he reached it, he knew it would be a junk, not matching the desired profile in any way.

Hua desperately hoped he would be the one to find the *Oriental Orchid*. He remembered too clearly the way his heart had beat and his mind had blurred when the Grail missile pursued him across the eastern end of Deng Xiaoping International. He carried air-to-surface missiles on his pylons, and he would dearly like to return the favor.

140 Kilometers East of Lufeng, South China Sea
September 26, 11:00 P.M.

The *Oriental Orchid* was now the *Flower Girl*, home port Macau. The original name had been painted out despite the dire predictions of Ned Cooksey who said one should never change the name of a boat.

The new name had been carefully stenciled in place by Angelo Malgretto, standing in the rubber dingy and using black paint. As soon as it had dried to the touch, Malgretto and Wehmeier had used a thinned wash of gray paint to coat the entire hull and superstructure of the cruiser. They had used roller applicators and had not worried about achieving an even appearance. The yacht now appeared well-worn, uncared for, and weathered.

On a steel pedestal mounted to the deck of the flying bridge and extending through a hole cut in the overhead canvas, Cooksey had mounted his large radar antenna. The radar scope was mounted on top of the table in the salon, but was currently at rest, and the antenna was covered with canvas. Cooksey's thin whip antenna was bolted to the right side of the flying bridge bulkhead.

Wehmeier was not exceptionally worried about being detected, even if anyone were looking for them. They were well west of the normal shipping channels, on an apparent course for Taiwan. While the yacht could make thirty knots, he was maintaining an easy pace of twenty knots through the smooth seas.

There was no hurry.

Kowloon
September 26, 11:40 P.M.

Dinner had been composed of an excellent roast duck in orange sauce, and as far as Kerry could tell, there had been no hint of a British influence in the meal. He supposed that Stephen Dowd hadn't outvoted Jacqueline Broussard in any aspect of the Anglo-French-sponsored meal. Wisely, he had not mentioned his observations to either Dowd or Broussard.

It had been an interesting evening for Ebbing had brought along two of the principals in Boehm-Bussmeier-Kraft, Matthew Kraft himself and a Saudi named al-Qatar. Kerry had found both men to be congenial and socially at ease, but he thought that both could also be absolutely ruthless under the surface. His conversation with Kraft and al-Qatar had been an exchange of bantering jibes related to the Astroliner and the AeroSwift, accompanied with good-humored smiles. The smiles, though, had been thin, on the brink of evaporation.

Though he did not say anything to anyone else, he also thought it interesting that Kraft and al-Qatar had flown to Hong Kong early, rather than flying aboard the AeroSwift on grand opening day. He wondered if they were afraid of flying or of missiles.

After dinner, Kerry and Broussard had gone up to their rooms to get jackets, then taken the ferry to the Island. They rode the tram to the top of the Peak, Broussard's first visit to the high-rise observation area.

There were quite a few couples borrowing the view, but they found an opening on a bench and sat together. The lights of the city interfered with the stars to some extent, but the view of the multicolored Victoria District and Kowloon across the bay was breathtaking. The lights shimmered on the night, and the perfume of flowers drifted with the breeze moving across the Peak.

Kerry, who didn't think of himself as much of a romantic, thought it was probably the most romantic spot on earth.

"It *is* beautiful," Broussard said.

"Better than Paris?" he asked, taking her hand in his. It

was soft and warm, and she squeezed his own hand delightfully.

"Would you make me choose between them?"

"I'm thinking ahead, Jacqueline."

"You are so certain that Pacific Aerospace will be the selected company, are you not?"

"I'm pretty confident, I guess."

"And when Aerospatiale-BAC is named the winner, you will quit your job and come here to attend me, correct?"

Jesus. That was a tough one.

"Or, let us say that BBK is awarded the contract," she said. "Then, you will come to Paris?"

"You ask difficult questions, Jacqueline."

"I ask the same questions that you ask."

PARTING SHOTS

TWENTY-ONE

Kai Tak Airport
September 27, 9:12 A.M.

"The days have sped by," she said, feeling quaint for having said it in that manner.

"Too fast for us to have found very many answers," Kerry told her.

Broussard knew what he meant. Wehmeier and Cooksey were still fugitives. General Chou, and to some extent, Yichang Enlai, still looked inward, to a People's People, for the source of their problem. Yichang's interest was renewed because Zhao Li had received another communique from the People's People, this time as a fax from an undisclosed origination point. Again written in Chinese characters, it was a collection of rhetoric forbidding Westerners to enter China Dome. Sun Chen had chosen not to release it to the press.

And there were few solutions to the puzzle that was Daniel Kerry and Jacqueline Broussard. Like the finished jigsaw variety, they fit together in a special way. In each other's arms, there was tenderness and fever, comfort and insatiable lust. Apart, there was the tension of competition and the reality that their paths were not meant to do more than cross for only an instant in eternity, then continue on their separate ways.

As they sat in Air France's departure lounge, Broussard could not help but feel that the end had come upon them long before she expected it or wanted it. The next days would contain frantic activity and then the exultation, or damnation, of the contract award. Their time was past.

Kerry sat in a chair directly in front of her, leaning forward, his elbows on his knees and his hands twisting the Styrofoam cup that had held his coffee. He was wearing a navy blue blazer and gray slacks, and she thought he had not ever before appeared so debonair.

It was not, she knew, a description that he would apply to himself.

"I think," he said, "we ought to cash in your ticket and take a boat to Macau. We'll see how depraved life can get."

"Henri expects me. I am to be his hostess for the guests on the Concorde II."

"I was joking."

"I am not in the mood for jokes, Dan."

He smiled, but it was a wistful smile.

"I'll just have to look forward to October fifth, then."

"I expect that Henri will keep me busy."

He raised an eyebrow.

"I think our little . . . what?"

"Fling?"

"Fling is over."

"We've had this conversation before, Jacqueline."

"At that time, I was angry."

"At me?"

"I do not remember."

"And this time?"

"I am . . . I do not know. Thankful, perhaps."

The muted female voice on the public address system announced her flight for the second time, in both English and Chinese.

He smiled as they stood up.

"You are laughing at me."

"I am not," Kerry said. "I just think you're the most mercurial woman I ever met."

She retrieved her purse, then took his arm. He led her toward the line forming at the door to the concourse.

As they reached the door, she stopped and turned to him. *"Au revoir."*

He bent his head down to kiss her.

Tender, as she knew he could be.

But it had the taste of goodbye.

125 Kilometers East of Lufeng, South China Sea
September 28, 11:47 A.M.

Hua Peng eased the throttle back and let the Shenyang F-12 lose altitude. His wingman stayed with him.

The boat on the surface was ten kilometers ahead of him, about thirty kilometers off the coast. It was on a track for Hong Kong or perhaps Macau, judging by the wake shining in the overhead sun.

It was not a fast boat, and as he closed the distance to it, he could understand why. It appeared to be ill-kept, sun- and salt-weathered to an almost silver finish. The closer he got, the more distinct were the weather streaks.

Hua banked easily to the left, watching Captain Jiang, Blue Dragon Two, in his peripheral vision. The second F-12 stayed with him.

A few moments later, and at six hundred meters above

the sea, he turned back to the right so that his path would cross that of the boat at a right angle and just aft of its stern.

Crossing the wake, he noted that the flying bridge was sheltered by a canvas top, but he was able to discern one person sitting at the helm. The stern was littered with cardboard. A perfectly disreputable vessel.

Jiang said on the interplane frequency, "I think he is a refugee from the 1960s, Major."

"You are probably correct. We could have the navy stop him, but they would only find two days' worth of marijuana."

On his kneepad notebook, he wrote down the coordinates and the yacht's name: *Flower Girl,* home port Macau, fifteen meters length, cruiser, oversized radar antenna.

The home port alone told him that the boat probably ran drugs. He was not, however, searching for drug smugglers.

"Where is the next one, Dragon Two?"

"Bear to the left, One. Fifteen kilometers."

80 Kilometers East of Lufeng, South China Sea
September 28, 2:19 P.M.

The two warplanes that had buzzed them two and a half hours earlier had unnerved Kurt Wehmeier somewhat. He did not know quite what he should make of them.

Angelo Malgretto had been on the bridge at the time, and Wehmeier had watched the aircraft from a cabin window. They stayed low, headed east, but he could not tell if they were looking for other boats before they were out of sight.

Cooksey had been napping all afternoon, and when he

came up from his bow cabin, Wehmeier told him about the military airplanes.

"Looking for us, no doubt about it."

"What makes you think so?"

"It was your picture in the taxi, old man. They just tracked it as far as the boat, that's all."

Cooksey was probably correct, but in that correctness, Wehmeier took heart. If the disguised boat had been recognized, they would surely have been approached by a naval ship by now. The aircraft had not even made a second pass.

"We seem to have passed the first test, then."

"Oh, I think so, mate. We're home free."

Cooksey searched the cabinet over the sink for a glass, then had to wash one of the dirty ones from the stack in the sink. He did not wash it well, but Wehmeier assumed the straight scotch would kill any leftover germs.

He checked his watch, then got up from the settee and crossed the salon to the desk built into the rear bulkhead, next to the companionway. The radios and radio telephone were mounted on the wall above the desk.

He lifted the telephone from its hook and dialed the telephone number.

It took some time for the satellite links to align, then the telephone rang four times.

And for the first time, he got an answering machine.

It told him to dial a different number.

The new number rang three times before it was answered.

After they exchanged their Doctor and Disease passwords, the man said, "You have a problem."

"I do?"

"They have the airport buttoned up tight."

"In what way?" he asked.

"There are fields of sensors to detect intruders at the ends of the runways, and the transports will be escorted by Chinese fighter aircraft on their approaches."

"Is that all?"

"The airplanes will also land downwind."

"I see. That is interesting. That is unexpected."

"I thought we were going to get all screwed up with this scheme, Wehmeier. You gave them too much to worry about."

He was accusing Wehmeier of the sin of performing his job too well, the job the man had wanted him to perform in the first place.

Wehmeier also noted the use of his name. He was no longer bothered by it, but he almost called the other man by his own name. The game played two ways, and Wehmeier had long known for whom he was working. He resisted the temptation to utter it, however. It was always advantageous to keep some information back. The future might well present a better time in which to use it.

"That is good," he said. "The idea was to give them much to worry about, and you wanted all of this attributed to the People's People."

"But you can no longer achieve the objective."

"Their silly defenses do not pose a problem. What I have planned for the first of October will occur on the first of October."

"You are certain?"

"Absolutely."

There was a sigh of relief on the other end.

Wehmeier responded to it by saying, "Make certain my transfers are accomplished on the afternoon of the first."

"It will be done."

He hung up and turned toward Cooksey, who was seated

at the table with his work of art. He had now added other boxes and video monitors to it, and it was becoming an ungainly sculpture.

"The Chinese," Wehmeier said, "will have military escorts for the airplanes, and they have installed some kind of motion detectors at the runway ends. Also the SSTs will land downwind."

Cooksey laughed.

Deng Xiaoping International Superport
September 28, 5:20 P.M.

The chartered China Airways Boeing 737 landed smoothly on the runway in front of the terminals, exited at a taxiway, and was directed into a parking position at Terminal One. The engine noise died.

Sun Chen stayed in his seat and watched the man standing in the open end of the jetway maneuver his controls and walk the jetway up against the side of the airliner. As far as he knew, it was the first use of the jetways.

He heard the door being opened, then Zhao Li appeared at the head of the cabin.

"Welcome to Deng Xiaoping International Superport! Chairman Sun, honorable members of the committee, and esteemed judges, we are at your disposal."

The men on board began to stand up and collect their luggage from the overhead compartments. All twelve members of his committee were present, as were two of the SST judges and eight experts from the bureau of air transport. Fifteen of the aviation specialists and five judges had departed this morning for Paris, Los Angeles, Berlin, and

Moscow. They would return aboard the competing supersonic transports.

Zhao worked his way down the crowded aisle as Sun replaced his papers in his briefcase.

"Chairman, I am most happy to see you!"

"Mr. Zhao, I wish that we could sell your enthusiasm. We would be far richer than this airport will make us."

Zhao smiled. "I have a surprise for you, Chairman! We have completed a block of rooms in the terminal hotel, and you and your committee will be accommodated right here."

Sun thought that his assistants, who had worked so diligently on finding appropriate housing for all of those attending, would be dismayed. He said, however, "That is wonderful. Now, we may work day and night."

Zhao did not know how to take the statement, but continued smiling. He took Sun's briefcase and hanging bag and led the way up the aisle.

For the benefit of guests, and especially for the Committee for Airport Construction, the second level of the main terminal had been completed. It was the level at which passengers boarded or disembarked from their airliners. Sun exited the smooth white tunnel of the skyway into a world he had seen only in architectural renderings.

He stopped just outside the doorway to absorb the impressions a newly arrived traveller would have, and he was satisfied.

The ceilings were five meters high, providing a spacious feeling. The floor was covered with an aqua carpet, though islands of white ceramic tile were placed under the profuse plantings of tropical shrubbery. The dividing walls were white with lines of aqua tile for trim. Near each of the jetway entrances were seating areas for passengers, and the seating and railings followed the white-and-aqua theme.

Across the wide corridor which circled the dome were the ticketing facilities for the airlines. The counters and baggage-handling ports appeared bare now, but he could imagine them bustling with activity. To the left and right, except for the jetway entrances, the open expanses of glass provided a clear view of the airport grounds.

It felt light and airy; it would not oppress visitors to southern China. At the moment, it also felt cavernous and empty, with only his small group attempting to fill space.

"I like it very much, Mr. Zhao."

Zhao bowed his head. "I am happy you are pleased, Chairman."

The group followed the circular walkway until they reached a cross corridor which led into the core of the dome. They took elevators to the eleventh floor, where the core was the reception lobby for the hotel. It was pleasant, with the light from above filtering down.

The hotel occupied the ninth, tenth, and eleventh floors and was an entity unto itself. Two concentric rings of rooms on each floor were divided into suites, dining rooms, lounges, spas, exercise gymnasiums, and conference facilities. This was not to be a cheap hotel. Each suite would rent for a minimum of six hundred dollars American per day, but the amenities would justify the expense, a tax-deductible business expense in most cases.

The committee and its associates were not required to check in. Zhao himself guided Sun over the bridge crossing the atrium and into a corridor leading to the outer ring of suites. Directly at the end of the corridor was a set of double doors, nicely carved in oak. On the right door was a small brass plaque with raised bronze letters reading: "Chairman's Suite."

He wondered how visiting presidents or premiers would feel about that designation.

Zhao opened the door, and Sun stepped inside.

It was an immense space, likely ten meters by fifteen meters, cushioned in ankle-deep beige carpeting. The walls were covered with ecru silk. Three low couches upholstered in pale blue surrounded a huge low table lacquered in dark blue. The seating arrangement faced the window wall. Against one wall was a recessed bar with six stools. A huge basket of fruit, flanked by large vases filled with flowers, rested on the bar. Against another wall was a lacquered Bombay chest. A large table of highly polished teak, with six chairs girding it, was placed under a hanging crystal light fixture in the right rear corner. Original paintings and Chinese tapestries adorned the walls, and clear crystal vases, lamps, and figurines were used as accessories. The total effect was one of casual warmth and ease. It was a nice blend of the modern with traditional Chinese culture.

Zhao took him to the couch grouping and showed him the control panel set into the edge of the large table. Pressing one button caused a panel on the far side of the table to slide back and a television set to rise. More buttons and slide controls activated a hidden stereo system. Soft, almost unheard, music filled the sitting room. Another button opened a recess to reveal a telephone.

"There are four bedrooms, Chairman, each with their own bathroom." Zhao motioned expansively with his hands toward each end of the room, where a door was centered in each wall.

"Is there a panic button?" Sun asked.

"A panic button?"

"Should I become lost."

Zhao smiled at his little joke, then directed a bellman arriving with Sun's luggage toward what he called, "the master accommodations."

The airport administrator reminded him that the first meeting of the committee and the airport supervisors would be at six-thirty, followed by dinner, then backed out of the suite and closed the door softly behind him.

Sun Chen wandered around the suite, poking his head into the bedrooms. From the fruit basket, he selected an orange and peeled it as he walked. He felt somewhat lost, exactly as he had told Zhao. His parents, and especially his grandparents, would not have believed such a place. There was room in this suite for at least six extended families. In a place where sixty people could live well, one Western businessman would relax from a difficult day at the bargaining table.

Dan Kerry had sent him a book of poetry, and he recalled a line from the American Carl Sandberg and altered it, speaking aloud in the huge and quiet room, "Capitalism, creeping in on cat's paws."

Sun stood by the window and looked out at the vast concrete expanses of the Superport. He wondered what he was doing to his country.

His early enthusiasm for economic progress suddenly seemed misdirected. He should be doing more for his people than creating lavish hotel suites.

September 28, 7:41 P.M.

Yichang Enlai ate his dinner with General Chou, Major Hua, and Major Yang in the squadron mess in Hangar Two.

From Chou's disgruntled demeanor, Yichang assumed that the general was in residence at the airport by order. He had probably been told to remain at Deng Xiaoping International until the grand opening ceremonies and the flight tests had been completed.

Yichang poured more tea for all of them from the enameled china teapot and asked, "How is it possible that this one boat could disappear so easily?"

"It is a small boat, Director," Yang said.

"And a large ocean," Hua finished for him. "It could well be in the Philippines by now."

"My reports from the authorities in Manila say that they have not seen it," Yichang said.

"They cannot track their own boats, I would wager," Hua said.

Yichang supposed that it was true. He knew nothing of the sea, but he suspected the hiding places were many.

"I should think," General Chou said, "that your fugitive, this Wehmeier, learned of the police hunt for him and decided to seek southern waters. We will not see him again."

Yichang hoped fervently that he would see none of the men on his short list. However, he would also rest better if he knew where they were.

"I would like nothing better, General. I fear, though, that we will hear from Wehmeier, or one of his ilk, two days from now."

"Let them write wild and condemning letters," Chou said. "I certainly do not care."

"The letters, I do not worry about. It is the missiles I worry about."

"No one, absolutely no one, will launch a missile at those airplanes, Director. Our defenses are extremely solid."

"I hope so, General. If an airplane is shot down, our careers will also be shot down."

Chou harrumphed.

Major Hua appeared worried.

Yichang asked him, "Major, how many vessels have been identified? What procedure are you following?"

"The naval command is accumulating the data," Hua said, "on their computer. Daily, they send us a listing of contacts or sightings that have been made. At the end of each of our flights, we telephone our data to them, and they enter it in the database."

"Could I see what you have?"

"Certainly."

Hua got up and crossed through the partition to his office. A few minutes later, he returned with a file folder and handed it to Yichang.

It was a thick folder. Yichang opened it and found a stack of computer printouts that he estimated comprised a hundred pages. Also in the folder were small yellow pages ripped from notepads.

"What are the notes?" he asked.

"They are the notations made by the pilots."

"So everything on the notes is now in the database?"

"Of course," Hua said, then tempered his response. "That is, I assume it is so. I have not examined everything closely."

"May I borrow this file?"

General Chou said, "It belongs to my command."

"I understand that, General. I will bring it back to you."

Chou provided his approval with an angry wave of his hand.

Kowloon
September 28, 9:17 P.M.

Kerry had just gotten back to his room, carrying a plastic bucket of ice, after having dinner with Bergen and Yelchenko, and his room felt extremely empty.

Broussard had only been gone a couple days, but her absence was a glowing omission that he wasn't yet ready to admit to himself. Given her stubbornness, though, he thought that sometime soon he would have to deal with the reality. She wasn't likely to back away from the position she had taken; she would stay with Dubonnet and Aerospatiale-BAC and Paris.

He knew damned well that the Concorde II wasn't going to be a Chinese aircraft.

She wasn't going to phone him, either, another manifestation of her stubbornness. He had found himself checking for messages at the desk frequently, even though there was no reason why she should feel compelled to call him and announce her safe arrival in France.

Kerry tossed his suit coat on a chair, then mixed himself a light scotch and water. He stood at the window and looked down on the colorful lights of Nathan Road. The street was jammed with people and automobiles.

What did she want? A firm avowal of love? Kerry didn't think he had uttered the word "love" since Marian had left him alone in Colorado. It was no longer part of his vocabulary.

And what the hell did he want, himself? He had been content for so long with short-term relationships that he had abandoned anything that looked as if it might run over a couple of months.

His commitments were to company and country and the freedom to explore both. He couldn't imagine dealing with a shared life.

No. It was gone.

But he thought he might check the desk one more time for a message. He picked up the phone and called.

No messages.

Standing there with the phone in his hand, he took a different mental snapshot of himself.

Why in hell should he wait for her to phone? It worked two ways.

He dug his wallet out of his hip pocket and found the short list of telephone numbers. They had been compiled by the Sunlight detective agency since most of them were unlisted.

Broussard's was an unlisted number.

He dialed it and waited.

Two rings, then: "You have reached the correct number, no doubt. Now, you must leave a message."

Damned answering machines.

At the tone, he said, "Jacqueline, dear. Having lousy time. Wish you were here. Love, Dan."

He had hung up before he realized quite what he'd said. He was about to make another call and leave another, clearer message when someone knocked on his door.

He crossed the floor and opened the door.

Yichang Enlai stood there, clutching a file folder.

"I hope I do not intrude, Mr. Kerry."

"Certainly not, Director. Come in."

The security man came inside, and Kerry motioned him to the chairs at the table as he closed the door.

"Would you like a drink? I only have scotch, I'm afraid."

"A small one, please."

He mixed the drink and took it to the table, settling into a chair opposite Yichang.

He eyed the folder. "What have you got there?"

"It looks to me like a great deal of work, I am afraid. I was hoping you would help me with it."

Yichang had a staff as large as Boston. Kerry wondered what made an American special.

"You have a feeling for that which we are searching for, I think," Yichang said.

Opening the folder and spilling the pages on the table, he explained the identification process the air force and navy were using relative to the vessel they were seeking.

"What I fear, Mr. Kerry, is that they are content to amass all of this information, which proves that they have been performing their assigned task, without actually looking at what they have collected and compiled. I do not believe anyone has analyzed the data."

"All right. They wouldn't be the first outfit to do it that way. What's on the sheets?"

"The computer printouts list the dates and times of visual contacts by either a naval ship or an aircraft. The name or registration number of the vessel is listed, as well as the approximate coordinates of the sighting and the bearing. Additionally, there is a short description."

"And the notes?"

"Those come from the pilots. We will need to compare them with the printouts to be certain the information was entered."

"Let me have half of that stack," Kerry said.

It looked like a long night, but he didn't have anything better to do.

Edwards Air Force Base
September 27, 3:32 P.M.

Terry Carroll knew he was acting like a mother hen. Don Matthews had told him so.

While he could have taken the day off, he hung around the lab, getting into Dennis Aikens' hair and taking periodic excursions to the hangar to check on the final preparations of the Astroliner. Cliff Coker was doing the same thing with the Astrofreighter.

Each of the prototypes had at least three hundred hours of flight time, but this trip was going to be different. He was going to be responsible for the lives of 168 passengers and seven crew members, counting himself, and he didn't care for the numbers. Or the types. Carroll had never been one to pal around with governors and movie stars and political electees. In fact, since Vietnam, he had had a distinct aversion for the Washington variety of politician.

But they were in his hands now, and he wanted to be damned certain that everything his hands touched on the airplane worked flawlessly.

He and Coker left the lab and walked across the tarmac to the hangar for the fifth time that day.

"Trade you," Carroll said.

"Uh huh. I've been thinking about it, and I'm just happy as hell to only have the four Chinese on board."

"Reba's coming along," he cajoled.

"Maybe I'll meet her on the other end," Coker said.

Inside the hangar, the two Astros were parked end for end, and most of the external access panels on both had been closed. The final systems checks were all but completed. In the morning, he and Coker, along with Aikens, would go over the checklists and make certain that every item had been initialed. Tomorrow, too, the cleaning crews would go through the cabins for the final run-through with the vacuums and polish.

On the thirtieth, the Astros would be moved to Los Angeles International where the tanks would be topped off and the liquor and food loaded. There were to be no flight kitchen trays for this flight. London Broil and Maine Lobster were being prepared in individual and generous servings by some Hollywood restaurant. Even the crew and the inspectors on the Astrofreighter would receive the royal dinner treatment.

The two of them walked beneath the Astrofreighter and eyeballed the access door seals and locks, then climbed the ladder to the crew door on the port side. They entered the crew compartment, which was just behind the flight deck. The space was outfitted with a restroom, a small galley, and two bench-type seats. The backrest of the seats could be raised, creating bunk beds. It was designed for long-haul flights which required relief crews, but would accommodate the four inspectors. If they wanted to move around a little, they could use the pull-down seat behind the pilots and opposite the flight engineer. With the navigational equipment installed in the Astros, a navigator was no longer necessary, but the fourth seat on the flight deck was available for FAA inspectors, instructors, or senior pilots giving check-rides to younger flight crews.

A few technicians were still working in the plane, but Carroll and Coker walked around them and poked into darkened recesses with their flashlights. Aft of the crew compartment was the cargo bay, and they made a slow circuit of it, walking carefully to avoid the rollers built into the floor. The cargo area had exposed ribs protected by rub-rails which ran the full length of the deck. Overhead were conduits, junction boxes, and equipment bays. They paid particular attention to all of them. The airplane's systems were powered externally, and they tripped circuit breakers and looked for red and green indicators. Everything checked out satisfactorily, except for the infrared threat detector.

Half an hour later, they moved to the Astroliner and started into the same routine in the cabin and in the rear cargo bay.

When they reached the cockpit, the two of them settled into the pilot's seats and followed their inspection checklists, working through all of the circuit breakers and systems readouts.

"I've still got radar and infrared threat receivers," Carroll announced.

"Problem is, Terry, I thought I had 'em, too. We were getting a green indicator, if you'll remember, even when the system was down."

"One of the techs, Mohammed . . . whatever his name is, checked them out a couple days ago. Everything was fine."

"He use the test cart on 'em?" Coker asked.

"I don't know."

Coker crawled out of the right seat. "I'll go out and power it up, and we'll try it."

"Roger."

Carroll initialized the receivers mounted on the engineer's panel while Coker left the cockpit to get the cart. He would wheel it around to the back of the airplane and fire simulated radar and infrared signals at the tail-mounted antennas and sensors.

He got back in his seat, and ten minutes later, both indicators began flashing on his instrument panel. Looking to the right, he saw the flashing "Lock-On" letters on the copilot's panel, as well as on the engineer's panel.

Mohammed was right. Everything was in order.

TWENTY-TWO

100 Kilometers South of Pratas Reef, South China Sea
September 30, 5:17 A.M.

The interior of the *Flower Girl* had deteriorated almost as badly as the exterior. Paper wrappers, empty cigarette packs, and a few liquid and hard matter spills decorated the carpet. Cardboard boxes were stored under the coffee table. Clothing was tossed haphazardly about, resting on tables, couches, and the desk. In both the fore and aft cabins, the lockers were crammed with Grail missiles. The stern deck was littered with brass shell casings, the result of their practice with the AK-47 assault rifles. Cooksey's electronic gear was spread all over the banquette table and on one of the settees fronting it.

Wehmeier did not much care what it looked like. Beer cans and scotch bottles rolling around on the deck irritated him, though, and while he waited for his eggs to cook, he gathered them up, carried them up to the afterdeck, and flung them into the sea.

When he went back below, Angelo Malgretto was just emerging from the bow cabin.

"You're up early," Malgretto said.

"I was hungry," he replied.

Wehmeier was not a social person; he much preferred

his own company, and the past thirteen days of confinement in a small boat at sea with Cooksey and Malgretto had frayed his nerves. He was also not a sailor. His stomach had rebelled a number of times during periods of high seas. Riding out a typhoon was an event he would not relish.

On the ocean, he had found he could not predict what his surroundings would do to him. He knew he had not seen them at their worst, but he sensed the awesome and uncompromising power that could be released, and he was eager to leave the life of the sea behind him. Better, he thought, were the back streets of any city in the world where he knew what the dangers in the shadows meant and how to cope with them.

"Well, I am next in line," Malgretto said.

Wehmeier scooped up his two eggs with a spatula and placed them on pieces of bread that had gone stale days before. They had run out of salt, so he applied pepper liberally. When he moved away from the tiny galley, Malgretto stepped in and began breaking his own eggs on the side of the skillet.

With his foot, he kicked a shirt off the couch and sat down to eat. On the coffee table in front of him was a sheet of paper with the calculations he had made. He studied them while he ate.

"Today's the day?" Malgretto asked.

"Yes. At eight o'clock we will start moving north. Three hundred and thirty degrees by the compass. We will maintain twelve knots of speed."

"And that puts us in place at the right time?"

"Or very close to it. I have allowed extra time for course adjustments if they are necessary."

Adjustments would quite possibly be necessary. If Wehmeier was not a sailor, he was also not a navigator.

Their meanderings about the South China Sea were conducted with best guesses. His intent was only to stay far offshore and out of the primary shipping lanes and fishing grounds. The current position of the *Flower Girl,* as he had marked on the navigational chart, might be off by as much as twenty kilometers.

Still, he felt confident that, as they neared land, he would identify some landmark, probably to the south of their targeted area of operations. Once he saw land again, he could alter course and eventually locate Bias Bay. Wehmeier had never been there, but Malgretto had accompanied Hyun Oh and Ibn Saldam to the bay to meet Ku Chi.

"And what if we encounter Chinese ships or airplanes?"

"You will be fishing from the afterdeck. This is a pleasure fishing boat, after all. We will all be wearing disguises."

"I hate fish."

"If you catch one, which I doubt, you may cut the line."

"And you?"

"I will stay below, just in case they have my picture."

"What about Ned?" Malgretto asked from the stove. "That hair of his is a beacon."

"We will convince him to shave his head."

"The bloody hell you will!" Cooksey barked from the companionway to the bow cabin.

"How about gray?" Malgretto said. "We still have some of that gray paint yet, and we could paint your head."

"I'll wear a cap, but that's as far as I go."

Cooksey came on up to the salon level, took a look at the eggs Malgretto was cooking, and wrinkled his nose. He pushed the Italian aside and opened the cabinet under the sink, searching for his last bottle of Scotch.

Wehmeier looked forward to the next day with a desire that was nearly palpable. He was impatient to complete his contract and secure his ten million dollars, as well as rid himself of these buffoons.

"We will change the disguises," he said. "I will shave my head."

"Then you had better get out in the sun and bake it," Malgretto said. "Otherwise, your head will only draw attention."

"And that," Cooksey added, "we don't need."

Deng Xiaoping International Superport
September 30, 8:30 A.M.

With some fifty thousand square meters of floor space to choose from in the seven terminals, Sun Chen had selected Yichang's office as his headquarters during his short stay at the airport.

He had vetoed his use of Zhao Li's office since it was becoming overrun by early arriving journalists. The correspondents, in fact, seemed to be taking over everything, especially the lounges which had been opened for the days of the celebration.

Yichang contented himself, when he was in the security center, with usurping Wu Yhat's desk. He was sitting there, ignoring the incessant itching of the stitches in his left forearm, when Zhao called him.

"Turn on Channel Six, quickly!"

Dropping the telephone, Yichang rose and went into his office to crouch in front of the television set and switch it on.

Sun and one of his assistants looked up from where they were sitting side by side behind the desk.

It was a news segment from a Hong Kong English-language

station, and the young Chinese woman in front of the camera was reading from a paper she held in her hand: " '. . . decry the stupidity of a Chinese leadership which will not respond to the voice of the people. Let it never be forgotten that the people rule, and in this instance, the people have said that Westerners do not belong in our land. The people have spoken, and it is the leadership which must absorb the responsibility for what will take place at Deng Xiaoping International Superport tomorrow.' That is the end of the message which, again, was received by this station less than thirty minutes ago. Our reporters are now contacting government and airport officials, and as soon as we have more, you will learn about it on Channel Six."

Yichang flipped to a Chinese channel in time to catch the end of a similar broadcast.

He stood up and turned to his superior.

Sun's face appeared drained of blood.

"I assume, Chairman, that since their last communique did not receive a public airing, the People's People have gone directly to the media."

"It would appear so, yes." The man's voice was stiff with anger or fear. Yichang could not tell which.

"How do you wish to proceed?" he asked.

Sun sat back in his chair. In Yichang's chair.

"I suppose that Zhao is even now overcome with telephone calls. I will have to hold a press conference." He looked to his aide. "Arrange that for eleven o'clock. And tell Zhao to say nothing to the media."

The assistant shot for the door.

"Director Yichang, what is in your mind?"

"These people have claimed responsibility for five deaths, Chairman. I think they would like to claim responsibility for many more."

"Yes. However, we have a steamroller before us. It is not about to be stopped."

"Chairman—"

Sun swung around to look out the windows.

"Over there, in Terminal Six, a banquet is being prepared for fifteen hundred members of Chinese industrial and airline interests. Their aircraft will begin arriving at one o'clock. And in Terminal Seven, a buffet for over a thousand correspondents is being readied."

Yichang was aware of the preparations. Earlier, when he wanted to be alone, he had gone up to the twelfth floor only to find it in confusion. Workers were setting up tables and covering them with white linen. Chairs were being carted in by the truckload. Chefs of every description had taken over the kitchens, and the clanging of pans and cutlery did not support meditation. The entire floor would be devoted to six different banquets for the important visitors arriving tomorrow.

He knew also that the hotels in Hong Kong were already filling with the dignitaries who would attend the grand opening, but who were not arriving by way of the supersonic transports. Many of the early arrivals, impatient to see the airport, had called to request personal tours, and Yichang—not wanting to offend anyone of influence and prompted by Zhao Li—had detailed some of his security personnel for duty as impromptu tour guides.

"The leadership," Sun continued, "will arrive in the morning. Do you want to turn their airplane back?"

"No, Chairman."

"You are confident that the runways are safe? As well as the approaches to them?"

"I place my confidence in Major Hua and General Chou,"

Yichang said. He did not know where else he could place it, when it came to the air defenses.

Sun nodded minutely. "And your search for the People's People?"

"My list has not grown shorter, Chairman. We have not been able to locate anyone on it."

He did not mention the hours that he and Kerry had devoted to poring over the printouts of ship sightings, primarily because those hours had been unproductive.

"I see no other recourse," Sun said, "other than to proceed with what has been planned for a year. We will simply have to intensify the security arrangements and I will go down and meet the reporters and deny the validity of the threats of the People's People."

Yichang saw no way to intensify what was already intense. He and Wu Yhat had composed the work schedules, bringing every available man on duty for extended tours. Through Inspector Maynard Wing, he had contracted with off-duty Hong Kong and Kowloon policemen to augment the airport security personnel.

"Of course," is what he said.

Paris, France
September 30, 7:30 A.M.

Broussard and Dubonnet ate breakfast together at Grand Vefour on the Rue Beaujolais, as they had done many times over the years. The cafe dated to prerevolutionary times and had the solidity and patina of age and history behind it.

Dubonnet looked awful. She thought that his carefully styled hair appeared thinner. The aristocratic face was drawn, and his cheekbones were prominent over the hollows of his cheeks and under the dark sockets into which his eyes had sunk. Normally, he appeared trim and fit for his advanced age, but she thought he had lost a considerable amount of weight. His immaculate suit appeared to hang on a rack of skeletal bones.

Had she been gone only six weeks?

He toyed with his poached egg as if he were willing up the determination to eat it.

"Father, are you ill?"

"Ill? I am not ill."

"You are not yourself, either," she said.

"I am getting too old for the pressures of this business, Jacqueline. I think that, once we have secured the Chinese contract, it will be time for me to retire."

She felt her heart sink. He wanted the contract to be the pinnacle of his career, to retire at the top, though she could not imagine him as a retired old man, puttering in his gardens. Every day of his life had been full of activity, and surely, retirement would kill him.

Loss of the contract would also kill him.

She knew how much it meant to him, but she suddenly did not know how far he would go to get it.

That damned Kerry had started the niggling little doubts that now crowded her mind. She no longer knew in whom she could place her trust.

Henri Dubonnet had fought with the French underground in World War II. He had never given up a battle in the war, and in the years afterward, he had never admitted to a loss in the world of commerce.

"Toward that end, Jacqueline, I have secured a number of promises."

"What are you talking about?" she asked as she placed a dab of butter on her toasted croissant.

"You are far too young to assume the managing directorship."

"As if I wanted to assume it."

She did.

"Also, the directors would be highly leery of a woman in that position."

Naturally.

"So, upon my retirement, Sir Jonathan Braithwaite will become the managing director. And you, my dear, will be named as the deputy managing director."

"Father!"

"It is true."

If Henri said it, it was true. He would have locked in the promises as solemn oaths. She felt her eyes mist as she thought of the possibilities. To be elevated to that executive position as a woman would bring her renown throughout Europe. She would make judgments that affected thousands. The responsibility inspired awe, and the rewards could be fabulous.

Dan Kerry could come to work for her.

She immediately banished that thought. Kerry was more evenhanded in dealing with minorities and women than she had first thought him to be, but even she could not see him accepting employment that had the appearance of being a gratuity.

He would not, she saw now, be a kept man, as her skier and her sea diver had wanted dearly to be.

As she would not be a kept woman.

She and Dan Kerry did not share a common destiny, she thought, and therefore she was free to pursue her own.

But the message on the answering machine. . . .

He had mentioned love.

For the first time.

But to be the deputy managing director. . . .
Unless. . . .
"There must be a condition in this, Father."
He smiled, somewhat grimly. "There always is, yes."
"The condition being that we must secure the contract."
"Yes."
She frowned.
But Dubonnet smiled again. "I don't believe that to be a problem, do you?"

Deng Xiaoping International Superport
September 30, 4:45 P.M.

Gerhard Ebbing saw Kraft and al-Qatar into their taxi at the ground transport transfer facility, then got back on a people mover headed for the terminals.

The car was crowded. Already, tours were being organized, and everywhere he looked, he seemed to see people. It was a diverse population; Americans, South Americans, Europeans, and Asians made the trek up from Hong Kong to see the new amusement park.

Ebbing had once gone to the Disney park in Paris, and the engineer in him was fascinated by the accomplishments of the entertainment conglomerate. He supposed that there was some of the same fascination for Deng Xiaoping International Superport in the minds of international tourists.

The subordinate terminals were off-limits for tours presently, and the rail car passed the first three platforms briskly and braked to a smooth stop at the platform for Terminal One. Ebbing exited in line with a group he suspected was on a world tour from Portugal.

While their guide explained their location, Ebbing bypassed the group and used his key on the restricted elevator. He rode up to the sixth floor, got off, and walked down the corridor to the office.

Sung Min was at her desk near the door and smiled at him as he entered. Zemenek and Bergen were the only two present, and they were patiently wading through copies of some computer printouts that Kerry had produced for them yesterday morning.

Ebbing pulled a chair away from one desk and dragged it over to Zemenek's desk.

"Anything?" he asked.

Bergen pointed to a handwritten list on a yellow legal pad. "Gerhard, these people don't see well."

"What people?"

"The sailors and pilots who compiled this thing. They take wild guesses about the length of a boat."

"We know for certain that it is forty-four feet."

"Sure. But the observers say, 'about fifty feet,' or 'perhaps forty feet.' Or the equivalent in meters. We're culling out anything from thirty to sixty feet, and so far, we've got, oh, ninety boats."

"Do we know where they are?"

"We know where they were."

"How long ago?"

"Anything from a week ago to two days ago."

"How about you, Pyotr? Do you think this is a fruitless exercise?"

The Russian sipped from his coffee cup, then said, "It may be, but do we have something better to do? It may be a miracle if we find something here, but we may also be in need of a miracle."

Ebbing leaned forward and rested his arms on the desk. "Three people in a boat. It does not seem as if they should pose so much of a threat that a squadron of fighter aircraft, a dozen ships, and the Lord knows how many of us converted spies should be worried about them."

"The SA-7 missile," Zemenek said, "is what poses the threat."

"How effective is it, though? From what Hua told us, it has rarely brought down a large plane."

"It has hit airplanes as high as six kilometers, though, Gerhard," Zemenek said.

He grimaced at the thought. "Yes, I know. An accident, perhaps."

"If three men in a boat fire six or nine missiles quickly," Bergen said, "an accident is bound to happen."

"From the boat? You are now thinking this?"

"It they cannot get near the airport, they could still make the attempt from the sea."

Ebbing thought about that. The AeroSwift, the Concorde II, and the Tupolev 2000 would all approach China Dome from the west. They would not be flying over the South China Sea.

"Given that presumption, Ernst, the Americans are the most exposed."

"Yes, they are."

Zemenek's and Bergen's deadpan faces stared at him.

"You aren't thinking? . . ."

Bergen grinned. "I have to admit, Gerhard, that I thought about it. Not doing anything. It could eliminate some strong competition. Then, I had to admit to myself that it is not simply an airplane. It is also one hundred and sixty-some souls, even if the souls might be a bit haughty. I would not want some omission on my part to hasten these souls on the journey toward their maker."

Zemenek did not make the same confession, and as Ebbing took a handful of the printouts and began to go over them, he wondered if Zemenek knew something he and Bergen did not.

It was possible. The Russians were in as much need as the former East Germany.

And, he thought bitterly, neither the Russians nor the Germans were in as much need as the BBK shareholders.

Deng Xiaoping International Superport
September 30, 5:50 P.M.

For the afternoon, Kerry had closeted himself on the twelfth floor, in a lounge called the Little Dipper. The noise of workers setting up for the next day's festivities didn't bother him. The clink of china and silverware was a fairly welcome background noise.

He had found a big coffee urn and made a pot of coffee, and with his portable telephone, he was quite content in a booth by the window wall. As he went through the printouts for the tenth or eleventh time, making notations in the margin, he allowed himself to be interrupted by telephone calls to Tokyo and the States. He had talked to Duff twice, to Jackson once, and to Carroll twice. Dennis Aikens had called him three times, looking for reassurances about the conditions at the Superport. Aikens was suddenly aware of the real, political world, as opposed to the scientific, engineering, aviation world, and he wanted to know that his babies were going to be safe in the hands of Chinese baby-sitters.

Mickey Duff had the F-16 in Tokyo, after a long flight from California via Anchorage. He was excited about his escort assignment.

All through the afternoon, a steady stream of aircraft had

been landing on Runways 27 Left and 27 Center. Most of them bore the logos of Chinese air carriers—Sichuan, Northern, China Airways—and had been parked at Terminal Seven. Several were charters from World and TWA, carrying television and print reporters he assumed, since they had been parked on the opposite end of the arc of domes, at Terminal Six.

All four of the helicopters seemed to be in the air constantly, and the Shenyang fighters had been on steady rotations. The grounds around the terminals and the perimeter fences were under scrutiny by security people in cars and pickups. Even a few fire trucks had been pressed into service as mobile security forces.

He poured himself another cup of coffee, wondering how soon he was going to float away, and picked up the sheaf of pilots' notes. Yichang had gone through them the first time since they were mostly written in Chinese, and he had jotted occasional translations on them. Fortunately, the computer had done the translations from the original Chinese to English for the printouts.

He and Yichang had verified, the night before last, that all of the sightings listed on the pilots' notes had made it to the printouts. That wasn't the problem; the problem was that not all of the information in the handwritten notes had made it to the printouts.

Some of the pilots had written down details that the computer apparently didn't want to have, and Kerry was adding those details to the printouts. He had been doing it for four hours.

He looked at the next note: Chinese junk, twenty-five meters long.

Turned it face down on his reject stack.

Next note: *Flower Girl,* home port Macau, fifteen meters length, cruiser, oversized radar antenna.

The length was right. He leafed through the printouts until he found the *Flower Girl.* Just below the line of the entry, he wrote: oversized radar antenna.

Picked up the next note.

Then realized he was performing a routine, rather than thinking.

Kerry went back to the printed letters he had just inserted. And asked himself, "Why?"

He picked up the phone, one which was issued to airport personnel and which required only a four-digit number for phones in the airport complex, and punched in the number for Hangar Two.

The man on the other end answered in Chinese and Kerry asked for Major Hua in English.

He came on a couple minutes later, "Yes, Mr. Kerry?"

"I'm curious about an entry on one of these pilots' notes, Major."

"Which is that?"

"Has to do with a yacht called the *Flower Girl.*"

"Ah, that is mine. I remember the name."

"You noted an oversized radar antenna."

"Did I? Yes, perhaps I did. There have been so many boats, I forget the circumstances. Let me think a moment." He thought for more than a moment, then said, "I believe it was rather a run-down boat. Captain Jiang made some comment about it being a refuge from the sixties. I think I assumed that old hippies, as you called them, would be in command of a cargo of marijuana."

"But why the antenna?"

"It seemed out of character for the boat," Hua said. "It was covered with canvas, but I recognized the shape."

"Out of character? What do you mean by that?"

"Most small craft, if they have radar, have a much smaller antenna, Mr. Kerry. They are intended to warn one of nearby shipping, or perhaps to watch for threatening storm cells. This one was considerably larger and suggested a capability for aircraft search."

Kerry mused over that for a moment, as Hua seemed to do.

Kerry said, "That kind of capability could worry me this week."

"Yes, sir. It could worry me also."

"Do you think you can find the boat again?"

"What was the home port? I do not remember."

"Macau."

"We will check there, and I will call General Chou."

"Thank you, Major."

He called the office on the sixth floor, got Bergen, and told him about his conversation with the major.

"Damn," Bergen said. "I think you two have got something. Better than anything we've come up with."

"My thought," Kerry said, "would be to delay the opening until someone finds that boat and either approves it or sinks it."

"Hold on."

Kerry heard him talking to others in the office.

"Dan, Gerhard is undecided, but Dowd and Yelchenko vote with us. We're the only ones here, so I can't get any more votes."

"I'll call Sun."

His conversation with Sun Chen, whom he located in the security center, was short. There would be no delay in the airport's grand entrance into the world.

He called Jackson at his office, but Mollie said she'd have to run him down at LAX and have him call back.

He did, twelve minutes later.

"What have you got, Dan?"

Kerry told him.

"A radar on a forty-foot boat. That's it?"

"It's an important radar, P.J."

"Could be. What do you want me to do about it?"

"Delay the flight by a day."

"No fucking way. I just got United to loan me a couple gates. Terry's coming in with the plane later. We've got governors and cabinet secretaries coming out our ears. I'm hosting a dinner for the early birds tonight, and I'm not going to get up there and say, 'Thanks, anyway, folks.' "

"It's just for a day, P.J."

"I'll see you tomorrow, Dan. Sweet dreams."

Los Angeles International Airport
September 29, 8:15 P.M.

The breeze was from offshore, and Carroll had been placed in the stack for a landing to the west. There were three commercial aircraft in line ahead of the Astroliner.

"Kerry tells me this would never happen at China Dome," he told the three others on the flight deck.

Matthews was in his copilot's seat, Dormund at the engineer's position, and Dennis Aikens rode the jump seat.

"Yeah," Matthews said, "but tell me how many tons of metal is going to be in the approach lanes when they're operating fifteen runways."

"It'll be interesting," Carroll agreed.

At five thousand feet, as he came around to the west in

his orbit, Carroll had a million-dollar view of the Pacific. With the sun way down on the horizon, the sea's surface was a slate-gray. No clouds, but a few sailboats were beating shoreward. Coming around to the east, he had a ten-cent view of Los Angeles. An inversion had trapped the brown cloud over the downtown area, and the streetlights just coming into operation were diffused and muddy.

Nine minutes later, they were cleared on final with gear and flaps deployed, and Carroll had the ILS lined up and linked to the onboard computer. The Astroliner flashed across South Gate and Watts at 250 knots. Down on the right, he saw that Firestone Boulevard was a string of gridlocked headlights and taillights. As they approached Inglewood in the failing light, he missed the midday view of blue swimming pools in backyards. A few patio lights were placed so that they reflected off the pools.

"Right on glide and centerline," Matthews reported.

The computer was making the approach, of course, and Carroll was beginning to expect nothing less than perfection. He glanced at the throttle cluster and saw them click back a fraction.

He assumed that Dennis Aikens had a self-satisfied smirk on his face, but he didn't turn around to confirm it.

The parallel set of runway lights widened as they got closer, then the airplane was over the approach lights. He switched his view to the video monitor as the nose began to block his vision of the runway.

"Still on track," Matthews said. "Speed two-two-oh."

A few seconds later: "One-nine-oh."

Then: "One-eight-oh."

With the nose held high to maintain lift, the main landing gear trucks touched down smoothly. He barely felt the contact. Speed came off quickly, and the nose began to settle.

As soon as the nose gear touched down, Carroll announced, "I've got the airplane."

"You have the airplane. Cutting off the automatic systems," Matthews echoed. "Done."

He ran the engines into reverse thrust, and when the speed was down to 120 knots, started applying some brake.

"That was very nice," Aikens said.

It was probably the first compliment he had heard out of the chief engineer in a year, Carroll thought.

"We're just here to serve, Dennis, but we serve very well."

The ground controller turned them off onto a taxiway and directed them toward the United concourse where P.J. Jackson had borrowed, begged, or stolen a gate.

Two gates, actually.

With the Astroliner's long nose, he couldn't pull into his parking place at a ninety-degree angle to the building and still have the jetway reach out far enough to match up with the passenger door. With the help of the man on the ground waving flashlights at him, Carroll parked on an angle, utilizing two spaces.

Jeff Dormund shut down the engines.

There was a hell of a crowd inside the concourse, their faces pressed to the windows, as they got their first view of the Astroliner. The flashes on cameras were going off like a mini police action. Matthews waved at them through the cockpit window.

"Last American stop," Carroll announced. "Next stop, Hong Kong."

Aikens unbuckled and stood up. "I'm going home and see my wife. If she'll let me in."

"Or still recognizes you," Dormund said.

"See you here early in the morning?" Aikens asked Carroll.

"You will. I'm staying with the plane tonight."

"Oh, come on."

"Damn right. We'll fuel up in a bit, then I'm stretching out in the cabin." Carroll pointed toward the mob in the terminal. "I'm not letting one of those nuts try to get a closer look."

TWENTY-THREE

Los Angeles International Airport
September 30, 3:30 P.M.

P.J. Jackson was in his element. He and Valerie stood at the door to United's international departures lounge and welcomed their guests. Supporting the value of this junket was the fact that not one of those invited had turned down the invitation. If something important, like world order, happened to be on their desks, they postponed world order.

He had had only one complaint, and that was from his twin. Paul had assumed somehow—P.J. had no idea how—that he was going along, to be seen and to mix with the political cream of the crop. He had even shown up uninvited at the dinner the night before, and P.J. had had to have another place set for him. Later, after dinner, telling him that he wasn't going along had been bittersweet. Jackson had enjoyed twinges of elation inside while attempting to console Paul with the fact that there just weren't enough seats. So many celebrities had been turned down, etc., etc. . . .

"Good afternoon, Mr. Vice President. I'm happy you could join us."

"It seems like the event of the year, if not the decade, Mr. Jackson. I was pleased that I could clear my calendar."

Yes.

"May I introduce my wife, Valerie?"

Valerie was happy, too, and that made Jackson happy.

The Vice President moved on to talk mutual business with the Speaker of the House.

He surveyed the group building in the room, more than a few of them clustering around the bar, then shifted to the windows to look out at the Astroliner, and thought of them, not as his guests, but as advertising. Despite appearances to the contrary, this wasn't a freebie. Every one of them was going to be a testimonial for the Astroliner, whether they knew it or not. In China, he would circulate them among the Chinese emissaries and let them extol the virtues of the American supersonic transport.

Jackson was extremely pleased with himself.

He glanced out the window and saw the caterer's truck pulling away from the aircraft. The food was loaded. The liquor was loaded. It was a good thing that it was going to be a short flight. Otherwise, they'd arrive in China with a bunch of loaded passengers.

At a tap on his shoulder, he turned and found Ken Stephenson.

"Damn, it's about time, Ken. I thought you were going to take a cruise ship."

Stephenson looked over the crowd. "I see only four of our directors."

"They're the only ones who said they could make it."

"You're certain?"

"I invited them all, Ken. You think I'm stupid?"

"No. I just wish more of them felt as if they had an obligation to support this enterprise."

"They only worry about the return on investment," Jackson said. "You know that."

Stephenson turned toward him, his face close in the increasingly thick mob of people. "Have you heard anything more out of China Dome? From Kerry?"

He decided he wouldn't worry the president.

"No developments that concern us," he said.

Los Angeles International Airport
September 30, 4:45 P.M.

Carroll, Matthews, Dormund, and the four moonlighting stewardesses had been told by Jackson two weeks before to get themselves appropriate dress for the inaugural flight. The seven of them had gone out and been fitted for matching uniforms.

Carroll, who had never liked uniforms much, felt pretty good in the silver-gray gabardine slacks and tailored jacket. He had given himself captain's rings on the sleeve cuffs and gold braid on the bill of the cap. He wore his Navy wings over the left breast pocket and the PAI logo over the right. The women appeared well-refined, too. They had objected to the requirement to wear the jackets, but he'd told them they were aboard his airplane as representatives of the company, not as bait for the passengers.

His jacket was on a hanger in the locker at the rear cockpit bulkhead, but he had kept his dark gray tie in place when he took his seat.

"Let's have the seat belt signs, Don."

"Damn. I'd forgotten we were in the passenger business." Matthews flipped the switch.

Carroll switched his microphone to the cabin public address system. P.J. Jackson wanted this to be professional.

"Ladies and gentlemen, this is Captain Carroll. On behalf of Pacific Aerospace Incorporated, I want to welcome you aboard for the maiden flight of the Astroliner supersonic transport."

Pause for the cheering to die down.

He couldn't hear anything in the cabin. Maybe they weren't cheering.

"Very soon, we will be moving away from the terminal, and we anticipate takeoff at four-fifty-five. Our cruise altitude will be sixty thousand feet at a speed of Mach two-point-four, and we will be following the Arctic route. The estimated flight time is four hours and five minutes, and we should arrive in China around one o'clock on the first of October. As you know, we are a day ahead of Hong Kong, but we will lose that day when we cross the International Date Line. Not to worry, though; we'll get it back on the return flight. About twenty minutes after takeoff, we will join with our sister aircraft, the Astrofreighter, and for any of you who desire, it should be an excellent photo opportunity."

Everyone in that cabin knew the value of a photo opportunity.

"Please remain in your seats until the seat belt sign is extinguished. We thank you for joining us, and we are positive that this will be your most enjoyable and memorable flight."

He switched off the PA system.

"You're a natural, Terry," Dormund told him.

Matthews was talking to a ground crewman who was patched into the intercom system via a jack on the exterior. The tractor's tow bar was connected to the nose gear.

"We're set, Terry."

He released the brakes.

"Take us away."

Matthews relayed the order, and the Astroliner began to back slowly away from the terminal.

"You see Reba back there?" Dormund asked.

"I saw her."

"And?"

"And I'm in love."

"Get in line, Captain," Dormund told him.

After the tractor released them, he and Dormund went through the checklist and cranked up the turbofans.

"Greens," Dormund said. "We've got beautiful engines."

Matthews announced taxi clearance from ground control. "Two-seven right, Terry. They want to show us off on the close runway for the spectators."

A few thousand aviation aficionados had gathered at LAX to watch the takeoff. Their faces were all around, pressing against the glass of the terminals.

"We're worth it."

No doubt because of the spectators and the cabin full of household names, there was no waiting in taxi lines. The Astroliner was cleared ahead of a few United, TWA, Delta, and Continental passenger liners, and Carroll reached the end of the runway without having to use the brakes once.

"PA One, Los Angeles Air Control. You are cleared for immediate access to the runway and takeoff."

"Roger, Los Angeles. PA One copies immediate clearance," Matthews said.

Carroll still leaned forward to peer through the windscreen and check the skies to the left and right.

"See anything, Don?"

"A bird just off and climbing west. Nothing coming in."

He continued his roll, slowing a bit so as not to jar the passengers as he turned to align himself with the centerline. He could only see the line at the far end of the runway because of the visual interference of the nose, and he used the view on his center screen to accomplish the alignment with the center of the runway.

"Power, Jeff?"

"Anything you want."

Without slowing, Carroll advanced the throttles, and the Astroliner instantly picked up speed.

The spaces in the dotted centerline, seen through the video monitor, began to get closer to each other and to blur.

"One hundred knots," Matthews announced.

One hundred and sixty-eight people. He didn't like this.

"One-twenty."

"Jeff?"

"Everything's perfect, Terry. No abort here."

"One-seventy."

"Now, I feel the difference in weight," he said.

"It's distributed just right," Matthews said. "And only twelve thousand pounds of luggage."

One hundred and sixty-eight people travelling light.

Two hundred thousand pounds of fuel. One hundred tons.

"One-ninety. Rotation coming up."

Carroll gripped the yoke, but tried to do it lightly, as if he wasn't worried about cartwheeling into the Pacific.

"Rotate."

He eased back on the yoke, and the nose gear quit rumbling.

A second later, the main gear released their contact with the earth.

The end of the runway disappeared from the screen, and

was soon replaced with the white flash of beach, then the blue-green of the Pacific Ocean's shallow waters.

"Gear up," he called.

"Gear. Up and locked. Speed two-five-five knots."

Carroll waited until he had 275 knots of airspeed, then ordered the flaps retracted.

"That was very nice, PA One," Air Control told them. "You'll make the six o'clock newscasts. You are cleared to eighteen thousand at three-zero-five for fifteen minutes, then further cleared to sixty thousand."

"Roger, Los Angeles," Matthews said. "Eighteen thousand for fifteen, then sixty thousand. Three-zero-five."

Carroll eased into the turn as they climbed, then leveled the wings at the proper heading.

"Okay, Don. Let 'em get to the trough."

Matthews killed the seat belt sign.

"Jesus," Dormund said. "The telephone lines just lit up."

Carroll looked back to the display to the right of the engineer's station which monitored the automatic switching of the telephone circuits. Amber lights indicated all thirty of the lines were tied up.

"Well, hell," Matthews said. "These people have been away from a phone for nearly half an hour."

"We'll start getting complaints that we don't have enough lines," Carroll said.

Sixteen minutes later, after they were on autopilot and making Mach 1.6, Coker checked in on the company frequency.

"PA One, this's Two."

"Go ahead, Two," Carroll said.

"I have you visual, two miles ahead of me."

"Bring it in tight for about ten minutes, Cliff. Let them

look you over in flight, then we'll go to the planned separation."

"Coming up on you. In ten, I'll move out a mile to your right."

The sun was low on the left as the pair of Astros headed for Alaska. Later, he would explain their flight path for the passengers who were unaware that the trip was shorter going over the top of the world rather than skirting around the waist of the globe.

Carroll adjusted the tinted screen on his side window to keep the sunlight from interfering with the digital readouts on his panel.

He checked the chronometer on the panel. They had about ten minutes before the flight deck tours were to begin. Carroll had objected to the exercise, but Jackson wanted any of the passengers who desired to do so, to have a quick look into the cockpit.

"Over here," Matthews said.

Carroll looked to the right to see the Astrofreighter about two hundred yards off their right wing. Coker waved at them.

"God, she's beautiful," Dormund said. "You realize this is the first time I've seen her in the air?"

Carroll had never flown the chase plane, so he hadn't seen either of the Astros from this vantage point, either.

"Born to fly, Jeff. Ain't nothing going to keep her down."

They were interrupted by a knock on the cockpit door.

"Check it, Jeff," he told the engineer.

Dormund left his seat and went back to unlock and open the door.

Reba came in, carrying a mug of coffee. She moved right past Dormund and up to Carroll's elbow.

"I thought you'd like some coffee, Captain, after that gorgeous takeoff."

Let's see. I'm married to whom?

Taya Wan, *China*
October 1, 2:15 A.M.

The *Flower Girl* was moored two kilometers offshore, just inside the protective arms of the points on either side of the bay. There was a mild chop rolling in from the open sea, and the yacht rocked slightly in it. A breeze coming off the coast rippled the waves, creating a few whitecaps.

There were another dozen vessels of various sizes spotted around the bay, but Wehmeier thought of them only as protective coloration. He would ignore them, and if any of them attempted to interfere, it would soon thereafter be on the bottom of the bay.

Since arriving a couple hours before, they had been making preparations. The stern deck had been cleared of shell casings, and six folding canvas chairs and two tables had been placed around the deck. He wanted the external appearance to suggest that there were more than three people aboard.

The curtains were drawn over all the cabin windows against prying eyes with binoculars from other boats. In the salon, the two one-hundred-watt overhead lights were illuminated.

Just inside the companionway to the salon, leaning against the rear bulkhead, were nine SA-7 missile launchers. They had spent some time cleaning and inspecting the launchers, as well as the AK-47 assault rifles. Twenty-four magazines for the rifles had been loaded with 7.62-millimeter rounds, and the magazines had been taped together in pairs, end-to-end, for rapid exchange.

Wehmeier did not expect an assault against the yacht, but he was prepared to repel it if it came. The missiles were not designed for surface targets, but would work well enough at close range if some ship or small naval vessel decided to investigate the *Flower Girl.*

Running his hand over the smooth and unfamiliar contours of his head, Wehmeier was satisfied with his own appearance. He had shaved his head and his upper lip, allowing the sun to darken his skin. Cooksey told him he looked like a proper storm trooper. He would wear Bermuda shorts and a Hawaiian shirt with a bright flowered print.

Cooksey had absolutely refused the disguise Wehmeier had planned for him, but Malgretto was amused by it and had shaved the dark hair from his legs and chest. He would wear a blond wig and a woman's bikini swimsuit as he sat on the afterdeck throughout the morning. From the distance of another ship or an airplane, the two of them should dispel any suspicions.

As soon as the weapons were prepared, Malgretto professed no interest in Cooksey's paraphernalia and went below to crawl in his bunk. Cooksey slid into his seat at the banquette and began flipping switches. Wehmeier stood next to him and watched.

"I'll make but two revolutions to test it, old man. I don't want to arouse suspicions."

Wehmeier knew that radars emitting energy could be detected by other radars, Cooksey was avoiding, or at least diminishing, that possibility.

"Very well, two turns," he said.

The cathode-ray tube in an oblong aluminum box placed at the inside edge of the table glowed green as it warmed up.

It was simply a blank screen. Next to it were two medium-sized video monitors, and all three faced Cooksey.

"I will use full power on the antenna in order to obtain a one hundred and ten kilometer range," Cooksey said. "I will need the generator."

Wehmeier walked over to the desk and used the remote ignition system mounted on the bulkhead next to the radios to start the fifteen kilowatt generator. As soon as it began running, the salon lights brightened perceptibly.

He went back to the table to watch the first real test of the radar. If it had problems, Cooksey assured him that he would have ample time in which to correct them and to refine the calibration.

From their mooring in Bias Bay, the 110-kilometer range of the radar gave them an adequate coverage of Deng Xiaoping International Superport and the surrounding area.

The electronics specialist turned on the second monitor, which was the visual display for his computer. From the menu on the screen, he selected an item labeled "Radar Record."

Then he flipped a toggle switch taped to the side of the radar screen.

Instantly, a thin white line shot out from the center of the screen and began to rotate around the focal point. It travelled more slowly than Wehmeier thought it should, and he attributed the slow speed to a shortfall in power for the antenna motor.

Cooksey had a magnetic compass resting on the table next to him, and he quickly checked it, then rotated a switch which shifted the numbers on the edge of the radar screen until they matched the compass.

The white line completed one revolution, leaving in its wake several bright blips.

"That's the thirty kilometer range," Cooksey said, thumbing another switch. "Now, the one-ten."

He spun another rotary knob, but it was unlabeled, and Wehmeier did not know what it controlled.

Wehmeier did not see a change on the scope, but as the line swept to the south-southwest, several more blips appeared.

The antenna made one more turn, again lighting up targets in its path, before Cooksey shut down the power to the antenna, then to the radar scope.

He switched his attention to his computer monitor. After tapping a few keys, an image of the radar reappeared, replaying what Wehmeier had seen on the radar scope.

As the blips appeared, Cooksey explained, "The first sweep was aimed at sea level, close in. These are the vessels around us."

"How close are they?"

"See the scale here at the bottom? It matches the crosses on the radar scan. The closest boat is a bit over two kilometers away."

"Good."

"Now we're in the one-ten range, and I aimed the antenna upward so that we're skipping over the surface targets. What you see showing up on the screen are three airplanes."

He waited until the second pass, then said, "Two of them are flying away from Kai Tak Airport, and one is inbound. They are all probably airliners."

"This is very good, Ned."

He was truly amazed that the man had put all of the wires in the right places and gotten it to work.

"Well, it's surplus American equipment. It was fair to start with."

"It requires no further work?"

"Not that piece, chappie, not a lick. Now, we just wait for one o'clock."

Over Paris, France
October 1, 12:19 A.M.

The Concorde II took off on schedule from Charles de Gaulle International Airport, leaving behind a large crowd of well-wishers and a tired seventy-piece brass band.

The pilot, Captain Mark Howard, made two low-level, lazy circles over the City of Lights before heading north and beginning to increase altitude.

It was, Broussard thought, a terrible time of the night to be starting a journey, but they would cross eight time zones toward the east and arrive in China just when they were supposed to arrive.

Broussard and Dubonnet sat in the front row, on the right side of the cabin, and she had the aisle seat. The front row offered the most leg room, and she was happy to have it. She thought it likely that some of the long-legged men in the other rows would make her an offer of a great deal of money for her seat by the midpoint of the flight.

Across from her, in the first two rows on the left side, were the four Chinese men from the Committee for Airport Construction. The judge and one of the aviation engineers spoke passable English, and she had spent a full day with them, showing off the company's construction facilities. The two English-speakers were somewhat enamored of her, she thought. Whenever she glanced their way, they smiled hugely at her. The four of them had more than adequate leg room. It was important, she thought, that the judge feel as if he was comfortable.

As they gained altitude, the festive air of the dinner and party prior to takeoff began to return. The conversation level rose, and the lights above the seats and the aisle were brightened.

She looked to Henri, but he was peering through his porthole. She did not think he had slept well the night before, and with the long evening prior to departure, he appeared completely exhausted. The dark circles under his eyes had grown, and his stature seemed to have diminished. She wanted so to help him through this, but did not know how she would do it. He refused to rest, and often, his mind seemed to be elsewhere. He was so accustomed to his decades-long regimen of bed before ten o'clock that this evening had to be working against him as jet lag would.

Captain Mark Howard announced on the public address system that they were at 13,000 meters of altitude. The large digital indicator on the wall in front of her indicated the speed was Mach 2.43. It seemed quiet in the cabin, and the ride was perfectly smooth. She thought that their finicky passengers would be pleased.

Howard was doing well. She knew he was a superb pilot, and at one time, she had thought him a handsome and dashing man. However, when he asked her to dinner on her first full day back in Paris, she had discovered that he had become somewhat drab and predictable.

When the seat belt warning was extinguished, the stewards and stewardesses began popping corks from champagne bottles and moving down the aisle with stemmed glasses stacked on trays. Broussard unbuckled her own belt and stood up, balancing herself on the arm of the seat.

Dubonnet looked up at her, then started fumbling with his own belt.

"Henri, you must stay right there. I will circulate with our guests."

"Nonsense, Jacqueline."

"Do as I say. Try to sleep."

"With this noise? It is not possible."

"Try."

He gave up and said, "Perhaps for a short while."

She turned first to the Chinese judge, who was trying to juggle his wineglass and a clipboard.

"Mr. Xing, please feel welcome to explore as you wish. If you knock on the door to the flight deck, someone will admit you."

"Thank you, Mademoiselle Broussard."

"And if there are any of the guests you haven't met yet, I will be happy to introduce you."

He smiled his gratitude, and she began to work her way down the aisle, stopping at each row to talk to government officials and industry leaders. She even made polite talk with the cinema actress she detested.

Deng Xiaoping International Superport
October 1, 10:20 A.M.

The main control tower at China Dome, Number One, was twenty stories tall and stood to the southwest of Terminal One, a half-mile away. From it, the controllers had an uninterrupted view of every runway, from the commercial passenger to the commercial cargo strips.

The top level floor was a hundred feet across, with a circle of consoles placed beneath the windows, which were canted outward at the top in order to deflect sunlight. The floor just below it did not have windows. It contained ninety-six radar consoles manned by the air controllers. Kerry had just toured it and found four of the consoles in operation, more than enough for the traffic expected that day. One air controller was military, dedicated to the operation of Hua's squadron and the helicopters. He had been given the call sign Serpent.

Serpent had heard of no sightings of their quarry, Dagger.

In the center of the top level was a raised floor with another circle of consoles managed by the supervisors. And at yet another raised position within the inner circle was the rotating chair of the chief controller.

Yichang introduced Kerry to the chief controller, then took him around the perimeter of the tower, explaining some of the features. When they had completed the circle, the two of them sat in the chairs before two inoperative consoles.

"Director Yichang, I don't mind telling you that I'm a worried man."

Yichang looked at his watch. "In forty minutes, General Chou will arrive to take command of the operations, Mr. Kerry. After he arrives, he may assume the role of the worried man."

"Excuse me, but I don't think he's too worried."

"He may not show it," Yichang said, "but I believe he is highly concerned. If he were not thinking of his career, he would not be here today."

Kerry looked out at the miles and miles of landscape available to the controllers. All morning long, aircraft had been arriving from New Delhi, Hanoi, Islamabad, Seoul, Tokyo, Manila, Singapore, Bangkok, Sydney, Christchurch, and other exotic and relatively nearby cities. They were now ringing Terminals Four and Five, with a couple Boeing 727s parked at Terminal Three. It seemed strange to watch only incoming flights. Nothing was going out of China Dome, as if extremely bad weather had been predicted.

The newly arrived aircraft made the airport suddenly feel as if it were real. On the field, vehicular traffic had also increased. Maintenance people moved among the aircraft, fueling and servicing them. Out on the runway ends, he saw several sedans parked. Dowd, Bergen, and Yelchenko were with some of Yichang's security men, double-checking the sound sensors that had been placed in the approach lanes.

All four helicopters were airborne, flying security around the perimeter.

"What do you suppose we have missed?" Kerry asked the security director.

"I would be quick to point out that, in your idiom, all of the bases are covered. However, I continue to hold the dreaded thought that the People's People have outfoxed us several times."

"Or Herr Wehmeier."

Yichang acknowledged the possibility with a nod, but said, "I do not know what else we can do. Except to wait, naturally."

"I wish I was flying the damned plane. It's better than waiting."

"There is one thing, Mr. Kerry."

Yichang was looking through the windows at the airplanes on the ground.

"I know."

"Airplanes have been coming in at the rate of one every nine or ten minutes. None of them have been attacked."

"None of them are SSTs."

"They all carry important personages."

Kerry had no answer for him. Still, he couldn't bring

himself to admit that Yichang and Chou had been right all along.

There was no elevator stop at the top floor of the tower since its shaft would have obstructed vision across the tower. Instead, a spiral staircase emerged through the floor close to the central position of the chief controller. As Kerry looked in that direction, General Chou's head came into view.

Kerry and Yichang stood up and crossed the floor to meet him.

After a round of good mornings, Kerry asked, "Has there been any further word about the *Flower Girl,* General?"

"The yacht? No. I think we are wasting our time in searching for it. No doubt, by now, it is in southern waters."

Kerry looked at his watch.

Chou said, "There is nothing to fear, Mr. Kerry. Soon, the fighters will take off, and everything will be secure."

Try as he might, Kerry couldn't share the general's optimism. He moved to a console on the southwest side of the tower and leaned on it to stare at the Shenyang fighters sitting outside Hangar Two.

They still looked like MiGs to him, and they looked like MiGs that had a few deficiencies.

October 1, 10:50 A.M.

Major Hua Peng briefed his pilots in the dining area, sitting around one of the large tables.

"We will want four aircraft in the air at all times, until 1230 hours, when all six must be aloft. Therefore, we will take off at staggered times, at half-hour intervals. Dragon

One and Two will go first, so that we may return once for refueling if it proves to be necessary.

"Each airplane is armed with two air-to-air defense missiles and four AS-8 air-to-surface missiles, as well as the cannon. Weapons are not released unless specifically directed by the mission commander, General Chou.

"Our patrol route will encompass a fifty kilometer distance from the airport, with an allowance for examining the South China Sea up to seventy kilometers from the coast. The maximum altitude will be five thousand meters. We will maintain subsonic speeds in order to conserve fuel.

"There is a light wind from the west-southwest, so the incoming aircraft will be landing on 27 Left. At 1250 hours, we will mass to the northeast of the airport to rendezvous with the supersonic transports. Each transport will land singly and will be accompanied by a pair of F-12s. You are to fly fifty meters off the wingtips of the transports, and you are to have chaff and flares active and ready for ejection."

"What if," Captain Jiang said, "we see a missile so late that we cannot use countermeasures?"

"All of the airport's radars will be active, Captain. A missile should be noted in time."

"Still?"

"Then, by order of General Chou, you are to intercept it with your aircraft. Attempt to eject from the airplane before the collision."

His aviators were suddenly a solemn group.

"Please keep in mind that each of the transports carries at least 165 people of stature. To have them killed on Chinese soil would reflect badly on our nation for years to come."

He waited a moment for that to sink in, then continued, "For the benefit of the spectators and the international correspondents, this activity is to appear much as a flying circus. We are merely escorting our esteemed guests to the airport. As each transport lands, you will peel off to the left and right, climbing at forty-five degrees, using afterburners momentarily. It is to be a spectacular stunt, and we will impress the correspondents."

His tone told them they would be impressive, or else.

"Once you have left a transport safely on the ground, circle back to pick up the next one in line."

"There are five transports," Major Yang reminded them, "but you will not converse directly with the pilots. All communication will be through the air controller, Serpent, and I will be in the tower with him."

"Additionally," Hua said, "there will be an American F-16 accompanying the two American airplanes. It is unarmed, except for countermeasures, and it will make the approach with you.

"Are there any questions?"

There were none, so Major Yang briefed them quickly on weather and flight conditions.

Hua dismissed the group, and he and Jiang left the hangar for their aircraft. They were the first off, and Hua hoped with all of his heart that it would be he who first saw a threat.

If there was to be one.

October 1, 11:02 A.M.

Gerhard Ebbing was nervous, as was Pyotr Zemenek, he thought.

Sitting around the office with only Sung Min to cheer

them was fruitless, so he called the control tower and asked General Chou for permission to come to the tower.

The general granted the request, but it was with patently obvious reluctance.

Ebbing and the Russian went down to the transport sublevel and took the people mover, which was full of a tourist group, to the tower, having to press the button on the forward panel to get it to stop there.

Just off the platform, a double set of locked doors greeted them, but Chou had called down, and they were admitted readily by a security guard carrying an AK-74 5.45-millimeter assault weapon. It was the first time Ebbing had seen guards with weapons, and the sight only heightened his anxiety.

They took the express elevator to what was in reality the nineteenth floor and got out into a small foyer. A large sign on a steel door shouted "No Admittance," at them, and they bypassed it for the stairs to the top floor.

Emerging onto the tower floor, Ebbing bypassed a scowling General Chou and stepped off the raised dais to the main part of the floor. Zemenek followed as he headed for Kerry and Yichang, who were sitting at a couple of the consoles.

He smiled, "You gentlemen seem to be in a merry mood."

"If so," Kerry said, "it must be an Irish wake."

Over Kerry's head, he saw two of the Chinese fighter aircraft rushing down a north-south runway, side by side. They took to the air swiftly, and their landing gear retracted almost as soon as they cleared the ground.

A controller on the other side of the tower was talking to someone, and Ebbing turned to see an Ilyushin 76 approaching from the east. It was marked for the North Korean airline. On the ground to the east, he saw a DC-9 moving into a parking place at Terminal Five.

"So much activity after so much somnolence," Zemenek remarked.

"It seems to be very normal," Ebbing said. "I am encouraged."

Kerry grinned at him. "See what you can do about encouraging me, Gerhard."

A smattering of chatter in Chinese drew his attention to one of the controllers, and he watched Chou leave the raised platform and move over to the controller.

Ebbing and his colleagues moved up behind the console, also.

The radar console was a repeater, showing the screen from one of the radars on the floor below. There were several blips showing on it, each of them identified by letters in a small, square box. And each of them belonged to airplanes from Malaya, Tahiti, Laos, and Burma.

Chou said, "The SSTs are not yet in our radar range, but they have all made radio contact. The airplanes coming from the west are now under Chinese air control."

"How about the Astros, General?" Kerry asked.

"Japanese air control has notified us that they are in touch with PA One and PA Two."

The time was getting close, now, Ebbing thought, trying to overcome the feeling that he was attending a funeral.

October 1, 11:50 A.M.

Sun Chen had abandoned Director Yichang's office for a quiet walk on the eighth floor, which was unfinished. The floors were of bare concrete, and steel studs, not yet hidden by drywall, seemed to hold up the ninth floor.

He had also abandoned his platoon of assistants, and he was relishing his solitude.

As he paraded himself along the outer wall of the dome, he noted the many airplanes parked at the other terminals. For these few days, Deng Xiaoping International Superport would begin to appear as he had always seen it in his mind. It was a powerful vision, and he was proud of it. He also envisioned the time when those airplanes out there were paying landing fees and airport use fees. The meters on the fuel tanks would be rolling, toting up a modest profit. The passengers would be strolling through the immense facilities, spending their dollars and drachmas on souvenirs of South China—postcards and miniature dragons. The air would hum with their contented chatter.

If all went well today.

Sun had overcome his earlier melancholy, and he was once again focused on the future of China.

General Chou Sen had assured him that every possible contingency had been identified and was subject to immediate countermeasures.

Yichang Enlai, conversely, was considerably more reserved, and he made no promises.

The unfortunate aspect was that Sun relied more heavily on Yichang's instincts than he did on Chou's.

And so he worried.

Perhaps he should have listened to Daniel Kerry, who had wanted to postpone the grand opening by twenty-four or forty-eight hours, just enough to upset any plans made by possible saboteurs.

But there were all of those people now crowding his . . .

the Republic's concourses. And too many of them carried pencils and notebooks and recorders and cameras.

With which they would record the new door opening on history . . . or the fatal tragedy that slammed that door shut.

Though he would prefer to continue walking in blessed silence for several more hours, until it was all over, Sun sighed and decided his responsibilities required that he be somewhere near the center of decision making.

He supposed that was the control tower, so he left his path and headed toward the elevators.

1,795 Miles North-northeast of Hong Kong
October 1, 9:05 A.M.

Matthews checked his navigation readouts and said, "We're four minutes off the pace, Terry, but right on track. Not too bad."

Carroll agreed. They had run into a stronger jet stream than predicted, but the Astroliner had bucked them gracefully. He was still holding Mach 2.4, the maximum allowed by the computer. The Astrofreighter was still in formation, a mile to his right. Coker had experienced no difficulties. He had reported that the Chinese inspectors were having a grand time. Everyone had enjoyed their steak and lobster luncheons.

"What's the distance?" he asked.

"Seventeen hundred and ninety-five miles. We hold this altitude and speed, call it an hour and two minutes."

"We have to spend a little time slowing down, Don."

"Details," Matthews said.

Dormund had propped the cockpit door open a couple inches, so they could listen in on the party taking place in the cabin. Several of the entertainers had dug out guitars and were leading the whole cabinload of passengers in singing some golden oldies. Carroll assumed that most of the passengers didn't know the words to anything that wasn't golden and olden.

They had been through "Faded Love," twice, a bunch of Buddy Holly's songs, a few Elvis, some Willie Nelson, and were now into "Michael, Row Your Boat Ashore." Carroll was enjoying it.

Until a voice sounded in his earphones, coming in on the company frequency.

"PA One, Top Dog. You reading me?"

He toed his transmit button. "Got you, Mickey. How's tricks?"

"Tell me where you are, and then I'll let you in on my tricks."

Matthews read off the coordinates from his NavStar readouts.

"Hokay, Big Bird. I'm six hundred miles south of you at angels four-oh. I'm going to go hell-bent for the China mainland and hope you can figure out how to catch up with me."

"Catching up with you is no sweat, Top Dog. You're going to have to get something with more speed than a tricycle."

"This tricycle is fun. Bet you can't do a barrel roll with your cargo."

Carroll thought about Reba and decided he didn't want her on the ceiling of the cabin.

And thought that that was still a possibility.

"In about half an hour, Don," he said, "we want to strap them in. Good and tight."

Deng Xiaoping International Superport
October 1, 12:12 P.M.

Kerry had moved up to the raised portion of the control tower and taken a chair next to the console that was in contact with Major Hua's squadron and the helicopters.

The operator, also known as Serpent, had mentioned to Hua that Kerry was present, and the squadron commander, being sensitive to Kerry's limitations, had instructed his pilots to converse in English.

Though he could understand the transmissions taking place, he also understood that nothing of importance had been noted by any of the fighters in the air.

The radar screen in front of the operator had been filtered so that only Hua's Shenyang F-12s appeared on it, each identified by its call sign. He saw that Blue Dragon One was moving south along the coast. Blue Dragon Two, Hua's wingman, was twenty miles off the coast, moving south in parallel.

The coastline appeared as a ragged gray line on the screen. Hua was approaching a large indentation in the coast.

"Serpent, Blue Dragon One."

"Go ahead, One," the operator said.

"I am going to orbit Bias Bay once."

"Copied and approved, One."

The blip on the screen seemed to move slowly as it made a large circle of the bay.

Two minutes went by, then the speaker blurted, "Serpent, I have found *Flower Girl!*"

Kerry leaned forward.

"Making another circuit," Hua reported.

General Chou moved closer to listen.

A minute dragged by.

"Serpent, is Mr. Kerry present?"

Kerry took the microphone the operator handed to him.

"Right here, Dragon One."

"The boat is anchored several kilometers offshore. The radar antenna is covered with canvas, and two people are on the stern deck."

"What do they look like?"

"I have used my binoculars, but the only people I see are a bald-headed man and a light-haired woman in a swimsuit. They are sunning on the deck and apparently drinking."

"Obviously," Chou said, "you are mistaken about the boat, Mr. Kerry."

"What do you think, Dragon One?" Kerry asked.

"The appearance is one of innocence."

"You wouldn't run in there and drop a missile on them?"

"Not in one hundred years," Hua said.

"Well, Mr. Kerry?" the general asked.

"Maybe we could ask for a naval boat to check on them, General?"

Chou appeared as if he were going to refuse the request for a minute, but then relented. "I will ask."

He turned and barked an order to a sergeant in Chinese.

The console operator took back his microphone.

"Blue Dragon One, Serpent. A naval unit is to be dispatched to investigate. You may return to your patrol."

Kerry happened to think it was a mistake, but he didn't see what he could do about it.

TWENTY-FOUR

Deng Xiaoping International Superport
October 1, 12:30 P.M.

The observation deck of Terminal One throbbed with mankind. Discreet blue velvet ropes suspended between chromium stanchions protected the six areas where tables had been erected for the banquets, but the horde of print and broadcast journalists had invaded the main terminal, and they tended to go where they wanted to go. A platoon of service personnel in white pants and red jackets, their faces not revealing their disenchantment with overbearing guests, scurried about and attempted to replace the stanchions when they were moved and the velvet ropes when they were bypassed.

The correspondents were having a glorious day. Wherever they turned, premiers and presidents, or their deputies, were in plain view, defenseless against camcorders, microphones, and pencils wielded like the swords they could be. Celebrities and the stars and superstars of the entertainment world mingled with the political and commercial figureheads; the reporters were driven to schizophrenia, Sun thought. They did not know whom to pursue.

Sun Chen had been diverted from his course toward the control tower and the center of decisions by Zhao Li who insisted that his presence was necessary on the top floor of the dome. He did not think that was true, but allowed himself to be redirected.

Zhao acted as his guide in the fleshy jungle and remembered names for him as he towed him from one group to another. Sun made amiable conversation, the points of which he could not remember thirty seconds later. His mind was on the skies, and as the time of arrival grew closer, he found himself pressuring Zhao toward the northern wall of the dome.

He wanted to have a clear view of the supersonic transports when they landed. He looked forward to the arrival, and he hoped they arrived safely.

But he had his doubts.

Over the Formosa Strait
October 1, 12:32 P.M.

Twenty miles to Carroll's right, the coast of China shone like crisp salad greens under the high sun. Some of the villages looked like cucumbers. On the left, the island of Taiwan took up most of his ocean.

The Astroliner was steady at 22,000 feet above the smooth blue surface of the strait, and Carroll had bled off speed until the readout displayed Mach 1.5. Cliff Coker had moved in closer with the Astrofreighter and was now a half-mile off to the right and slightly behind. On the radar at a thirty-mile scan, he had identified six aircraft. Two of them were Chinese military, and four were civilian transports en route to or from Japan.

Don Matthews had an aeronautical chart spread across his

lap, and he had been trying to identify the coastal towns and villages they had passed as they flew parallel to the coast.

"Damn, Terry, there's one hell of a lot of towns."

"There's a hell of a lot of people to fill them, Don."

"Yeah. Okay, that's Hanchiang at our three o'clock. Four hundred miles to Bias Bay. We're right on with the NavStar."

The air corridor that had been established for them was relatively narrow. The Chinese did not want them flying over the mainland, citing interference with domestic air corridors. The SSTs were to stay between twenty and thirty miles off the coast until reaching Bias Bay when they would turn inland for a straight shot to China Dome. Carroll thought the Chinese were being downright paranoid, but in earlier discussions with Dan Kerry, Kerry had suggested that it would take several years, maybe a decade, before China really accepted a role as an open nation. Kerry thought there would be several changes in the powerhouse of Beijing before any real changes were made.

The opening of Deng Xiaoping International was, in itself, a hell of a step in the right direction.

The passenger cabin had quieted down some as they lost altitude. Carroll could imagine most of his charges up against their portholes, many of them getting a first look at China.

"Let's strap them in, Don."

"Roger that, Captain." Matthews flipped the toggle switch to turn on the seat belt sign.

A couple minutes later, Matthews said, "Up there, Terry. Eleven o'clock, and a couple thou above us."

"You have him on radar?"

"Just. Call it twenty-six miles."

Carroll saw the tiny glint in the sun and toed the transmit button. "Hey, Hot Dog, PA One."

They hadn't established a call sign for Duff, so Carroll just called him whatever he wanted to call him.

"That's Top Dog to you," Duff came back.

"You want to put the brakes on? We're at angels two-two and sliding under you."

"My brakes are all worn out," Duff said. "Comin' back to you."

As Carroll watched, the F-16 shot steeply skyward and then rolled over on her back. Approaching them inverted at supersonic speed, the Falcon closed the distance between them rapidly.

When he was almost directly overhead, Duff applied up elevator and looped down toward them, disappearing from the view of the Astroliner's cockpit. A few seconds later, he pulled up on Carroll's left wing.

"Hi, guy!"

"Fancy meeting you here," Matthews said.

"Got your camera?" Carroll asked Duff.

"Thirty-six-shots worth."

For those in the passenger cabin who might have been alarmed by the appearance of the fighter, even with the giant "General Dynamics" lettering on the fuselage, Carroll switched on the PA system and announced, "Folks, this is Captain Carroll. Out on our left, you may have noted another airplane. That's an F-16 demonstration aircraft, flown by Pacific Aerospace's Assistant Director for Aeronautical Engineering, Michael Duff. He's going to shoo—take some pictures of us since this is something of a historical occasion."

Carroll thought that "shoot," wasn't a good word today.

He looked out his side window in time to see Duff waving at the passengers with a Nikon.

There was always the chance that their approach and landing would be completely uneventful. If that were the case, Kerry had decided they needed a cover story for the guests. The escort by the Chinese F-12s, when it came, was to be explained as part of the ceremonial arrival.

Conversely, there were probably a few intelligent people among those in the cabin, maybe even the politicians. They read the papers, and they knew what had been happening at China Dome. The appearance of the military aircraft was going to make them uneasy. If they were brave, they would keep their opinions to themselves. Carroll hoped so, anyway. He didn't need a cabin full of panicky people. He didn't need the democratic process taking place, led by artful politicians, whereby the passengers voted to skip the stop at China Dome.

"PA Two," Carroll radioed. "Bring her on in."

The Astrofreighter closed on them, and Carroll soon had a flying wedge with himself at the point. The other airplanes flew a hundred feet off his wingtips and slightly behind.

In the order of things important, both the Astrofreighter and the Falcon were expendable. If it came down to it, Carroll would let either of them absorb stray missile fire.

On the radio, tuned to the company frequency, he warned both Coker and Duff, "PA One's backing off to Mach one."

"PA Two."

"Top Dog."

"All right, Don. Get hold of that air controller and get us clearance to ten thousand. We'll get the party rolling."

Deng Xiaoping International Superport
October 1, 12:34 P.M.

The control tower was much like a temple, Yichang Enlai thought. No one spoke out loud.

In the background, from overhead speakers, were the radio calls among various aircraft, but they were muted. The people in the tower, when they spoke, did so in soft voices that were just above whispers.

The tension was almost visible.

It was certainly physical. Yichang felt it in the tautness of his shoulder muscles. He had all but forgotten the soreness of his arm, and twice, he had inadvertently pressed on his left arm against the console edge, resulting in sharp jolts of pain.

The repeater radar screen at his left had a large number of blips on it, all identified. Off the coast were the three American airplanes, neatly identified in the small boxes next to the blips. One hundred and sixty kilometers to the northwest were the three symbols representing the other supersonic transports. In the last half hour, the three of them had converged and, according to the data blocks next to the symbols, were flying at 3,000 meters and 550 knots airspeed. The controller was beginning to separate them by altitude.

The air controllers had been in contact with all of the SSTs, using the airport's standard frequency for arriving aircraft. The military craft were conversing on a separate frequency. In the tower, both sets of radio conversations overlapped and sounded confused.

Kerry, who was sitting in the chair next to Yichang, had his head cocked to one side, listening to the various radio dialogues taking place. Yichang supposed that the former fighter pilot was able to separate out the important information. He himself missed most of it.

Kerry leaned in front of Yichang to ask the man at the console, "Would you ask Blue Dragon One if the naval cutter has arrived in Bias Bay?"

The *Kanchou* was en route.

The operator bypassed Major Hua and punched the numbers of a keypad, which appeared on one of the console displays. He had dialed directly into the naval command frequency. "White Bear, this is Serpent."

"Go ahead, Serpent. This is White Bear."

"What is your position and time to contact, please?"

"Serpent, we are twenty-two nautical miles south of the target. Anticipate arrival in thirty-five minutes."

"Thank you, White Bear. Serpent out."

Kerry looked at Yichang. "That's too damned late."

On the screen, Yichang noted that Blue Dragon One was staying in the area of *Taya Wan,* flying an orbit to the north of the bay. Hua was obviously as concerned about the boat as Kerry was.

Yichang turned and looked toward General Chou. He was in the central seat of the tower, where he had telephone sets at his fingertips and could observe the screens on nearby consoles, and he did not seem to be paying very much attention to Kerry, Ebbing, Zemenek, or Yichang. Perhaps he had not noticed that Hua was still flying off the coast at a time when he was supposed to be grouping his squadron to the northeast of the airport.

Reaching across to the screen, Yichang tapped his forefinger against the symbol for Blue Dragon One.

"I see it," Kerry said.

"He is watching. Let us let it be for the present, Mr. Kerry."

Kerry was not satisfied, judging by his expression, but seemed to accept what must be.

The speaker in the ceiling above them carried the air controller's radio transmission from the floor below them, "Pacific Aerospace One, Deng Xiaoping Air Control."

"This is PA One, Deng Xiaoping."

"Current conditions are as follows: barometric pressure of three-zero-point-one-one, wind easterly at four knots, gusting to six knots, visibility high. We will be landing you on Runway two-seven left."

"Ah, Deng Xiaoping, PA One has a request."

"Go ahead, Pacific Aerospace Zero-One."

"Pacific Aerospace Zero-One requests clearance for a landing on Runway nine right."

"Uh . . . hold on, please."

A second later, the telephone next to General Chou rang, and as it did, Yichang and Kerry left their seats and hurried to the raised dais.

"Certainly not," Chou was saying into the telephone.

Almost simultaneously, Yichang heard transmissions from the BBK, Aerospatiale-BAC, and Tupolev pilots, all demanding to be recognized by the controller.

The general looked up at the ceiling, toward the speakers.

"General," Kerry said, leaning over a console to speak to him.

"I am busy here, Mr. Kerry."

"Sir, the pilots of all those transports are requesting permission to land downwind."

The hard planes of Chou's face tightened even more. "A previously agreed tactic, Mr. Kerry?"

"Yes, General."

Chou's lips remained stiff.

"Think about it, General. If whoever is out there is listening on a radio scanner, they no longer have time to change their launch position."

"This is a dangerous proposition, Mr. Kerry," Chou said.

"Not with the length of these runways, sir."

Chou looked around the floor. Everyone, from the foreigners to the tower personnel, was watching him.

The general did not appreciate giving up a position that he had already taken, especially for an American, but finally pulled the telephone close and said, "Very well. Let them use nine right."

"Thank you, General," Kerry said.

Yichang followed Kerry back to their watch position at the console and pulled a castered chair over to sit next to him.

He could not help but feel that Kerry had won a small battle with the general, but that in winning it, he might have forsaken a future battle.

Yichang's shoulder muscles tightened yet further.

October 1, 12:41 P.M.

Gerhard Ebbing had watched the mini-drama between Kerry and Chou with some foreboding. He was relieved when Chou gave in, but he knew he would not feel any release from the fears flitting about his mind until the AeroSwift was safely on the ground.

Matthew Kraft had called him twenty minutes before, asking for the position of the airplane, and after Ebbing told him, had sounded quite jubilant. Kraft and al-Qatar were in the main terminal where, he said, Sun Chen had just broken out the champagne.

Ebbing could, in fact, hear the background noise of the party over the telephone. He had thought at the time that the difference between the atmospheres in the terminal and in the control tower could probably be measured if only he had the right instrument. He would have to design it.

Someday.

Today, he would stand with his friends Zemenek and Kerry and brood over the fate of five airplanes.

And the fate of his unlikely new friend, Jacqueline Broussard.

He wondered if Kerry was thinking about her.

As they stood staring at the moving symbols on the screen, he heard the controller vectoring the SSTs to a new holding point to the northwest of the Superport.

General Chou called someone at Terminal One to announce a slight delay in the landing schedule.

The military controller's voice came over the speaker: "Blue Dragon One, Serpent."

"Blue Dragon, go ahead."

"The rendezvous point is moved to radial three-one-zero, three-zero kilometers, three thousand meters altitude. Confirm."

"Blue Dragon copies radial three-one-zero, three-zero kilometers, three thousand meters. Executing."

22 Kilometers Northeast of Taya Wan
October 1, 12:52 P.M.

On the squadron net, Hua Peng told his aviators to meet the SSTs at the designated coordinates, then added, "Dragons Three and Four will escort the first aircraft. Five and Six will accompany the second. Dragon Two, fly high cover until I join you."

"Two will comply."

"Three."

"Four."

"Five copies."

"Six."

Captain Jiang would be wondering why Hua had changed the order of flight, but he was disciplined enough to obey without question. Hua watched as Jiang's F-12 performed a wingover to break out of his formation off Hua's right wing, then streaked away to the west.

He was at 4000 meters of altitude, cruising slowly at 325 knots, and he had been holding a rectangular orbit north of Bias Bay for some time. Like Daniel Kerry, he was suspicious of the *Flower Girl,* but he had nothing more than instinct on which to base his suspicion. General Chou would no doubt have words with him about his failure to immediately execute his part of the exercise, but since the *Kanchou* would not reach the bay before the American SSTs were scheduled to overfly it, he would delay.

As he came around to the north in his circle, the three American aircraft appeared on his radar. They were clearly identified, flying at 3300 meters of altitude and Mach 1 airspeed. The rate of closure was rapid.

Hua continued his orbit.

Banking into the southerly direction, with his antenna deflected to its lowest point, his radar picked up the returns of the ships in Bias Bay. He identified the *Flower Girl* by using directional keys on his targeting panel to place an orange circle around the blip on the screen.

"Serpent, Blue Dragon One."

"This is Serpent."

"Serpent, Dragon One. I respectfully request that the incoming SSTs be directed to make their turn inland immediately, before reaching Bias Bay."

"One minute, Dragon One."

Hua waited, easing out of his turn and staying on a course to the south. He imagined a debate taking place in the control tower. General Chou would not want to alter the approved air corridors at the last minute.

Waiting.

His radar screen displayed a sudden strong pulse.

"Serpent, Blue Dragon One."

"One, this is Serpent. Please wait."

"Serpent, the *Flower Girl* is operating a strong radar in an air search mode. I am investigating."

Southern China
October 1, 12:55 P.M.

P.J. Jackson was seated in the cockpit jump seat behind Terry Carroll. He was strapped in place and wore one of the communications headsets.

He had been talking with the flight crew about China. It was a first visit for Matthews and Dormund. Both Carroll and Jackson had been to Hong Kong a few times, and Jackson had steamed through the South China Sea on a number of sea tours.

"Pacific Aerospace Zero-One, this is Deng Xiaoping Air Control."

"PA One. I read you, Deng Xiaoping," Matthews said.

"Your corridor has been moved to the north. Turn right immediately to a course of two-six-five."

Matthews looked over at Carroll as he said, "Roger that, Deng Xiaoping. Turning right to two-six-five."

Jackson felt a chill run up his spine. Something was wrong.

Carroll told Matthews, "Kill the autopilot."

Matthews reached out for the center pedestal and snapped the switch down. "Autopilot disengaged."

On the company frequency, Carroll said, "PA Two, Hot Dog, turning right. Stay with me. Execute."

Carroll made the turn smoothly. The right wing dipped,

and the coast came around until it was dead ahead. The passengers wouldn't know this was an unplanned course.

Jackson leaned forward so that he could look out of the side windows on the left and right. Both the F-16 and the Astrofreighter stayed right with them.

Jackson was not one to interfere with any flight crew, much less his own. When it appeared that they were on the new course and the air controller wasn't going to instruct them to make any other changes, he asked, "What the hell was that about, Terry?"

"Damned if I know, P.J."

"Can we use the company frequency to talk to Kerry?"

"I'll find out."

Carroll talked to the air controller, and then switched frequencies. Kerry came on a few seconds later.

"PA One, Kerry."

"P.J. here, Dan. What's going on?"

"The squadron commander changed the corridor," Kerry said. "A last-minute diversion, I think. It's nothing to worry about."

The shoreline slipped under the long nose, and they were in China.

"So tell me what else is happening."

"We have a suspect boat, but it's under surveillance. You're not going to come anywhere close to it. Other than that, nothing. The downwind approaches appear to be clear."

The air controller was talking to Matthews on the other frequency, telling them to decrease altitude.

Carroll reduced his throttle settings manually, and the Astroliner began to descend.

"You a little less anxious this morning, Dan?" Jackson asked.

"No."

That didn't help Jackson, at all. He still felt troubled by his decision to overrule Kerry on delaying the flight.

"Terrence," Kerry said, "you be ready for anything."

"My adrenaline level's up there, Air Force guy, but the Navy will get us through," Carroll said. "Stay close by on this freq, will you? We can't hear what the military people are doing, and I'd kind of like to know."

"The military aircraft are on the way to your rendezvous. You should be seeing the other SSTs soon, as well as five Shenyang F-12s. There's a sixth one around, also. Plus, there's four choppers hanging around the airport, but they won't interfere with you."

"Copied," Carroll said.

Mickey Duff interrupted. "Dan, Mickey here. These guys know I'm friendly, right?"

"You're expected, Mickey."

Kerry cleared off the air as Matthews leaned forward and pointed with his left hand. "Over there, everyone. At eleven o'clock."

Jackson saw China Dome for the first time. It was still far off, and they would pass it to the north, but the clusters of domes and the white expanses of the multiple runways were a stunning sight.

"Damn," he said. "I thought all along that Kerry was just feeding me a bunch of hyperbole."

Taya Wan, *China*
October 1, 12:57 P.M.

Malgretto continued to pose in his bikini and wig on the stern deck, but Wehmeier had gone below to the salon after removing the canvas cover from the radar antenna.

He had stood behind the banquette settee, watching over Cooksey's shoulder as the man made three revolutions with the radar, capturing the images into the computer's memory.

Now, Wehmeier found himself checking his watch against the digital alarm clock Cooksey had taped to the top of the second monitor.

"They are behind schedule," he told the Brit.

"That's all right. There's no hurry, chappie."

"I wish we did not have to use the radar."

"I've got to know where the birds are."

With the radar shut down, Cooksey replayed the sequence from the radar scan, then froze the image. He pointed out each of the blips on the screen, saying, "Up here to the northwest, on the fringe of our coverage, are the three transports coming from the west. These two, and these three, are probably Chinese military aircraft. They're headed for the same place. This one, over here to the west, I don't know. It may be another airliner bound for either Deng Xiaoping or Kai Tak."

He moved his finger to the right of the screen.

"Two of these three, to the north of us, must be the American SSTs. I don't know what the third airplane is, but it is smaller, judging by the strength of the radar return. They seem to be flying together. Then, down here, about twenty kilometers away, is another that I do not know."

He advanced the image through two sweeps.

"It is moving south, and it is a small aircraft. It could be a military aircraft."

"We will not use the radar again," Wehmeier said.

"I will have to."

"No. Listen to the scanners."

"Very well. I will try."

The radio scanners had been locked onto the frequencies

used by the airport's air controller and the incoming aircraft. Some of it seemed like gibberish to Wehmeier, but Cooksey understood it well enough.

He would have to.

"What are they doing now?" Wehmeier asked.

"It sounds to me as if they're stacking the SSTs to the northwest of the airport, in preparation for landing them. We aren't getting the military transmissions, but I suspect that the fighters will act as escorts. They are probably making a great deal of it, Walter."

"No doubt. I will go back up to the deck, now, in case that airplane takes another look at us. Call me when you are ready to begin."

"Sure thing, old man."

"Don't do it without me."

"Of course not."

Wehmeier always liked to see whatever he could see when others were about to die.

45 Kilometers West of Deng Xiaoping International Superport October 1, 12:59 P.M.

Captain Mark Howard had tried to order her off the flight deck, but Broussard had prevailed. She had lifted the hem of her skirt to keep it from becoming soiled and knelt on the deck on a cushion between the two pilot's seats. She gripped the back of each seat with her hands. A spare headset squashed her carefully styled hairdo.

As they circled at 2,500 meters of altitude, she had occasional glimpses of the other SSTs. The Russian airplane was a thousand meters above them, and the AeroSwift was another thousand meters above it. Both of them, she had to admit to herself, were magnificent airplanes. Below the AeroSwift by perhaps 500 meters were five fighter aircraft.

Every airplane was circling, waiting for the American airplanes to join up with them.

Kerry had probably arranged it this way, she thought. It was something he would do, to gain more attention for the PAI aircraft.

And she wondered where Kerry was.

Was he worried, as she was?

Daniel Kerry, you should be worried about buying me dinner next week. Should you not?

She missed him. When she closed her eyes, she could see his face.

No.

It was not going to be.

Nothing coming over the radio from the air controller indicated that anything was amiss. The air controller's voice was perfectly calm.

She should go back and check on Henri. He had not been able to sleep, and his color was not good. She was afraid he was deathly ill.

The carrier wave in her earphones evaporated as the air controller transmitted: "All SST aircraft, this is Deng Xiaoping Air Control. The order of landing on Runway Nine Right will be as follows: Pacific Aerospace Zero-One, AeroSwift One, Concorde One, Tupolev One, Pacific Aerospace Zero-Two. American Falcon, you are approved for landing with Pacific Aerospace Zero-One, but you will use Runway Nine Right Center."

All of the aircraft acknowledged the directive.

"What is that? What is this Falcon?" she asked Howard. He leaned back and turned his head to her. "It sounds like a military F-16, mademoiselle. Apparently, they brought their own escort."

Again, Kerry had done the unexpected.

He complained about her startling changes of mood or attitude, but he was the prime example of his own complaint.

Perhaps that was one of his charms. From day to day, he would probably not be the same.

She thought her own unpredictability was one of her own charms.

Broussard had not explained that charm to Kerry. He was not likely to believe her.

Deng Xiaoping International Superport
October 1, 1:07 P.M.

"The boat radar is no longer radiating energy, Serpent," Blue Dragon One radioed.

Kerry tapped the sergeant at the console on the shoulder, and the man, resigned to Kerry's continual interference, simply passed him the microphone.

"Dragon One, Kerry. What do you see?"

The radar repeater showed the SSTs and the F-12 strike aircraft gathering in the northwest, some twenty miles away. Blue Dragon One was still circling above Bias Bay.

"Mr. Kerry," Hua said, "the woman on the boat is starting a charcoal fire on a grille hung over the side on a boat railing. The man is standing beside her, and both of them appear to be drinking."

"The radar antenna?"

"It is motionless, though the canvas cover is now removed."

Shit. There's something wrong about that boat.

But Kerry didn't know what it was.

General Chou suddenly appeared at Kerry's shoulder.

"Are you satisfied now, Mr. Kerry?"

"No, General, I'm not. We've got—"

"I think not, sir," Chou said. "Sergeant, order Blue Dragon One to join the rest of his squadron."

The sergeant relayed the order, then Chou turned to the civilian monitoring the Deng Xiaoping Air Control console and said, "Tell the air controller to bring in the first airplane."

Yichang Enlai, standing next to Kerry, said, "General Chou, would it not be possible to leave the one airplane—"

"We have wasted more than enough of our resources on this fantasy, Director Yichang."

Chou turned and walked back toward his chair in the center of the tower. His back was as straight as an ironing board.

Kerry spun in his chair to the vacant console where he was sitting. It was shut down at the moment, but a headset and a separate microphone rested on the desk. Normally, the operator sitting here would be in direct telephone contact with one of the controllers on the floor below, and the screen in the slanted panel above the desktop would echo what the controller was seeing.

On the top right corner of the control panel was a large square button with a Chinese character etched into its plastic. He punched it.

The console lit up as power flowed to it.

Below the power button were the slide and rotary controls for several different radios.

"Which of these is the UHF radio?" he asked Yichang.

Without saying a word, the security director leaned forward and pointed to the middle unit.

Kerry found the power switch and turned it on. On the keypad next to the display, he tapped in 222.6, the company frequency normally used by Pacific Aerospace.

He glanced at the radar repeater screen on the console next to him and calculated a heading.

"Falcon, Kerry."

"Go ahead, boss, you've got a Falcon."

"Mickey, abort the current mission. Go to one-one-oh and light off the afterburner."

Duff didn't hesitate. "I'm gone."

A second later, Duff asked, "What am I doing?"

Taya Wan, *China*
October 1, 1:09 P.M.

When Cooksey yelled up from the salon, Wehmeier whipped around and went down the companionway at a run. He left Malgretto throwing hamburgers on the smoking charcoal grille attached to the gunwale railing.

The Chinese fighter plane that had been hanging around to the north of them had turned tail and gone west, and Wehmeier figured they were pretty much in the clear.

"What do you have?" he asked the Brit.

"Look at this."

On the third monitor, the one to the left of the computer monitor, Wehmeier saw a clear video picture of green hills interspersed with yellowish rice paddies. The picture unrolled rapidly, scrolling down the screen, but the scenery did not change much. More hills, more rice paddies. A flash of a village passed down the right side of the screen.

"Your man in the United States did well, old chap. The video data link is perfect."

"This is coming from the Astroliner?" Wehmeier asked. He knew that it should, but he could not quite believe that his plans were achieving fruition.

"Exactly! We're using their camera in the nose of the aircraft and tapping our transmitter into the circuit. What we're seeing is what the pilot is seeing, if he is using the video system."

"Which way is he going?"

"That, I cannot tell you. That's why I need the radar again."

"No."

"Just one sweep. I've got to know when to kick in with the rest of it, old man. Otherwise, it's all for naught."

"Just one rotation," Wehmeier said.

South China
October 1, 1:11 P.M.

"Where the hell's Mickey going?" Matthews asked.

"I don't know," Carroll told him, "and we're not going to worry about it now."

Carroll had the Astroliner on a course of 180 degrees, losing altitude at a rate of 300 feet per minute. They were currently at 4,000 feet AGL and making 350 knots. The airport was twelve miles away, to his left oblique. He was following the directions of the air controller exactly.

They were on the autopilot, linked up with Deng Xiaoping's Instrument Landing System, and Carroll was making manual changes ordered by the tower by feeding the information to the computer.

On his left, China Dome crept slowly to the north. He

saw a flash of silver in the sun as the F-16 bypassed the Superport to the north.

"Pacific Aerospace One, you are coming up on final."

"Roger, Deng Xiaoping," Carroll said. He had taken over direct communications with the controller from Matthews. He was broadcasting on both the controller's frequency and the company frequency.

"AeroSwift One," the controller said, "take up a heading of one-eight-five degrees. Descend to two thousand meters."

"Copied, Deng Xiaoping," the German pilot said. "I am going to two thousand meters, heading one-eight-five."

The BBK Enterprises aircraft was about nine miles behind them.

"Pacific Aerospace One, turn left to nine-zero degrees. Maintain your current rate of descent."

"PA One, roger. Turning to nine-zero."

Carroll dialed in the new heading, and the airliner went into a perfectly balanced bank and turn, leveling her wings as the radio compass readout came up on 090.

"Airspeed two-eight-zero," Matthews said.

"Let's have the video, Don."

"Video coming up."

Carroll's center screen blinked, then showed him undulating green fields. Through the windscreen, the Superport's right runway was lined up with the Astroliner's elongated nose.

"Eight miles out," Matthews said.

"Looks damned good to me," P.J. Jackson said from the jump seat.

Carroll resisted telling the chief operating officer to shut up. Jackson was good, though, about not interfering.

Matthews had relaxed his seat harness and was leaning up close to the yoke, his eyes scanning the ground ahead.

Carroll knew he was looking for suspicious vehicles or for someone to jump up from behind a tree, hoisting a SAM launcher in their direction.

"Indicated airspeed two-six-zero. Two thousand, one hundred AGL," Matthews said.

The controller notified them, "On course, on glide path."

"That is the longest damned runway I've ever seen," Carroll said. "We want to put her down at about one-nine-oh knots."

"Copy one-nine-oh," his copilot said.

The Distance Measuring Equipment (DME) readout just below the eyebrow panel showed him at seven miles out.

The airplane lurched.

Jumped upward, fell down.

"What!" Matthews yelped.

Carroll grabbed the yoke, prepared to override the computer.

The yoke felt as if it were frozen solid. He couldn't shove it forward or draw it back.

The nose swung to the right.

And lined up on Terminal One of the dome complex.

Carroll attempted to roll the airplane back to the left.

But nothing happened.

"Disengage autopilot!" he yelled.

Matthews slammed the switch down.

And still nothing happened.

TWENTY-FIVE

Taya Wan, *China*
October 1, 1:11 P.M.

The nose camera of the Astroliner was angled farther downward than Cooksey and Wehmeier had anticipated; they could not see as far ahead of the plane as they wanted. The monitor gave them a perfect view of the green fields leading toward the runway, but the structures of the airport remained out of sight, too far above and to the right of the camera's eye. Only the radar, as Cooksey had maintained, had told them when the airplane was on its final approach.

Wehmeier stood behind Cooksey, captivated by what he was watching on the monitor. He thought of those endless kilometers of green fields as the prelude to disaster. Every nerve ending in his body tingled in anticipation. The sensation was not new to him. On every operation he had ever undertaken, the same heightened sense of godlike power had been present, but this time, the peak was much greater, and the rise toward it all that much better. Any other awareness of his being could be set aside. This was what his life was about.

Death.

Angelo Malgretto had come down to watch, too. Standing beside Wehmeier, he said, "Neat stuff, Ned! I told you before, Walter. This guy's the greatest."

Cooksey was seated at the table, but his back and shoulders were rigid with his concentration. As soon as he had turned on the high-frequency transmitter and pressed the button to send the first digitally encoded transmission, the receiver Mohammed Dakar had installed in the Astroliner's central control pedestal—connected to the aircraft's own antenna—had closed a microswitch. Closing that circuit prevented anyone aboard the airplane from disengaging the autopilot. Cooksey now controlled the major flight controls by way of the autopilot.

In front of him on the table was a blue box with a pair of joysticks and several slide switches. He had explained to Wehmeier that the right stick operated the Astroliner's ailerons and elevators and the left stick managed the rudders and throttles, and with the airliner's power-assisted controls, Cooksey's effort was minimal. Without touching the sticks, he could change headings, speed, and nose attitude with the slide switches.

At the moment, he rested his hands lightly on either side of the box, with his thumbs on top of the sticks. He had turned the airplane slightly to the right of its landing path, but he had done so by guesswork since he could not yet see the runway on the video screen.

"I think," Cooksey said, "that the pilot must be fighting the controls. He will be panicking."

"Think of it!" Malgretto said. "He knows he is dying, and there is nothing he can do about it!"

"Can he take it back?" Wehmeier asked.

"Not at all, old man. Look at the picture. He may be

fighting it, but the video is solid as a rock. She's all mine."

And then at the top of the monitor screen, the first of the domes came into view.

The picture shifted minutely as Cooksey made some adjustment with his joysticks and the plane went farther to the right.

Wehmeier's hands quivered as he imagined the impact.

Those on the airplane would die.

And perhaps fifty percent of those in the terminal. No. More. Sixty, seventy percent.

The death toll could reach fifteen hundred, maybe two thousand.

All of them the greedy, oppressive, manipulating members of the establishment who thought they controlled the world.

He would show them differently. It was he who could manipulate their ultimate world, that of life and death.

And Wehmeier had a flash of personal insight.

It was possible that his paymaster was in the terminal. If so, Wehmeier would lose his ten million dollar payment.

No. He was to be on one of the supersonic transports.

The man had not been forewarned of Wehmeier's revised and spectacular ending for the American Astroliner.

But what if he was in the terminal?

The hell with it. He could live on the three million he had in hand.

The thrill of the kill could not be overcome by filthy money.

"Speed it up, Ned," Wehmeier said. His anticipation of the ending was almost orgasmic.

"Nonsense, old man. Enjoy every moment."

Deng Xiaoping International Superport
October 1, 1:12 P.M.

"Dan! Dan!"

Kerry heard the call on the console speaker. The voice was firm, but there was a distinct edge of hysteria in it. He mashed the transmit button on the desk microphone.

"Got me, Terry."

"I've lost control."

Jesus Christ!

Kerry looked up to his left to see the Astroliner coming in. The two Shenyang F-12 fighters accompanying her banked away to the left and right, escaping a possible malfunction. The airliner veered away from the runway.

Kerry automatically calculated the projected track.

Toward the terminals, possibly the main terminal.

"Tell me about it," he said as calmly as he could. He fought the urge to yell. His adrenaline production went to peak.

"The damned autopilot won't release, Dan. Somebody's overridden me."

The fucking boat!

Kerry didn't question Carroll's interpretation of the problem. The man knew his airplane too well. There was a remote transmitter somewhere, and only by killing the transmitter would Carroll regain control.

It was the boat.

The thought of consulting with General Chou was a fleeting one, gone almost as soon as it formed in his mind. Chou would want to argue the merits, and Kerry had a deadline.

"Mr. Yichang," he said, "tell Major Hua to sink the goddamned boat."

Yichang took one glance at General Chou, then fired a

rapid order in Chinese to the sergeant at the console next to Kerry.

Kerry hit the transmit button. "Mickey, where are you?"

"I heard, Dan. Just went feet wet."

"See the boat?"

"I think so. There's a bunch of them out here."

"You've got to take it out."

"I know."

General Chou shouted across the tower, "Mr. Kerry!"

October 1, 1:12 P.M.

With all his being, P.J. Jackson wanted to leap over Carroll's shoulder and grab the control yoke. There was in him a nearly irresistible urge to control his own destiny.

Next to him, Jeff Dormund sat sideways, staring toward the front. His hands shook as if he also wanted to grab something, do something.

Both Carroll and Matthews were fighting their control wheels, trying to push the aircraft back to the left, to gain altitude, to change anything. Terry Carroll's right hand gripped the throttle cluster, attempting to shove them forward.

They wouldn't move.

The speed continued to drain off, the orange numbers of the digital readout blinking as they changed downward: 215 . . . 214 . . . 213 . . .

Matthews, with his ingrained thoroughness, kept calling out the numbers. "Airspeed two-one-oh, altitude six hundred."

And amazingly, Carroll went on the PA system.

"This is Captain Carroll. We have something of an emergency up here, folks, and I would like to have you prepare for a possible impact. Please put your heads down and use the cushions as your flight attendants instructed you earlier. Do it now, please."

The domes appeared to become huge in the windscreen, and all Jackson could think was that Kerry always had to be right.

Taya Wan, *China*
October 1, 1:13 P.M.

Major Hua Peng was westbound at 400 knots and 3,000 meters of altitude, listening to the transmissions on the military frequency, when an amazing thing happened.

The American F-16 appeared ahead of him in almost head-on silhouette, but 500 meters below him. He knew that it had to be supersonic, utilizing full afterburner.

It was there.

It was here.

And then it was gone, screaming beneath him in the blink of an eye, the sun flashing off its metallic surfaces.

Even as he slammed his F-12 into a hard left turn, he radioed, "Serpent, Dragon One."

"Serpent."

"The F-16 just went by me. What is happening?"

"It is confused, Dragon. Wait . . . Director Yichang tells you to sink the boat. Immediately!"

Hua came out of his turn leveling the wings and shoved the throttle past the detent into afterburner. He felt the pressure of full thrust as he was pushed back into his seat.

The F-16 was far ahead of him, just reaching the bay. It was in a shallow dive, its speed brakes now deployed.

Hua eased the stick forward a moment, putting his nose down and increasing the rate of his acceleration.

"Blue Dragon One, Serpent. General Chou countermands that order. Turn back now."

The F-16 was aimed toward the wrong vessel.

"Copied, Serpent," Hua said, but he had absolutely no intention of abandoning his course. His career was over, but not his life. He had to live with himself.

He did not know what frequency the F-16 pilot was using, but assumed that he would also be monitoring the International Distress Frequency on UHF 243.0. He flicked his transmitter to that frequency.

"F-16 pilot, this is F-12 behind you. Bear to your left. It is the gray boat with the radar antenna."

A second passed.

"Gotcha, F-12."

Hua was up to 650 knots now, a thousand meters off the water as he reached the bay. He banked slightly to the left to line up behind the F-16.

The boat was five kilometers away.

The American fighter was a flat and bright reflection of sun three kilometers ahead of him. Hua did not even glance at his radar screen to verify his estimates of distance.

The American fighter was almost touching the surface of the water, slowing quickly. His hot exhaust was a red dot against the blue of the bay.

And the pilot did another amazing thing.

He lowered his landing gear.

Automatically, without thinking of it, Hua armed his cannon.

"Blue Dragon One, this is General Chou. You are to abort this mission immediately!"

Hua did not hear the general's order. His mind was on another plane of consciousness.

His total focus was on what was taking place ahead of him, now at a distance of three kilometers.

Hua dumped his speed brakes.

Pulled his throttle back.

The F-16 was barely clearing the surface of the water. Hua would swear the wheels were touching the tops of the waves. He was still moving at more than three hundred knots.

The F-16 lined up directly broadside of the yacht.

A figure appeared on the afterdeck of the boat, scrambling about, lifting some dark object to its shoulder.

A missile erupted from the stern deck, but the distance was too close, and it went wide of its mark before the heat-seeker head could lock on. And with a head-on shot, the missile would probably never find a strong enough heat source.

Hua jigged his F-12 to the left, just in case the missile's target-seeking head found him.

It did not.

Hua was certain the F-16 pilot was going to drive the fighter directly into the hull.

And at the last moment, he pulled up a fraction.

The extended landing gear and the centerline external fuel tank smashed into the flying bridge structure, and wood, canvas, and metal pieces exploded into a cloud of debris.

The impact caused the fighter to throw its nose down, and just before it crashed into the sea three hundred meters to the far side of the boat, Hua saw the pilot eject. The seat arced upward from the cockpit, the parachute deploying, though not fully, before the pilot hit the surface of the bay.

The figure on the stern deck rose unsteadily from where he had been knocked down by the collision. It was the woman in the swim suit. She had a rifle now, and she took aim toward the pilot in the water.

Hua was thirty meters above the surface and 500 meters away when he depressed the firing stud of his cannon. The tracers peppered the sea to the stern of, and on the near side of, the boat. He applied back pressure on the control stick to walk them up to the stern, then added a small amount of left rudder, and the 23-millimeter shells punched gigantic holes in the boat from the transom to the bow, a meter above water level.

One shell caught the woman standing on the stern deck. She exploded and disappeared.

And then he was over the boat and past it. He banked into a hard right turn and started back.

The dialogue on the radio was confused and overlapped, but he heard General Chou screaming his head off.

Deng Xiaoping International Superport
October 1, 1:15 P.M.

"Got it!" Carroll yelled.

On the video screen, he could see thousands of faces pressed in awe and fear against the smoked glass of the dome.

He rammed all four throttles full forward against their stops and hauled back on the yoke.

"One-nine-five! Not too much, Terry!" Matthews called out.

The stall-warning buzzer sounded off.

"Gear up. Full flaps."

"Roger. Gear coming up. Full flaps already deployed."

It probably seemed closer than it actually was, especially to those in the dome, Carroll thought. He estimated they cleared the top of the dome by a couple hundred feet.

"Speed coming up," Matthews said. "Two-one-oh."

Carroll eased the nose down a trifle.

The stall warning quit shouting at him.

"Everything looking good here," Dormund said.

"Jesus H. Christ!" P.J. Jackson sighed. "If my stomach wasn't back there behind us, I'd throw up."

Carroll eased the nose down a bit more as the airplane recovered lift. He banked slightly to the left, back toward the runways and away from the domes. The last dome zipped by below them.

"Where are the F-12s, Don?" he asked. He didn't want a midair collision at this point.

Matthews scanned the skies. "Well clear, Terry. One out to the left and the other a mile away on the right."

He switched on the PA system again. "Captain Carroll here, folks. Our little glitch has been corrected, and you can relax now. We'll be on the ground in a few more minutes and I'll buy you all a drink."

Switching the selector switch to the tower frequency, he said, "Deng Xiaoping, this is PA One."

They were over the far eastern end of the runway at 400 feet of altitude, continuing into a left turn when a breathless controller came back to him, "Go ahead, Pacific Aerospace Zero-One."

"We've had our fly-by, and it looks great to us. Request permission for a full circle and landing."

"Permission granted, Pacific Aerospace Zero-One. AeroSwift One, you are directed to hold at your present altitude."

The Astroliner responded well when Carroll attempted slight changes in the controls. It felt good to him, and he couldn't help thinking, "So much for the goddamned computer."

"I think, Don, we'll do the next one hands-on. How about we skip the ILS link this time?"

"Good damned idea, Terry. You breathing all right?"

"Just starting to," he admitted. He wanted to check his pulse rate, but he was afraid to let go of the yoke.

"Damn," Jackson said. "You guys just got a bonus."

"I want to be chief pilot," Carroll told him.

"You're already chief pilot."

"I want to be a well-paid chief pilot. One who doesn't fly passengers."

"You got it. Anything else?"

"I want a long session alone with a tech named Mohammed Dakar."

"You think he's involved?" Jackson asked.

"Damned sure of it."

"No promises on that one Terry. I'll have to call as soon as we're on the ground and have him picked up."

"Okay. I hope I get a kiss from Reba."

South China Sea
October 1, 1:22 P.M.

Kerry, Yichang, and Ebbing reached ground level, and shoved through the doors onto the tarmac just as the Guard One helicopter set down outside.

Behind them, before the doors swung closed, Kerry thought he could still hear Chou yelling at them. It was probably his imagination.

The general had come unglued when no one would respond to his orders, and Kerry figured his credibility was forever gone.

The copilot of the helicopter held the door for them, and they piled into the back, Kerry sliding across to the right side.

Before they were even strapped in, Yichang yelled above the roar of the turbine, "Take off!"

The Gazelle leaped from the ground like its namesake, and Kerry fought for balance as he tightened his lap belt. He pulled the headset from its hook and fitted it over his ears.

They were five miles away from the tower, skimming the ground at 190 miles an hour when Kerry looked back and saw the Astroliner flaring into her landing profile. The main gear touched down, and a few seconds later, the nose gear followed. The runout was perfect.

He reached across Ebbing, who was in the center seat, and tapped Yichang on the arm, pointing back.

Yichang turned to look. "That is one down."

"How are you doing, Gerhard?" Kerry asked.

"I am saving my heart attack for later this evening," Ebbing said. "I would hate to spoil the afternoon."

Yichang directed the pilot to switch the military frequency into the intercom, and Kerry heard Serpent instructing two F-12s to join up with the AeroSwift for her landing.

Chou came on the radio personally then, demanding a situation report from Major Hua. He was trying to control his volume and timbre, Kerry thought, but the voice was still shaky.

"Serpent, this is Blue Dragon One. The F-16 rammed the boat . . ."

Kerry closed his eyes in pain.

". . . with his gear extended, and I followed with a strafing run. The Falcon crashed in the bay, but the American pilot is waving at me from the water. He has a flotation device. . . ."

Kerry felt the relief wash over him.

". . . The yacht is still afloat. There is a fire aft. I can see no movement aboard. The *Kanchou* has just entered the bay, but is eight kilometers away."

A few minutes later, they were over the bay, and the smoke from the burning boat clearly marked the pilot's course. Hua's fighter was a couple thousand feet above them, making a large orbit.

Just before he reached the boat, the pilot altered course to the right, and Kerry saw that he was making for Mickey Duff, whose orange Mae West marked his position a quarter-mile south of the yacht. He slowed and went into a hover twenty feet above Duff.

Kerry looked down to see Duff grinning back at him. There was blood on his forehead. His deputy made violent gestures toward the boat with a pointing finger.

Kerry waved back at him.

On the intercom, Kerry said, "He wants us to get to the boat, first. Take me over there and drop me off, then come back for Mickey. You need the room in here, anyway."

"Director Yichang?" the pilot asked.

"Do as Mr. Kerry suggests."

The Gazelle banked away and headed for the boat.

"You have a fire extinguisher?" Kerry asked.

The copilot passed a large one back to him.

"I will go with you," Yichang said.

"You don't have to."

"I want to secure any evidence."

While the chopper hovered to starboard of the bow a few

feet above it, Kerry and Yichang released their belts and made their way out the door held open by the copilot. The downdraft of the rotor whipped their clothing with frenzy. Like the old and reliable Huey, the Gazelle had landing skids rather than wheels, and Yichang sat on the floor and reached down with his feet for the skid. When he found it, he stood upright, waited until the boat came up at him with the rise of a wave, then pushed himself off. He landed sprawling on the bow.

Kerry gripped the fire extinguisher against his side with his left arm, settled on the jamb of the door, found the skid, and leaped to the deck. He landed on his feet, but his momentum carried him forward, and he tumbled onto his right shoulder. He nearly slid into a gaping hole from a cannon shell. He pushed himself to his knees, then onto his feet. The deck was tilted.

Yichang was already on his feet, a pistol held muzzle-up in his right hand. Kerry hadn't known he was armed.

The helicopter lifted away abruptly, dipped its nose, and headed back toward Duff.

The topsides of the cruiser were a mess. The flying bridge was all but gone, including the bridge decking, which was also the ceiling of the salon. Except for a few stringers and broken pieces of teak protruding from the port and aft cabin sides, the salon was open to the sky.

Incongruously, Kerry thought of it as a convertible.

He saw another helicopter approaching, one of the Super Frelon military choppers. Major Hua came over low, dipping his wings, then headed west. He might have been getting low on fuel.

"This boat's going down in a few minutes," Kerry said.

It was listing about ten degrees to the left, and the angle seemed to increase steadily.

"Perhaps we will not worry about the fire," Yichang said. "I do not think the fuel tank was hit."

The smoke rising from the stern deck was thick and black, but Kerry couldn't see the source of it because the back wall of the salon was still standing. He started aft along the narrow side deck, holding onto his extinguisher with his left hand and grabbing the jagged edges of the cabin with his right hand.

He hadn't gone three feet before he looked down into the cabin and saw the bodies.

Or what was left of them.

"Son of a bitch! You won't need the pistol, Director."

The 23-millimeter cannon shells had penetrated the hull of the cabin before detonating. If it weren't for the two heads, one bald and one red-haired, lodged against the near side of the cabin, Kerry wouldn't have been able to count bodies. Not much was recognizable in the cabin. Pieces of shattered metal, plastic, video monitors, bent Grail missile launchers, cushions, and dishware littered the deck. There were also large chunks of flesh and pieces of human limbs. Thin, reddish blood coated it all.

Kerry choked back a gag reflex, looked away, and continued working his way along the side deck. When he reached the stern, he found the cushions of a transom-wide lounge were on fire, started by hot charcoal dumped from a brazier. He aimed the hose of the extinguisher and squeezed the handle. The whoosh of white vapor killed the flames instantly.

He tossed the extinguisher aside and checked the deck. There was blood and a few fragments of tissue. Whoever had been standing here had been blown clear off the boat.

The cabin doorway was already open, the door blown away. Kerry went down the few steps to find Yichang already in the cabin. He had come over the top, through the broken front windshield. He had a plastic bag clutched in one hand and was sifting through the debris with his other hand.

"What are you looking for?"

"Hands. I can get fingerprints from hands."

Kerry resisted another urge to vomit. He kicked through some of the debris, but he wasn't a cop. He didn't know what to look for.

To the port side of the companionway was another set of steps. He heard water sloshing in the bilges, but thought he'd take a quick look down in the stern cabin.

He heard the whine of turbine engines and the beat of rotors, and he looked up to see one of the Super Frelons hovering a hundred yards away. General Chou was in the open doorway, waving frantically at them.

Kerry ignored him and went below to the stern cabin. The boat coughed and tilted some more. It felt as if it was becoming more sluggish in responding to the slap of the waves against the hull.

One cannon round had penetrated the cabin, leaving a huge hole in the hull through which daylight spilled, and the cabin was a war zone. He quickly checked the small head and the closets, which had had their doors blown away.

Nothing.

At least, nothing that he thought was important.

The cabin was a sea of foam rubber from the exploded mattress of the bed. Kerry shoved aside a pile of foam and shredded blankets. Only the box spring remained, and he was about to leave it when he saw the corner of a black box imbedded in the springs.

He walked around the bed, kicking loose trash aside and leaning against the twenty-degree tilt of the deck. Scooping remnants of bedding to one side, he found a black attaché case fitted into the springs. He pulled it free and popped the catches.

Cash. A bunch of it.

Papers, documents.

Six tape cassettes.

"Did you find treasure, Mr. Kerry?"

Yichang was standing in the doorway.

"I did. Take a look."

He shoved the case across the box spring.

Yichang rifled through it. He folded papers, unbuttoned his shirt, and shoved them inside. The tape cassettes he placed in his pocket. Then he shut the case and looked up at Kerry.

Kerry raised an eyebrow.

"The bag of money will keep General Chou at bay."

"I see," Kerry said.

"Not that he is corruptible, Mr. Kerry. He will turn the money in, but he will also not inquire about other evidence until I have a chance to examine it."

The boat lurched again.

"Shall we go, Mr. Kerry?"

"After you, Mr. Yichang."

TWENTY-SIX

Deng Xiaoping International Superport
October 4, 1:20 P.M.

The five supersonic transports were aligned in a single row two hundred meters from the front of Terminal One so that the people on the observation deck could see them. Jacqueline Broussard thought that every one of them carried the special flavor of the 21st Century. Though they were ungainly on their long-legged landing gear, their fuselages and wings were exceptionally sleek. She would be proud to represent any one of them.

Her own SST was parked second from the left side. She sat in her chair and kept her eyes on it as Sun Chen and his assistants announced the winning bids for the major air carriers. They took their time doing it, building the suspense, even though the winners in this category were all but ordained: United . . . Delta . . . Quantas . . . Lufthansa . . . Air France. . . .

Sun and his aides had their backs to the supersonic aircraft, standing before two tables and a podium at the northern wall of the dome. There was an irritating feedback in the microphone—suggesting that even the high-tech airport was subject to glitches—and Zhao Li rushed forward to correct it.

All of the competing vendors were seated in a block of

chairs facing the Chairman of the Committee for Airport Construction, and behind their seats were strung velvet ropes intended to keep the nearly two thousand guests and reporters at bay.

Several sets of bright lights shone from behind her, lighting up Sun for the television cameras.

The air carrier representatives were assigned to the special seating, though some of them now filed up to the front to collect their certificates as Sun announced the names of their companies. In the front rows, Broussard sat with Henri Dubonnet, Francois Miter, and Stephen Dowd. Next to them were the Russians. On the other side of the aisle from her were Ernst Bergen, Gerhard Ebbing, and Matthew Kraft. Behind them, Kerry sat with P.J. Jackson and Ken Stephenson, the latter two of whom she had met just a couple days before.

Whenever she looked at him, Kerry grinned at her. She did not like it and thought that he was attempting to initiate some response from her. They had not had one moment together to talk since her return to China Dome. A variety of activities, and especially the examinations of the aircraft, had intervened. She and Henri, who appeared much healthier after recouping his sleep, had devoted their time to entertaining and shepherding their guests around the airport and in Hong Kong and Kowloon.

Kerry, Dowd had told her, had been involved in a number of hearings following the events of October 1. She still found the scheme, as it had been explained to the media, almost fantastic. The ground crews for all of the supersonic transports had examined their aircraft, but only the Astroliner had been tampered with.

She stared ahead, watching Sun make his announcements, but she could feel Kerry watching her. She vacillated between ire and desire. She had never thought the words to be so closely related before.

Finally, Sun Chen said, "Now, we come to the decision of the judges and the awarding of the supersonic transport contract."

Broussard, as well as Kerry, Ebbing, and Zemenek she thought, had been partially stunned when they learned, on October 1, that Sun would have no part in the decision. He had announced the names of the judges, and his had not been among them. They had been lobbying Sun in subtle ways for months on end, and it had all been to no avail.

One of the chairman's assistants handed him an envelope, and Sun opened it slowly and carefully. The buzz of the crowd behind them died away. Broussard held her breath.

"The supersonic transport contract is awarded to . . . Pacific Aerospace Incorporated."

She let her breath go in one long and quiet sigh; she had known it would be this way.

The Americans in the crowd behind her yelled and whistled. Stephenson stood up while shaking hands with Jackson and Kerry. Henri got up and crossed the aisle to shake the PAI president's hand, then came back to stand beside her.

He took her hand.

She tried to smile, but she was close to tears.

Henri squeezed her hand, and she looked to him.

"I'm sorry, Henri."

"There is nothing for you to do any longer, Jacqueline," he said. He looked infinitely sad.

"You are firing me?"

"Yes."

"Thank you, Henri."

October 4, 2:20 P.M.

Sun Chen and Zhao Li circulated through the mass of people. He shook hands with the representatives of the air carriers who had been successful. Now that it was over, Sun was immensely relieved. He had not been aware that the stresses had been affecting him as much as they had.

They encountered the Pacific Aerospace contingent in the crowd, all of them with champagne glasses. Kerry introduced him to people he had not yet met—pilots and crew members.

Mickey Duff, the F-16 pilot, had a large bandage on his forehead and his left hand was wrapped in a fiberglass splint.

"Your hand, Mr. Duff?"

"I broke four fingers in the ejection, Mr. Sun. Your doctors told me I would fly again, and that's all that counts."

"The People's Republic owes you a great debt."

"I think you just paid it, sir."

"Nevertheless, a ceremony is planned at which our military would like to recognize you, Captain Carroll, and Major Hua. You will accept?"

"I would be honored, Chairman."

"And so you shall be."

He turned to Terrence Carroll. "You will also attend, Captain?"

Carroll grinned at him. "I already got my kiss, Chairman Sun, but sure, I'll be there."

Sun did not understand the reference, but did not pursue it.

He looked at Kerry. "You are impetuous, Mr. Kerry."

"I agree."

"However—and I know you will not repeat this—I appreciate your overruling our military."

"I am sorry if I angered General Chou."

Chou was retiring. He was not prepared for the new world.

"I will accept your apology on his behalf. I hope you will be staying at . . . China Dome?"

"Dan will be our man on the scene, Chairman Sun," Vice President P.J. Jackson said.

"I will be talking to you frequently, then," Sun said and let Zhao lead him onward.

They talked to several others, including the losing vendors—Kraft seemed the most upset, all but refusing to talk to him.

Then Broussard stepped out of the crowd to intercept him.

"Chairman, I am happy that I had this past year to get to know you."

"And I you, Mademoiselle. What will you do now?"

"I do not know. My job with the company is now terminated."

Sun thought that a delightful event.

"I think Mr. Kerry will offer me a position," she went on.

"Would you accept?"

"I do not think I could work for Mr. Kerry."

"That is most fortunate," Sun Chen said.

Hong Kong
October 4, 4:40 P.M.

Inspector Maynard Wing had allowed Yichang Enlai to invite Kerry, Dowd, Bergen, Yelchehko, and Ebbing to accompany them. Yichang thought their presence was necessary to the deliverance of poetic justice.

With Wing's four plainclothes detectives and the hotel manager also in the party, it required two elevators to take them to the seventeenth floor of the Hong Kong Hilton.

They got out and walked down the long hallway, following the manager. When they reached the suite, the manager bent over and opened one of the twin doors, then stepped aside.

Maynard Wing stepped forward and pushed the door open, and the whole group filed inside.

Matthew Kraft and Hakim al-Qatar were seated on the couches before the window, facing each other across the coffee table. They had been in heated discussion, Yichang thought, and they both looked up, startled, when the group filed in.

Hakim al-Qatar's mouth dropped open.

As far as Yichang knew, al-Qatar was in the clear. They were not here for the Arab.

Kraft stood up, his face red in anger. "What is happening? Gerhard, what are you doing?"

Ebbing flipped the tape cassette in the air, catching it with his hand. He tossed it one more time.

"It was I, Matthew, who recognized your voice on this tape. Talking with Kurt Wehmeier. How could you do this to our countrymen, Matthew?"

Ebbing's voice had a raw edge to it. Yichang thought the man was struggling to withhold his fury.

Hakim al-Qatar said, "What is this nonsense?"

Kraft said, "I don't know what you're talking about."

And Kerry, as Yichang might have expected, stepped around Ebbing and marched across the room. One of Wing's detectives reached out to stop him, but Wing waved the man back.

Kerry went around the coffee table and faced the much smaller man.

Kraft backed away from him, perhaps reading the hate in Kerry's face.

Kerry only swung once, his right fist rising from his side in a swift blur. There was power and emotion behind the strike, and his fist caught Kraft on the left cheek and nose. Blood spattered and the lightweight Kraft flew backwards, his legs catching the sofa. He tumbled over the back of it and crashed to the floor.

"Charley Whitlock sends his greetings," Kerry said, then turned and walked toward the door.

Yichang went with him, thinking that Charles Whitlock would have approved.

He wished he could have made the same statement.

Hong Kong Harbor
October 5, 10:20 P.M.

The moon was low in the east and cast a broad band of soft white light across the slow waves that rocked the idled water taxi. The neon lights of Kowloon reflected their reds and blues and greens off the water's surface, swirling and dancing in the night.

The boat's pilot sat at his helm, his ears capped with the headphones of a Sony Walkman.

Kerry reclined in the rear seat of the boat and studied Broussard. She had told him that Dubonnet had fired her, but she still sported a smirky little smile. No doubt she would spring a surprise of some sort on him.

She sat on the front edge of the seat next to him, shaking her head negatively, her dark hair catching the moonbeams.

"You won't work for me?"

"We do not get along. We would be at each other's throats."

"Part of the time, probably. But the rest of the time?"

"What would I do for you, Daniel?"

"I don't know. We'll work something out."

"I have already taken another job."

"Oh." He was disheartened. He had thought that, finally, something would work in their favor.

"Dan, you left a message on my machine."

"Which you never returned."

"I was busy. You spoke your naughty word."

"Which one?"

"Love."

"I did, didn't I?"

"Did you mean it?"

"I almost called back to correct it, then decided it was correct as it was."

She settled back in the seat, and pulled his arm around her shoulders. The breeze off the bay was cool.

"I am to be the Director of External Public Relations for the People's Republic."

"Here? At China Dome?"

"Yes."

He smiled at her. "You want to share a room for a while?"

"We will see how much time passes before you or I change our minds."

"Shall we try for fifty years?" he asked.

"Let us try for that, love."

About the Author

William H. Lovejoy is a successful author of high tech thrillers, espionage novels, and mysteries. He lives in the Colorado Rockies where he is at work on his next novel.

WARBOTS by G. Harry Stine

#5 OPERATION HIGH DRAGON (17-159, $3.95)

Civilization is under attack! A "virus program" has been injected into America's polar-orbit military satellites by an unknown enemy. The only motive can be the preparation for attack against the free world. The source of "infection" is traced to a barren, storm-swept rock-pile in the southern Indian Ocean. Now, it is up to the forces of freedom to search out and destroy the enemy. With the aid of their robot infantry—the Warbots—the Washington Greys mount Operation High Dragon in a climactic battle for the future of the free world.

#6 THE LOST BATTALION (17-205, $3.95)

Major Curt Carson has his orders to lead his Warbot-equipped Washington Greys in a search-and-destroy mission in the mountain jungles of Borneo. The enemy: a strongly entrenched army of Shiite Muslim guerrillas who have captured the Second Tactical Battalion, threatening them with slaughter. As allies, the Washington Greys have enlisted the Grey Lotus Battalion, a mixed-breed horde of Japanese jungle fighters. Together with their newfound allies, the small band must face swarming hordes of fanatical Shiite guerrillas in a battle that will decide the fate of Southeast Asia and the security of the free world.

#7 OPERATION IRON FIST (17-253, $3.95)

Russia's centuries-old ambition to conquer lands along its southern border erupts in a savage show of force that pits a horde of Soviet-backed Turkish guerrillas against the freedom-loving Kurds in their homeland high in the Caucasus Mountains. At stake: the rich oil fields of the Middle East. Facing certain annihilation, the valiant Kurds turn to the robot infantry of Major Curt Carson's "Ghost Forces" for help. But the brutal Turks far outnumber Carson's desperately embattled Washington Greys, and on the blood-stained slopes of historic Mount Ararat, the high-tech warriors of tomorrow must face their most awesome challenge yet!